CONTROL

THE DESPOT CHRONICLES #2

CONTROL

ANDY T. HANSON

4 Horsemen
Publications, Inc.

Control
Copyright © 2024 Andy T. Hanson. All rights reserved.

4 Horsemen
Publications, Inc.

Published By: 4 Horsemen Publications, Inc.

4 Horsemen Publications, Inc.
PO Box 417
Sylva, NC 28779
4horsemenpublications.com
info@4horsemenpublications.com

Cover & Typesetting by Autumn Skye
Edited by Jen Paquette

Library of Congress Control Number: 2024935570

Paperback ISBN-13: 979-8-8232-0447-7
Hardcover ISBN-13: 979-8-8232-0448-4
Audiobook ISBN-13: 979-8-8232-0488-0
Ebook ISBN-13: 979-8-8232-0446-0

ACKNOWLEDGMENTS

To the stoics and the skeptics, and everyone else who feels out of place in a world of absolutes.

"Stars, hide your fires, let not light see my black and
deep desires."

- Shakespeare, *Macbeth*

CONTENTS

PROLOGUE

DOLLY

Grinding gears and the low shriek of stressed metal hinges brought an abrupt end to the flow of Maisie's storytelling. Dolly was standing in front of the kitchen counter a few feet from the coffeemaker, waiting patiently for the pot to boil. Her eyes had gone immediately to the hatchway upon the first creaking grind, along with everyone else's in Boyd's Clubhouse. They all saw Nate "Novccaine" Barker duck clumsily into the chamber as soon as the hatch opened wide enough for his skinny little frame to squeeze past. The room stayed silent while the little man threw his weight against the hatch to jam it back closed.

Dolly looked around the room and could tell neither her husband nor Maisie were particularly pleased with the man's timing. *They did tell him to come here after his shift,* Dolly reminded herself when she too felt the beginnings of frustration over Cainey's intrusion. She could understand their annoyance. Maisie had been finding her groove over the past hour. She had started the story in fits and starts but fell into a steady rhythm after a time. The story hadn't quite progressed beyond their first few months aboard the Nest before the small man's disruption, but Dolly had known where it was inevitably headed and, so, had done her best to tune Maisie out for the most part this past hour. She felt no urge to recall any of the painful memories Maisie was elaborating upon. Although Gabe's death was a deep scar on her soul, and she still felt his loss every day, Dolly didn't like the uncomfortable feelings that arose within her whenever people spoke of him.

Dolly wasn't ashamed of remarrying—she loved Boyd with all her soul. It was just strange to remember those early days. The memories always brought with them some feelings of betrayal, though she knew they were unfounded. So as Maisie spoke, Dolly focused on serving breakfast to Larry, Maisie, Boyd, and Jed, and then she made herself a plate and focused on the meal, and then she focused on the dishes, and now that those were finished, her focus was on the coffee. She had even thought she might slip over to the oak library after handing out the steaming mugs, but Cainey's arrival meant she'd need another mug, and most likely another pot, so it was Dolly who was first to speak after Cainey's intrusion. "Hey, Cainey. You want coffee?"

"Uhh, yeah," the small man answered after a quick glance around the room. "Thanks, Dolly. Lots of cream."

Dolly reached up to open a cabinet and withdrew a coffee mug but could still see Cainey out of the corner of her eye. He was striding toward the black-and-white island, his eyes locked firmly on the beautiful pilot staring down at her hands in bewilderment. Dolly did not at all like the look on the whip-thin module garage maintenance worker's face. Cainey had always creeped her out a little. *And it looks like he's found a new target for his perversion,* Dolly thought, feeling bad for Jordana while simultaneously determined to warn her to watch out for the guy.

"Any problems down there, Cainey?" Maisie asked him when he arrived alongside the island. "Hey, Cainey! Yo, Barker, you listening to me?" she asked, pounding her palm against the countertop for added emphasis in drawing his attention.

Throwing back his shoulders, Cainey began to shake his head quickly. He tried to play off the awkward leering he'd been snapped out of into a deliberate gaze around the room. Finally, his eyes landed on Maisie, and he gave her a casual answer. "No problems. I took care of everything, like I said."

"Your supervisor didn't come up to you at all?" Boyd asked him.

"Why would he?" Cainey scoffed. "The son of a bitch is never in the module garage anyways. And nobody went running to him with any secrets. I told ya—I took care of everything. I cleared the place out completely, and no one was the wiser for it. The rest of my shift went by like clockwork."

"Who is your supervisor, exactly?" Boyd's tone told Dolly he was not at all pleased with Cainey's flippancy.

"Why?" Cainey asked indignantly. "It's like I told ya—he don't know shit. The motherfucker never leaves his fucking pleasure quarters. He leaves the garage's operations to his footmen, and I cleared all those bastards out of there. Don't worry, Priest. I know what I'm doing."

"I hope so, Novocaine," Boyd said with a growl, "for all our sakes."

"Oh yeah, I received a heads up call over the secure comm's line on my way here from Rafferty," Cainey said as an afterthought. "Him and Harrington are headed this way. They want to meet Ms. Revere." Novocaine's creepy gaze fell back to Jordana. The copper-toned beauty glanced up from her hands to lock eyes with Cainey. Their eyes did not stay long in contact, and when Jordana quickly glanced away, Dolly smiled to herself to see the disgust that lay within them.

"Why the hell don't I have one of these secure comms devices by now?" Boyd asked sourly.

"Sheffield is the one who builds the things," Cainey explained. "Take it up with him. They do take a bit of skill to operate though," the little man added, half under his breath.

Dolly thrust a hot mug at Cainey's chest to shut the man up before her husband got truly angry with him. "Wait a minute," Jordana suddenly barked as Dolly started back to the coffee pot. "Does he mean *President* Rafferty and *Hubert* Harrington, AOA's CEO?" she asked, horrified.

"Uhh," Maisie began, "well, yeah. They're a major support to our resistance operations."

"Are you kidding me?!" Jordana asked in exasperation.

"What's wrong, Ms. Revere?" Boyd asked.

"What's wrong?" Jordana responded in an incredulous voice. She took a few seconds to settle herself and then began her explanation. "Look... I can tell where this story is going. I know that this Schef fellow and your commander must be pretty dreadful people and all and maybe they took advantage of some truths, but I'm sorry to be the one to tell you all that they are indeed *truths*."

"What do you mean, Jordana?" Maisie said with alarm, a rare show of weakness in the young Sagal.

"I mean Schef and your commander might have used their beliefs for nefarious purposes, but what they told you about the infection is fairly close to the mark," Jordana said, looking Boyd dead in the face. "Have AOA or the government leaders actually ever explained to you all that happened nine and a half years ago? Do they have an explanation for the infection?"

"Not really." It was Maisie who answered, the fear in her voice gone now and her usual calm control ruling once again. "No one has really thought to press them much. We've had other things on our plate. I'm not nearly done with our story up here, after all. We haven't exactly had a lot of time for any prosecution of the past."

"Yes," Jordana began, "I can see that, I guess. But haven't you all ever wondered over the incredible nature of this place you call home? I mean ... how about all the materials for this station, for example? Have you never wondered just how in the bloody hell they got all this composite steel up here?"

"By shuttle," Maisie said, zero confidence in her voice.

"What, piece by piece? Much of it was hauled up in shuttles, I'll grant you that, but more of it wasn't. It would've taken ten thousand trips. Think about it."

They all pondered the idea for a moment. It was Maisie who once again voiced the question that must've been on the tips of all their tongues. "So how did they get it here, then?"

"They had technology advanced enough to form the steel right out of the moon dust itself, some matter conversion technology or something. They built this whole epic facility in less than two bloody years, for Christ's sake."

"Well, yeah. We all know their tech is amazing." This time it was Larry who spoke up.

"Amazing?" Jordana made the word a scorning of Larry's intelligence. "I get that you've had your hands full with this Witenagemot or whatever, but have you never thought about just how unbelievable this place and all the tech inside it truly is? The things President Daniel

Rafferty and his council of world leaders backed, the things they allowed Hubert Harrington and his AOA to do, brought the infection and this last horrible, blood-filled decade down upon us all. And now you are inviting them to come meet with me like I'm some exhibit in a museum. I want nothing to do with those traitors." Jordana pushed herself up off the stool and moved toward the hatchway. "I'm sorry, but I can't break bread and trade secrets with those men."

"Wait, Jordana, please!" Maisie wailed, grabbing Jordana's forearm. The pilot glanced back, and the two beauties locked eyes. "We all know the world governments and AOA have a deal of blame on their shoulders for everything that has happened. None of us have forgotten that nor let them off the hook for it. But it's the past. We have too few friends left up here to turn down any help. Please, just stay for a few minutes. Boyd will kick 'em out before they are able to pester you or anything."

"Yeah, Ms. Revere," Boyd put in, "the bastards know not to overstay their welcome in my place."

"You all just don't understand," Jordana said with a sad reluctance. "It's not just that they're to blame for the unfortunate spread of a virus that happened to escape containment or something, which would be bad enough, but ... you see, Maisie," she said, placing a hand on the younger woman's shoulder, "they knew all along that humanity would be wiped out, and they said nothing. They kept silent only to ensure that they would survive the catastrophe. That is why this station was built. Not as some scientific habitation project, but as a refuge to run to. Well, it's perhaps a bit more complicated than that, but basically that's it."

Maisie wasn't sure what to say. "But wha..." Maisie managed after a few beats. "What are you saying, Jordana?"

The pilot withdrew her hand and let it swing once again by her side. She drew in a deep breath, and with an uncomfortable look etched across her face, began to answer, "Arlo Bailey—my group's leader I told you about—he discovered it was part of the deal they made with the people, or beings or whatever, who gifted them all this amazing tech."

"No," Larry muttered under his breath.

Jordana didn't let the interruption phase her. "AOA made first contact with these tech givers, so the governments were then forced to go through Harrington as an intermediary for all negotiations with them. It was all documented in AOA's files. Arlo hacked into their mainframe the day the infection spread and discovered all of this right there, plain as day. So anyways, the government leaders quickly formed a secret council upon learning of AOA's discovery, and along with AOA, they were then told by the tech givers about their plans to destroy humanity and take control of the Earth. The tech givers promised to spare a few thousand people—AOA and the governments were allowed to pick who—all they had to do was build this station and follow any orders they issued to the letter, without hesitation. These tech givers told AOA and the government council that they needed a base of operations when they came to claim Earth. Apparently, their attack on humanity would render the planet uninhabitable, and they would need a safe base to monitor the invasion. They promised the residents of this station that they would be spared and even allowed to stay behind after the tech givers left to conquer their next planet. Branch 1 wasn't really designed to house AOA and the VIPs but rather the tech givers themselves. And in order to keep Harrington and Rafferty and the rest of them sweet during the station construction process, these tech givers promised AOA and the council a steady stream of advanced technological blueprints, even beyond the tech that they would need to be able to fly up here and construct this station. The tech givers promised them the stream would be steady and continuous until they arrived for the invasion—if, that is, AOA and the governments followed all their instructions to build in secret so as not to alert the public. They were further ordered to prepare no defenses against the invasion, to just keep everything business as usual. And with their miracle tech, they were able to accomplish that very thing."

Dolly's head was spinning, her coffee duties forgotten. She was not surprised, however, to find her beloved husband had remained calm in the face of the pilot's sickening news. He asked a follow-up question almost right away, with no discomfort in his voice. "If all that is true, then where in the hell are these supposed 'tech givers'? It's been ten years almost. When are they coming?"

"They were scheduled to arrive five years ago; at least, that's what they told AOA. Arlo thinks the whole timeframe and their plans for invasion that they shared with AOA were all a lie. 'A ruse of sorts,' he says. Arlo does think the tech givers are truly coming, though, or at least planned to come, but it most likely won't be until after the infection dies out. He figures they didn't tell the governments and AOA the real means of attack. The infection was the real weapon they used. You see, they never planned to render the Earth uninhabitable. After all, they're most likely coming for the planet's resources. They wouldn't want to destroy it. So Arlo figures they lied to AOA and just used them to build this station. These tech givers simply slipped the infection into their tech stream, and AOA went ahead and fabricated it without even realizing what it was. The Alphas too."

"What?!" Maisie shouted. "Did you say Alphas?" Jordana gave her a tentative nod, and Maisie plowed on, "The Alphas are real?"

Jordana gave her head another affirmative nod before drawing in a quick breath to answer. "Arlo found out about them too when he broke into the data files. AOA received the infection in a package with a dozen other exotic infections. They had no idea what it was and just went ahead and fabricated it. But apparently, the tech givers had ulterior motives for giving the tech, which was most likely to slip this infection in and get it fabricated so they could release it. It was like a Trojan horse, basically. Once all the Alphas were fabricated, they did what they were programmed by the tech givers to do and broke away from AOA's control to release the infection on the world and then manage its spread."

"What do you mean they fabricated the Alphas?" Boyd asked her. "I thought the theory was that they were people infected with a specific strain of the infection."

"Are you telling us that not only is the Alpha theory true, as my father and the other four scientists working alongside him in Branch 1's labs believed, but that AOA has known that for certain all along?" Maisie asked, disbelief and heartbreak warring in her voice.

"Uhmmm... Well, yes, I'm sorry, but they are indeed real."

"What the hell are they, then, if not people?" Boyd asked.

"Well, neither Arlo nor myself are scientists or anything, or even medical doctors, such as your father," she said, nodding at Maisie, "and he only had so long to review those data files before the infection got out of control and he was forced to flee, but Arlo is pretty sure they are some kind of symbiotic, sentient generals for those poor souls who have become infected. The Alphas basically monitor the hordes. In the early days of the infection, they made sure enough people were kept alive after contracting the infection to have enough of these *Damned*, as you call them, to keep the infection spreading on and on. Basically, the Alphas are some sort of fabricated, biological AI that acts as the brains of the infection weapon system. Arlo even thinks the infection can be modified for different species. He thinks these tech givers have done this same thing before on other planets. It may even be the reason they haven't come to claim the Earth yet. Maybe one of the planets they tried to conquer fought back. Maybe the bloody bastards are all dead."

"Well, at least you end your bad news with a hopeful thought," Boyd said into the silence that followed Jordana's spiel. "Only thing I don't understand is why these tech givers would need this station if the infection is their means of attack. Seems like quite a lot of effort and expense to put into some meaningless decoy."

"Who knows the minds of aliens?" Jordana retorted. "Maybe they had AOA build this place as a failsafe, a backup plan in case they arrived too early, or in case humans reacted rashly and nuked the planet. Or maybe they need the station because they can't survive in Earth's atmosphere."

"Well, the gravity and atmosphere in this station are identical to that of Earth," Boyd pointed out.

"True," Jordana conceded. "But that can all be adjusted in the control room, can't it?"

"Probably," Larry allowed.

"It could be a thousand reasons is all I'm saying. Perhaps it's cultural, and they don't like to set foot on the soil of their conquered world."

"Conquered world?" Maisie's voice was full of bewildered woe. "You sure make these tech givers sound charming."

"And it was your leader's bright idea to send a spy plane up to the forward command headquarters of this interstellar and genocidal alien species?" Watching her husband, Dolly knew what he must be thinking. Boyd had grown to distrust any person who sought power for any reason. It's what caused him to drag his feet over joining Maisie and her resistance for those first months. So she knew her husband was highly skeptical of this Arlo Bailey, sight unseen.

"Have you been down to Earth lately, Priest?" Jordana asked Boyd angrily. "We, as a group, my people and I, decided it was worth the risk. We had the satellite data. The station was dark. No one was home, so to speak. The Bruderschaft, as we call ourselves, weighed the odds and bet that beings who were already five years late wouldn't show up on the very same day we launched a recon vessel to investigate their station."

"Fair enough," Boyd said with a hint of a grin.

"Listen," Jordana broke in before Boyd's grin could stretch any farther, "I've held back some elements of my mission from you chaps. I apologize for that. And I hope, given my peculiar rescue, you can understand it." She paused for their acknowledgment. "My people, the Bruderschaft, they are planning on following me up here. I do have a sitrep message to relay to them, but afterward, I am supposed to get the Lunar Dock ready to receive the E-11 that my people will be arriving in."

"You can't let them come, Ms. Revere!" Boyd coughed out. "It's not safe up here."

"It isn't safe down there, Priest."

"But I don't understand," Larry Holderman said, a red blush rushing across his face. Every eye in the room fell to him, and the bald, beer-bellied goof was forced to elaborate or his concerns. He tugged back another long snort of his flask before speaking. "If your people, the Bruderschaft, if they thought these tech givers might be on their way someday, then why in the Sam Hill did they want to hang out in the one spot they was sure to find yas?"

"Our plan was only to stay up here long enough to rest and get in a few harvests in the greenhouse," she explained. "We just wanted to stock up on everything we'd need to build a settlement. We were going to use Cardinal's Nest's imaging satellites to find a secure valley back on Earth, preferably one on an island free from any Damned and with a flat area large enough to land our E-11, temperate to grow crops and secluded enough to be able to hide it from imaging satellites in case the tech givers do eventually show up. We would take all our gathered food and supplies and build a safe haven there to ride out the rest of the infection."

"I'm sorry, Jordana," Maisie said in a peculiar voice.

"Sorry?"

"You and your brothers and sisters in the Bruderschaft made it all the way across the Atlantic, then nearly the entire width of America, braving Damned all the way, finally arriving at your destination, to find that not only does it exist, but the launchpad has interplanetary craft in good enough working order to get your people to true safety, then you manage the flight up here, survive a crash landing, get stumbled upon randomly by a solitary collector module crew just before your oxygen runs out, only to learn that the safe haven you were hoping for is occupied by despots and cowards. So, I'm sorry, and I'm ashamed."

"It uhh... It," Jordana muttered in response, "it's a bit disappointing, to say the least, but it's hardly your fault. That's obvious. I appreciate the sentiment, however. And I am truly grateful to both you and Jed, of course," Jordana directed this at Larry and then the tall, dark and stoic module pilot still seated alone at the dining room table, "but I have a responsibility to my people. They're counting on me to get my message out today. I will not fail them, especially not by delaying just to spend time exchanging pleasantries with humanity's greatest traitors. My people need to know what to expect up here when they arrive."

"You really believe that's likely? They're truly coming?" Boyd asked pointedly. "I know it's rough on Earth, but like I was saying, your people coming here is a bad idea. There's no telling how the Witenagemot will react."

"They'll react as they always do ... in their own interest." Maisie raised her head and straightened her shoulders as she spoke. "But it might not matter."

"Wha..." Boyd started. He cleared his throat and tried again. "How can you say that, Mais? After all we've seen them do these past years... Are you trying to sneak an army in here to depose the Witenagemot? I thought I knew you better than that. Bloody uprisings are not the answer!" Boyd turned to Jordana. "How many of you are there in this Bruderschaft?"

"87," she said with pride.

"Maisie, what could you hope to accomplish with 87 against the hundreds of loyal residents the Witen has up here?"

"I'm in no way advocating violence here, Priest.' Maisie's voice was animated with righteous fury. "I'm simply saying that if we help Ms. Revere get her message out, and then find a way to get the Lunar Dock ready to receive the Bruderschaft's E-11, we may be able to convince the people to finally rise up as one and shake off the Witenagemot's rule. There need not be any bloodshed at all, at least not any innocent blood. Once the residents see Jordana and her people for themselves, all of the Steward's lies will be exposed. Revolution will be inevitable after that. And with you and I leading," Maisie spoke to her mentor earnestly, "we can ensure the revolution plays out as peacefully as possible."

"What's this about finding a way to get the Lunar Dock *ready*?" Jordana broke in to ask. "I thought you said the entire station was already operational."

Everyone in the Clubhouse looked over to Jordana. Dolly finally broke the momentary silence. "It's like Maisie said, honey. There's a lot more of our story up here to tell ya."

"I'll tell you the rest on the way," Maisie promised Jordana, wearing the strangest of smirks.

"On the way?"

"I can get you to the control room so you can get your message away. If, that is, you will swear to do your best to convince your people to join our resistance."

"Whoa, whoa!" Boyd's face turned red with panic as he spoke. "You can't do this, Mais. I mean... I get it. Maybe the Bruderschaft showing up would swing the people into an overthrow of the Witen. But you'll never be able to get the damn message out in the first place. We got no friends down Branch 1. You show your face anywhere near there, and no one will ever see them bright hazels of yours ever again."

"I know a way in, Priest," Maisie said evasively.

"Okay, so you know a way in. You still have no idea how to get the message past whatever tech they're running up there. You didn't suddenly become some expert computer hacker in the last few seconds, did ya?"

"I know someone who can do it," Maisie answered in that same annoying, evasive voice.

"Someone you can trust, I hope."

Maisie ignored the comment. "Well, what do you say, Jordana? Do we have a deal?" she asked, extending her hand with a smile.

Jordana looked at it for a few seconds. She then made a show of looking into every face scattered around the room, finally snatching Maisie's outstretched palm to shake. "Deal," the pilot agreed in her slightly pretentious English accent.

Maisie gave her a bright, warm smile and kept the shake going for a deal longer than necessary. When she finally did break the shake, Maisie turned on her heel and headed for the hatchway. An expansive arm wave indicated that Jordana should follow her. "Come on, Jordana. Let's get you out of here before Rafferty and Harrington arrive."

"Be careful, Maisie," Boyd yelled after his protégé as she moved to stoop through the hatchway. Maisie didn't bother responding to the worried instructions. The hotheaded, stubborn resistance co-leader simply ducked out of the Clubhouse and off into insanity. Jordana slammed the hatch shut behind them, its echoing crash serving as punctuation for the disaster of the women's irrational departure.

CHAPTER 1

JED

They led Colton Murphy to an empty chair in front of an empty black desk. The desk faced a larger version of itself thirty feet across the tiled floor of the Grand Rotunda. Perched behind this larger austere black desk sat the Steward, with a stern face and crossed arms. The desk was elevated on a five-foot platform in a fashion Jed figured was meant to deliberately evoke an average courtroom scene, recognizable in every corner of the vast United States. From his raised position, the Steward, a man once known as Harclay Aponyaschefski, surveyed the gathered masses.

The survivor of the Infection Event had quickly packed back on all the weight that had melted off him during his time among the Damned. Jed couldn't quite tell from his vantage point, but he was pretty sure the middling-sized, fox-faced man had the beginnings of a beer gut pushing against his black tactical blouse. All of the Witen members had begun wearing a uniform of one type or another over the last few days. The Steward was currently clad in the black tactical blouse and slacks, along with a pair of the black leather tennis shoes of AOA's former security squad. However, the Steward's gear was ornamented with gold stitching around the collar, two perfectly rendered golden eagles stitched atop each shoulder and a five-inch gold "W" in a swooping Old-English script on the right breast pocket.

Jed forgot about the black-and-gold clad Steward for a moment to ponder just who was producing all the needlework so quickly. Then it came to him.

Duh, the synthetic fabric clothing printers at the shopping center in Branch 4's recreation district.

Jed had never actually seen the things in operation himself. The fancy gizmos were operated out of public view. They could print any design of clothing on file in any size with any alteration. The rec district had several different clothing storefronts, but all the material was actually fabricated by the same five machines in a big operations room behind the shopping center. All users did at the storefronts was select an outfit from one of their interactive kiosks, and the damn thing would slide out a minute later on a speedy little conveyor belt, directly to the storefront attendant manning the checkout stand.

Jed was lost, marveling at Cardinal's Nest's wonders, when the Steward's head snapped quickly in his direction. He had been harboring a tiny amount of hope that his position near the rear of the crowd might help keep the Steward's gaze from falling on his slight figure. Jed had no overt reason to worry about his status in the eyes of the Witenagemot, but neither was he fool enough to believe the amount of time he and Larry Holderman spent in the company of the priest and the dead doctor's daughter had gone unnoticed by the Witen.

The aforementioned two were toxic, for sure. Maisie, for one, had never stopped railing openly against the Commander, and his cronies' unrighteous power grab, from the moment her father's head left his shoulders right up to this very second. Conversely, the priest had been more aware of the precarious nature of inflaming the Commander, or any Witen member just now, and so he'd adopted a more tactful approach to his vocal opposition this past week. But either way, Jed knew the Witen was watching them both closely and were therefore watching their associates closely. So, Jed Redding had no illusions; he had some work to do if he wanted to continue enjoying the low-profile life to which he'd been so accustomed. Plus, Jed and his friends, Stevie Hyun, Alice Stark, Dolly Duchesne and her husband Gabe, along with Jed's partner, Larry, were even now standing right next to Father Boyd and Maisie. So, in retrospect, Jed realized the Steward's eyes fixing on him firmly was an inevitability.

Thankfully, the dreaded gaze lasted only a few seconds when it finally came. The Steward sharply snapped his attention toward the slender and seedy man who had seated himself at the desk across from him. Colton Murphy was the little man's name, a cafeteria attendant and accused rapist—that's all Jed knew of him. The man fit the image of the creepy little abuser too, sitting hunched over in the black metal folding chair. From his position in the gathered crowd, Jed could only make out half of the man's face. Lank, greasy, rat-brown hair fell over Murphy's eyes, casting the other half of his face in deep shadow. The half Jed could see was sharp featured and clean-shaven. From the looks of it, someone in the Witen had worked him over pretty well, then went and slapped some makeup on the battered abuser in a half-assed fashion. Jed guessed the Witen wasn't afraid of looking bad for working over the as yet un-convicted man; they had spread word around of Murphy's ill deeds and obvious guilt so effectively these last few days that few present were likely to have much sympathy for the guy. Still, they did make the attempt with the makeup. That said something to Jed; at least they were making an attempt at looking proper and impartial. They could've just hanged the man from the oculus in the dark of night, without a soul present to account. No one aboard would've dared said shit. Jed figured, under the circumstances, the Witen's attempt at holding court for all to witness justice was a promising sign in an otherwise gloomy sea of eventualities.

He knew the priest was of a like mind with him in this. Though, Jed also knew that Maisie most definitely did not see things that way. The poor girl had yet to find her brother. A week had passed with no sign of the boy since he screamed that mournful cry after the Commander had killed his father before his very eyes. Maisie's pain was a liability in large public gatherings right now. It made Jed nervous to have her so close by. Maisie was capable of saying anything, and right now, Jed and Father Boyd, and all their closest friends and associates, needed to be making efforts to get *off* the Witen's radar. *God, I hope the priest can keep her in check during this damn farce of a trial.* The Steward had already spotted them all standing together. If Maisie made a scene, Jed Redding knew he'd most likely be lumped in with her. He felt just awful for the poor girl, but right now, cooler heads needed to prevail.

Neither the Steward nor the Commander had made any appearances around the station this past week. Jed figured the Witenagemot had most likely been too busy establishing their bureaucratic hierarchy. They'd had their footmen *patrolling* the halls for days now, though nobody was really sure how to behave toward them. Their authority hadn't really been contested too heavily yet, at least not that Jed had heard, and with his passion for gossip, he most likely would have heard. But neither was their authority carrying any sort of real teeth as of yet, and they hadn't really been pushing it. Jed took it all to mean the kinks were still being worked out. Only yesterday, they had been issued something the Witen was calling the "New Destiny Constitution." It was essentially just a list of rules and regulations and something called a "Chain of Command Reference Guide." So today was the first day the eyes of all the members of the Witen would directly be on the residents. *All except for the Commander himself, it seems*. Jed couldn't see the man once named Jasper Montrois anywhere in the rotunda. He spotted Captain Alvarez and all six Lieutenants peppered throughout the chamber but, oddly, no sign of the Commander. Regardless, he knew it was a day to keep his head down. Jed just hoped his friends around him knew that as well. Poor, sweet, heartbroken Maisie most of all.

The Sagal girl's cracked, anguished voice quickly doused cold water on the fires of that hope. "We can't let them do this, Father!" she said in a voice so loud it could be heard eight rows deep into the densely packed crowd. "We can't give into their authority. Not once! We have to stop this. The man needs to be tried by the people, by a jury of his peers... Isn't that the saying or whatever?"

"Indeed, it is Mais." The priest's voice was pitched at a far lower volume as he calmly answered the enraged young girl. "It is, in fact, a strong piece of propaganda for communal responsibility. Only thing is, right now, that form of aspirational rhetoric would be drowned out in the darkness. No sufficient appetite for rebellion or its promises exists among the masses gathered here today. We definitely don't have the right vehicle here in this Colton Murphy to rally their decency and morality anyway. The man is most certainly guilty, Mais. We can't be seen to be on his side now. We already have a long march uphill with these people," Boyd added with a thumb to indicate the residents around him. "I lament the lack of due process, as it were, but that's the way the mob is leaning just now. I'd love to overthrow the bastard that murdered your father today, Maisie, here and now, you know I would, but it just isn't feasible. We have to bring the people along with us in order to stand any chance. We can only walk as fast as our slowest person, and this past week should have illustrated to all of us just how many slow people we got up here with us."

Gabe chuckled at that. And when he'd gained his composure enough to speak, added, "You damn sure got that right, Father."

"How is any of this funny to you, Gabe?" Maisie demanded of the man whom Jed himself would've definitely classified as one of the priest's *slow people*. The nitwit didn't even have the presence of mind to respect how emotionally fragile the young girl was at this moment. He just jutted out his brutish jaw and scowled at her in response. "I'm sure this Murphy creep is guilty too," she told the fishery crewman after a moment and a deep breath. "But do you all believe his crime is worth the sentence the Witenagemot is sure to give him for it? We all know the only justice they understand. We all saw Montros hack my father's head from his damn shoulders and then raise it up like some kinda sick trophy. Is that what y'all are gonna let this society up here become? Has one great ... great ... ca-catas-catastrophe... Yeah that's the right word. Has this one great catastrophe destroyed our collective sense of what is right and what ain't? Wasn't America extremely opposed to cruel and unusual punishments? I remember learning it was supposed to be, anyway. We can't let them do this. Surely, all you wise elders of mine," Maisie added with an eye roll, "you can see we have to try and stop this. We definitely can't be seen to be approving of this!"

"Don't worry, Maisie," Gabe cut in, "everyone around can hear you plain as day. They all know you don't approve. Trust me."

Jed looked around him to see that Gabe sure hadn't been lying; every head within Jed's view was turned their way, taking in every word of Maisie's invective. A steady pounding noise of steel on hard ceramic suddenly crashed its way through the crowd, drawing attention back to the mock courtroom. The two Lieutenants who had led

Colton Murphy to his lonely table were now stationed across from each other in the center of the makeshift court. Jed recognized the thin-framed black man on the right as Lieutenant Woodson, while he figured the ginger woman on the left with the square shoulders was most likely Lieutenant Dobechek. The pair stood at rigid attention next to the two A's in the AOA logo stenciled in giant maroon and silver lettering at their feet. They wore the black tactical gear of the former security squad, ornamented in the same fashion as the Steward's, with finely stitched single golden bars over each shoulder in place of Aponyaschefski's pair of eagles in repose. The Earth was framed like some heavenly harbinger in the center of the oculus directly above the logo the black-and-gold uniformed lieutenants flanked. Jed's gaze rose up to that glorious sight as the rest of the crowd's was fixed firm on the lieutenants maintaining their stiff positions of attention while they pounded the butts of their black-shafted, four-foot-long axes against the pristine and seamless floor of the Grand Rotunda.

It wasn't more than a few heartbeats before the pounding of the axes was the only sound to be heard throughout that cavernous chamber. Jed's gaze fell down from Earth just in time to see the Steward clear his throat before speaking to the residents gathered silently around the mock courtroom in a rough crescent. "Let me start by thanking all of you for coming here today. While the task before us here is no cause for celebration, I would be remiss if I refrained from conveying our appreciation to all of you. You've done all we've asked so far, and I'm proud of the righteous and cordial relationship that has blossomed among us these past few days. Starting a new path toward an unknown future can be precarious, even in the best of times, and so, your respect and adherence to sensible law and order during this tumultuous transition has been beyond commendable. All but for one of you. One man here has flagrantly flouted our laws—nay, he's insulted basic human dignity. That individual sits across from me here today," the Steward said, gesturing with an open palm to the man below him. "The Witenagemot has come to the decision that, for the sake of trust and transparency between the residents of Cardinal's Nest and its ruling council, the trial of this immoral individual will be held in a public tribunal commission format, according to the applicable bylaws of the New Destiny Constitution, so that all may witness. So that you may all sleep sound at night knowing criminality of any kind amongst us shall be weeded out with extreme prejudice. Your safety and security are the Witenagemot's only concerns, and no one here shall be allowed to threaten that great trust." The Steward's eyes pierced the crowd, falling in an attack dive like that of the eagle represented on his shoulders onto the enraged figure of Maisie Sagal. It then flicked rapidly between the young girl and the large priest beside her. The crowd followed the gaze. Soon, all eyes present, apart from those of Jed and his gathered friends, were turned toward the dead doctor's daughter and Father Boyd, her partner in booze peddling. Jed saw a variety of emotions warring on the faces of those residents near him in the press: anger was there, so was pity, but it was mostly anxious confusion that reigned.

"Today, you shall all witness the justice of the Witenagemot." The Steward's ringing voice drew the crowd's collective attention back to him. "We ask for your decorum and cooperation throughout these proceedings. Remain quiet and settled, or you shall be removed. This will be your one and only warning on that account. Our footmen stand at the ready all throughout you in the crowd."

Jed looked at the crowd in front of him, searching for said footmen. He could only make out a few of them nearby. The Witenagemot had indeed uniformed all their members over the past few days. Their fancy clothing printers had made golden dress coats with finely embroidered black Old-English "W's" on the right breast pocket for the supervisors, two of whom stood a few rows up from Jed. The footmen were harder to spot in their gray version of the former security squad's tactical blouse, trousers and tennis shoes, complete with golden "W's" on right breast pockets. Those gray uniforms had a way of blending into the sea of riotously colored clothing adorning the bodies of the residents around him, and Jed gave up the search before it had even really begun.

"They have been empowered by their lieutenants and the sacred authority of the New Destiny Constitution itself. They have been granted discretionary authority to deal with any disturbances here today. But I trust that their efforts will not be necessary. I think I know you all well enough by now to be sure of that." The Steward paused to allow a confused murmur that came across as only partial agreement ripple through the crowd. "This assembled commission, which I chair with full authority, has a supreme mandate to seek justice. But we must, at the same time, balance that sacred trust against the best interests of our residents. As such, the Witenagemot has judged it prudent to protect the identity of the victim in this case. We felt it would be only cruel to force her to face her accuser in such a public setting. Knowing this, we decided to have her prepare a sworn statement that shall be read by Lieutenant Dobechek, after which, the defendant will be allowed to respond to his accuser and offer up any defenses he may have. So, I'll remind you once more to be mindful of your decorum and to wait until this proceeding has concluded and you have been excused before leaving the Grand Rotunda. Now, without further ado," the Steward said, aiming his open palm toward the still rigid Lieutenant Dobechek, "Lieutenant, will you please read aloud the sworn statement?"

Dobechek snapped to attention and marched, axe slung over one shoulder, to an open space of floor just in front of the Steward on his dais. Jed went to his tiptoes to get a look at Colton Murphy as the lieutenant withdrew her pocket tablet from her black tactical blouse. Beneath the lank, greasy hair, Murphy's eyes now darted back and forth, looking at anything and everything. *Searching for an escape route,* Jed guessed, though he knew the poor fool didn't stand a chance of clearing the encroaching mob all about him, even if he did spot one. *There ain't no escaping this place, anyhow,* Jed thought. It was slightly possible, he supposed, that the man might pull an Elias and elude his captors for a few weeks, but just as it was bound to happen with Elias before very long, the Witen would catch him in the end. Cardinal's Nest was a huge place, it must be said, but it wasn't *that* huge.

Murphy's eyes finally held steady on a fixed point once Lieutenant Dobechek cleared her throat and began reading the victim's sworn statement off her pocket tablet. "Last Friday, Day 3 of the New Era, I was working the dish sinks in the kitchen of the main cafeteria alongside Colton Murphy." Jed turned from the accused to watch the big lieutenant placidly read the sworn statement. "We were pushing the cart of dried dishes through the kitchen to the stacking shelves near the back," Dobechek continued, "when Mr. Murphy pointed to the opposite back corner of the kitchen. He told me to look. I turned and saw that the large meat cooler door was left open. Mr. Murphy said we should close it. I told him to do it himself, but he was strangely insistent and made me come over to the cooler with him. Once we arrived at the cooler's open door, I noticed we were all alone in the kitchen. It was near shift's end, and most of my shiftmates had already left for the night, and the late crew wouldn't be arriving for another half hour. Mr. Murphy must've noticed the fear on my face when I realized we were all alone because he chose that moment to push me into the open cooler. I landed on my back on the hard metal floor, bashing my head in the process. I must've been knocked unconscious because the next thing I knew, I was waking up with Colton Murphy ripping my pants and underwear off me. I was still groggy, so at first, I could barely resist him. I remember slapping at him all weak and woozily. He then grabbed both of my wrists in one of his hands and drove the elbow of his free arm into my chin, slamming my head back down against the floor. The last thing I remember before blacking out again was him saying, 'You want this, bitch! Don't act like you don't. Quit your damn squirming.' I woke up sometime later with him inside of me, raping me. I remember thinking it had to be a horrible dream, but then the pain hit, and it was all too real. I screamed and screamed, but he had closed the cooler door when I was unconscious, so no one but us could hear. I remember him laughing and telling me to be quiet, that he'd be finished soon. I remember him smiling above me. And I remember aiming for that smile when I bashed my head into his. The headbutt managed to get him off of me, and I was able to scramble to my feet, though I was only able to make it to the door and push it open before Mr. Murphy wrapped his arms around me from behind and flung me back into the cooler. I started screaming at the top of my lungs again, which made him try and close the cooler door once more. So I rushed him, and we quickly began a struggle to control the door. After a few moments of fighting back and forth, he managed to throw me back to the ground and pull the door closed. I was exhausted, woozy, and terrified at that point. I remember just lying on the ground in frozen shock as he pulled his penis back out and looked down at me with cold, dead eyes. I thought I was going to get raped again, and most likely killed, but before he made it one step toward me, the cooler door was flung open. Two of my colleagues had not yet left for the night and had heard me screaming from inside the cafeteria hall. They saw what was plainly happening and immediately restrained Mr. Murphy. My colleagues then tied up Mr. Murphy. Then one of them went to seek out our proper authority in the Witenagemot." Lieutenant Dobechek tucked her pocket tablet away as soon as she was done reading.

The gathered crowd remained silent as she marched back to her position beside the first maroon A in the massive logo. No sooner had the lieutenant snapped back to attention than the Steward pounded his fist down on the tabletop in front of him to quell any whispers among the crowd. Heavy silence reigned once more. Jed was sure the Steward was enjoying the tension and his supreme control over it. The man hadn't actually broken out in a smile, but Jed could see it there in his eyes. The Steward's voice was full of serene reverence when he finally did speak. "Mr. Colton Murphy, please stand, sir." Murphy got to his feet right away, albeit with utter disdain in his every motion. "What say you to these charges, Mr. Murphy?"

"I say she's a lying bitch, hiding behind y'all's pocket tablet." Murphy's voice was as greasy as the rest of him. "Nothing ever happened," he added with dripping contempt. "And if y'all was able to question her in this bullshit court, you'd figured that out quick enough, but I ain't about to protect that lying whore. I'll tell ya who that bitch is—"

"Do that, Mr. Murphy," the Steward cut in to say, in a voice that displayed its first hints of anger, "and you will forgo your right to a defense, your tongue will be sliced out with a hot knife, and you will be blown naked out an air lock. Your victim is a brave woman, and this tribunal will not tolerate any slander against her, nor disclosure of her identity. Understand that, Mr. Murphy, before you dare open that lying mouth of yours again," the Steward ended, a finger pointed at Murphy's chest.

"How very impartial." Jed heard the statement plain as day, even though he was sure the priest meant to utter it under his breath, if at all, judging by the look on the clergyman's face.

Many in the crowd had heard it as well; faces were once more turning their way. "Silence was requested, ladies and gentlemen," the Steward reminded the crowd in a commanding voice, "and silence we shall have. Hold your tongue, Father," he said, shifting his pointing finger to Boyd's chest.

"It's a fair point though, ain't it?" Maisie shouted.

Jed felt the thickening tension ratchet up with each silent moment that followed the young girl's shout. "You think Mr. Murphy isn't getting a fair shake, Ms. Sagal?" The Steward's question only added to the simmering tension. "Perhaps you and Father Boyd would care to serve as this man's counsel. Do you think you can defend his actions, Ms. Sagal?" When neither Maisie nor the priest had an answer for him, the Steward pressed on. "No? What, nothing to say to that?" Still, the pair remained silent. "I understand your distraught condition, Ms. Sagal, so I will go ahead and overlook this disruption, though the good Father ought to know better," he added with a serpent's smirk aimed at the priest. "But interrupt these proceedings again, and you shall be removed from here ... forcefully, if need be. Understand?" Father Boyd gave the Steward the nod of acknowledgment he was seeking. Maisie however, never lost her scowl of disgust as she stood firm, not giving the Steward the satisfaction of cowing her. The man on the high throne behind the large black desk must've decided not to push the issue, despite Maisie's defiance. He turned his attention back to the accused rapist before him. "You name the victim a liar, Mr. Murphy. Is that correct?" he asked after a few beats.

"You're goddamn right," Murphy confirmed.

"You say nothing happened, yet the two colleagues mentioned in the sworn statement report that they caught you just as described. They confirmed all that they could of your victim's story, in fact. They flung the cooler door open to discover your innocent victim bloodied and battered and half-undressed, lying on the floor with you standing over her, your vile cock in your tiny little hand, ready to finish raping the poor, helpless woman. Both of those heroic men are here today and are more than willing to testify to what they saw. Would you care to call them forward, Mr. Murphy? Perhaps they'll tell a different story if you question them. Who can say? I do know they are eager for the chance to confront you, though." Murphy had no intention of calling the two men who caught him in the act to testify—that was plain to see. His shoulders were hunched, and Jed could once more make out his eyes darting all about the rotunda. The stupid asshole must've only then been realizing that his bluster and arrogance were not going to carry him safely through this mess.

"They're fucking liars, too," Murphy barked out suddenly in a bitter voice.

"Well then, let's call them forward so you might name them such to their faces," the Steward said, motioning to someone in the crowd.

"Fuck that. They'd only lie more," Murphy responded feebly.

The Steward held up his hand to forestall his prior request to the unknown person in the crowd. "Have you any other defense for your actions, Mr. Murphy?" The smugness in the Steward's tone rolled down from his lofty perch, curdling Murphy's hopes utterly as it engulfed him. Jed could see on the man's face that defiance was fading, and fear had taken its place. The Steward must've seen it as well, for a smile did finally slide across his sharp features, for a few seconds at least. "Well, Mr. Murphy, what say you?" The man only spit in answer. Though in his fear, his spittle was thin and pathetic. "Be seated, Mr. Murphy," the Steward commanded. Murphy was flustered. He clearly wanted to argue, to plead his case before an interested party. Unfortunately for Colton Murphy, no such body existed aboard Cardinal's Nest Station just then. He sat down without a word. "I am ready to make my ruling," the Steward announced to the assembled residents. "This tribunal was commissioned by the Witenagemot Council and sealed with the approval of the Commander to weigh the evidence of this case with solemnity and a blind heart. As chair of this tribunal, it is my duty to issue the final verdict. So, in accordance with the requisite statutes of the New Destiny Constitution, this commission finds the defendant, Mr. Colton Murphy, Cafeteria Attendant #22, guilty of rape, an egregious violation of the New Destiny Constitution and the Commander's peace."

"Well, this commission can eat my ass," the convicted rapist howled back at the Steward. "You psycho motherfuckers ain't got no power over me," he told the Witen with transparently empty conviction.

"I beg to differ, sir," the Steward growled right back at the man with sour menace. Echoes of the retort could be heard throughout the chamber as the Grand Rotunda, which had become silent as a tomb. The hairs on the back of Jed's neck stood up as a faint sound, just on the edge of hearing, touched his ears a moment later. The residents around him heard it as well; it was no illusion. The sound grew louder with each passing breathless second. *Footfalls*, Jed surmised. *A heavy tread.* It was obvious in the crash and cadence. Equally as obvious to Jed was who must be delivering those footfalls.

Confirmation came a few breaths later. Jasper Montrois, the man Jed and all his fellow residents were now supposed to call the Commander, stepped out from behind the Steward's raised desk to glower at the crowd through his scarred face and milky white right eye. Where had he come from? Where had he been? Jed couldn't say. But as soon as he materialized, black axe in hand, to stand above the silver O of the floor logo, Jed chided himself for not predicting his entrance sooner. *These guys sure get off on the theater of all of this shit,* Jed thought as the Commander raised his right, axe-wielding arm above his head. The Commander was uniformed in the identical gear of his fellow officers in the Witen. His gold-trimmed black uniform was set apart only by the single, seven-pointed, golden star shimmering in pride of place above each shoulder.

"I am justice," the bear of a man promised the residents. "This is my holy instrument," he added, pumping his black battleaxe up and down twice in gnarled, long-fingered hands. "From this day until the end of days, whatever blood stains its blade shall serve only to further sanctify its righteous vengeance. See it, my residents… Know it… Fear it." The crowd was still, in a hypnotized silence, and if they were anything like Jed, too discombobulated to resist the magnetism of the Commander's testimony and exceedingly afraid of that black battleaxe. If they were like him, they remembered the damage that wicked edge could inflict. The Commander lowered his axe back to his side as he turned to face the elevated judge. 'Steward, you were chair of the tribunal commission for this man, Colton Murphy. Will you confirm to me your judgement?"

The Steward cleared his throat as he leaned forward in his chair. "Colton Murphy has been duly convicted, according to the applicable bylaws of the New Destiny Constitution, of the egregious violation of rape," he told the Commander with what seemed to Jed like forced ceremony.

"Very well then. Steward, the block, if you please," prompted the former security commander, his axe-less hand held out in expectation.

Jed watched from the still silent crowd as the Steward bent, slowly coming back up with a chunk of rough-cut lumber. Jed took it for a thick log cut fresh from The Meadow's forest. It was roughly two and a half feet high and two feet in diameter. All the bark had been stripped from it, leaving only the raw green wood underneath. The Steward awkwardly leaned over the desk to pass off the bulky hunk of timber to the waiting arm of the Commander. Jed could guess what the block was for; it didn't take a wildly imaginative mind to puzzle it out. He also thought having the crude device at the ready undercut the Witen's claims of righteous justice a bit. It made the whole thing seem premeditated in a way that flew in the face of their supposed purpose for this spectacle.

Though, if anyone else felt the same as he, they kept their beliefs as privately as Jed kept his. The silence was pervasive, almost penetratingly so, as the Commander walked with the chopping block under one arm and his gleaming battleaxe in the other hand toward the center of the logo's silver O, just as Lieutenants Dobechek and Woodson sheathed their long axes across their backs and moved toward the convict still seated before his lonely black desk. Too late, the disgusting fool finally understood the block's implications. He bolted straight up from his chair, bashing his thighs against the desk in the process.

Murphy was mid snarl, mid agonized gasp, and halfway through a half limp, half fierce defensive punch when the two lieutenants arrived at his side. Dobechek batted the offending arm aside contemptuously as Woodson grabbed hold of Murphy's other arm, bending it back before smashing him flat on the desktop. Then Dobechek, the scowling ginger officer, snatched hold of Murphy's other arm, wrenching it back to meet its twin. Murphy kicked and bucked. He did try to break free; no one can say he went to the block meekly or contritely. Regardless, the two lieutenants had him standing before the Commander alongside the freshly cut chopping block in a few short seconds. To add literal insult to injury, the crowd, who had been against the man from the jump, was now openly taunting and ridiculing the pathetic convict.

Montrois turned from Murphy to once again raise high his wicked weapon. He made a slow circuit in place with the axe held up in an arm thicker than Jed's leg and more muscled than a bull's shoulder. Jed guessed he was trying to gain the crowd's attention. *Again, with the theater,* he thought, exasperated. *We get it already. You have our attention, you fascist bastard.*

"I trust all of you have read the New Destiny Constitution by now," the Commander began. "So you will all know the penalty for an egregious-level offense then." Jed hadn't read the damn Destiny Constitution, but he could guess the penalty. He guessed *egregious-level* was going to be a pretty loose term used by these Witen bastards in the days to come as well. "I implore you all not to look away," the Commander said to his subjects in a voice that sounded more like an order than a plea. "Our footmen will mark those of you that do." *All stick and no carrot,* Jed thought with a resignation laced with both fear and sorrow. "For there to be peace, there must be justice. And true justice must be witnessed. The Witenagemot will not hide in the dark. The Witenagemot is the justice of Cardinal's Nest Station. The Witenagemot is *humanity's* justice. And *I am* the Witenagemot. Now, witness my justice." The Commander lowered the axe and turned back to the captive still squirming in the unyielding arms of the two staunch officers. "Any last words, Mr. Murphy?"

"You... y-you can't," Murphy stuttered, disbelieving. "You can't do this. You f-f-fuckers got no fucking right. Let me go!" he shouted in the faces of the lieutenants.

He was still shouting at the officers to let him go when the Commander stepped up to smash an open-palmed slap across the sputtering man's face. "Make him kneel," he ordered his subordinates. Without hesitation, Woodson and Dobechek drove their captive to his knees. Murphy never once stopped squirming for freedom as they bent him over the chopping block at the very center of the shiny silver O. Dobechek had been leaning on Murphy's back to keep him still but backed off when her leader stepped into position. She instead held the much smaller man in place with a firm hand pressed down on his shoulders. Woodson quickly added his strength, pinning the man firmly to the thick block of timber.

The black axe flashed up without warning. Jed had just enough time to look over at the priest before the cruel steel fell back down to its savage purpose. He didn't know what he was hoping to see, exactly. Did he want the priest to shout an end to the madness? Did he want the self-proclaimed clergyman to keep his tongue and suffer through the debacle silently with all the rest? In that moment, Jed couldn't be sure. Even after the Commander slashed his black executioner's blade down on the back of Colton Murphy's neck, while Father Boyd held his tongue and dropped his eyes, Jed still wasn't sure. Even after the rapist's head dropped from the block to roll away with its greasy brown hair slapping at its blind, dead eyes, Jed *still* wasn't sure.

"Elias!" The shriek exploded like a stick of dynamite in a library throughout the crowd. Jed, along with the rest of the residents, turned to face the voice. Maisie Sagal was already shoving her way through the press of bodies by the time Jed laid eyes on her. "Elias!" the girl screamed again, this time from six rows deep.

Jed followed Maisie's line of sight to Elias Sagal. The boy was slouched against the colossal archway of Branch 6. The crowd wasn't far behind in tracking the boy. The chattering started almost immediately but reached a quick crescendo as Maisie, who had just broken free from the mass of people, sprinted to her brother's side. Jed was dozens of yards away, but he could clearly see that the boy did not look good. His clothes and face were caked in a thick layer of dust and grime. He looked frail and weak, like he needed to lean against that archway frame just to stay upright. Jed shuddered to think of how the boy must have been living these past few days. *God, when's the last time the kid ate anything?*

Exuding its sad herd mentality, the crowd, as one, moved toward the Sagal children. Jed and his friends flowed over with all the rest, though soon, the priest started shoving a more aggressive path through the crowd. Dolly, Alice, and Stevie were right on his heels. Jed followed with Larry Holderman at a more stately pace. Jed Redding didn't like the idea of intruding on the children's reunion. It didn't seem right to him. He mostly followed the crowd to the Sagals' side to intervene if any of his fellow residents decided to be as overly intrusive as only a post-Infection Event resident of Cardinal's Nest Station could truly be.

When he and Larry did arrive at Maisie and Elias's side, Jed had a small moment to admire Dolly, Stevie, and Alice Stark, who were all pushing back against the nosy crowd. Only Father Boyd was inside the 10-foot cordon the women were enforcing. The priest had his hand on Maisie's shoulder as she was bent low, still calling out to her brother and attempting to look into his downcast eyes. Jed burst through his friends' impromptu barricade and turned to add his presence just as Maisie stood up and shouted at the crowd, "Please, just give us some space, people! Go home! Get lost, for all I care. This ain't none of your business."

"You heard her, folks," the priest boomed in support. "Show's over, anyhow."

"I don't believe that's your call, Father." Jed turned toward the cold voice to see the Steward surrounded by Lieutenants Dobechek, Woodson, Masterson, and Schwambach. The Commander stood just behind the encircled Steward. Lieutenants Gregson and Dirks stood just behind him. The lieutenants had cleared a wide swath of residents, their axes held in front of them, to make their way to the Sagal kids. The crowd that only seconds before had been as rowdy as a death-metal concert fell ominously silent once again. The Steward reigned in a smirk as he added, "Let me remind you this is still an official Witenagemot tribunal proceeding. Only the Commander has the authority to dismiss the assembled residents."

"Have you some other poor fool's head to hack off today, Jasper?" the priest blurted in response.

The collective gasp that rippled through the crowd was frightening enough to send a shiver down Jed's arms. Lieutenants Dobechek and Masterson stepped angrily toward Father Boyd as the Steward responded with an outstretched finger, "Watch yourself now, Priest. Perhaps you haven't yet read the New Destiny Constitution. I understand you've got a lot going on in that liquor lab of yours, but failure to know the law is not an excuse for breaking it. The Commander is to be referred to only as such. Violations of this simple rule will be punished at the discretion of the ranking authority on scene." The Steward turned around to face his leader. Jed looked over at the gorilla in the black-and-gold uniform as well. The Commander didn't seem to be paying any attention to what was unfolding in front of him. Jed was pretty sure that both his milky eye and his good eye alike were fixed firm on Stevie Hyun, still standing guard near the Sagals.

Jed thought he saw Stevie notice their tyrant's gaze just as the man you should never call Jasper snapped his attention toward Father Boyd. "Speak my true name, Priest," he told the failing clergyman in a voice so flat and emotionless it chilled Jed through and through.

Boyd wanted to say something snarky; Jed could see him swallow back a dozen witticisms. In the end, though, the priest looked toward Maisie and saw something there that evidently made him think better of pushing the buttons of a recent headsman. "The Commander," Boyd finally said to the floor in front of him.

Jed was afraid the begrudging public capitulation wouldn't be enough for the decapitator-in-chief. Instead, the Commander nodded once at the Steward and immediately turned his mangled gaze back to the redheaded beauty. That stare worried Jed. He didn't know what was drawing his ruler's eyes to the wife of the man's former friend and squad member. The Steward's face was slightly puzzled when he turned back to the priest as well, though the look only lasted for an instant.

"The boy needs help," Father Boyd sullenly told the Steward.

Masterson and Dobechek stepped back a few paces from the priest as they turned to the Steward to hear his response. "I agree," the tribunal judge returned with an impenetrable look on his face. "We shall see that he gets the best care available. After all, the Witenagemot exists only to serve its people."

"I can take care of my brother on my own, thank you very much," Maisie snapped as she stepped away from Elias and toward the Steward.

"Can you?" the Steward asked, as though he'd been awaiting the setup. "'Cause I'd have to strongly disagree. I believe it would be highly irresponsible of our council to allow this poor, weakened boy to remain under your sole care. We have no wish to add to your troubles, Maisie. The Witenagemot is not blind to your state, but your father freely agreed to the terms of the Final Tournament. He lost, Ms. Sagal, and now it is incumbent upon each resident to come to terms with that fact—yourself included."

"Oh, go to hell, you jerk!" Maisie screamed as she rushed toward him. Thankfully, Dolly managed to reach her before either of the two nearby lieutenants. Jed had a strong belief that neither of those Neanderthals would have been quite so gentle or soothing.

"There it is, folks," the Steward said, addressing the whole crowd now. "Ms. Sagal, sadly, is clearly not fit to care for her poor, traumatized brother any longer, the brother who has, thankfully, returned to us after all these days. The boy clearly can't survive anymore i l guidance. I'm certain you all can see this as plainly as I do." The Steward paused to allow a few of the worst sycophants nearest to him to nod in agreement. "So, is there anyone here among us today willing to do the Witenagemot the honorable service of watching over young Elias as he recovers from his trauma?"

"Hey, no!" Maisie shouted out in a panic. "You can't do this. He's my brother. You have no right to take him from me."

"Oh, no, Ms. Sagal, for there you err," the Steward said with an ugly grin. "On the strength of the Commander's victory over your father, we have every right."

Jed could see the impotent, desperate rage in Maisie's eyes. He wanted to do something. He wanted to say something. But Jed found himself just as helpless as the young girl. He was frozen in place, casting his eyes from the encroaching crowd back to Maisie and the boy behind her, still leaning against the archway with his eyes staring at the floor.

"I'll take the boy." Jed had been looking at Elias when the shout rang out from the crowd. His eyes flung toward the sound, landing on Helena Heathcoat standing five rows deep in the press. She stood out like a wine stain on a white dress in the sea of residents. Helena was nearly a head taller than everyone around her. Her tan turtleneck, with its black checkered pattern, along with her tight black leggings and white low-top sneakers, were quintessential Helena style, blending remarkably well with the prim posture and smirk she currently sported.

A beat later, he heard Alice Stark splutter in horror, "E-E-Elle, wh-wh... what the hell are you doing?"

"I have a spare room, sir," Helena bellowed across twenty feet of rotunda floor to the Steward. "It's just me in my two-bedroom quarters now. I'd be honored to care for the boy. I promise to do you and the Commander proud, sir," she assured them.

"Elle, you go too far," Alice Stark yelled at her wife with heartbreak in every syllable. "He ain't yours, Elle. You can't take him from the only family he's got left. Please, these madmen aren't worth all this. Please, talk to me. You don't have to do this, Elle. I understand you're angry with me, but we can settle all that without dragging these innocent children into it."

Helena did glance at her wife, but Jed saw only bitter resolve on her face. She didn't even bother responding to her life partner. Instead, she turned quickly back to the Steward with an obsequious and compliant manner on her face and in her body language. Without delay, the Steward turned back to the Commander, who was still staring at Stevie Hyun. Montrois broke off his leer long enough to nod at his subordinate. "Very well, ma'am," the Steward said, turning back to Helena. "Lieutenants Dobechek and Masterson, if you would kindly collect the boy and deliver him to this honorable resident."

The officers instantly marched toward Elias. Maisie twisted free of Dolly's grip. "Run, Elias! Stay hidden. I'll come find you. Run!"

Elias didn't budge. The dirty, drawn, and weak young boy didn't so much as lift his head. Dobechek was on him in two short heartbeats, while Masterson broke off to restrain Maisie. The frog-faced officer lifted the young girl off her feet with one arm. The priest made to stop him but broke off halfway through his first step. Jed couldn't name him coward, for he hadn't moved in the slightest to stop Masterson. Neither did Larry Holderman or Gabe Duchesne. Even Dolly, Stevie, and Alice, who had been the more zealous of Maisie's defenders so far, didn't move to interfere. As Dobechek bent over to clasp Elias's hand in her own and lead him off toward Helena Heathcoat's waiting treacherous arms, neither Jed nor any of his friends moved to the rescue.

"*Now* the show is over," the Commander growled as Elias was passed off from Lieutenant Dobechek's care to that of Helena Heathcoat's. Meanwhile, neither the tyrant's dark eye nor his light ever once left Stevie Hyun. "You may all go back about your business," he told the crowd. "Lieutenant Masterson," the Commander called to his officer, still without shifting his gaze from Stevie, "let Maisie go."

Masterson released the kicking and screaming young girl in his arm. The Commander then turned without another word and headed for Branch 1's enormous archway. Jed watched Stevie shudder with relief when the Commander's eyes were finally lifted from her. Masterson shoved past the priest an instant later, while Maisie beat uselessly at the man's retreating back. The lieutenant shrugged off the assault as the minor nuisance it was and joined up with the rest of his councilmembers within a few steps. Maisie was left in a shuddering, ineffectual heap at Father Boyc's feet. Jed could do no more than watch on with numb despair as the Witenagemot Council marched sedately from the mayhem and straight toward their sanctuary.

CHAPTER 2
ELIAS

Helena Heathcoat drenched the pancakes in maple syrup. Elias had not lacked for carbs or protein during his stay with Ms. Heathcoat. The elegant older woman had a hearty breakfast ready for him every morning before he left and a full three-course dinner waiting when he returned every evening. The food was delicious, too. Elias had never eaten so well in his life. But with the intense training the Witenagemot had been putting him and the perhaps 50 children left in the Integration Program through lately, Elias had needed every last morsel just to keep his energy levels up. He was pleased, with that in mind, to find today's breakfast menu featured pancakes. Ms. Heathcoat had made the dish several times over the last few weeks. She never failed to spoon a hearty dollop of the dairy farm's fresh-churned butter on top of his stack before drowning his plate in a thick pool of sweet, greenhouse-special maple syrup. It made for a fantastic carbo-load, and thus, was the perfect dish to prepare Elias for the important day ahead.

I had best bring it today. Ricky sure ain't gonna take it easy on me, Elias thought before marveling at just how much he cared. Elias could remember being utterly bereft of care and interests only a few weeks earlier. He thought back to the lost soul he'd been in the wake of his father's death and was stunned at how far he'd come since then. *I got the Steward to thank for that,* Elias reminded himself. *You better not fail him today.*

"How are the pancakes, Eli?"

"Delicious," Elias assured Ms. Heathcoat around a mouthful of sugary stickiness.

"Good. The Steward tells me you got yourself a big day today, so you be sure to eat as much as you can. I can always make more if you like."

"No, this'll be plenty," Elias assured his host. "Thanks, Ms. Heathcoat."

"How many times have I told ya to call me Elle?"

"Yes, Elle," Elias replied.

"Thank you, Eli," Ms. Heathcoat said through a grin. "Oh yeah I got eggs cooking for you, too," the tall, short-haired woman added, rising to her feet and turning toward her kitchen. "This place is now the quarters of Elle and Eli," Ms. Heathcoat told him, turning back suddenly with a warm smile on her face. "At least until the Witen calls you on to bigger and better things," she proposed with a wink.

Elias only smirked back as he forked up another bite of pancakes. Their relationship hadn't always been quite so affable. Elias hadn't wanted to go with Ms. Heathcoat that day back in the Grand Rotunda. He hadn't wanted to go with anyone anywhere, in fact. His feet and stomach had betrayed him that day, that was all. Elias had been hiding out in the tunnels and vents of the Nest's substructure since the Commander defeated his father. He'd been feeling such shame and sorrow that Elias was sure he could never face the world again. He'd intended to hide out until his heart stopped beating.

Elias had been in such a bad place, so dissatisfied with his very own skin and soul, that the only thought he could hold in his mind was a primal desire to no longer exist, though he lacked the courage to do anything about it, beyond hiding away in the darkness, hoping to become a part of it. But somehow, in his hunger and thirst-driven delirium, he'd stumbled his way toward the Witen's trial of some sicko rapist taking place that day in the Grand Rotunda. Even now, the memory seemed unreal. He'd felt ill just to be seen by the other citizens. And when he'd seen his sister... well, the shame had been crippling. He could do no more than stare at the floor as his fate had been decided around him.

Elias had known that going with Helena was not what his sister had wanted. He'd heard her scream for him to run, that she'd come find him. But as much as he didn't want to upset Maisie, even a little bit more, he couldn't find the strength within himself to face her either. He tried to imagine begging her forgiveness for getting their father killed, but the thought near drove him mad. What if she screamed and told him she hated him? Or worse yet, what if she didn't? What if she held him and forgave him? Elias had tried to imagine a life where his sister would always know that his cowardice had killed their father. The thought had bugs crawling over his skin, just as it drove the breath clean from his lungs. How could he ever hope to look her in the eyes again? It was all just far too much, and so he'd kept his head down and allowed himself to be led off to the waiting arms of Helena Heathcoat.

Elias hadn't been a good guest those first couple of days, he was sure of that. Helena never complained, but he knew she took his coldness to heart. Not knowing the woman's motivations for taking him from his sister had made for some awkward meals in those first few days. Elias couldn't be around his sister without cracking up, he knew that, but neither did he want to accept pity and care from a woman who was clearly working against his sister's interests. He was confused beyond reason and, as a result, kept mostly to himself. Elias wasn't sure if he'd actually spoken a comprehensible word to Ms. Heathcoat at the start. Looking back now left him ashamed at his behavior toward his loving host. But of course, that was all before the Steward had showed up to take him for that long walk around the Nest's living quarters.

It was three days in, maybe four, Elias wasn't exactly sure. He and Helena were suffocating in the thick silence inside her dining room when the hailing bell chimed. Helena had gotten up to answer the door, and when she passed back through the room's narrow archway, none other than the Steward himself was trailing behind her. The man on whom Elias had once fixed a firm fascination proceeded to politely invite him on a stroll about the living quarters' alleyways with which the boy was so familiar. To his present shame, Elias had only reluctantly, and extremely sullenly, accepted the invitation, staring down at his shoes for the first few dozen meters of that fateful walk. It took a bit for Elias to break through his choking fog of guilt and heartbreak before the wise words of the Steward began to consciously register in his mind.

"None of this is your fault, Elias. I hope you can understand that," the Steward had said after a turn down Alleyway IV in Violet Corridor.

"I know," Elias had replied with a great bit of distance still obvious in his voice.

"That's good," the imposing man had assured him. "It wouldn't be fair if the tragic events of the past few weeks had to be compounded by the destruction of your curious soul, Elias."

He hadn't known what to say to that. The statement seemed strange coming from a man as august as the Steward. Elias had never spoken to the guy. He figured he was nothing more than one of a hundred or so other kids aboard station in the eyes of the Witen's number-two man. So, Elias hadn't responded, unless avoiding eye contact by staring down at his toes was a response.

"Your father was an incredible man, Eli. May I call you Eli?" Elias had managed to lift his gaze long enough to look the Steward in the eyes as he nodded his confused and reluctant approval. "I understand if you question the sincerity of that statement, coming from me, but I swear to you it's the truth. I greatly admired the man. His death was the one sour tragedy marring the core of the pristine fruit that is our Witenagemot. It was wholly unnecessary. It need not have been, Eli... But for fate, I suppose. I hope you can find a way to believe me when I tell you that the Commander and I did all we could to avoid it. But your father was who he was ... and fate played out the way it did. Eli," the Steward paused over his name, drawing in a breath to mask clear emotion, "it's my belief that our ancestors watch over us all, even now, from some distant plane. They can see us. I do believe that. I believe your father sees you, Eli. And I believe he is damn proud of you because he is now blessed with the great privilege of seeing the man you will one day become. And I'll bet it's that knowledge that's putting his soul at peace after the failures of his final days. Your father knows now the error of his resistance, I'll bet. Yet he has the consolation of knowing it was all a part of fate. A fate that blossoms bright around you now, Eli. Your father's eyes couldn't be opened in life, but his folly need not be a disaster. You can set it to rights. You see, Eli, your father—great man though he undoubtedly was—clung stubbornly to a dead way of living, thinking, and being as fundamental humans. In that old, dead way of being, which your father did gloriously champion, the entitlement of the individual was revered above all. Your father felt that old, fundamental human entitlement so profoundly that he could not reckon with all the ways the realities of his present circumstances had shifted the true priorities of life. Is any of this making sense at all, Eli?"

Yes and no, Elias had wanted to answer. The Steward had been using some big words that were hard to follow, but he did feel, on some level, that he understood what the man was trying to tell him. It seemed to mesh with things he'd been frustrated with his father about before the Final Tournament had ever even begun. Elias remembered begging his father not to fight Carrie's husband. He remembered how much he idolized the security staff and how much he'd wished his father did as well. And all those memories seemed to add up to some sort of agreement with the point the Steward was trying to make. Even so, Elias felt a tightness in his gut. He didn't think it was honorable to agree with the sentiments of a man his father had so clearly counted an enemy. The Steward's voice had been consoling and honest, but Elias had been pretty sure the man was still denigrating his father's memory despite the calming tone and poetic language, none of which sat well with Elias in that moment.

Perhaps the Steward had recognized that feeling on his face because he'd placed a comforting hand on his shoulder and said, "It's okay to feel some anger toward the Commander and me, Elias. Despite how wrong your father may have been in his priorities, he was still your father. I get that, Eli. I do. The Commander does, too. We understand how emotionally charged you so rightly may be. That's why I didn't drop in on you and Ms. Heathcoat right away. I had a boy of my own once. You remind me of him a great deal, in fact. Anyway, my prior experience taught me that a few days of cooling off would be most prudent and ... uhm ... beneficial." The Steward had released a few sad chuckles with that.

The news of the Steward's son, coupled with his clear emotion at his memory, along with his comfort in showing it all to Elias, brought the boy's attention completely off his shoes and onto the lines of life running chaotically across the emotion-stricken face of the man once known as Harclay Aponyaschefski. "What's his name, your son? What happened to him?" Elias had asked the questions too fast to realize how intrusive and rude they were. Obviously, whatever had happened to his son wasn't pleasant. Any idiot using his brain instead of his mouth would see it as clearly taboo subject matter. But Elias had been drained, physically and mentally. He wasn't in a good headspace and so forgave himself the lapse in decorum.

The Steward, for his part, had been incredibly gracious. He gave no indication of anger or annoyance as he went on to answer Elias's impertinent questions. "His name was Walter," he said with a sad smile. "Wally, we called him, his mother and me. She and I were separated years ago... Couldn't agree on anything, you see, apart from the nickname, that is," he added with a glint of dark humor poking through the sad grin. It passed in a flash. And as they came around yet another twist in Violet Corridor, a tempest of encompassing grief rolled across the Steward's face. "I remember being so afraid that first day. Nobody knew what was happening. People were turning on each other, regardless of whether or not they'd been turned into Damned. Everyone was trying to flee the city, so the roads were jam-packed, making sitting ducks of all the unfortunate souls stuck there to the roving hordes. It was hell on Earth, in other words. So, when Wally and I made it to those caves in Sharpe's Woods unscathed and unhunted, you can imagine how relieved I felt. I dared to believe we could survive out there. We both did. Then we started making supply runs. I swear, each run was harder than the last, with more and more of the gray bastards to hide from. Oh, gee, forgive my language there, Eli, if you would." Elias had shaken his head to dismiss the unnecessary concern. "Well, anyway... I guess I'm just trying to explain that I should've known back then that it was all bound to end badly. Hell, I probably did know on some level. Wally was a few years your senior, but just a kid, nonetheless. I should've put up more of a fight. I should've put my foot down and forbid him from leaving that last time. But I... I... I was weak, Eli, and I let him go. He never came back. The Infection Event claimed him, right along with all the countless others."

"Oh," Elias had dumbly responded. In fairness to himself, he didn't know what else to say. No adult had ever been so frank with him in his life, save maybe Carrie Montrois. The heavy emotional territory he and the Steward were trudging down left Elias lacking the conversational ability to participate with anything beyond an "oh" and maybe an "uh huh."

"We all made mistakes in that old world, Eli," the Steward had told Elias, stopping a few feet from one of the many Holographic Interface Information Kiosks (HIIKs) located at alleyway junctions. Elias was no match for the magnetism of his presence. His eyes had locked onto the Steward's only a few inches above him. The Steward wasn't a very tall man; Elias lacked only a handful of inches to top him, but even so, there was something in the man's presence that seemed to radiate dominance and authority. Although, he also somehow maintained an endearing approachability all the while. "Your father's mistake was opposing life's new realities and resisting the Witen's necessary supervision. Mine was allowing my son to believe in a dead hope, in hope for a dead world. I let him believe that he needed to keep us alive in order to outlast the unoutlastable. If I held him back from that last supply run, if I had told him the truth I knew even then, that the once beautiful and glorious hope of the old world was dead forever, then he'd have been there with me to be rescued by the Commander and his squad, and it wouldn't have to be me alone accounted as the sole survivor of the Infection Event on Earth. But it all went the other way, Eli, and that's just the way it is. Nothing to be done for it now. Fate was what fate was. My son and your father were martyrs to humanity's new age, Eli. That's just the way it all went. Now, that doesn't have to make sense to us, and we don't have to like it, but it is what it is, nevertheless. We all made mistakes, and we can't rewrite the past. All we've got is the road before us. The Infection Event has marked our rebirth as a species. And for whatever reason, through whatever strange turns of fate, you and I have found ourselves among the survivors. You and I are among the pioneers of the new world, Eli. And we need you, Elias. God knows we need you, kid."

The bold earnestness of the statement threw Elias for a loop. Here was this important, influential man treating him like an equal and appealing to him on the most basic of levels. Elias had been too caught up in his own grief to recognize or appreciate how exceedingly unlikely it was that he should count himself among the final 500 human beings left alive in the universe. A wave of shame washed over him. Everyone aboard station, indeed, everyone who'd ever drawn a breath on Earth, had lost someone because of the Infection Event. Was his particular grief superior to everyone's so as to excuse closing himself off from the responsibility implicit in being one of his species' last few survivors? Elias did not think so. He had dug deep to touch his pain in the hope it would rise up and wash away this newfound guilt the Steward was laying on him, but it had caught in the webs of his mind, and deeply confused though he still was, Elias found himself taken in by the Steward's reasoning. He could not help but send his imagination shooting off in a thousand different directions, pondering just what it was the Steward and his Witenagemot could possibly need of him.

That was, until he remembered his sister. Maisie, like their father before her, was the Witen's unambiguous enemy. He had nearly fainted just thinking about adding "siding with his sister's foes" to the crushing shame he already felt over his cowardly involvement in their father's demise. Adding such a betrayal to the tangible corruption in their familial bond was the last thing Elias had wanted to do. He suspected he needed to be working toward her forgiveness and understanding, not away from it. Maisie was ever on his mind in those first few days in Ms. Heathcoat's living quarters. He'd missed her terribly, though he dreaded facing her. Elias loved his sister, and he needed her probably as much as she needed him, but the fear of discovering a true and insurmountable gulf between them had kept him away. It was better not to know, to avoid confirmation one way or the other, or so he tried to tell himself anyway.

Elias had been utterly confused, in other words, and the Steward must've seen that plain on his face as well. He somehow intuited the exact struggle Elias was grappling with. "We need your sister as well. I can only imagine how conflicted you must be. I'll bet that being seen walking and talking with me has got you pretty anxious, wondering just what Maisie might think. She'd most likely be pretty angry, I'd bet, and rightly so. I mean, my Commander killed your father, after I facilitated the whole circumstance in the first place. She's got every right to hate us, and so do you, Eli. But I trust that both you and your sister will come, in time, to understand how crushed we in the Witen are by your father's death, and how we had no choice. I trust that the both of you very good souls will come to feel the heavy responsibility that lays on the shoulders of every citizen of the Witenagemot, a responsibility that I'm sure your father now fully understands and readily condones from his peaceful plane in the great beyond. I speak, of course, of the responsibility we all have to each other to protect this station and one another, to ensure good harvests and well-maintained life-giving machinery, and to ensure the security of our entrusted responsibility by adhering to the rules and laws of rightful authority. That's really all us in the Witen are trying to do, Eli. We aren't cruel or heartless or unreasonable either, kid. We know the recognition of our new heavy responsibility will dawn on each Witen citizen in their own time. Your sister has some very righteous anger to work through. The Commander and I understand this, and it's another reason why our system of order we call the Witenagemot and its New Destiny Constitution is the perfect system to oversee the birth of our new world. You see, the Commander *is* the law. Thus, he can choose to ignore the laws stipulated in the Constitution when a situation calls for it. Your sister Maisie has been violating the New Destiny Constitution's laws left and right. But the Commander has great reverence for her and your father, and for you for that matter, and so, he has ordered the Witen to refrain from confronting her. You see, he has no wish to compound her suffering, nor yours. We deeply regret stripping your guardianship away from Maisie. I thought it was in your best interest, however, and the Commander *very reluctantly* agreed with me. He only has the best interests of both you and your sister at heart. Truly, you must believe that. He wants only to do right by both of you. It just about killed him to have to cause more grief to your family by sending you off with Ms. Heathcoat. But he had to 'cause he cares about you, kid."

Elias had tried to imagine the milky eyed, scarred behemoth of a man that was the Commander of the Witenagemot feeling any extra care or reverence or sympathy for anyone, much less a member of the Sagal family. The razor-sharp, black battleaxe always either in his hand or strapped to his back whenever he was seen in public seemed to belie any sort of understanding or lenient disposition. Yet somehow, Elias supposed the wholesome sincerity in the Steward's face spoke to the truth of his assurances. After all, the Commander was Carrie Montrois's husband. How could her spouse not have a kind and understanding nature at heart? *Right?*

Before Elias had been able to answer himself, the Steward had continued with his entreaties. "The Commander trusts your sister will come around after she blows off whatever steam is lingering within her. If he were a lesser man, or if our Witen were unworthy, innocent hurt and broken folks like you and your sister would be chewed up and spat out by the negligent mechanisms of holy bureaucracy. Luckily for all of us, the supreme authority wielded by our Commander allows him to ensure true justice never falls victim to those sorts of irrational ministrations ever again. So, fear not for your sister, Eli. She will be taken care of. I'll even guarantee to you here and now that, before too long, she and you both will come to feel the weight of our responsibility and join us as productive and active citizens of the Witenagemot. You two will be happily reunited soon enough. I'm sure of it. But regardless, I guarantee she'll be looked out for until that day, and you as well."

The Steward was wearing a genuine smile by then. Elias found himself smiling back, though with only a minimal inventory of muscles engaged in the effort, for he was still wary of the man despite his bold promises that explicitly addressed Elias's particular concerns. Then, he'd found a voice from somewhere within him to ask the question he'd stopped his curiosity from addressing only moments earlier, "What is it you guys need from me?"

"Well, Eli, *we*, meaning every citizen of the Witen, need your help ensuring our security and survival. We hope that you will come to answer the call of our collective responsibility. We need men like you, Eli. This society may have to endure up here for years, decades even, who knows. We need to prepare the next generation to take up the mantle of the Witen's officers and footmen and we have high hopes that you will join us in that endeavor. I've heard great things about you, Elias. By all accounts, you're a smart and tough kid—exactly the type of man humanity needs in this moment. We are starting an Integration Program next week, and although I don't know you well enough to ask, nor do I deserve a favor from you, it is my wish that you will be among our first class of students. Many of the children around your age, with the support of their guardians, have signed up for the program, but the Commander and I know what a great loss it would be for the Witen, and humanity itself, if you were to absent yourself."

Elias couldn't help but feel flattered, then as much as now, but he was still racked with reservations. "What is an *Integration Program*?" he asked in a soft voice.

"It's what we're calling the Witen's assimilation course. It will be a 25-week course, much like a boot camp. You know what a boot camp is, right?" Elias had nodded and the Steward continued his explanation. "Well, it'll be a bit like that. We need to build up the physical bodies right along with the intellects of the next generation in order to ensure they are worthy to carry on the cause and claim spots as footmen, or even officers, of the Witenagemot. The Integration Program will be full of courses in a variety of fields and disciplines, and it is the great hope of both the Commander and myself that, by its completion, the next generation will indeed be prepared to fulfill their responsibility. It won't only be children such as yourself, either. All of our newly minted footmen will be taking many courses right alongside you. Folks of all ages and all walks of life working together to ensure humanity achieves righteous glory in the new world, ushering in a triumphant and auspicious destiny for all of us."

"Oh," was once again all Elias was able to muster in response to the Steward's electric orations.

His awkward confusion hadn't daunted the Steward, thankfully. The man had simply smiled at him while tapping the ballcap atop his head. "It's a lot, I know, and I'm not asking for any kind of answer from you today. The way I see it, you can run to your sister and try and work through your shame, or you can join us on day one of the Integration Program on Monday in The Meadow. I swear, it really won't affect either my or the Commander's regard for you, nor your sister, no matter which of these paths you choose. I just wanted to have a moment with you to make my plea, man to man. Yesterday is gone forever, Elias. I'll bet that if either you or I could change it, we would both rewrite it in a way so your father did not have to die. I'll bet, too, that you and I know the only way that rewriting could possibly work. I think you're special, Eli. And I think you can indeed see what your family just could not ... and still will not. Something tells me you're the strong one of the Sagal bunch. And all of me is sincerely hoping you'll come to realize that yourself as well over these next few days." The Steward added another warm smile before placing his hand back atop his shoulder. "Whatever you decide, or don't decide, I hope that you don't take it out on Ms. Heathcoat, though. She is a good woman just trying to do her part to live up to our collective responsibility. I know she and your sister have a bit of drama between them, along with Ms. Heathcoat's wife, but you know how women can hold grudges, right? In my experience, Eli, it's always best to exempt yourself from any such nonsense," the Steward told him, wearing a look of life-earned wisdom. "They'll work it all out before too long and find some other drama to occupy themselves with, you watch," he added with another soft chuckle. "Anyway, Ms. Heathcoat deserves a break, I think. In the end, there's never really a good excuse to be a dishonorable guest. Good manners can be an elusive discipline to master, but they remain an extremely important one, nonetheless." That last had stung Elias a bit, as he realized how childish he had been toward Helena those first few days. So, he nodded once again but kept eye contact a few beats longer to make sure the man knew he would strive to do better when it came to Ms. Helena Heathcoat. "Very well then, Eli, you can head on back to her ... if you wish. I hope to see you Monday. Though, as I said, the Commander, the Witen, and I will all understand either way. And my office hatchway will always be open to you."

The Steward had left him at the alleyway junction after that. There were no footmen lurking nearby to ensure he walked back to Helena's quarters, either. It seemed they were trusting him. At the time, that trust had only increased his raging confusion. But for whatever reason, he had indeed walked back to Ms. Heathcoat's without deviation. And for whatever reason, that Monday morning, he also showed up for day one of the Integration Program.

They were dropped off in four nearly full repulsion trolleys to find the Steward standing rigid at the center of The Meadow's football field with Lieutenants Schwambach, Woodson, Dirks, and Dobechek aligned a few yards behind him, copying his posture of firm attention. The officers all wore their black tactical pants and blouses trimmed in gold. Their insignia of rank on each shoulder and finely embroidered

W patches on each right breast pocket popped with importance and authority from yards away.

Elias had nearly not been there to see the intimidating view. He had managed to catch the trolleys in time that morning, but only just. With every step from Ms. Heathcoat's quarters to the trolley depot in the central hub, he had fluctuated between commitment and intransigence. It seemed he was tugging himself two steps forward, only to pull one step back. But somehow, he'd gotten there just in time. And even after he'd arrived at the depot to find roughly 50 or 60 other kids about the same age, give or take 3 or 4 years, already lined up with their parents or guardians standing beside them, holding their hands and whispering advice and encouragement in their ears, he still couldn't be sure he was making the right choice. Though, it was indeed heartening to see the amount of support there was for the Integration Program among the residents and to see how many people had so profoundly felt the "heavy responsibility," as the Steward had called it; so much so they were entrusting the Witen with the care and nurturing of their children. Nevertheless, Elias was still unsure as he boarded the last trolley in line.

Each trolley car was five paces wide with three rows of double facing seats; one pair in the front, one in the back and another sandwiched in between. Elias had climbed into the front row of the mirrored pairs, sliding all the way over to the first spot to sit with his back facing the conductor's cab and his right leg and side pressed up against a pair of perpendicular safety bars. Tessa Rodriguez had sat across from him on that trip, and if it hadn't been for her burning, chestnut eyes shining out at him from a radiantly warm face framed by a flowing tangle of ebony locks, Elias would've most likely stared at the floor and tortured himself with confusion over his choices all the way to The Meadow. But Tessa did something to Elias that he couldn't quite explain. She had a way of removing him from whatever moment, no matter how benign or intense, and inducing a treacherous grin of delight to stretch across his lips and throughout his mostly dormant soul. Elias had been glad to see Tessa among the children, to say the least. It had certainly added to the lightening of his confusion, maybe even more so than seeing all the other children and their parents combined.

However, his puckish grin was gone quick enough after he glanced to Tessa's left and spotted Ricky Allanson on the bench beside her. The blond Ricky had been glaring at him with clearly cruel intentions pulling at the muscles around his fat, wormy lips and narrowed, chalky-blue eyes before shaking off the annoyance after one calming breath and a subtle returned glare from Elias. Then he'd gone right back to wrangling his soul's glow over Tessa's proximity, interspersed here and there with fits of stewing in his confusion for the rest of what felt like an interminable trip to The Meadow and day one of the Integration Program.

Something about the ceremonial image they'd all witnessed that morning, though, after hopping off the repulsion trolleys and crossing The Meadow's footbridge, of the Steward and his lieutenants all decked out in their imposing uniforms had lifted any lingering struggles of the mind left over from the trolley ride. It had been a powerful sight. There was something about the five Witen councilmembers standing so self-assured and sharply disciplined that made them dazzle among their surroundings. They weren't much more than smudges and dots inside the monstrous, multi-climated chamber when Elias and the other Integration Program Initiates had first crossed the footbridge, but even so, they had drawn the eye. Certainly, none of the children had been unsure where they were supposed to gather in that gigantic facility.

Elias had been somewhere in the middle of the gaggle of kids that had approached the silent and perfectly still councilmembers. He couldn't say for sure whether or not he would've reacted as the kids in the front did after the Steward abruptly nodded and the four lieutenants behind him snapped into motion, shouting orders and shoving children into some semblance of order, but he was a realist and ever did strive to stay humble, so he allowed himself to admit he most likely would've screamed and recoiled in fear just like all the others. But Elias had been near the middle of that gaggle, alongside a bewildered Tessa. The pair had managed to fall into the slowly shaping formation lines before any of the lieutenants had been able to shout in either of their faces. They had managed to avoid that particular character trial that morning, but many more that day, and for the weeks to come, were soon to follow, and not even God himself could've avoided them all.

The rest of that first day in the Program was hazy now. Elias could recall little with any surety. Those first few weeks had been so chaotic and challenging, both physically and mentally, that it had all sort of melded together in his mind now. Only the image of the five Witen officers, dwarfed by the gargantuan chamber around them, and yet, undoubted masters of every square inch of that space, along with the slow trudge of the initiates toward them had stuck out clearly among the rest.

Elias had fallen in line with the Integration Program quick enough, it was true. Despite his penchant for lonely freedom, Elias had always enjoyed a bit of routine and structure, too. He'd thrived, in fact, under the relative constraints. The Integration Program had come to replace youth sports as his source for daily structure. Elias loved team sports. He gloried in being a part of a well-practiced and finely tuned ball club. So, a large part of him had reveled, and even excelled, in the militaristic, boot camp atmosphere of the Program. He did still have his moments of doubt in those early days, many in fact, but their pull on his decisions and will had weakened, just as his physical body had strengthened.

There'd been countless times while running lines on the gaming fields, or struggling up and down The Meadow's hills carrying a 30-pound rucksack on his back, or racking his brain for answers during a strenuous course exam, when he had wanted to shrug off the burdensome responsibility the Witen was constantly reminding him and the other initiates and footmen of, and just quit and run to Maisie. But he'd pushed through those moments, somehow, and had even come out laughing on the other side. He'd also been comforted early on to learn he wasn't alone among the initiates in his doubts. Many of the other children, Tessa Rodriguez chief among them, had questioned their parents' and guardians' decisions to give them to the burgeoning Witen, with its clear propensity to engage in violence for the greater good. Thankfully, for all their sakes, there had been the Steward's weekly lectures, along with their Truth In History and New Destiny Constitution courses to set all their minds at ease. Elias, and all the Program Initiates who'd made it as far as him, had learned that the Witen had done, and was now doing, only what was necessary in these wholly unprecedented times.

By now, all the initiates, Elias right along with them, fully and truly understood their collective responsibility and were thus eagerly seeking the incredible honor of serving humanity in its most desperate hour as footmen of the Witenagemot. Hence this morning's heaping helping of pancakes and scrambled eggs—Helena Heathcoat's way of helping him prepare for the contest to claim the highest honor of all in the Integration Program. For it was this morning, in just 35 minutes, that the Challenge Contest to determine which initiate would be the first to claim the title of Initiate Supreme was set to begin. Elias had excelled in every course the Witen had thrown at him. He'd even topped many of the footmen with his test scores in at least a half dozen of the various Station Systems, New Destiny Constitution Law, and Truth In History courses that the initiates took right alongside those footmen. He'd tested top of the class in every physical challenge as well. His two-mile run time was the very best in the whole Program, full stop. And he'd only had four footmen best him at chin-ups, sit-ups, and push-ups. As far as initiates went, only Ricky Allanson had done more chin-ups. Elias had bested him at sit-ups, while push-ups had been a tie between them.

Ricky Allanson, with that weaselly smirk ever plastered to his pinched face, had shown himself the clear threat to Elias claiming the universally coveted title of Initiate Supreme. He swore the boy would be the target of his challenge today. He saw no benefit in wasting time with any lesser foe. Ricky was the kid he'd have to beat to win in the end. So, he would cut through all the bull and just challenge him straight away. It was true that all the kids eligible did present their own unique challenges. Elias wasn't so cocky as to believe otherwise. Many of them were pretty damn talented, actually, not to mention the fact that they were likely just as fit as him by now, especially the three or four older girls and boys in the challenger pool. After all, he had to rank in the top 25% of the Program just to have a right to take part in the Challenge Contest at all. Even knowing this, though, and absent any arrogance whatsoever, there still was little doubt in Elias's mind that he could best them all.

It was entirely possible that all his planning for who to challenge and when was completely in vain. Another top-tier initiate could always challenge Ricky before Elias was even given the chance, and then Allanson would get the satisfaction of getting to call him out. Elias was irritated and unsettled by that scenario. *I'm sure the other initiates know it's in their own best interest to challenge someone more in their own league,* Elias told himself, shrugging off his momentary irritation. An initiate at least received a Program Merit for winning any single challenge, so it made little sense for a lesser competitor to challenge either Elias or Ricky, knowing the odds were greatly stacked against them. Elias was nearly certain that they would be rational and seek the Merit, for that in and of itself was a heck of an accomplishment to flaunt, as well as a slick medal to pin to your Witenagemot Initiate dress uniform. He had an inkling that Lieutenant Schwambach, the Master of the Games, understood that the initiates would take all that into account as well. Elias guessed the lieutenant would choose the weakest initiate from the contest pool to challenge first and then trust the contest to take care of itself from there, leaving Elias and Ricky for the last challenge just by its natural course.

However it all might play out that morning, a lack of sugar and carbohydrates slowing him down was certainly no threat. Elias decided to stop fretting over the challenge process as he forked up another mouthful of pancakes. Better, Elias figured, to go over the many obstacles of the Challenge Course itself and try to map out the best route possible in his mind. The challenge part of the contest was meant to deliberately evoke the Final Tournament and its challenge system, but the actual form the contest took was quite different. First of all, there were no death match fights. Instead, there was an elaborate obstacle course stretching the entire width of The Meadow's gaming fields. Challenger and victor started beside the forest and The Meadow's hazy blue suspensor field boundary. The first to snatch the pennant from its cradle inside the small steel tower at the opposite end, just in front of the soft hill alongside the desert boundary, was the winner. Unlike in the Final Tournament, though, the winner had the right to challenge their next opponent, not the other way around. Although, like the Final Tournament, one loss did put a competitor out of the Contest completely. In the end, the Integration Program would bestow upon the last man standing the high honor of Initiate Supreme, until next month's Challenge Contest.

Elias swore to himself over another bite of his breakfast feast that he would indeed be the first to claim that honor and never relinquish it, for Helena Heathcoat's sake, if nothing else. *These are some damn good pancakes, after all,* he observed with a contented chuckle. *Time to earn the privilege of her care and make her proud,* Elias vowed with refreshed vigor. *Time to beat Ricky Allanson and wipe that smarmy grin from his fat lips and pale eyes once and for all.*

"Elbow! Hey, that's a foul!" Elias shouted out in frustration. He'd been so upset by Kyle Erkov's elbow smash into the nose of Tessa Rodriguez just as she was set to overtake him that he'd momentarily forgotten himself. Lieutenant Schwambach snapped his head around so fast to glare down at him from his elevated judge's platform it shot a shiver rippling down Elias's spine. "Apologies, Games Master," he managed to splutter out after an everlasting silent moment. Elias heard Ricky Allanson's hushed laugh from the formation rank directly behind him. A few of Ricky's cronies in their three-rank by five-row squad formation joined in the low laughter after Lieutenant Schwambach cast one last grimace toward Elias before turning back to the action on the challenge course.

It took nearly every drop of Elias's will to remain calm and in place inside Program Squad 3's tight formation, positioned near the center obstacle apparatus of the challenge course, as those soft chuckles washed over him. He knew his face must be bright red, but to his relief, he occupied a spot in the formation's front rank, where none of his rivals could see his face's betrayal. It wasn't until he noticed Tessa out of the corner of his eye as she flung herself over the top of the cargo net obstacle that his seething rage over shaming himself before Lieutenant Schwambach, a founding member of the Witenagemot and Master of the Games, finally abated.

Sadly, it was fear and helpless anxiety that came rushing in to replace it. Tessa was now a dozen paces behind the long-legged Kyle Erkov. She'd lost major ground after that elbow, an elbow that, now that Elias thought on it, might not have actually occurred. After all, the Master of the Games had not noticed the foul, and surely Lieutenant Schwambach had a better view of the action than he did.

How dare I even doubt him? Elias scolded himself. *Lieutenant Schwambach is a glorious hero-warrior of the Witen.* He'd obviously seen something Elias couldn't. Perhaps Tessa had only slipped just as Erkov's arm went flailing, and it only appeared egregious from Elias's perspective. After all, he'd learned throughout his Truth In History courses, and the Steward's lectures, that one's perspective could affect reality in any number of ways. *You shouldn't have shouted out, Eli, either way,* he reprimanded himself. *Remember the lessons of the lectures,* he thought, imploringly, just as the Program Creed popped in his head. *The officers have no bond but to that of the Witen and the New Destiny Constitution,* he chanted in silence. *Their lives are ended. Now, they are but stewards of the future. From this comes their clarity of mind. From this comes their wisdom. Trust in their loyalty. Emulate their example.*

Whether or not it was a slip or a flagrant elbow, the only reality that mattered now was that Tessa had lost a lot of late ground to Erkov. She was closing, though. Elias could see her eat up yards with each smooth, rapid stride of her nimble legs. Ricky's laughter died quickly as each second made the shrinking gap between the competitors plain, even to their obstinate eyes. All that lay before the pair of contestants now was the mud crawl beneath barbed wire two feet off the ground, then a 30-yard sprint to the final rope climb up a sheer 15-foot steel wall where a black pennant emblazoned with the golden W of the Witenagemot awaited the first competitor to snatch it from its cradle and so declare themselves victor of the challenge.

Kyle Erkov was a close friend of Allanson, and both were well aware of Elias's fondness for Tessa. He knew Ricky didn't just want his man to win but was rooting for Elias's friend to lose, and badly. Tessa had only just qualified for the Challenge Contest. She and Elias had been figuring her to be challenged early on, most likely by one of the younger kids. But after no one had challenged her in the first few races, Elias began to smell Allanson's grubby fingers all over it. Ricky used his popularity and influence with the other initiates to antagonize Elias at every opportunity he could throughout the Program's past weeks. He and his friends were relentless. Sadly, Tessa had become an unwilling pawn in that unwelcome contest on more than one occasion, much to Elias's dismay. Knowing all that, Elias began to realize Ricky and his buddies were saving her for a later race, to force her to run against a far superior opponent, and thus be embarrassed for the crime—as Ricky saw it, anyway—of daring to befriend Elias Sagal. He guessed rightly, too, that it would be Allanson's goon, Kyle Erkov, the smug, self-satisfied asshole, who would be the one still around late in the contest to challenge her. All of which made the gasps of horror that replaced Allanson's low laughs as Tessa pulled within a half dozen steps of Erkov before they reached the mud crawl come as music to Elias's ears.

He yearned to shout encouragement to Tessa, to urge her on to the finish, but caught himself well before the words were formed. His eyes even flashed nervously toward the lantern-jawed Master of the Games a time or two, just to make sure the revered figure could not smell his thoughts and intentions on him. Thankfully, Lieutenant Schwambach's eyes were locked on the course, and Elias was able to stifle his shouts before they ever squeaked out. Tessa didn't seem to need his meager cheers, anyhow. She shot beneath the low roof of the mud crawl on a headfirst slide, gaining herself a good four paces on Erkov. The lanky-limbed, pale-complected thirteen-year old, known to the Integration Program as Initiate Kyle Erkov, had been timid when approaching the messy obstacle, despite having already soiled his immaculate uniform on his previous run. He'd come to a full stop before the entrance to his particular channel through the apparatus and had even seemed primly reluctant to plunge into the thick muck covering the ground beneath the barbed wire. Tessa had shown no such reluctance and so made that major gain on her competitor. Erkov disregarded his cocktail party decorum quick enough, though, once he glanced back over his shoulder halfway through the obstacle and saw how close the dark-haired eleven-year old was to overtaking him.

Erkov emerged from the clinging mud first, flapping his arms in the air beside him to rid himself of the black muck. Tessa was not far behind. They even seemed to set off on the 30-yard sprint at nearly the same exact moment. Certainly, whatever lead Erkov may have gained with that slip of Tessa's, that Elias had mistakenly perceived as an elbow, was all but vanished now. Elias's whole body gave one shuddering twitch that he only just wrangled before he broke his at ease position inside his unit formation. Tessa was right on Erkov as they reached the 15-foot tower wall. They both even took their respective ropes in hand in near flawless unison. *Tessa might just win this challenge!* The thought had Elias's heart pounding like a hummingbird in heat with anticipated joy. He imagined Tessa pinning the award to her dress uniform. He could picture her chestnut eyes shining out at him with well-earned pride. Elias was delighted by the premonition. He knew how hard Tessa Rodriguez worked. For some reason, which continually irritated him, the Program officers hadn't fully seen that yet, so it pleased Elias to know she'd earn their respect with this undeniable act. She'd beat the much taller, much stronger, and much older boy, who had dishonorably challenged her, right before their very eyes.

The hope for that sweet justice swelled to bursting in the first stage of Erkov and Tessa's ascent. Three long strides right out the gate had Tessa up the wall a good two feet ahead of Kyle. Her next stride up the daunting vertical face, though, brought about the first tears in the bulging balloon of Elias's hope. The quick strides before it seemed to come with no hesitation, but she lingered over the fourth. Elias could even now see the tremble in her arms as her once firm grip slowly slipped away. Erkov saw it, too. Elias watched his mouth form words, saw Tessa's head shoot toward him, and then saw a grin spread across the pale boy's bony face. In the next instant, Kyle Erkov was three strides past her and halfway up the wall. Elias saw Tessa dig deep for some last reserve of energy, saw how much she struggled to bring it about, and then, to his grief, saw her energy abandon her completely. His heart sank in his chest just as Tessa crashed to the turf flat on her back some seven or eight feet below.

Erkov would never be overtaken now. He was a mere three or four strides from the top of the wall. Ricky Allanson saw the inevitability as well. Elias could hear his panicked breaths morph into a low, satisfied chuckle. He felt the anger rise within himself once more with the return of Allanson's laugh. His eyes, though, were still on the course, and the commendable and impressive display to which Tessa Rodriguez was treating him and the rest of the gathered initiates of the Integration Program. She must've had the wind knocked out of her. How could she not have with such a high drop? But she hadn't lingered long on the turf. She was up and back at it within a few quick heartbeats. Tessa truly was an amazing girl. Her will simply refused to break. Elias realized that, knowing all he did of the character of Tessa Rodriguez, he should've expected nothing less of her. He watched on, proud of his one true friend, as she snatched the rope back in her hand so vigorously she seemed to border on anger rather than zeal and set to climbing, despite the fact that Erkov had already reached the summit and snatched up the black and gold pennant.

The sight of him waving the pennant back and forth at the top of the tower like he'd just mounted Everest, contrasted with Tessa struggling step-by-step up the wall's planks just below him, suddenly made Elias realize that if Tessa hadn't fallen, he might have actually found himself having to face her in this Contest. There was only him and Ricky left to be challenged, after all. He supposed a part of him always knew that was a possibility, but his fondness for her had forced those thoughts to the very recesses of his mind. But as Erkov's childish behavior stoked the fierce burning forge of his desire to defeat him, Elias tried to imagine making himself similarly motivated to defeat Tessa. In the end, he decided that, though he would never actually say it to her face, he was contented that she should lose. It was a raw hatred for the opponent that made it easier to channel his inner drive, or so Elias had come to discover, anyway. *Didn't the Steward say something like that in one of his lectures once?* Elias pondered. *Yeah, it was "hate brings clarity" or something like that.* The memory of the Steward's quote brought with it a balm for the guilt he felt in not being sad for his dear friend's loss. *It's better that she loses so I don't gotta run against her.* The truth of that was very plain to Elias, for he looked inside his heart and saw with certainty that he could never even pretend to hate Tessa Rodriguez.

Then, invading his contention with his friend's defeat, came sudden flickering images of his father, morningstar in hand, clashing violently with a hulking brute wielding a black battleaxe, the memory broken by cloudy dream-memories of a gigantic wolf and his hands clutching tightly to tufts of the beast's shaggy gray fur, along with a red-hazed image of just his right hand clutching not dense, warm wolf fur, but rather the spongy wooden hilt of a blood-covered dagger thrust deep into the excessively thick neck of an enormous, dark-brown bull with impossibly wide horns. Elias always knew, on a basic level, that the giant, axe-wielding brute with the scarred and muscular arms was the Commander, but the flickering images of his memory always cast his features as indistinct and unknowable, seemingly washed out behind a dark, shadowy fog. As for the wolf and bull, Elias couldn't begin to say. He'd dreamed of them the night before the last match of the Final Tournament, and they'd kind of just stuck around since. But the images usually only invaded his dreams. Elias chalked it up to the stress of the Challenge Contest that he should be so assaulted by them in his waking life.

Whatever the reason the images chose to invade his conscious peace, Elias had no time to grapple with them. He shrugged off their menace, shoving them back into the dark corners of his mind, locking them there alongside all other thoughts and worries from those dark times before the light of the Witenagemot. Perry Sagal was dead. Elias was lucky enough to be able to be his legacy, and all on account of the commitment and fortitude of the Commander, the Steward, and the captain and lieutenants of the Witen. Elias knew all other contrary thoughts were useless baggage now, not fit to interfere with the supreme mandate of the Witenagemot, nor the glorious future for mankind they were building.

Lieutenant Schwambach's harsh whistle pierced the silence inside The Meadow, making it easy for Elias to shrug off the last dregs of his dark memories. "Alright, that's enough," the lieutenant shouted out at Tessa through cupped hands. She was only three paces up the wall but was refusing to quit. Elias saw it as testament to her spirit, though a part of him also understood the lieutenant's point as well. The contest was over. Erkov was still standing at the top, waving the pennant. There was no doubt about who had won. Elias knew Tessa just wanted to finish. She hated to leave anything undone. But there were still more challenges to run, and they couldn't all wait around for her forever. "Come down from there, and return to your squad. The race is over. You've lost. You too, Initiate." This last was spoken by the Master of the Games to the gangling idiot still waving the pennant like a toddler at a parade. "Come down from there, and stand before me. Let's not waste any more of my time. Get over here, and make your challenge."

Is this it, then? Elias really didn't think so. True, there was only him and Ricky left for challenging among the contestant pool, but even so, Elias guessed the odds still weren't quite 50/50. The smart money was on Ricky being the one Kyle Erkov would challenge. He guessed that Ricky not only wanted the satisfaction of challenging and beating Elias, but the extra praise for having won two challenges that day as well. Elias figured, too, that Kyle Erkov was a big enough sycophant that he'd gladly throw the race to make sure Ricky Allanson, his idol, would accomplish those feats. Elias also knew that Ricky was aware of all that, too, and would not pass up the advantage it presented.

It irked Elias something awful to know he'd have to endure the farce that would be a race between Ricky and Kyle before he could finally run the course himself, but he endeavored to level his head and focus on only what was in his control, namely, all the various obstacles of the long course. After a moment, his mind was swimming with obstacles and the myriad ways to master each of them as Kyle Erkov began to jog with slow pomposity toward the judge's platform.

"I present the course pennant, Games Master," Erkov said through labored breaths after arriving in front of the elevated platform.

"Very good, Initiate," the Master of the Games said lazily. "Leave it at your feet and speak your challenge."

"Yes, Games Master," Erkov responded while dropping the pennant and still trying to catch his breath. "I challenge Elias, Traitor's Son!" he finally screamed, after filling his lungs.

The name was a knife to Elias's soul, a dagger to his honor. It brought back every horrible, clashing image of morningstar versus battleaxe, along with the haze of howling wolf and dying bull, from the thick shadows of his subconscious, but he let nothing show. Every officer present in The Meadow turned to look at him. Elias refused them any display. To help with that, he had the small satisfaction of knowing Ricky Allanson must fear to face Elias himself. Instead, he was hoping his lackey could take him down. That knowledge managed to lessen the sting of the insulting moniker Erkov had called him out with, enough so that his head was still held high with firm, square shoulders as he stepped out of formation. Elias marched with no hesitation to the challenge course's starting line to show he accepted the challenge of the dead-man-walking known previously to the world, and the Integration Program, as Initiate Kyle Erkov.

"Initiates, ready?" Lieutenant Schwambach bellowed across The Meadow's gaming fields. Elias responded with a raised right arm crowned by a firm thumbs-up. To his left, he felt more than saw his opponent mirror his action. Kyle Erkov stood a good five inches taller than Elias. His two-year age advantage had aided Erkov in the weight department as well. They had roughly the same build, though Kyle Erkov's limbs were a deal more gangling than Elias's more toned and proportioned ones. Elias wasn't sure if being the lighter and smaller opponent put him at a particular disadvantage in the Challenge Contest, but standing at the starting line of the course alongside the bigger kid made him a bit uncomfortable, a bit unsure. He hated himself for the feelings but couldn't deny they were there in those moments just before the start of his first ever challenge race. They lasted all the way up to the moment Lieutenant Schwambach raised his right arm high above his head and shouted, "Begin," dropping the outstretched arm.

And so it was that Elias was a step behind the older Erkov off the starting line. Erkov had been granted a 30-minute rest period, just like those granted to the victors of the Final Tournament's challenge matches. So, he had his wind back, which made it hard for Elias to gain any ground on him before they reached the obstacle. It was the tire agilities obstacle up first. Two running lanes lay side by side with each lane containing ten rows of tire pairs. Kyle Erkov had bounded through his first two pairs of tires, with a one-foot-ahead-of-the-other strategy, before Elias had set a toe inside the first tire in his lane.

The fear of being outmatched by the older boy threatened to overwhelm Elias and only increased after he failed to gain any ground on Erkov throughout the rest of that first obstacle. *Remember who you're running for, Eli,* he demanded of himself as he set off after Erkov upon jumping clear of his last tire. *Remember all they've done for you. Remember what you owe them.* The self-demands spurred Elias on throughout the intervening 10-yard dash between the tire agilities obstacle and the 25-foot beam wall climb obstacle. So, as Elias grabbed hold of the second beam of the wall and planted a foot on the first beam, Kyle Erkov was only one beam ahead of him. The wall was constructed of two vertical pillars planted deep in the ground five yards apart and sticking up 25 feet in the air. The pillars were connected by smaller horizontal beams, spaced anywhere from two to four feet apart, creating an irregular ladder of sorts. Each competitor must ascend the daunting ladder, flip themselves over the top, and then climb down the other side.

Erkov seemed to hesitate as he neared the obstacle's summit. Elias was quick to seize on the opportunity. Though he had a healthy fear of most of the normal things people feared—heights included— Elias also possessed an ability to disregard it in critical moments. This was no different. He reached the top beam just as Erkov did, but unlike the older boy, he flung his right leg over the precipice with no delay, completely ignoring the vertigo-inducing sight and feel of the action. Erkov had already been over the tricky obstacle twice before, but even that experience didn't seem sufficient to chase away his apprehension in flinging his leg over the top beam in order to start his descent. Elias opened up a two-beam gap between himself and Erkov thanks to the gawky boy's reluctance at the obstacle's summit. Erkov did manage to get over his fears before too long, however, and Elias was only a step or two ahead of him as they embarked on a sprint before the challenge course's next gut-wrenching obstacle.

Hurdles followed the 10-yard sprint after the beam wall. Six 4-foot hurdles were staggered the length of a 20-yard stretch of gaming field. Elias leaped up just before the first hurdle and planted his palms on the crossbeam in order to pivot himself up and over the simple apparatus, only seconds before Kyle Erkov did the same two feet to his left. The following two hurdles were cleared by Elias in the same quick and easy fashion as the first, but the fourth had him digging deep for a little extra strength. He cleared it on the first try, but it hadn't been as pretty to see as the first three. Some of his fears about being overmatched by a physically superior opponent wouldn't be fended off any longer, especially as he struggled to drag himself over the fifth hurdle. Flipping himself over to the hurdle's far side, he caught a glimpse of Erkov darting past him. Kyle reached the sixth hurdle ahead of Elias, and he could have succumbed to despair then and there, but something made him dig deep to touch the comfort of his resolve. Kyle was better at certain obstacles, while Elias held the advantage in others. He might as well accept that. *Come on, man. Keep your head, and stay with him,* he berated himself, clinging tight to that burning resolve.

Elias was indeed *right with him* as they completed the last hurdle. They even remained neck and neck for every stride of the 10-yard dash to the next obstacle, the balance beam. A beam rested atop two tires spaced 15 yards apart above a shallow trench filled with muddy water. Erkov was first on the beams, but Elias was only a step behind. Each competitor flung their arms out to either side for balance as if they were a child about to play airplane. Elias was quicker on the long, treacherous beam than the older boy, opening a 2-yard gap halfway through the obstacle. Elias felt a grin threaten to touch the corners of his lips, but he shoved it down. He knew that, just as he couldn't let falling behind Erkov break him, he couldn't let dumb pride lead him into an otherwise avoidable mistake either.

Elias endeavored to remain on an even keel. And so, he couldn't say what made him lose that focus on the very next stride to dart a glance at the assembled initiates in their squad formations, but nonetheless, that's exactly what he did. His eyes sought out his squad. They passed over his empty spot in the front rank of Squad 3's formation and came to land on a pretty, dark-haired girl in the formation's last row, third from the left. Tessa Rodriguez was as rigid and stoic as the rest of the initiates around her, but the dried blood below her nose, along with the purple-and-yellow bruises spreading out below both her chestnut eyes made her stand out among the others. *No... There...*

But there was no elbow, Elias tried to tell himself. *She slipped. She just... She slipped.* Elias's eyes sought out the Games Master perched eight feet off the ground on his judge's platform. There was nothing on the lieutenant's face, save boredom, perhaps.

Doubt gripped tight to Elias's gut in that moment. It would've rendered him incapable of continuing the race were it not for his eyes finding the Steward, now standing just beside the judge's platform. The Witen's number-two man was standing alongside the Commander and every lieutenant of the Witen; even Captain Alvarez and Supervisor Chairman Mikkelson—in his fancy gold suitcoat with its special black stitched trimming around cuffs and collar—were there. Elias didn't know when exactly the Steward and Commander and all the rest had arrived, but seeing them now, and especially spotting the encouraging smile currently animating the Steward's face, allowed Elias to push away the image of the battered Tessa, and all it could mean, and refocus once more on the race.

Erkov had retaken the lead due to Elias's wavering on the balance beam, though it was only a pace or two. Elias ate up the ground between them in the first 10 yards of the 20-yard sprint to the next obstacle in line. He was set to overtake him when Kyle Erkov glanced back and noticed. Elias saw the elbow coming as soon as Erkov launched it, but his incredulity at the fact that it could possibly be happening caused him to react late to the blow's threat. He managed to skid and slide to a halt while throwing his upper body to the side in order to duck the incoming blow, but the maneuver left him off-balance, and he tumbled unceremoniously to the turf. The attempted elbow smash had spun Erkov in a complete 360. He was still on his feet when Elias went sprawling, though, and was able to scramble ahead a good five paces before Elias Sagal even got back up. Elias delayed himself even further after he paused to glance once more at the still bored Games Master surrounded by his fellow officers of the Witen, none of whom seemed to be in the least angered by Erkov's flagrant abuse of the contest's rules. Even the Steward remained unmoved by the clear foul. *Why aren't they saying anything?* Elias asked himself. He truly didn't understand. *Maybe it's all a test, Eli,* he thought with dawning horror. *A test you're freaking failing big time, man.* "Dammit," Elias muttered low enough that nobody, Kyle

Erkov included, could hear him. Then he took off in pursuit of the long-legged boy.

He had his questions, he had his doubts, but there were no answers for any of them here and now. He told himself he could settle all that later. Right now, there was only beating the asshole who had flung that illegal elbow at him, the jerk who had called him "Elias, Traitor's Son," the pathetic bully who must really have landed the very same elbow he just missed Elias with down upon the bridge of Tessa's nose. Elias let his anger over all of it replace his doubts and questions. He recalled the Steward's preaching on the value of hating your opponent. *Maybe that's the lesson, Eli,* he posited to himself. *The Steward must know I have to hate this guy. That must be why they let him hurt my friend and why they didn't do anything to stop him hitting me. So, hate him, Elias. Just freaking beat this asshole already.*

Rage was indeed a good motivator. Elias felt the lessons of his Truth In History courses, as well as the Steward's lectures, come alive inside him. His bitter hatred of his foe was clarifying, even invigorating. It allowed him to take back all the advantage Kyle Erkov had gained after his cowardly elbow attempt. The cargo net obstacle was next up. The competitors reached its base at the same moment. Elias felt the burning rage propel him up and over the 12-foot net. He glanced once more at Squad 3 as soon as he landed on the ground on the far side. This time, he sought out Ricky Allanson. Elias wanted to see the fear in his eyes as he realized Kyle Erkov would never catch him. The dismay and apprehension he saw there in the blue eyes of his nemesis served to kindle his searing fury anew, almost making it a joyous thing in which to revel. And so, revel in it he did. Its fuel rocketed him a dozen paces ahead of Erkov as he approached the second to last obstacle.

Elias dove headfirst into the mud crawl in much the same way Tessa Rodriguez had done in the previous race. Not caring about the cold, clinging wetness of the mud, Elias crawled through its grime with relentless forward motion. He planted his head right down in the muck and cared not as it seemed to spread across every square inch of his face. Elias cleared the mud crawl before Kyle Erkov had ever even entered it. However, he didn't let this knowledge slow him down on the last sprint of the challenge course. He flung himself up the rope against the wall leading up to the final tower platform and the sacred pennant with careless abandon as soon as he reached it, and when he attained the top, he was amazed to discover himself barely winded. He remembered being on the edge of total exhaustion all the way back on the hurdles. Elias was astounded to realize what a true difference unlocking his joyous rage had done to his physical capabilities.

Reaching out for the black-and-gold pennant, his mud-splattered hand hesitated just before snatching it from its cradle. Finally, it fell right back to his side. Elias turned from the pennant to face Kyle Erkov, who had only just reached the base of the wall below. Elias waved for the older boy to climb the rope. Erkov responded with a puzzled expression but took the rope in his hands, nonetheless. Elias waved once more for the older boy to join him atop the wall. He could feel the tension inside The Meadow grow with each second as Erkov shook his head and began his ascent. The initiates and officers were just as quiet as they'd been only seconds earlier, but there was now a palpable tension that Elias was sure every last one of them was feeling. He shrugged the tension aside, clinging tightly to the surging hatred for his foe.

Erkov finally placed a hand atop the wall and moved to drag himself up to the platform where Elias waited. The older boy's confusion still remained on his face, although Elias Sagal could now see some blossoming hope mixed in as well. It made the kick he planted square in Erkov's face, just before he could finish pulling himself up, all the sweeter. An audible groan did escape a few of the assembled initiates' lips after that, perhaps even a few of the officers' as well. Elias paid no mind. Instead, he watched Erkov crash like a limp noodle to the turf 15 feet below. Elias then spat down at the crumpled boy at the base of the tower wall before turning to pluck up the black pennant with its gold emblazoned W. Elias did not flourish it as Kyle Erkov had. He simply jumped down from the tower platform with a slight assist from the rope, then moved to stand over the older boy's limp body.

Elias saw that the flat of his foot had connected square with the tip of the boy's bony nose; the lower half was snapped off to one side. Elias could also see a few missing teeth in both Erkov's upper and lower jaws, as well, with his mouth hanging slack and wide open as it was. He saw, too, the older boy's chest rising and falling in a steady rhythm. Elias turned from the unconscious competitor before him to give a nod, hoping it conveyed Erkov's condition to the assembled initiates and officers. The officers, for their part, seemed unconcerned about Erkov; none had made a move to check on him nor issued any orders for their subordinates to carry out that chore. They were stone, each as unreadable as the next. Elias was pleased with their disinterest. He sauntered casually away from Erkov in the heavy silence of The Meadow, along the challenge course, to toss the pennant down in front of the judge's platform and the Master of the Games who sat atop it.

"I present the course pennant, Games Master," Elias said with no sign of exhaustion after glancing at the Steward and receiving the smallest of approving nods. The gesture, tiny though it was, felt immensely gratifying, but Elias fought it, trying instead to cling to his anger. He used his forearm to wipe mud from his face, taking the time to right himself. He couldn't let contentment seep in now. After all, there was still the last race. There was still Ricky Allanson.

"Very good, nitiate," Lieutenant Schwambach said, sounding interested for the first time all day. "Speak your challenge."

"I challenge whoever is left," Elias answered, avoiding the indignity of having to actually speak Ricky's name aloud.

Some chuckles rippled out from the assembled squads, but the laughter died quickly after Lieutenant Schwambach swung around on his seat atop the judge's platform to face the three formations. "Who is left?" he asked the initiates.

Allanson snapped from at ease to attention and stepped one pace ahead of his formation rank. "I am," he half squeaked, half shouted at the Master of the Games.

"Very well, Initiate Allanson," Lieutenant Schwambach prompted. "Do you accept the challenge?"

Ricky looked around him for a long moment before turning back to the Master of the Games on his high perch. "I must decline, Games Master," he finally blurted out.

A gasp rolled through all three squad formations. Even Lieutenant Schwambach seemed nonplussed. He was speechless for a long moment before he finally found his voice. "Excuse me, Initiate? Did I hear you correctly? You're declining the challenge?"

"I would like nothing more than to prove my worth to the Witen, and to yourself, Games Master, but the medical aide told me to sit out the challenges today if the injury I suffered to my knee while winning last week's Pop Fitness Challenge started to flare up. I'm sorry to say, Games Master, and I really wouldn't say anything unless I had to, but my injury is really getting to me here, just standing in formation. I would happily accept the challenge regardless, but like I said, I was warned very strongly against it by the Program's medical aide. And while I don't doubt that I could easily beat Traitor's Son, even despite my injury, I feel it would be in the best interest of the Witen, and humanity's fate, that I should make sure my leg heals completely, so I'll be able to contribute my full potential in the future."

"Well spoken, Initiate," Squad 3's leader, Lieutenant Woodson, broke the silence that followed Ricky's explanation. "Humanity's fate is far too important to gamble on anything, even these hallowed proceedings. Go ahead and step back in formation, son, and good on you for fighting through the pain here today."

"Yes, Squad Leader. Thank you," Allanson shouted out with what Elias felt was obviously false bravado as he stepped back into his rank.

Allanson was the lieutenant's favorite, which made it easy for Ricky to get away with his tormenting of all those who incurred his wrath. But even Elias, who'd suffered most from Lieutenant Woodson's adoration of Allanson, was surprised to hear the squad leader defending the blond boy's refusal to race. Worse yet, as Elias glanced around at the assembled officers, he saw they were either unmoved by the proceedings or were obviously agreeing with Lieutenant Woodson's appraisal of Ricky's cowardly act. *He ain't hurting,* Elias thought with disgust. *He wasn't limping at all earlier. No way the med aide said any such thing. He's lying! Can't they all see it?* Elias looked over at the Steward. Surely, he wouldn't approve of the asshole's obvious lies. The look he found on the Steward's face, though, was one Elias could not decipher. Whatever it was, it was clear that the Steward wasn't about to voice any sort of complaint. *This asshole is clearly afraid to face me,* Elias thought of Ricky, *yet he still somehow stays on their good side.* It made no sense to him.

"Well, I suppose that's it, then," the Master of the Games said, cutting through Elias's confusion. "Okay, Initiate Sagal, you are the Initiate Supreme." Lieutenant Schwambach began a slow clap after that, which slowly spread throughout the formations. "Congratulations," he added, just as Lieutenant Masterson, Squad 2's leader, stepped up to Elias.

"Congratulations, Initiate," he said, taking Elias's hand into his own and squeezing tightly throughout a lengthy handshake.

Lieutenant Gregson, Squad 1's leader, was next to step up and shake Elias's hand, adding a "Congratulations, Initiate," as well.

Next came his own squad leader, Lieutenant Woodson, whose "Congratulations, Initiate" seemed begrudging.

Lieutenant Dirks, Master of Training, and Lieutenant Dobechek, Master of Studies, were the last lieutenants to step up and shake his hand. It seemed Lieutenant Schwambach was contented to stay up in his high perch. The two masters' "Congratulations, Initiate" were both spoken in much more neutral tones in comparison to that of Lieutenant Woodson's.

Supervisor Chairman Mikkelson's grip was sweaty, while his "Congratulations, Initiate" was hasty.

Captain Alvarez had a firm yet friendly grip during his handshake, and by the time Elias heard his "Congratulations, Initiate," his confusion and anger at not being able to run against Ricky Allanson had faded away, being replaced with amazement over actually achieving his goal. He was getting the praise of the Integration Program's officers he'd been craving, the praise he knew he deserved.

So, by the time the Steward had offered his congratulations along with an extra confidential and knowing wink and grin, Elias was feeling pretty damn good.

Only after the Commander had enclosed his hand inside his giant paw before grunting out, "Congratulations, Initiate," did the bittersweet draft of confusion resurface once again to gag him. The Commander had stepped up right alongside him after his intimidating handshake and Elias's eyes had flicked back to his squad's formation. In particular, the last rank, third from the left. Tessa still stood in position, her head still high, still appearing impassive, but her eyes, those chestnut orbs that so beguiled Elias, held a sorrow in them that tainted the glow he'd been basking in only seconds earlier. He'd done it. He was Initiate Supreme. Helena would be so proud. He should've been ecstatic, but dark, desolate doubt and cryptic confusion disrupted the possibility of any sort of celebratory mood, even as the Commander of the Witenagemot himself stood alongside him, raising his arm in triumph while quieting the still-clapping formations.

"Initiates," the scar-faced gorilla-man barked out the first words he'd ever uttered to all the initiates throughout the Integration Program's many weeks. The ranks of initiates quickly ceased their clamor. They were on pins and needles to hear their Commander. Elias knew he ought to be as well, but despite a monstrous internal struggle, he couldn't shove the tortuous sight of Tessa's bruised face and eyes brimming with sorrow from his mind. "I present to you the first ever Initiate Supreme," the Commander proclaimed, shaking Elias's upraised arm.

Almost as one, the assembled formations roared out their pleasure in his victory. Its genuine nature did shock Elias a bit and even managed to strip away some of his inner torment, but only some. He had achieved the goal he set out to accomplish, but it seemed the world would never let anything be simple. Instead of reveling in his glory, as Elias felt was just, he found himself grappling with unwelcome doubts. It wasn't fair. *Well, to hell with my stupid doubts, then!* he suddenly decided, recalling the clarity he'd achieved on the challenge course, and remembering that it was simple hate and anger which brought it about. Elias swore to keep things clear and simple from then on out. He'd just stay angry. He would keep hate, with all its freeing clarity, forever close.

CHAPTER 3
THE COMMANDER

The soft trilling of his hailing chime woke the Commander from another fitful night's sleep. He'd been dreaming, as ever, but the precise form of dread he'd been facing down in his subconscious was wiped clean from his reckoning upon the opening of his eyes. It was only the emotions dredged up by the constant nightmares that stayed with him come the morning. So, inevitably, he was irritable as he smashed down the hatchway intercom button on his bedside table. "What?" he asked whoever it was at his living quarters' hatchway.

"Commander, sir, this is Footman Morison with your wake-up reminder, sir. It's 0900 hours now, Commander, sir," the nervous footman on the other end of the intercom answered in a shaky voice. "There was a special order from the Steward in my shift duties list this morning to ensure I rang your hailing chime as a wake-up reminder at this time, if I hadn't seen you out of your quarters yet, that is. I apologize for the intrusion, sir, but I... I..."

"No need for that, son, you're just following orders." The Commander cut through the man's fumbling with a voice he hoped sounded a bit softer than his initial response. "Inform the Steward I'll be there directly."

"Yes, Commander, right away."

The Commander didn't know the man from Adam. He couldn't keep all the new faces inside the Witenagemot straight. Of course, he didn't need to. He had the Steward and his lieutenants tending to such mundane details as staffing and personnel. Plus, the Commander figured it was better to keep his distance with the rest of his subjects, to stay ever above them. He couldn't be pulled down to their level. How could he ever sit in judgement over them, then? No, it was for them to know him and his laws, not the other way around. *You shouldn't feel guilty about sounding grumpy when one of them comes before you, either,* he told himself. *Guilt is far too slippery a slope. It ain't but a step or two from playing favorites.* No way could the Commander allow such blasphemies to take root in his heart now. He needed to grow colder and harder, if anything, not less. All the blood spilled to attain the fragile order he and his men had instilled could easily become pointless and lamentable if he allowed himself to drop the burden of leadership, even for a second, even for something as desirable as a kind look and a bit of friendly conversation. Those were the desires of Jasper Montrois, and resurrecting him, even for a heartbeat, would destroy the Commander completely and humanity's great last hope—the Witenagemot—right along with it.

He knew the Steward would agree with him. He wouldn't care how brusque the Commander had been to his errand boy. The Steward was the most practical of them all. It was he who showed the Commander the truth, tearing away the last stubborn remnants of the blinders that had been laid upon his eyes by AOA, the government pretenders, and countless generations of people just like them. It was also the Steward who then possessed the good sense to trust in a man once known as Jasper Montrois to be the supreme guardian of the Witenagemot. The Steward proved the worthiness of their cause with that act, the Commander believed, and secured his trust from then on.

His number-two man understood the order of things better than any. He would never presume to reprimand the Commander for his manners. Despite this, though, he still figured the Steward would be perturbed about his late arrival for their inspection of the Nest's fishery. The Commander was supposed to be there at 0900, not just waking up. So, he'd likely be annoyed by the Commander's adherence to his own particular schedule, but he'd also understand the Commander's flexing of his authoritative muscle. Really, the more the Commander thought on it, the more he figured the thin ex-lawyer would not only understand but approve. *Hell, he probably worked my tardiness into his precious damn schedule,* the Commander thought with an inner grin. *I'm sure he makes the lieutenants, supervisors and footmen wait on him in turn.* Such were the nuances and subtleties of authority. It was all just an art of sorts, really, he realized.

As the Commander rose from his Alaskan king bed in the center of a plush carpeted and finely furnished master bedroom, with that thought settling its obvious truth on his mind, a yawn crept up on him. Embracing it, the Commander stretched his back and shoulders and then used the momentum to stumble the first few steps toward his private bathroom. The bathroom, as well as the bedroom it was attached to, was lavish and gargantuan in comparison to those found in the domiciles of folks in Blue Corridor or any other such residential sector over in Branch 4. The Commander thought nothing of this disparity. Not out of a sense of pompous entitlement but as a sign of power. It was only right that the Commander of the Witenagemot should be quartered in the luxury VIP chambers once occupied by Hubert Harrington, formerly CEO of the Advancement Operations Alliance. It would send the wrong signal to the ignorant, impressionable masses if the Commander were to show deference to anyone, on any matter, not the least of which being the housing arrangements for the station's ruling regime. The Commander was in charge. He deferred to no one. His due was the lord's portion, in all matters. He'd come too damn far to shrink from the vanities of power now.

So, after he finished drying off from a quick wash, neither did he feel guilty about tossing his towel down on his salmon-colored tile floor beside his spacious shower with its clear glass walls dividing the far third of the bathroom from floor to ceiling. The Commander knew a council-vetted servant of the Witen would be along sometime today to tidy up his messes and prepare his meals. Complacency led to idleness, which bred resentment, which in turn gave rise to rebellion. It was a leader's job, then, above all others, to keep his charges focused on their tasks alone. Survival, preservation, perpetuation— such were the lofty labors with which the Witen had been tasked. Thus, the pressure on the Commander to succeed in his duty of keeping his charges focused and obedient was far graver and more urgent a pressure than ever lay upon the shoulders of any man or woman who'd ever lived. His indifference to the messes he left in his wake was justified in this way. It all kept the servants busy. The lieutenants and supervisors all doled out plenty enough work to keep the footmen and other servants of the Witen busy as well. No one was ever overly taxed, by any means, but neither would any of them ever be allowed to grow close to that scourge of sanity known as idleness.

And so it was that, even though the Commander was perfectly capable of pressing and preparing his own uniform, he nevertheless felt nothing but a world working in perfect order as he stepped into the set of black tactical pants and shrugged into the gold-trimmed, black tactical blouse that had been laid out for him last night by a servant. All was as it should be. Control was locked firm in his grasp. If a little comfort had to be a byproduct of the Witen's righteous authority, then so be it. The Commander would bear it as a commander should.

Shoes strapped tight and the creases in his blouse crisp and sharpened, the Commander then stepped through the large portal leading into the hallway off his bedroom and headed for his kitchen. Rushed or not, he wasn't leaving his quarters without a cup of coffee. A servant was already there when he arrived. She was a small, squirrelly woman. He'd seen her around his quarters on a number of occasions. She irritated him a bit. She was meek to the point that the Commander could barely even hear her when she addressed him. Thankfully, not much needed to be said just then. She'd anticipated his wants and had the percolator ending its cycle just as he stepped into the high-ceilinged, austere, white-walled room. The Commander pointed to a to-go mug beside the coffeemaker, and the servant quickly got the hint. She topped off the mug, adding just the right amount of sugar and correctly forgoing any cream. He snatched the beverage from her a bit more forcefully than he'd intended, but he was impatient for the caffeine. He was about to step out among his people. He couldn't afford for bags under his eyes to undermine the scarred, bearded, and implacable visage he always presented to the public at large. The flock needed to see what the Commander had endured for them. They could never be allowed to see anything that conflicted with the hard, brutal, ruthless man they all feared.

He had to sip the piping-hot coffee, but soon, the drink was doing its work, and the Commander was feeling ready to step out into his station. He ran his hand through his beard, pulling apart a few tangles and knots, as he made his way through his spacious quarters toward the hatchway. Mug in hand, he paused before the portal to straighten his blouse one last time and pass a final hand through his dark hair. A slow, easy breath and another sip of his coffee buoyed him out into the Grand Alleyway, an immense arcade 40-feet wide and 80-feet tall, cutting straight as an arrow down the center of Branch 1. The middle of the Grand Alleyway was divided in half by a line of flowering pink and violet hibiscus bushes planted in three-foot gray planters. Its walls and ceilings had a soft gray basecoat but were slashed everywhere with elegant streaks of maroon and silver. The giant AOA logo that previously occupied pride of place in the center of the Grand Alleyway's ceiling, painted in gigantic maroon and silver letters 20 yards long, had been painted over crudely with a mismatched gray. The Commander did not see this as an eyesore, however. The logo's erasure had been one of the very first orders he had ever issued. It symbolized his ascension over their corrupt authority. The logo had kindled a hatred in his heart that dragged up painful memories he'd been doing his best to bury. So, he'd deemed it immediately necessary to make the Witen's new sanctuary an AOA-free zone. The sight of the crude patch job was a mark of beauty in the Commander's eyes. To the left of his quarters, as he exited, lay the control room, about 10 yards away. The Commander turned right upon exiting, though, leading him toward the gaping archway emptying into the Grand Rotunda 100 yards away. All along the walk, he passed by the residences of his fellow councilmembers on both sides of the imposing alleyway, each spaced out a good deal from its closest neighbor. His Witenagemot underling's apartments might not be quite as regal as his own, but by no means could they be termed meager in either dimensions or amenities.

The Commander's long legs ate up the yards in no time. He wasn't pushing himself or showing any outward signs of haste. His legs were just long. His body was just strong. He was just relentless. It all had the effect of making the world seem slow around him. He could've hopped aboard the repulsion trolley that was always stationed just outside his quarters' hatchway, but the Commander enjoyed the walk. It felt like doing something. It settled his roiling mind. The ride surely would have gotten him to the fishery just inside the giant archway of Branch 3 quicker, but it couldn't have been more than an eight-minute walk, a negligible difference in the Commander's eyes. He arrived to find the Steward standing outside the large hatchway leading into the facility, alongside the fishery's staff supervisor. The man was conspicuous in his gold dress coat with its elegantly stitched black W on the right breast pocket. The Commander recognized him as a Witen councilmember, but although he dug deep for it, the short, sandy-haired man's name wouldn't come to him.

Thankfully, the Steward saved him. He had been standing at ease with three gray-clad footmen behind him in identical stances, but he moved to indicate the supervisor with his arm as soon as the Commander got within a few feet of them. "Commander, sir, Supervisor McClellan and I welcome you to the fishery."

"Good morning, Supervisor," the Commander greeted the small man as he took his hand for a shake.

"Good morning to you, Commander," the man gushed in response. The Commander had become used to being the target of a bit of sycophancy these past few months, but Supervisor McClellan was putting all the others to shame with the fawning look in his eyes alone. He was clearly nervous, but there was what seemed to the Commander like genuine awe pushing away any reservations that may have served as safeguards to his obsequiousness.

"Easy, man," he told the fool, snatching his hand back. Saying nothing, the Commander passed the mug he still held off to the supervisor. His subordinate took it without a word and almost seemed excited for the opportunity to care for his leader's beverage. Fighting a pleased smirk, he turned to the Steward. "Good morning to you and your footmen, as well, Steward."

"I thank you, sir. As do my footmen, I'm sure."

"Good morning, Commander," all three footmen said in unison after snapping to attention.

"At ease, footmen," the Commander ordered them with an approving grin, which in turn drew out reciprocated grins full of undisguised pride. "Shall we then, Supervisor?" he asked, turning back to the fishery's top man.

"Yes, Commander, sir. Of course, sir. Right this way," the man gushed, stepping up to the terminal to open the entrance. A few quick taps of the screen and the 10-foot maroon-and-silver sliding door retracted into the bulkhead with a soft hush. "Follow me."

They were definitely in the fishery. The pungent, oily, marine stink that filled the Commander's nostrils within his first steps into the contained facility left no doubt. The smell failed to improve as McClellan led them toward the aquariums and live pools where the station's seafood population was cultivated and maintained. The three footmen fell into position around the Commander and the Steward, one to either side and one behind. The facility wasn't exactly packed with workers, but they passed half a dozen or so at various stations along the way, all of whom diverted their eyes and made their labors conspicuous and exaggerated as the Commander and his retinue passed them.

McClellan had the coffee mug tucked into the left hip pocket of his golden blazer now. It bumped along wildly as he walked, though the man didn't seem to notice. He was busy chirping away with a string of facts about each aspect of the impressive facility as they passed it by. The Commander barely heard him. He had his eyes and ears out for the things the man wouldn't be including in his audible report. Anyway, the Steward was doing all the questioning and praising, as each were warranted, so the Commander was free to drift from the guided tour, as it were. Everything seemed on the up-and-up, however, as far as he could tell. The Commander was growing bored with the whole tedious affair as a result, despite the incredible sight of the massive tanks and pools in the rear half of the facility, each stocked with one marine species or another. Supervisor McClellan must've picked up on his impatience because he abruptly clapped his hands together, ending his monologue and leading them away toward the processing half of the fishery.

The Commander turned absently to follow him, his Steward and footmen immediately following suit, when he noticed her and stopped dead in his tracks. A shiver of bright, resurrecting hope buzzed down his spine. His feet, unbidden by his conscious mind, stepped toward the impossible apparition. *Carrie?* He almost cracked up over the inner utterance of his wife's name alone. Another step toward her and the glorious mirage remained. His wife, his love, his life, his great loss, was standing in front of a 30,000-gallon aquarium with a pocket tablet resting in one arm as she surveyed the fish swimming within. The Commander made to shout out her name, the name he'd been aching to speak aloud for countless dark days, but before the beautiful sound of his wife's name could form on his tongue, she moved her head. As she did, Carrie's perfect face remained like a ghost of the other, still facing forward while the other shifted. He blinked, and the dual image was gone completely.

The woman who had worn his wife's face was now looking straight at him. She had the same red hair as Carrie, the same crystal-blue eyes and light splash of pale freckles, but she was different. She wasn't Carrie. He remembered then his bright hope at first glance and instantly resented himself for allowing such useless emotions to overcome him. He had buried the past. He needed to in order to rule. Hope was a weakness, a disease to his leadership. And yet, he'd succumbed to its empty promises in the blink of an eye. The notion angered him, even as images of his wife and daughter began to flood his mind, images he'd worked to bury deep—flashes of backyard picnics and Sunday morning breakfasts in bed, of the fear and misery in his family's eyes as he left for deployments, and the joy and relief in them when he'd returned, of Christmases and birthdays together, movie nights and family dinners. They all rushed in. His fists balled up and shoulders grew stiff as a stump in response.

In spite of the dozen eyes he could feel studying and judging his every move, the Commander stood stiff and took what time he needed to right his mind. He shut his eyes and tried to erase the past in his subconscious. Deep breath upon deep breath seemed to do the trick after a time. He reopened his eyes and now saw only the beautiful, somehow familiar, woman before him. All tragic memories of the loves he lost were staying away, or at least along the margins.

"Commander?" the Steward prompted with a cleared throat after a time. "Shall we follow Supervisor McClellan, sir?"

"What's her name, Steward?" the Commander demanded of the Steward with an outstretched finger aimed at the strangely familiar redhead.

"Her, sir?" the Steward responded after a moment of silent confusion. "I... I don't... I—"

"Yes, her," he cut off his subordinate impatiently. "Who is she? What does she do here?"

"She... Uhh... She... Well..." the Steward began before snapping out of his rare awkwardness and turning to shout at Supervisor McClellan, who had gotten a few yards away from them. "Supervisor, get back here, if you would."

McClellan turned around with an abashed look on his face and instantly jogged back toward them. "Sorry, Steward, sir. Didn't mean to get so far ahead of you. Is there a problem, sir?"

"No problem, Supervisor, merely a small inquiry," the Steward assured him. "The, uhhm, redheaded woman here," he said, indicating the woman still holding the pocket tablet by the nearby aquarium, "her name and job title?"

McClellan was thrown by the off-topic question for a moment. "Well, that is our main shift tank water quality tech, uhh... Mrs. Hyun, I believe. I did get that right, miss, didn't I?"

If McClellan had been thrown be the inquiry into her identification, then the woman could be said to have been floored by it. With a stiff confusion, she turned to look the Commander in the eye after the question was put to her. She answered the man in the affirmative after a time, but the Commander had been too lost in the blue oceans of her soul's portals to fully hear it. His mind was adrift so deep inside them that it took a few moments to realize why she was so damn familiar to him.

It's Abner's wife, Stevie. Abner Hyun, the onetime best friend of Jasper Montrois. The Commander had known them both for years. *How did I not see it before? How did I forget?* he asked himself as their staring contest continued. What was worse, he suddenly remembered this was not the first time this exact illusion had played out. Memories of an anxious crowd pressing close all around as he gazed into the turbulent blue eyes of his wife while she served as a guard against the rambunctious crowd, keeping them back from Maisie Sagal and her bedraggled little brother. It had been the same cruel hope that had grabbed him then as well, only to have the same vile truth smack him back down, he remembered with a sick, sinking feeling.

It scared him a little, his forgetting, which angered him in turn. He felt his grip on supreme control slacken a smidge. And a smidge was more than enough to unnerve him. Stevie Hyun was a woman the Commander definitely needed to avoid. "Get back to work," he shouted out suddenly in a thick voice. "All of you, everyone, back to work!" There were only three other fishery workers in shouting distance other than Stevie, and they were already engrossed in their duties. Even so, none dared voice an indignant complaint. "Lead on, Supervisor," he said to McClellan in a tone that brooked no argument.

"Uhh... Yes, sir, of course, sir," Supervisor McClellan stuttered, swallowing a nervous squeak. "Right this way, Commander, sir," he added, turning once again to lead the small inspection party toward the processing department.

CHAPTER 4

ALICE

"Ughh… Shit," Alice Stark moaned between spits. *Goddamn those fucking eggs,* she thought, recalling the scent of their frying reaching her nostrils, which in turn led to her adding a bit more putrid muck to the patch of floating regurgitation in the toilet bowl she was currently curled up around. *At least it's my own toilet,* Alice consoled herself during a bit more swearing and spitting after her final bout of morning sickness ran dry. It had been a close call, for sure. She had been at Stevie Hyun's place a few alleyways over when her friend had decided to make herself breakfast, after a good deal of encouragement from Alice, for the poor woman looked thin as a rail. Alice feared she'd been so distracted by the behavior of her husband Abner of late, as well as the strange and unsettling attention she'd been receiving from the Commander, that Stevie just wasn't eating anymore. It was when Stevie cracked the eggs and the hot pan hissed as she dropped them onto it that the triggering odor had cruelly assailed her.

Alice felt doubly shitty as she bent over her porcelain post for leaving Stevie mid-conversation to sprint back to her new quarters to vomit, but Alice wasn't ready for anyone to know about her condition just yet. Alice herself had not quite wrapped her own head around it all yet. She felt terrible for ditching her vulnerable friend without explanation, but the fear that confronted her when she thought of using Stevie's bathroom to vomit, with its obvious flaw of being far too close in proximity to her friend to disguise her lavatorial activities, had forced the quick flight upon her.

I'll go back there and tell her I thought I left my stove on or something, Alice decided, just as a soft knock tapped a rhythm on her bathroom hatchway. "Alice, you okay in there?" Maisie Sagal's voice came to her ears, half-muffled by the thick hatchway. *Oh no!* Alice thought with a sinking heart. *She said she'd be at Father Boyd's all day. Oh god, what's she doing home?* "It's okay, Alice... I know." Maisie's voice came to her once again. "Do you need a hand? I'm not about to judge or nothing, Ms. Stark. I'm just... Well, I dunno, I'm here to talk, or whatever, if you want."

The panic in Alice's chest was punctured by the sweet earnestness in the voice of her 13-year-old roommate. She should've known the kid was too bright to be able to hide her pregnancy. Maisie had probably known for weeks, now that Alice thought back on some of their previous conversations. Alice had been so wrapped up in the chaos of losing her wife, her lover, and her freedom, on top of the worry and confusion of her present circumstance, that she might not have been as sharp in her attempted deceptions as she might have hoped. Alice had felt the pangs of morning sickness, though that title pissed her off, seeing as how the nausea attacked her morning, noon, and night. She'd battled it throughout every day of her now 14-week pregnancy, but the frequently crippling and often unpredictable sickness had definitely increased to scary new levels the last six weeks. *Maisie probably couldn't help but figure it out, really,* she realized with a sigh.

"I'll be right out, Mais," Alice called out to the brave young girl on the other side of her bathroom's hatchway. "Just give me a moment, kiddo."

Alice finished washing her hands and rinsing out her mouth before stepping from the bathroom to find Maisie waiting just outside with a patient and kind look that seemed far beyond any child of her age. It was wise and comforting, that look, and Alice found herself eager to take refuge in its promises. It seemed to shout out a mature understanding. And the next thing she knew, Alice found her face pressed against the shoulder of her dead lover's daughter, sobbing a long-overdue release of months-long tension. "It's okay, Ms. Stark. It's okay," Alice heard the astute, hazel-eyed girl tell her.

"You knew?" Alice managed to gulp out the question as she lifted her head from Maisie's shoulder. "How?"

"The walls of this space station ain't that thick, Alice," Maisie answered with a slight blush. "I hear you nearly every night throwing up in there. I just haven't been able to bring myself to confront you about it. I was afraid it would come across as judging, 'cause I got hopes that you'll keep it for my dad's sake, and mine and Eli's, but I know it ain't my place to say that or anything. I know how confusing it must be to think about bringing a child into the world of the Witen, not to mention what Ms. Heathcoat might do when she finds out and all. And I just didn't know how to tell you all that. 'Cept I just now heard ya, and suddenly, I realized the only thing to do was to be honest and lay it all out. You see, I never thanked you for... You see, I was so happy when you decided to move in with me after they took Eli away—"

"I'm the one who should be thanking *you* for that," Alice broke in to assure her. "I had no other place to go. You took me in. You certainly did not have to do that."

"Yes, but... I did it 'cause I wanted us to be close, Ms. Stark."

"Alice, sweetie. Just Alice," she instructed her roommate.

"I was hoping we could form a real bond, Alice," Maisie continued with a blush and a smile, "where we look after each other, help each other out, and don't judge each other, but just, like, try and talk and understand each other and respect each other as equal people, or whatever."

"I was hoping for that for us, too, Mais," Alice assured her with emotion still cracking her voice. "I shouldn't have hid the baby from you. I'm sorry. I just... I... I was scared. I *am* scared."

"I understand, Alice. I do," Maisie said. "Let's you and me promise to be totally honest with each other from this moment on. My daddy loved you. I know that he did. I saw it in his eyes. And so, I'm willing to trust and love you, Alice. I'm, I don't know, *eager* to, really. You see, I think you and I are going to come to really need each other up here."

"Oh, honey, I got a feeling you're very right about that," Alice concurred with a loving smile washing away the anguish in her heart. "No more lies or secrets from here on out. I promise."

"Good," the girl responded with a refreshing enthusiasm in her voice. "That's good."

"I did love your father, Maisie, very much. I want you to know that. And I do love this child," Alice told her with a hand moving to caress the small swell of her tummy, "but things are so unsettled here, so … dangerous."

"I know," Maisie said. "I get that. I—"

"But then sometimes I think that I'm just using that as an excuse to run from my responsibility, an excuse to shield me from the inevitable confrontation with Helena, as well as having to be constantly reminded of Perry and that fucking monster killing him. I am confused beyond all reason, in short, Mais. And I've no real idea what I'm gonna do from one moment to the next," Alice added with an ironic smirk.

"We'll find the right answer for you—together, Alice," Maisie assured her in a trusting voice. "I would say we should make some snacks and talk it out in the kitchen right now, but I got some people coming by in a few minutes. I'm sorry about that, by the way. I know I should've told you, but it all kinda just came together this morning at the last minute."

"People? What people?" Alice asked in a puzzled tone. Her mind was racing with a thousand thoughts and fears, and the information Maisie had just thrown at her was out of place with all the rest. It took her a minute to clear her thoughts and focus on this new topic. "What are you talking about, sweetie? Who's coming here?"

"I was at Boyd's this morning, tending to my daily chores, which, now that the Witen outlawed the credit system, my daily duties over there have exploded, let me tell ya. The priest is taking trades now for his product, and I gotta find a place to store all the useless junk. Lord knows what he is gonna do with it all, or what he's gonna do when all the drunks constantly at his quarters finally run out of stuff to barter."

"Whoa, okay, okay," Alice cut into Maisie's rambling. "Back to the topic at hand. Who are these people on their way to our quarters?"

"Oh, right, sorry," Maisie said, shaking her mind back to the subject. "My head is, like, in a million pieces these days."

"I know how you feel," Alice told her patiently.

"Well, I was watering Boyd's hydroponics garden when Hubert Harrington and President Rafferty came barging in," Maisie started. "They had Mr. Spurnberg with them and a couple other people I didn't recognize, though I pegged 'em for AOA execs and government people. Mr. Spurnberg was a friend of my dad's, and I know he was no fan of the Witen. I heard a lot of his and Dad's conversations late at night in the days before the Final Tournament when they thought me and Eli were asleep. And I also know that AOA and the government people sure aren't happy about being kicked out of their luxury quarters, nor what Boyd calls, 'usurped from their seats of authority.' So, I guessed they were all there to talk the priest into joining in a conspiracy or whatever."

"I hope they sent you out of the room before they discussed any such thing," Alice barked indignantly.

"They tried." Maisie crooked her eyebrow.

"They tried? What does that mean?" Alice asked in a calm enough voice, though her anger with the negligent adults was swelling inside with each second.

"Relax. They never talked about anything, really. The priest wasn't having it," Maisie said, brushing off Alice's concern.

"Good," Alice interjected.

"He's been telling me for weeks now to 'let my anger-driven ambition rest,'" Maisie went on, clear disappointment edging her voice. "Every time I confront him with the latest bullcrap the Witen has done, he's got nothing to say about it. He just changes the subject. I didn't want to believe he was really doing nothing to oppose the Witen. I was telling myself lies that he was being dismissive only on the outside while secretly, underneath, he was plotting the Commander's downfall. But he hasn't been plotting nothing. He isn't gonna do anything about the goddamn Witen."

"Maisie," Alice called to her roommate, a touch of scolding in her voice.

"What?" Maisie shot back with defensive anger spicing the question. "I'm not a kid anymore, Alice. I thought you of all people would understand that. I've been through too damn much. We all have."

"I know you're far more mature than most girls your age," Alice allowed, "but you're still young. Father Boyd has lived, Mais. He's seen the world. It's given him experience. And I'm sure it's a bitter pill for him to swallow, but if he has decided to yield to the Witen and their demands, then maybe that's the wisest course to take."

"No, Alice," Maisie said with pleading now animating her voice. "How can you think that? That ain't the way my dad saw it. He knew they had to be stopped."

"And it cost him his life," Alice whispered.

"Yes, it did!" Maisie concurred, loudly and vehemently. "And we should give no less. He gave his life to stop these Witen jerks. We have to be willing to do the same, to honor his sacrifice, Alice. I know that opposing the Witen will be extremely dangerous, and it will most likely mean an unending parade of anxiety-racked sleepless nights ahead, but 'just 'cause the job is hard ain't no excuse to shirk it' as Perry Sagal himself often would say."

Alice was at a loss. She knew deep down that Maisie spoke the truth. A part of her had been secretly angry with the priest's capitulation to the Witen as well, but she always buried it under a dense blanket of logic and self-preservation. But Alice now saw that Perry's sacrifice did deserve to be honored. She understood in that moment just how pathetically she'd been behaving. Yes, she did have a deal of troubles on the horizon, but there were enough *at leasts* on her side to shame a saint. *At least* she was still alive (of the nine billion people who'd once roamed the Earth only four months back, she was one of only five hundred or so left), and *at least* she wasn't one of those poor souls who'd been turned to mindless monsters by the infection and left to wander the decaying streets, and *at least* she had friends with shoulders to cry on, and *at least* she had Maisie. They were both still here and kicking. Time had not run out on human decency yet. Enough strength of will still remained inside them to do something about it. "You're right, Mais," Alice said after a time. "Father Boyd is afraid. He's a failure, the poor man. He failed at being a priest and was impotent to stop the madness of the Witen. He's just hoping now that ignoring it all will fix everything. I don't really blame him. I can sure see the allure of that hope. I was content to turn my head from the plain truth, too, Mais. But no, you're right. We have to honor your father."

"Oh, thank you, Alice. Thank you so much," Maisie said before embracing her in an emphatic hug.

"I haven't agreed to anything explicitly now, Mais," Alice cautioned.

"No, no, I get it," Maisie assured her.

"So, finish your story, then," Alice prompted. "Is it the priest on his way over here now? Do you want me to try and help you talk him into joining in with AOA's conspiracy?"

"No, it's not the priest coming here. It's... It's... Well, everyone else," Maisie answered without looking Alice in the eyes. "You see, Boyd tried to rush them out of his place as soon as they mentioned why they was there. They were telling him how they needed a place to meet that would be off the Witen's radar. Harrington himself said he was the one who figured Boyd's shop would make the perfect place 'cause of all the regular foot traffic in and out of there every day. They all figured no one in the Witen would think it odd for all types of people to be visiting his place. Then, when that was going nowhere, they tried appealing to Boyd's vanity by telling him how no other resident has the ear of the people quite like he does and how he is uniquely positioned to be the lynchpin to all their plans—something about his 'innate coordination abilities' or something like that. But, like I said, Boyd wasn't having any of it. He actually tried to physically shoo them out of his shop. That's when I got the idea to offer to hold the meeting at our quarters instead, with you as the lynchpin. I told them how much everyone loves you and how easily you can inspire the people or set them at ease with barely a word. And well, they went for it."

"At our place!? The lynchpi—I don't..." Alice began. "I'm not so sure tha—"

"We should be able to pull off one impromptu meeting here without the Witen coming down on us," Maisie cut in to assure her. "I didn't offer our place as a permanent gathering spot or nothing, or your guaranteed help or anything. We need to find something much more safe and hidden for that kinda thing, of course. But the resistance to the Witen needs to stop wasting time. This morning's meeting is the big first step we all need to take. It's important, Alice. Don't ya see?"

Maisie had her at a loss for words once again. Alice found herself swayed by the arguments of the teenager but felt a twinge of irresponsibility in allowing herself to be moved thus. Though, as she stared deep into her hazel eyes, Alice thought back on the things Maisie had said: of wanting a person to rely on, a person to trust and respect. She slowly came to realize that she had almost given the young girl an oath without really ever promising anything in particular. Alice could not go back on that now. She was going to need Maisie. She owed her the rightful respect the mature and courageous girl had earned. "Okay, Mais. Okay," Alice finally said, relenting. "Let's get the dining room ready for our guests, then."

No sooner were those words out of her mouth then their hailing chime rang out into the cramped quarters. "That'll be them," Maisie said, making for the hatchway. But after she ordered their quarters' hatchway to slide open with a soft hush of compressed air, the person who stepped into the room was someone Maisie was definitely not expecting if the sudden shock on her face was any indication. "Stevie?" Maisie managed to splutter the name of the skinny, freckle-dusted, redheaded woman standing before her. "What are you doing here?"

"Hey, Mais," Stevie answered in a tone unaffected by the young girl's shock, "I just came to check on Alice. I take it you were expecting someone else."

"Uhh... Yeah," Maisie responded after a few beats.

"Who?"

"Hey, Stevie," Alice cut in before Maisie could offer up any answer, "I was just gonna head back to your place. I'm sorry I ran out of there on you. I just... I—"

"You had to battle a round of morning sickness. I get it, honey," Stevie offered, cutting off Alice's words. "Oh, don't give me that look. Of course I know. You and I have spent too much time together lately to hide it from me. Plus, you suck at it anyway. Deception is not your strong suit, my dear."

"Well, I-I didn't mean to lie to you or nothin—"

"No, no, Alice, I wasn't trying to imply that," Stevie cut in once more. "I just wanted you to know that you don't have to play any sort of games with me or nothing. I'm here for you no matter what. If you want to keep it a secret, then I'm only here to help with your cover-up. Whatever you need, Allie."

"Funny," Alice said with a lightness in her voice. "Maisie here was just telling me much the same."

"Us ladies are in this damn thing together," Maisie told the two older women.

"That we are, Mais. That we are," Stevie agreed, just as the hailing chime rang out once more. "I'm guessing that is whoever you thought I was."

"Most likely," Alice concurred. "It could get you in some trouble, Stevie, if you stay. Maisie needs me here for this, but you shouldn't risk yourself, too."

"Stop, Alice," Stevie said with an upraised hand. "We ladies are in this damn thing together, remember?" She paused long enough for Alice and Maisie's grins to settle firmly on their faces. "I'll go along with whatever you got going on here, but I will expect you gals to explain it all to me after it's over."

"Fair enough," Maisie said with no delay.

"Fair enough," Alice agreed after a beat.

"It's just an initial meeting, really," Maisie told Stevie as she moved to open the hatchway once again. "You won't be lost or nothing. Today is the first day of the resistance, Stevie." With that, Maisie depressed the hatchway entrance button, and Tom Spurnberg entered their quarters with a slew of the Witen's public-enemy-number-ones right behind him.

"Okay, first things first," Hubert Harrington said from his perch at the head of the Sagal family's oak dining table, "we should clear the room of any minors or anyone unwilling to swear full secrecy. This place is crowded enough as it is," Harrington added with a lip curled up in pretentious disgust.

All eyes fell to Maisie, who had seated herself right beside AOA's CEO. "I hope you don't mean me, Mr. Harrington," the incredible girl told him, as well as the rest of the room, in a crisp, clear voice.

"Of course I do, Ms. Sagal. You're what... Ten?"

"I'm thirtee—" Maisie started to respond before catching herself with a deep calming breath. "These are my father's quarters, Mr. Harrington. You are here at *my* invitation. I will stay."

"Ms. Stark, is it?" Harrington asked, turning his gaze to Alice.

"Alice is fine," she told him.

"Very well," the former executive allowed. "Alice, then. You are the guardian of this minor, are you not?"

"I suppose I am," Alice answered, only after sharing a knowing look with Maisie.

"Very well, then, while we do appreciate the assistance of your charge in setting up this meeting, we do not feel it would be ethical to conduct our intended proceedings in the presence of a minor. It's bad enough, quite frankly, that she knows as much as she does already. Let's not expose her to any more possible harm. Why don't you send her off to a friend's place for a few hours?"

"Maisie stays, Mr. Harrington." Alice found the calm from somewhere in order to say those words. She was pleased it came, given the rage she was feeling as she stared into the eyes of AOA's condescender-in-chief. "She stays, Hubie," Alice added with a bit of condescension of her own. "She's got bigger balls than any inside the hairy old sacks of you bastards. You ain't gods no more. You poor jerks are just one of us now. So don't think to order Maisie and me about in our own damn home. If you all want to destroy the Witen or get us all away from them somehow, then you're going to do it just like the rest of us. You're no longer special."

"She's right." Spurnberg, an AOA computer engineer, spoke up to agree with Alice before she could get carried away any further. "The resistance can't have any ego or else it loses its moral authority. We have to work toward equal peace for everyone. There are too few of us. Even with the people in this room and all our various like-minded friends, our numbers are still far too few for anyone to play a passive role. So, if you execs and ex-presidents," Spurnberg said, indicating Harrington and Rafferty in turn, "really want to help us defeat the Witen, then you better know you're gonna have to get your damn hands as dirty as the rest of us."

"We will pull our weight, Mr. Spurnberg. Don't you worry none," Harrington told him.

"Please, call me Tom," Spurnberg shot back.

"Why don't you go ahead and impress all us equals with your particular contribution to our resistance?" Harrington suggested.

"Actually, Hubie, I do, in fact, have a plan," Spurnberg assured him.

"Oh yeah, I'm sure you do," Harrington returned.

"Gentleman, please," Daniel Rafferty, former President of the United States, cut in. "This bickering is hardly the way for us to begin these hallowed proceedings. I know there is bitter feeling between the station workers and all those formerly quartered down Branch 1, but let us put an end to all that here and now. We truly do need to work together as one, with everyone pulling their fair share of weight, or as you say, Tom, 'getting their hands dirty,' especially if we are to pull off the proposal Mr. Harrington and myself and the government council have managed to devise over the last few weeks' worth of clandestine planning and fact-finding endeavors between the fifty or so of us."

"So, you've already got a plan, then?" Stevie spoke up to ask.

"We do, Ms.... Uhh?"

"Stevie is fine."

"We have an excellent and workable plan, Stevie," Rafferty assured her in his slow southern drawl.

"Excellent, eh?" Alice asked with deep skepticism.

"It's simple, yet effective. The very things every truly good plan has in common," Rafferty said as he leaned back in his chair.

"What is this simple plan?" Maisie asked.

Harrington glared at the young girl beside him for a good few seconds before making an effort to clear his throat and address the crowded table. "The Witen are fools. They've destroyed all the firearms and therefore left themselves vulnerable. There aren't enough of them to repel a well-timed incursion down Branch 1 and into the Control Room at the end of the Grand Alleyway. These good men and women you see with us today, apart from Tom here, who simply tagged along, are government officials, AOA execs, and the family members of both groups, all of whom have volunteered to participate in this assault. With your help, and your 'like-minded friends,' as old Tommy here put it, we will plot a way to rig the work schedule, undermine security protocols, and otherwise make Branch 1 as vulnerable as possible for this incursion."

"What are they gonna do in the Control Room, this 'assault team' of yours?" Maisie shrewdly asked.

Harrington did not look at all happy to do it, but he answered Alice's roommate. "AOA has several Launch Platform Satellites orbiting the Earth even now. All the data we had access to from these specialized platform satellites, before the Commander and his Witen launched their coup, indicated that perched atop two of those satellites was a fully serviceable and launch-ready Star Hawk. Fully serviceable and fully stocked, you understand? Meaning, each of those Hawks currently has fourteen M4 rifles sealed discreetly away in the hidden weapons locker in their cargo-bay floors. And, oh, by the way, each of these Star Hawks are completely controllable via remote stations inside Branch 1's Control Room."

"Your genius plan is to fly a bunch a guns to the station so we can grab 'em somehow?! Which, by the way, you can't do anyway 'cause The Witen destroyed the hatchway controls for Branch 2." Maisie's scorn matched what Alice currently felt.

"There is an emergency air lock hatch inside the Control Room that empties right out onto the lunar surface," Harrington added dismissively. "We can load everything right through there. Then we charge back out of the Control Room with the rightful balance of power clearly visible in the hands of the brave assault team."

"But the threat will be just as empty as The Witen realized it was," Stevie told him. "You can't fire 'em any more than they could. It would destroy the station. They blew all the guns up to keep any away from the hands of some lone nut who might go off and forget about his fragile surroundings, not because they feared their presence as a threat to their power. Your brave assault team will come charging out of the Control Room with nothing but metal clubs, essentially, 'cause they can't very well risk firing the damn things. And the goddamn Witen will surely know that. They'll simply plant every last footman outside the Control Room hatchway, ready to meet your brave fools with metal clubs of their own. Then more blood will be spilled, and the Witen will still rule in the end. This pointlessness cannot truly be your plan."

"Perhaps it does have its areas of ambiguity. Though I dare say, if your husband were to lend us his services, its chances for success would greatly increase," Harrington pointed out with acid in his tone. "Where is he now, Stevie? Do you know? We sure could use him. His sulking seems a bit childish and unhelpful just now. Wouldn't you say?"

"My husband played his part in the Witen's foolishness, Mr. Harrington. I'm not hiding from that," Stevie told him with an upturned chin. "I'm here to try and right that wrong."

"I'll bet Abner only did what he thought was best in the moment, Stevie," Maisie said in a warm tone that was out of place in the intense atmosphere. "I know you're still mad at him and everything, but we really could use him. I mean, not for this assault team ridiculousness, but for something someday, I'm sure. He deserves his chance at redemption, too, I think."

Alice watched as Stevie twisted away from Maisie's wise eyes to fight back tears. "Maybe you're right, Mais. Maybe. But I sure ain't roping him into your murderous scheme either way, Mr. Harrington," she finished, turning to the CEO in question.

"It's as good a plan as we've got, Mrs. Hyun." Rafferty spoke for the agitated Harrington. "But your husband's added efforts really would ensure the tide turned our way, no doubt about that. Will you really not consider just talking to him for us?"

"It don't matter what Abner's plans are, anyhow." Tom Spurnberg had become still and silent in his seat near the far end of the table from Harrington but had quickly stirred back to an impatient buzz.

"Why is that, Mr. Spurnberg?" Maisie asked the long-faced, clean-cut, gray-haired man.

"No message can get passed the cloaking tech, not without the unique Daily Passcode, anyway. And I hear the Steward forced you guys to hand over sole access to the Daily Code Generator to him, as well as all the rest of the station's security infrastructure along with it."

"There is no cloaking tech, Mr. Spurnberg! That is a spurious lie," Harrington told him in an affronted tone.

"There sure as hell is! I saw the program with my own damn eyes during your half-assed mainframe wipe, right before we were rushed aboard that E-11 all those months ago with the sound of growling and feasting monster-people filling the air," Spurnberg fired back in anger.

"You saw something you had no clearance for. A simple explanation surely exists that you do not have proper authority to view. You have taken five seconds worth of context-free words that flashed across a screen you were watching in an understandably agitated state, and your mind made connections that weren't there. End of story," Harrington harrumphed.

"You can trust us, Tom," former President Rafferty assured him. "What reason would we have to lie to you all? We are equals in this enterprise together, remember? AOA never developed any cloaking tech whatsoever, I promise you."

"Okay, fine," Spurnberg allowed. "What about the security codes for the Control Room hatchway, then? How do you plan on bypassing that without explosives or a hacker better than me, of which there are few who ever lived, and definitely none currently aboard station? Roddy Sheffield might be able to get there in the end, but no way that dude would help out with your bullshit plan. The man feels y'all betrayed him after the Witen's raid on the Control Room back before they were the Witen. And anyway, he's 'keeping outta the *Game of Thrones*,'" he says. But whatever. Point is you can't get in unless you got some bypass or override code or something. So, what is it? How you getting in? Huh? Tell me that. The Witen got in last time by holding a gun to your head for the codes, Hubie," Spurnberg said, addressing his old boss directly now, "but that trick ain't gonna work twice. The Commander and the Steward are very different sort of men, for one thin—"

"We have a solution for that problem." A woman who, up until that point, had remained largely unnoticed by Alice spoke up suddenly in a flat, controlled voice.

"What kinda solution?" both Maisie and Spurnberg asked in unison.

"What, you guys kept a secret set of override codes I'm not aware of or something?" Spurnberg pressed. "Is that it? 'Cause if that's the case, then I can offer a plan much better than the one you've proposed. A plan, that if executed properly, could end the Witen's tyranny in an eye blink."

"There are no override codes." The same woman who had spoken up before leaned out of the half-shadow in which she lurked to answer in the same flat, empty voice.

"Then how the hell do you plan on getting in?!" Spurnberg demanded.

"Let's just say, for arguments sake, that Harrington and his bunch could really get ya these override codes, Tom. What is it you plan to do with 'em?" Maisie asked.

"There are no damn override codes, nor is there any freaking cloaking tech," Harrington broke in to scream. "This meeting is utterly pointless if these imaginary fears and impossible means are to even be entertained."

"My plan could work without the override codes. I'm pretty sure, anyway. I haven't perfected the relay-hijack I'll need to pull off to do it, but once I do, it'll work—no problem," Spurnberg explained. "But if I were to have the override code for the hatch's security pad, then we could go as soon as today."

"Go where? Do what, Tom?" Alice pressed him a little.

"Well, it ain't super honorable or nothing, but it would fix our problem, for sure. It would definitely end the Witen."

"Just spit it out, man," Harrington implored.

"We've all heard by now about the two alternate Control Rooms located in the access tunnel system of the station, right?" After everyone at and around the table nodded their heads, Spurnberg went on. "Well, you see, each Branch has its own independent self-destruct system. They're each rigged with these incredible implosion charges that cause each Branch to be essentially swallowed up by the lunar surface beneath it, sparing the remaining Branches from any residual damage. Apparently, they were installed with the intent to be a last-ditch option for preventing the spread of a fire in a particular Branch or a catastrophic air-leak or something from going on to threaten the rest of the station. So, I propose we take over one of those smaller, far less secure control rooms, and I access its operating system in order to close Branch 1's gigantic hatchway and then lock out its Control Room, switching over main-station control to the smaller room that we'll have just taken over. We'll have to do it at night, I think, to ensure they're all there in their quarters. And then, well... Well, then we initiate Branch 1's self-destruct protocol on the bastards."

"No!" The woman who had been so emotionless before raised her voice now. "Absolutely not!"

Alice thought it strange that someone so clearly inferior to Harrington, as far as company rank, would be the one to take the lead.

Harrington didn't seem to Alice like the type of man to defer to anyone willingly. But, just as with her earlier outbursts, he never even glanced in her direction, much less offered any rebuke. "Many of the Witen councilmembers who now live down Branch 1 have family members living with them. We'd be flipping the self-destruct on them, too, Tom," Alice said in a soft voice meant to show she wasn't assaulting the gray-haired man's character.

"I said it wasn't very honorable," Spurnberg answered her with a sad shrug of his shoulders. "But y'all can't deny it would be effective."

"Maybe we wouldn't have to blow anybody up or anything. Maybe just locking down Branch 1, with the Witen inside, would be enough," Maisie suggested.

"Lock them away just to starve to death?" Spurnberg asked a bit apologetically.

"Well, maybe we could use the promise of supplying food for them through this air lock in the Control Room Mr. Harrington was talking about as a way to get some sort of concessions from them or something," Alice said, piggybacking off Maisie's postulation.

"No!" the nameless black-haired woman abruptly shouted. "AOA will not entertain any such wanton brutality on the innocent family members of the Witen councilmembers, not to mention the clear flaw of us not having these supposed override codes to give you. Nor will your relay-hijack trick work either. This station's security is impenetrable. No mere basic level computer engineer could ever hope to overcome it."

"If the security is impenetrable, then how the hell do you propose to get into the goddamn Control Room?!" Spurnberg asked, sounding exasperated. "You must have some way. We all promised each other oaths of secrecy here. We are in this together as equals, remember? So, out with it now—tell us how you plan to get past the Control Room's security hatches?"

"I'm not sure you've said or done anything here this morning that warrants us trusting you with that kind of information." Harrington spoke up before his smooth-skinned, cool-eyed subordinate. "None of you have demonstrated your worthiness of the sacred partner-ship that would need to exist for us to feel comfortable with such a disclosure. So, I believe we shall part ways here and now," he said, shifting to his feet.

"I hope that doesn't mean you're still planning to go through with your assault team nightmare, Hubie," Maisie said as the first of the assembled execs and government officials shuffled out of Alice and Maisie's dining room.

"We will act in the best interest of the station, Ms. Sagal, whatever that entails," AOA's CEO said in a smug voice as he looked down on her.

"As will we, Mr. Harrington," Maisie told the man, unflinching. "You don't really imagine we will sit by and let you do something so reckless and doomed, do you? If you all don't swear, here and now, to forget about your idiotic scheme, then we promise to go straight to the Witen with your plans. Don't we?" Maisie asked Alice and Stevie in turn.

"You're goddamn right we will, Mais," Alice said as Stevie nodded her head with vigorous support.

"Very well, ladies." The ageless woman with the flawless skin and the immaculately cold-featured visage spoke before Harrington this time. She was standing now. Alice could see the same emptiness that lived on her face and in her bleak, ebony eyes was present in her long, slender, geometrically pleasing frame as well. "But I remind you that's a two-way street. If you dare to pursue Mr. Spurnberg's harebrained plan, then know that the Steward himself will be hearing about it from Mr. Harrington and President Rafferty's very own lips."

With that, and not a word more from any of them, Harrington, the inexplicable woman, President Rafferty, and the other nine former VIPs exited the living quarters. A silence hung in the room between the four remaining residents. Finally, Maisie cleared her throat. "So, this plan of yours, Mr. Spurnberg... Is that woman right? Can you truly never perfect this relay-hijack trick of yours?"

"I can only try," Spurnberg told her. "I'm sure I'll get there in the end. That cold-ass chick was only trying to scare us off, I think. All they're after is their power. They want their luxury quarters back is all."

"What would you need?" Alice asked him.

"Time, for now. When the day comes that I figure it out, we will need some bodies for the raid on the alternate Control Room. Just enough to overcome the one or two footmen that will be pulling guard duty that night. Nothing crazy."

"We can get the people," Maisie said, looking in the eyes of the two older women.

"We have friends who will help, I'm sure," said Stevie, "but those AOA assholes sounded serious about ratting us out if they smell a plan. Whatever we do, we gotta do it quietly. We can't keep meeting here either. The whole damn corridor had to see all those AOA and government guys traipse in and out of this place. The Witen will surely hear about it before long. We have to assume from this moment on that we are being monitored."

"I think I know a place off the Witen's radar that might work for us. Plus, it'll be out of sight of AOA and the government twats, too. So we can eliminate the worry of them catching wind of any of our future plans and ratting us out. The place is probably on their secret charts, I'd guess, but they don't ever leave Maroon Corridor anymore. I doubt they'd send someone searching for our meeting place. What'd be the odds they'd guess the right antechamber to search for us anyhow?" Spurnberg put in. "You ladies just keep your heads down 'til I can scope out the scene and get a better feel for the place. Wait 'til I get back to ya before ya do anything."

"Will do, Tom," Alice told him. "You better be sure to keep an eye in the back of your head as well."

"You got it, Alice." Spurnberg was up out of his chair with those words, then out of the living quarters completely after just a few short beats. Alice, Maisie, and Stevie all exchanged glances in the suddenly silent room. Then, in unison, and utterly unprompted, all three of them stretched a hand across the wide table toward the other. *We ladies are in this thing together.* Alice ran Maisie's proclamation through her head on a loop, knowing absolutely that the other women to whom she steadfastly clung were thinking much the same. They stayed like that, hands interlocked atop the lacquered oak surface, for a long time, drawing on the strength of the other to steel themselves for the grim road ahead.

CHAPTER 5
THE STEWARD

Infection Event: Day 226

The jangling chime of the little entrance bell above the street door told Harclay Aponyaschefski he had a walk-in, a rarity in any circumstance but especially strange for a Sunday morning. When he factored in the closed sign clearly hanging across the half-glass entrance door to his practice's modest office, the unlikelihood of a walk-in client at that very moment was astronomical. Yet when he looked up from his computer to take in the two men casually strolling across his office, straight toward his desk, Harclay realized his previous calculations had suffered from the vital flaw of massive underestimation. Apparently, these AOA clowns were a bit more serious than first brush would indicate.

He thought he'd left their argument yesterday with a fairly clear understanding among both parties. Sure, neither party was very happy, but still, both had a firm grasp of where the other stood. The contentious snob show Harclay had to endure at the office of AOA's retainer hadn't gotten either party anywhere, ending in insults and threats. Harclay had been through with talking, and he'd told them all as much. They weren't listening. They took him for some small-town goober. They figured Harclay Aponyaschefski to roll over like all the rest. They were wrong. If they really weren't going to quit harassing his clients, then Harclay Aponyaschefski would take their asses to court.

In fact, that had been the last thing he'd told them in that pretentious and uncomfortable art nouveau conference room of theirs.

They had more insults and sneers for that but no real rebuttal as he'd left them to stew in the threat. At the time, he guessed they finally understood they were dealing with a serious man. Harclay assumed a mature corporation to understand when discourse was done and litigation had begun. But apparently, AOA was no mature corporation. They even sent over the same smug asshole that had flapped his gums all afternoon at him yesterday. They had to know Harclay did not like the man. They had to know sending him for an unexpected meeting early on a Sunday morning would not go over well.

So why do it? Harclay wondered. Were they just inept at handling legal liability? Could that be it? Could a corporation as seemingly powerful as them, with their reality-defying anonymity despite their undoubted financial might, truly be this maladroit at legal matters? Or were they playing at something else here? Harclay Aponyaschefski could guess at which was more likely, but it would be only that—a guess. This step of arriving unannounced at his office was truly unexpected. Factor in the two men they'd sent as emissaries and it made deciphering their intentions harder still.

AOA's first man to make it across the office to Harclay's desk was yesterday's lead antagonist: a man who went by the obnoxious moniker of Brent Ashly. Six-foot tall with blue eyes and slicked-back blond hair, Brent appeared more like a yuppie Wall Streeter than an international corporation's attack shark. But he could certainly talk some shit—Harclay had to give him that. The second man to come and stand in front of his pine desk was of a different classification altogether. Harclay had no memory of him from yesterday's shit show. That hellish marathon had been wall-to-wall stiff-neck lawyers, with a few Brent-types peppered in here and there. The man now standing a pace behind Ashly's right shoulder would've stuck out like a sore thumb in that gawky gaggle. He appeared in his late thirties or early forties. His faced was lined, creased, and scarred in a way that made placing exact age difficult. The man had the look of someone who has been places and seen things, the kind of places that stay with a person, the kind of things that leave their mark. He was dark where Brent was fair, brawny where Brent was slight, and menacing where Brent was risible. Harclay did not like to think any *thing* or any *one* could knock him off his game at this point in his life, but the piercing stare of the dark, silent man hovering just behind Brent Ashly was having a definite effect on his composure. The evidence of which manifested itself in the form of a pitiful, squeaky throat-clear before breaking his cardinal rule of never being the first to speak in a meeting. "Mr. Ashly, isn't it? What the hell brings you to my office this morning, unannounced and uninvited?"

"Mr. Aponyaschefski, sir, good morning to you. Please forgive our intrusion. It's only that you left us yesterday with the impression of a diligent and precipitative soul," Brent Ashly said as he sat himself down, unprompted, in the armchair in front of Harclay's desk. "And so we wanted to catch up with you one last time before you made any hasty decisions."

"*Hasty decisions*?" Harclay shot back, abashed. "Sir, I consider showing up at my office uninvited and far outside of anything resembling normal business hours and barging past a clearly visible closed sign, without the barest knock, to be a *hasty decision* on *your* part."

"Well, I can certainly appreciate your perspective there, Mr. Aponyaschefski, that I can. But the door was unlocked," Ashly responded from his quickly achieved position of comfort. "I take it you're in here working on filing a brief against my clients. Hell, you're probably ten minutes from polishing off the finishing touches. Ain't that so?"

"Five," Harclay told him with a righteous smirk. "But how does its state of completion have any bearing on your unorthodox and unmannerly visit?"

"Well, our employer," Brent began while running a hand through his slick hair and then using it to indicate the tall figure lurking just behind him, "you see, they aren't keen to see their name showing up in any legal filing. You can understand, I'm sure. AOA is very fond of their privacy. Public spectacles, such as the one you and your clients are cooking up, are to be assiduously avoided. They would prefer that you and I come to an agreement here and now before you take any unpardonable steps."

"Well, Brent, as you well know, AOA, through you and their other so-called lawyers who were cowering around you yesterday afternoon, already expressed this very position to me then. And you all well know what my response was. I don't care that you would prefer me not to file the suit. My clients will not be bought off, sir. Now, I'm getting pretty sick and damn tired of telling you that! Mr. and Mrs. Corbray have lived in that house for fifty-seven years, goddammit! Mr. Corbray's parents lived there for another forty before that. They will not be moved. Your money does not mean shit to them. All they have left in this fucked up world is that goddamn house and property. It's not a plot on a map to them as it is to your AOA friends. It's their home. And they ain't leaving, Mr. Ashly. So, why don't you and this thug you brought with you—like the amateur asshole you are—hop on back aboard your fancy corporate jet and fly off to your greedy masters to tell them that their precious anonymity isn't more important than the rights of two hardworking American citizens? Tell them they may have bought off everyone else in this cowardly town, but they won't buy me, nor the Corbrays either."

Brent didn't respond but to clap a slow, mocking clap. Then he took a pack of Camel Turkish Blend cigarettes from an inner coat pocket. Ashly tapped the pack a few times before sliding loose a single smoke. He leaned forward in the chair to reach into a pants pocket. Harclay figured he was going for a lighter but lost all interest in the man's unsettling behavior when the big guy behind him moved. Within five paces, the dark and weathered man was standing on Harclay's side of the desk. He looked up at the tall, menacing figure for only the barest glimpse before darting his attention back to Brent Ashly. AOA's lawyer had put the pack away and now sat with a smile on his face, the stubby white cigarette tucked away in a corner of his mouth.

"Call off your goon, Ashly. Are you crazy!? Who the hell do you people think you are? I'll thank you to get the hell out of my office right now before I call the cops."

"Ha huh!" Ashly burst out with what came across as genuine glee. "Go right ahead, my friend. Call 'em. I'll bet the dispatcher will send the chief himself to answer your call, you being the big important man you are around these parts. Oh, gee, would you look at that?" he said pointing to the giant man lurking beside Harclay.

"What?" Harclay asked, almost involuntarily.

"It seems your emergency this morning has been anticipated. They've gone and sent the chief ahead of time."

"What the hell are you talking about?" Harclay asked, darting quick glances around his office in desperate hope of catching a glimpse of Chief Ericsson. Ericsson was mixed up with these AOA guys, too, Harclay knew that, but he'd also known him before AOA came poking their noses into Millstone's governance. Ericsson was a good guy just trying to do the best he could with what he'd been given. He might have taken money from AOA, but no way would he sit idly by and let a citizen of his town be harassed in his own damn office. Only, Chief Ericsson was nowhere to be seen, try as Harclay might. There were but two other men in the office just then: one being the hulking goon beside him, and the other Brent. "There's no police chief here. What are you playing at, Ashly?"

"Oh, but there is, Mr. Aponyaschefski," Ashly told him as he brought the lighter up to torch the end of his cigarette. "Millstone's mayor... Uhh... Mr. Dawkins, I believe it is... Well, he had a sudden loss of confidence in Chief Ericsson's abilities. But as luck would have it, he soon met my good friend here," he pointed to the man lurking to Harclay's left, "and soon enough, he felt compelled to install *Chief Greymoor* in Mr. Ericsson's place, effective immediately. You see, Mr. Aponyaschefski, we feel that maybe you and the lovely Corbrays don't quite understand just how much this piece of property means to *us*. You forced extreme actions upon us. We're not taking this case lightly, Mr. Aponyaschefski, not by any means. We want this darn thing settled. And we shall have it settled. You see, I'm afraid you didn't really think through your actions yesterday. You feel strong about your case, about the Corbrays and their rights, as well you're entitled to feel. And it would be a noble and worthy cause to pursue, in any other circumstance. But not this one, Mr. Aponyaschefski—not this one. You see, my clients are different from other clients. A bit of hard reflection before our meeting yesterday might've helped you to see that truth plain enough. You see, Mr. Aponyaschefski, my clients, they just don't fucking care."

"They... What?" Harclay asked after a confused second.

"They don't fucking care about you or the Corbrays or any of the thousand other hicks just like them they've had to step over along the way. They don't have to. They own everything and everyone. And they're sick of humoring you, Harclay. They've decided to flex some of the vast power they've purchased just to shut you up. They've decided you and the Corbrays are a nuisance that needs to go away. They had to buy every last damn cop and government official in this little Podunk shithole just to be confident that they have the unchecked power to shut you and your clients up and force y'all to relent to all their requests, but they did it. They even went as far as installing Chief Greymoor to his current position. And they did it all to spite your persistent ass, Mr. Aponyaschefski. If you can take any balm for the assault on your noble character today is sure to be, let it be how damn annoying you are and the lengths you forced them to. But," he said drawing in a long drag of his Turkish Blend cigarette, "unfortunately for you, now must come the unpleasant part."

"What are you... Whaa ..." Harclay managed in response just as Millstone's new chief of police clapped a meaty paw on the back of his neck. "Hey, get the fuck off me! What the hell you think you're doing!?" he shouted at his accoster while attempting to squirm loose of his grasp.

"Stay still, Mr. Aponyaschefski, and this will go a lot quicker," Ashly told him from his languid lounge.

Greymoor snatched Harclay's left arm and forced it down, inner arm up, atop the desk. "Quit your fucking squirming," the police chief said into his ear, sending a shiver shooting down Harclay's spine. To his shame, it stilled him as well.

Brent Ashly leaned forward in the armchair, reaching for Harclay's captive arm, the cigarette bobbing slightly between his firm-set lips. "Okay, Harclay—mind if I call you Harclay?"

Aponyaschefski spat at the man for answer.

"Very well, then. Schef it is," Ashly conceded with a grin. "I understand that's what your friends call you. I think it's a fitting sobriquet for the circumstance. You see, when we leave here this morning, Chief Greymoor and I are going to be satisfied that we can trust you as we would a dear friend. Or else we won't be leaving," he added with a chuckle.

"Fuck you!" Harclay shouted at him, terror and rage surging through him in equal parts. "You can't just do this to people—force them to your will. You can't. This is still America, goddammit!"

"Well, we *are* doing this, Schef," Ashly told him through a patronizing grin. "Best get used to it, and fast." With that, Brent began to roll up the shirtsleeve of Harclay's captive arm.

"What are you doing?" he asked impotently. "Hey, stop that. Let go of me, goddammit!"

Brent got the sleeve past the elbow and leaned back in his chair. He locked eyes with Harclay for a moment, a moment in which he was hopeful that it was righteous anger evident on his face and not craven concern, but he couldn't be certain. Ashly took no note of it either way. He simply took another long pull off his cigarette as he leaned forward across the desk. "Now, here's what's gonna happen," he began in an almost bored tone, "the chief and I are going to illicit certain promises from you. Once we are satisfied you will indeed honor those promises, we will leave. And so long as you remain a good little boy and don't go knocking over any liquor stores in town or running any stop signs or filing any legal briefs concerning my client, then you will never have to see me or Chief Greymoor ever again. But," he added after a pause, "rest assured, the chief and I will get those sincere promises from you, Schef. That, my friend, is *my* promise to *you*."

"This is so fucking illegal," Harclay told them in a voice he was proud of. "I'll have you and your corporation's balls for this. You just wait and see. Harassing me like this... Who the hell do you people think you are?"

Ashly nodded at Greymoor, and no sooner did Harclay register the gesture than the massive lefthand of the chief was smacking its way across the side of his face. Harclay could hardly believe it. The blow stung and knocked him a bit loopy for a moment, but it was the pure indignity of the act that hurt the most. *Really, just who in the hell do these people think they are?* he wondered in disbelief. He couldn't credit the reality of his present circumstance. It was like something out of a movie, far too surreal to be accepted. But the second open-handed smack from Greymoor forced Harclay to deal with his unlikely reality.

"That's who we are, Schef," Ashly told him. "We're the people who can smack a lawyer around in his own damn office and fear no reprisal, legal or otherwise. So quit playing dumb. A few promises and we're outta your hair forever. Then you can wash the last few weeks from your mind, forget about the Corbrays and their shitty little piece of property, and go back to being the honorable hayseed you pretend to be."

"Just give the man the promises he wants, asshole." Greymoor's fetid breath came thick to Harclay's nostrils along with the imperative.

Harclay didn't respond.

"First promise I want you to make, Schef," Ashly said, "is that you will drop this case, as well as any residual cases, and furthermore promise to not take on any similar cases in the future."

"What constitutes a *similar case* exactly?" Harclay asked derisively.

Ashly answered with another nod to the new chief, and Greymoor responded with another massive smack upside Harclay's head. Then Ashly leaned in and said, "We'll trust you to make that judgement as each case presents itself."

Harclay's wits were wandering in the wake of the last blow. He was unable to piece together a comeback of any sort. *Or perhaps I'm just afraid to,* he thought with sudden horror over his possible cowardice. A groan and a spit were all he could muster. The groan was weak and humiliating. The spit was laced pink with his blood.

"Well, come on, Schef. Let me hear you say it," Ashly prompted.

Harclay wasn't certain if he'd planned to defy the man again. Regardless, it didn't matter one way or the other. Greymoor never gave him the chance. The burly, brown-eyed police chief simply tightened his grip on the back of Harclay's neck, forcing him to arch up and shriek with pain. Greymoor kept it going a few seconds before finishing off his cruelty with another smack upside Harclay's head.

"The words are easy enough to say, Schef," Ashly explained with mock honesty. "Just tell us that you promise to drop the case and abandon the Corbrays to fend for themselves. Say you're sorry for the inconvenience and irritation and that you'll be a quiet little camper from here on out."

"Say it," Greymoor urged, jerking Harclay's head about in his powerful grip.

Harclay almost did. The words were on his tongue, nearly out, but he caught himself at the last moment. A flash of the Corbray's exhausted and defeated old faces staring at him across this very desk entered his thoughts, giving him the strength he needed to stay silent in the face of the unprecedented criminality currently assailing him.

"Speak, you little shitbag!" Greymoor shouted into his ear before he must've felt a bit more shaking of Harclay's head and another open-handed smack were warranted as well.

"This goes on for as long as you like, Schef. The chief and I have the time. But know, too, that our efforts need not be limited to the confines of this office. We can smack you around in here for a few hours while you stay obstinate and defiant, and all that brave act will have gained you is the forced involvement of your loved ones."

"You wouldn't dare," Harclay told him. Though his heart began to sink as he realized if AOA were willing to beat an honest citizen in his own office right on Main Street, they were probably willing to take the fight to that citizen's family and friends as well. He was beaten. He saw that clear. He never felt so useless, so impotent. Harclay felt tears rising, yet suffocated by the shame of letting his attackers see him cry. He was lost in that moment and could not find himself.

"We will do whatever we have to," Ashly told him. "Because we can, and we must, like I already told you." Inhaling a slow toke of his cigarette before blowing it elegantly from his lips, the business-guised gangster stared at its cherry ember for a long moment. Finally, he snapped his gaze back toward Harclay. They locked eyes as Ashly rolled the cigarette over in his hand. Slowly, he began to move the burning cig toward Harclay's arm, still resting atop the table.

Greymoor clamped down on the appendage once again, immobilizing it, and only then did Harclay understand what they intended. "Okay, okay," Harclay said in a rush. "You win, okay? I promise. I'll drop the case, I swear. Whatever you say. You don—don't you... You guys don't have to do this. Come on, please. I promise I'll drop the case. Okay? You won't hear a peep from me, I promise."

"Well, Schef, my friend, that is indeed good to hear," Ashly said, pausing the cigarette's slow journey. "Promise us too that you will not contact the FBI or any other such useless organization. We would be sure to hear about it if you did and would be then forced to make good on our threats toward your family."

"Okay. Fine. Whatever," Harclay said, just wanting done with all this now. "I promise. I won't talk to anyone about AOA."

"Good, that's good," Ashly said. "We have a solemn pact then, you and I?"

"Yes, I suppose we do," Harclay allowed.

"Any pact worth a fish's fart needs to be sealed, though. Isn't that right, Chief Greymoor?"

"Sure does, Mr. Ashly," Greymoor agreed, his twin grips upon Harclay growing even firmer.

"What say you, Schef? Do you agree?" Ashly asked him.

"Agree with what?"

"That a pact must be sealed in some way."

"I guess. Whatever you say. Let's just end this."

"Very well, Schef, my friend," Ashly said, wearing the strangest smirk. Without warning, the man then darted his hand forward, pressing the cherry ember of his cigarette into the soft skin of Harclay's left forearm.

Harclay screamed and bucked and tried desperately to knock Brent's arm away with his freehand. The pain persisted, nonetheless. Ashly proved stronger than Harclay would've thought. Plus, Greymoor's viselike grip on his neck greatly impeded his efforts. The pain was worse than any he'd ever experienced. It was a darkness that swallowed him whole and left him a helpless shell. It mastered time. It knew no fear, no pity. It would stay forever. Hope burned like tinder before its majesty. And just when he was sure it would go on into eternity, the instant before madness enveloped his conscious mind for good and all, Ashly lifted the tortuous implement. The Camel cig was out now, Harclay could see that, crushed to ash against his skin. He needed to scream, but none would come. His body refused his orders. Pain forced him to bite down on his tongue, forced tears to stream from his eyes and his bladder to let loose the morning's coffee.

"There," Harclay heard Ashly say, from some place far away. "I'd say that seals our little pact nicely. Wouldn't you?"

Ashly didn't want an answer. That was plain. He wanted to laugh. And that's just what Chief Greymoor and Brent Ashly proceeded to do. Each grating cackle and huffed giggle was a lash against Harclay's pride. But he did not move. Harclay Aponyaschefski stayed glued to his desk chair, stewing in their disdain and his own filth, until he finally woke up.

The Steward opened his eyes to blackness, his bedroom dark and silent. He rolled over to grab his pocket tablet from his bedside end table. 0633 ST, the clock on the tablet's homepage read. His alarm was due to go off in a little over twenty minutes, but the Steward knew any hope of snatching a few more winks of sack-time was a hopeless proposition. *The goddamn dream*, he thought, irritated. It was one of a half dozen or so tragic memories that plagued him of a night. He hated them, almost as much as the fact that he could do nothing to stop them. No amount of pills or booze could keep the memories at bay. He had eventually consigned himself to a few moments of quiet meditation every morning in order to flush the anger and shame the dream-memories always drudged up. Last night's dream was a particularly difficult one to shrug off. The mornings after its visits always found the Steward spending a bit more time in his quiet meditation than normal, and today was going to be no exception.

Despite last night's unpleasant visitor to his subconscious, and the added meditation it caused, the Steward was still ready for the day long before 0900 when his trolley was scheduled to pick him up. He had a good forty minutes to dedicate to a good breakfast and a half dozen cups of coffee, as well as all of last night's sitreps from every last sector of Cardinal's Nest. He satisfied himself that certain situations were being handled as he directed while mentally marking others to keep his eye on. It seemed that all which lay beneath the supreme authority of the Witenagemot was in good order this morning, and so the Steward wore a small smile on his lips when he finally exited his luxury quarters at precisely 0900.

He was pleased to discover Elias Sagal standing at attention near his trolley in an immaculate blue Initiate's Service Uniform, with its elegant gold stitching around the collar and cuffs, alongside Marcia Dollingford, a footman of the Witen, in her similarly stitched and starched gray blouse and trousers, both of them with matching gunmetal-gray war hammer hilts poking up from behind their right shoulders. Dollingford had been assigned to the Steward's official security detail since day one—assigned by the Steward himself. The woman had all the qualifications he desired in his personal detail. Number one: ability, she was certainly no wilting-violet. Dollingford was stout-shouldered and well-muscled and athletic as hell. She stood only five-three but could best men and women ten inches taller in the hand-to-hand combat tourneys the Witen hosted every month for their footmen to showcase their worth. And second: she was loyal to the Steward in particular, almost to a fault. He figured it to be adoration. And so long as she was able to perform her duties when she was around him, then adoration was a damn good thing as far as he was concerned. It meant she wouldn't betray him. It meant one more person he could fully trust. Such folk were few and far between up here, so the Steward did not scorn the gift of the warrior-woman with the cute dimples and twinkling blue eyes.

And so, too, with Elias Sagal. He could see the idolization in the boy's face whenever he spoke with him. Seeing his nervous energy, the Steward instantly knew it, too, for adoration. Perhaps a different sort than Dollingford's, but adoration, nonetheless. After the Integration Program wrapped up for the season, and all the initiates were being placed in internships throughout the Witen's domain until next year's Program started back up with all those who failed to muster out this year, the Steward used his nearly unchallenged authority to place the boy with Dollingford and the rest of his detail. For as much as Elias clearly adored him, the Steward was ever wary of Maisie Sagal weaseling her way back between them. He needed to keep the boy as close as possible while the Program was in hiatus. An internship alongside Dollingford was the perfect answer.

"Initiate Sagal, at ease, son," he told the nervous boy. "Good to see you this morning. You as well, Footman Dollingford."

"Good morning, sir," Elias managed with an admirable calm.

"How goes the internship?"

"Very well, Steward, sir. I'm so grateful for the placement here in this prestigious unit."

"Well spoken, Initiate. It seems the Integration Program is working its magic on you," the Steward added with a chuckle to let the boy know he was being teased.

"Well, it's only his first morning, Steward, sir," Dollingford put in. "We'll hold back any critique of his performance until the day is over at the very least."

"Ha huh. Yes, Footman, quite right," the Steward agreed with a smile in his voice. "You listen to the footman now, you hear?" he implored Elias. "She'll steer you right. And remember, there are no dumb questions. Questions are how we explore the world. They aren't to be despised. Don't hesitate to ask Footman Dollingford or any of her compatriots anything about your duties. But when you get an answer, accept it and move on. Time's too pressing for us to doubt each other. I want you to get as much from this internship as possible now. Anything worth doing is worth doing right. Ain't that so?"

"Yes, sir, Steward, sir. I won't let ya down."

"I know you won't, kid. I know you won't," the Steward told the new intern with a pat on the shoulder as he hopped aboard his waiting repulsion trolley.

Four minutes later, his trolley was pulling up outside of Justice Hall. Elias and Dollingford were first to jump off the repulsion trolley, but the Steward wasn't far behind. He was feeling good now, last night's nightmare nearly forgotten and an ever exhilarating Third Day ahead. Such day-long adjudication marathons were fast becoming the Steward's favorite part of his burden of being a nameless officer in the Witenagemot. The pressure and stress his title brought to bear on his shoulders could be overwhelming. He needed the Third Days to take his mind off the Witen's vast responsibility.

Whenever he sat behind the massive cherrywood desk perched up on its five-foot dais, the burden lifted, and he could dive into the mundane. He could put his law degree to use. Each new pair of plaintiff and accused that came before him required their own often unique solutions. The Steward had gained a reputation for honesty and wisdom within the first few Third Days the Witen had hosted. They became a sort of episodic play that pleased the gathered residents as well as himself.

The recently installed pinewood double-doors were already open as the Steward approached Justice Hall. Dollingford had darted in ahead to ensure the room was clear of threat. There were at least twenty or so residents already gathered in the benched viewing gallery, but Dollingford must not have noticed any suspicious behavior among any of them. She simply elbowed a path through a patch of residents standing in the aisle between the benches for the Steward upon his first step through the hatchway. Though he was ever appreciative of the tenacity of his personal footman, the Steward did not rush to take advantage of her efforts. He paused a few steps into the room to gaze around and take its measure. Like always, few residents in attendance were able to hold eye contact with him for very long as he looked them all over. He stayed there, gazing about, until a silence fell over the square chamber. Only when he was certain everyone was fully quiet and paying all their attention to him did he step through the path Dollingford had won him. He made his stately way toward his adjudication desk, feeling every eye in the hall on his back.

The Steward smiled to see his cherry throne. The desk reminded him of the one used during that first court the Writer had held in the grand rotunda. Afterward, he had made the Commander see that the situation was not tenable. Surely, the desks could not remain there permanently, and surely, it was far too unnecessary a hassle to drag them all out every time they needed to have a trial. The Commander had quickly seen the truth in both those points, and so, instructed the Steward to find a more permanent solution. The Steward had taken on the task with the seriousness and dedication it deserved, and after a few sleepless nights full of blueprints and charts and endless research into everything from international law and history to philosophy and psychology, the Steward had the solution.

The Third Day, he'd named it, an open court where any plaintiff may bring a case before the Steward, who, by the authority of the New Destiny Constitution and the Commander's righteous victory in the Final Tournament, held adjudication powers checked only by the Commander himself. This open court would take place every third day, and so, with the name for the new court system easily construed from that point, the only question then left was where this Third Day process should be held.

Luckily, the Steward's deliberations had provided him with a ready answer for this problem as well: the old security staff's recroom. After they knocked down the wall that divided the room in half and then tore out the lockers back there, as well as the showers and plumbing, they were left with an open space roughly 45 feet wide and maybe 50 long with a 15-foot ceiling. Once they threw the dais up against the back wall and plopped a plaintiff and a defense desk ten feet in front of it, they still had quite a bit a room for the five rows of church-pew-like bench seating in the viewing gallery, each one of which was hand-constructed by a team of station engineers from three gigantic pine trees out of The Meadow's forest. And as simple as that, the rec-room was dead, along with any lingering connections to a best forgotten past. Justice Hall rose triumphant in its place.

This Third Day began like all others before it, and although each case presented had its own particular unique qualities, the hours proceeded without any real surprises. Just the usual civil complaints, i.e., noisy neighbors and other such petty personal grievances, along with accusations of hoarding and what the residents had quickly come to call in the wake of the credit system's disillusion as "portion hogs." Nothing to really set this Third Day apart from any other until late in the morning, just before the lunch break. The day's docket had seemed to clear early, and Dollingford was calling for any final plaintiff who didn't sign the chart and would wish to be heard to come forward, a routine occurrence at the end of every Third Day. Few ever took up the offered last chance, so the Steward was set about gathering himself up to climb off the dais and head back to his quarters to indulge in whatever his servant had prepared for his midday meal and was thus taken aback when a thin, nervous young voice shattered the room's relative silence.

"I have a charge to lay, Steward, sir," it said.

Many of the residents in the viewing gallery were already on their feet, making the speaker hard to pick out straight away. The Steward's gaze swung back and forth across the room before him, searching for the thin voice. He could see just about everyone else in the room doing the exact same. Murmurs started fast as heartache. Within three breaths, it seemed every person in Justice Hall was speaking. The Steward was forced to slam his gavel four or five times before the silent solemnity a courtroom deserved had returned. "Silence, ladies and gentlemen. We shall have order here," he told them all. "Now, whoever spoke, come forward and lay your charge before this court."

All those residents left standing quickly squatted back down. All but one. A girl. The Steward knew her. Well, knew *of* her. Her name was Clara Christie, an early dropout of the Integration Program. The girl had begged out after less than a week. The Steward had granted her request. The Witen had no place for the weak-willed, no room for quitters or loafs. He sent her off to Supervisor Chairman Mikkelson to be placed directly into the labor force. Just because she couldn't hack it as a member of the Witen didn't mean they couldn't find some use for her. The Steward had trusted Mikkelson to discover where she might best be utilized. The man had been doing that very same thing for AOA before the Witen's glorious ascension, and so far as the Steward could tell, everyone seemed to be performing adequately in their assigned roles. The Station was still running at maximum efficiency anyway.

The Steward didn't feel he really needed to be read into labor decisions any more than that. But judging by the irate supervisor rising, red-faced, and making his way toward the defense desk as Clara Christie made her way to the plaintiff's post, there was obviously some sort of problem with her job. The Steward saw, too, that the supervisor had risen from a place on the benches just a few feet down from Chairman Mikkelson himself, further cementing the Steward's belief that Clara Christie wasn't at all pleased with her labor assignment.

The Steward had noticed Mikkelson earlier in the morning—how could he not? The man was four-hundred pounds and breathed louder than any snuffling boar. Every small silence throughout the morning's deliberations were filled with his waking snores. But the Steward had thought nothing of the Witen's Labor Director and Supervisor Chairman's presence. The man attended most every Third Day, as did the majority of his supervisors, and none had ever been involved in any of the cases brought before the Steward.

It unsettled him to think about having to adjudicate negatively against a Witen councilmember. They were all oathbound and sworn to each other. The Steward was not fond of the notion of impugning a councilmember before the eyes of the public. The Witen's human fallibility ought not be displayed in such a manner, and it had been his understanding that the residents had all come to accept that as well.

He knew his supervisors and footmen could not possibly be perfect, but he thought the public knew better than to drag the Witen's dirty laundry before the court. Judging by the discomfort pouring off the residents present in Justice Hall just then, most all of them actually did understand the obvious faux pas. Certainly, no one seemed very eager to hear whatever Clara Christie might have to say.

No one, save young Elias, it seems, the Steward thought as his gaze fell to his personal security detail's new intern. The boy made eye contact with Clara more than once and seemed to be trying to convey some sort of support through his body language. *Now, what's that all about?* the Steward wondered. *I thought it was the Rodriguez girl the boy was pining after. Hell, man, he's a twelve-year-old boy. He's probably got the hots for every miniskirt who looks his way. This here is probably just a schoolboy crush on an older girl. Ha huh ha. You poor bastard, Elias. Get ready to be hurt, kid. Trust me, I've been there myself,* he recalled with an inner grin. "Ms. Christie, I believe it is?"

"Yes, Steward, sir. Clara Christie," the teen confirmed.

"Have you a charge to lay before this court?"

"I-I-I... Ughhh... I-I..."

"Relax, Ms. Christie," the Steward counseled the nervous teen. "Take a breath and tell me what brings you forward today."

"Well, Steward, sir, it's... You see, it's... Well..."

The Steward turned to the supervisor who had taken position behind the defense desk. Clearly, the man figured whatever brought Clara forward involved him in some way, so the Steward turned his attention to him. "Supervisor, what reason have you to rise to the defense desk?"

"I know what it is which brings Ms. Christie before you today, Steward, sir. She brought her complaint to my attention yesterday. But there was simply no satisfying Ms. Christie's complaints in any way that would accord with The New Destiny Constitution. And when I told her as much, she threatened to bring her complaint to you, Steward, sir, at today's Third Day. I warned her such nonsensical frivolities as those that *plague* Ms. Christie would not be received well in these solemn chambers. But she wouldn't be moved, sir. So when I heard her rise just now, I felt it prudent not to waste your time and just went ahead and stepped up to the defense desk."

"Is this all true, Ms. Christie?" the Steward asked the girl behind the plaintiff desk.

"Well, Steward, sir," the lanky, dark-haired teen began, "it's true as far as it goes, I guess. I don't think my complaint will shame this court or anything, though. I sure hope not, anyway. It seems pretty serious to me. And I didn't want to bring it to you, anyhow, sir. I was hoping Supervisor Naughton would just leave me be. I don't want to be seen as going against the Witen or nothing. I love the Witen, and I'm proud of what y'all are doing for all our futures and everything. I even wanted to be a footman," she added with a glance over at Elias. The boy had eyes only for her. Justice Hall might have been burning down around him and he'd have never known. His anguish over Clara's clear discomfort was plain as rain. "I just... I can't take it no more, Steward, sir," the teen went on, "and Supervisor Naughton's got me further into his debt now, not out. I just couldn't see no other way to end it all, sir."

"Speak your charge, Ms. Christie," the Steward prompted.

"Sir, I think it might be prudent to hear some of the background the Witen's supervisor network has accumulated on Ms. Christie before these hallowed chambers are subjected to her blathering madness," the supervisor broke in before Clara could speak.

"You're Supervisor Naughton?" the Steward asked the man behind the defense desk.

"Yes, Steward, sir, that is correct. I am Supervisor Naughton of the Witenagemot Council, currently in charge of the dairy and poultry farms. Ms. Christie was placed under my authority a few months back. She has been a constant thorn in our side ever since. Though, I'm pleased to report I have not let her incompetence affect the production of either farm under my purview."

"Incompe—? I'm not incompetent. The job is simple enough. How the hell can anyone be incompetent at it? He is lying to you, Steward. Trying to make me look bad," Clara told him in a voice that sounded so pitifully honest the Steward was forced to rethink his policy on the Witen's dirty laundry.

I'll do what's right here as best I can, for the boy's sake if nothing else, but not at the cost of the Witen's integrity, he decided after a few moments' serious reflection. "Just tell me exactly what your complaint against the good supervisor is, Ms. Christie. Calmly now.

No citizen has any need to fear a reprisal for speaking truth," the Steward told her. "Especially not in this hallowed hall. That is precisely the point of these Third Days: so that you, the good residents of Cardinal's Nest, should feel comfortable and safe, as well as confident in your rights and security. If you have a charge to lay against a Witen councilmember, well then, I can see how that might seem scary. But I assure you, I listen to every testimony in this courtroom with the same critical, unbiased focus as the next. I never perform the sin of prejudging a case. True justice is blind, Ms. Christie, and I am humanity's avatar of true justice within these walls. You don't doubt my commitment to impartiality, do you, Ms. Christie?"

"No, sir, of course not," Clara promised in a rush. "It's only... Supervisor Naughton and ... and his ... his friends, they scare me, sir."

"Well, I am not them."

"No, Steward, sir, you're not, sir. I-I... I just ..."

"Relax, and trust me, Ms. Christie."

"Yes, sir. Of course, sir," she answered after another quick glance toward Elias.

"Very well, then. What makes you so afraid of Supervisor Naughton? Take a deep breath and speak clearly."

"It started the first day the chairman sent me to the dairy," the teen began after the instructed breath. "It was just small favors in the beginning, like laundry or other little chores like that. He had us all doing them for him. If you didn't, you were guaranteed the worst job available. You see, every day before our shift starts, Supervisor Naughton assigns us our daily duties. If he owed you from an earlier favor or chore or whatnot, you got an easy gig monitoring the control board or something like that, away from the stinky animals, but if you were on his bad side, or *in his debt*, as he calls it, than you can expect to be on shoveling duty, or one of a hundred other equally nasty tasks we gotta do over in the dairy."

"Hmmm," the Steward cut in, "he was abusing his authority for duty assignments, then? Hmmm, that is serious. We cannot have the integrity of a single facility in our precious station compromised. I thank you, Ms. Christie, for bringing the issue to my attention. The supervisor and I will certainly be having a discussion in my personal office just as soon as we are finished here, I can promise you that."

"But… Well, that ain't all of it, sir," Clara spoke up, sounding a bit confused.

"No?" the Steward asked her after a few seconds of solid eye contact. "You sure about that, Ms. Christie?"

"Yes, sir," the teen obliviously answered. "The favors for good jobs is bad enough, I agree, but it's what the favors became that's brought me here today and got me so afraid of the supervisor and his friends."

"Steward, sir, if I may," Supervisor Naughton broke in. The Steward gave him the smallest of chin nods. "I welcome eagerly any discussion with you about the operations of the facilities under my care and my management. Any wisdom you would deem to impart upon me would be, of course, my great honor. But I believe Ms. Christie to be seriously troubled, and to allow her to cast her baseless aspersions in this open court today could only have negative consequences to the tranquility and cooperation the Witen has managed to foster over the last few un-un … unbelievable and … and … auspicious months. She is ill, Steward, sir, and I recommend she be remanded to Newton Hospital's psychological observation cell, where the good doctors and nurses of this station may examine her and devise a plan of action that is in Ms. Christie's own best interest. I presented this step, which I don't at all take lightly, by any means, to Supervisor Chairman Mikkelson last night, in fact. The Chairman reluctantly came to agree with my conclusions. It was our intention to bring this matter to you directly after today's Third Day had concluded, but seeing as Ms. Christie has pressed my hand, I am compelled to press for her self-interest detainment here and now."

The supervisor's plea provided a quick out of this mess for the Steward, but as he looked out on the crowd, he could tell from the faces he saw staring back at him that most felt the man's request to be a transparent attempt at injustice. The people were willing to look the other way to a point, but only that. The Steward understood this fundamental aspect of human nature better than most. How else could he have achieved his current status? He had to know people. It was its own unique skill. He had honed the craft back in his old-world days on the legal circuit. He didn't feel any danger of out-and-out revolt then and there, but he could tell if he swept this away without hearing the girl's whole story, there would definitely be some disillusioned souls shuffling out Justice Hall's cherrywood double-doors when this Third Day was officially called into recess.

Damn the bratty little shit for not taking the easy out I offered her. I would've moved her away from Naughton, at least. How could she not see that? The ditzy bitch is probably just too stupid to see the position she's putting me in, he thought bitterly. With how eager Naughton was to end this, the Steward was certain the girl's story was not going to be pretty, whatever it was. *Wait a minute. The Chair, of course.* The sudden memory was extremely welcome. The Chair offered a way for the Steward to allow her story to be told, if that's what it came to, and not lose the loyalty of his councilmembers in the process.

They'd found it the first week the Witen had taken up residence down Branch 1. It was tucked away under some cellophane in a back corner of Newton Hospital. They'd all took it for a massage chair of some sort at first, complete with a widow's-peak style, temple-rubbing helmet, à la Professor X, that was attached to the back of the chair and came down on your head like something out of a '50s beauty salon. But once they sat down in it, they realized the thing was not at all intended for providing comfort or tension release. The person sank down into it awkwardly, forcing the body into a sort of C shape, with the knees higher than the ass and head and neck beyond the chest. The arm rests were long with black on gold, baseball-shaped knobs protruding from the ends. So far as the Steward knew, the few people who knew of the chair's existence hadn't been able to even turn the thing on. But it had a unique design that made an impression on an individual at first sight. The Steward had thought such a powerful object was not to be derided simply because no one could understand what the hell it was for. He thought rather to take advantage of its intriguing ambiguity.

One particularly troublesome Third Day, an idea of how best for the Witen to benefit from the Chair's obvious effect, popped into his mind. He told them all the black, gold, and navy-blue monstrosity was a cutting-edge lie detection device AOA had been working on in secret, knowing that AOA would never refute the claim, and that the Witen could easily make people doubt AOA's denials if they did. The sleek-lined, composite-material chair with its crisscrossing, LED-lit wiring visible through the chair's clear back, was the perfect vessel for any wild claim the Steward could concoct. The Chair captured one's imagination, and the Steward knew instantly his claims of an unerring lie detection device would be readily accepted.

So, leaning on his prior stroke of genius to get him out of this new mess, he said, "I will hear Ms. Christie's claims." The Steward quickly pounded his gavel a few taps to quell the tiny uproar that followed those words. "Provided," he said, using the gavel to point at the teen now, "that you agree to sit in The Chair during your testimony and accept its judgement of your honesty."

Clara's eyes went to Naughton for a long time after that. Silence filled the hall, apart from the soft humming of the air-recyclers. The supervisor never so much as flicked his eyes her way. Naughton reserved his facial expressions for the Steward alone. The man was clearly angry.

"It's not that I doubt your claims of mental instability, good supervisor," the Steward told him. "You have earned your rightful power and authority within our Witen, but the residents do have their rights as well. We must never fall into the trap of putting our needs over the survival of this community. Not that I am accusing you of any such act, only that an honest man, as I expect every Witen councilmember to be, need not fear the lies of another, not when we have the Chair at our disposal. All present here know the unconquerability of the Chair. If the girl is found to be lying, she will be dealt with, and none here could dare then doubt the Witen's commitment to blind justice. Supervisor Naughton, all of your performance reports have indicated to me that you are an exceptional and well valued member of the Witen's council. The lies of one individual will have no impact on that standing. You have my word on that."

Naughton didn't know what to say—that was plain. He managed a nod after a time, so the Steward turned his attention back to the teen behind the plaintiff desk. "Well, Ms. Christie, will you submit yourself to the Chair?" Clara glanced around the crowd behind her for a while, but the Steward could see no one in particular share any gesture with her. It made him think of something he should've addressed earlier. "Where are your parents, Ms. Christie? Are they here today?" True, the girl was sixteen and a member of the labor force, which made her a full-fledged citizen under The New Destiny Constitution, but the Steward had a sudden hope the girl's folks might be wise enough to see that talking their daughter off the stand now was in her best interest.

Clara Christie's headshake and her soft, "No, sir, they told me not to come today," put an end to that sudden hope.

"Yet you came anyway?"

"I'm a working citizen with every right to."

"Yes, I suppose you are," the Steward conceded. "So, you will submit yourself to the Chair, then?"

"Yes, Steward, sir," Clara Christie said in a clear voice. "I don't intend to lie to you, so I've nothing to fear from any chair."

A slow breath, in through the nose and out again, had the Steward calm enough to speak in a tone betraying none of the emotions currently churning his guts. "Very well, Ms. Christie. Very well."

"I invoke the right of wergild!" Supervisor Naughton shouted out.

"Wergild?" the Steward asked, though he knew what the request meant. It was he who wrote the damn law, after all.

"Yes, Steward, I ask for the abrupt end to these proceedings on my promise to pay the wergild to my victim as granted to me by rights enshrined in our New Destiny Constitution." The Steward's jaw was not responding to his demands to close back up as he watched Naughton turn to lock eyes with Mikkelson. The Steward caught the fat man's small nod just before Naughton turned back to face the dais. "I am Ms. Christie's accoster, and I will admit my fault and guilt in all her charges. As a councilmember of the Witen, it is my right to then pay my victim the wergild as designated in the New Destiny Constitution."

"Half of your property, Supervisor Naughton," the Steward reminded him. "The wergild is half of your property. You will concede all this to Ms. Christie?"

"Yes, Steward sir, I believe I will."

"But wha...? I haven't finished my... What the heck is wergild, Steward?" Clara Christie asked in a deeply confused voice.

"All councilmembers are entitled to pay a wergild to any non-councilmember accuser to end all further litigation," the Steward told her, begrudging every word.

"But I haven't even explained what I'm accusing him of."

"And you shall never speak of it again," Naughton spoke to Clara directly. "The wergild ends this trial here and now. Both parties involved are to never speak of any details of this case, under pain of punishment."

"Punishment?" Clara uttered in confused horror.

"Sixty days in Branch 1's brig, Ms. Christie," the Steward told her with bitterness at Supervisor Naughton's invocation of the bylaw he had slipped into the New Destiny Constitution as a failsafe for the Commander's supreme authority.

"Sixty days?" Clara's voice broke as she directed her disbelief toward Elias.

The boy's confusion was written all over him. *Shit,* the Steward thought angrily. *Why did this have to be the boy's first taste of Third Day justice?* He was going to require a lot of one-on-one time in the near future to ensure his mind was still on the right track.

Damn Naughton, and Mikkelson, too. Just what in the hell kinda games are they playing with the residents? The Steward would have to squeeze a bit more information from the spies he already had reporting to him about Chairman Mikkelson. *Maybe I'll even figure a way to add a few more.* No way would the Steward allow a disgusting inconvenience like Supervisor Chairman Mikkelson to undermine his Witen. "That ends today's proceedings, then!" he suddenly shouted over the murmuring crowd. "Everyone out. Return to your duties if you have them. Go on," he yelled, encouraging the ignorant masses. "Third Day has ended. Clear the hall!"

CHAPTER 6

ALICE

"**T**here really is nothing left in this darn thing, Mais. I'm gonna have to go out," Alice Stark informed her roommate over a shoulder, her face buried deep in their all but empty refrigerator.

"We all just talked about this again last night, Alice," Maisie shouted back from their living room. "You know you promised Stevie weeks ago that you'd stay inside for the rest of the pregnancy. You're showing *way* too much."

"Well, I've changed my mind," she told the teen girl as she slammed closed the refrigerator door. "I'm not living like some hostage in my own damn home any longer," Alice informed her as she swayed and waddled her bulging belly around the corner and into the living room.

Maisie was busy lacing up her black canvas tactical boots on the edge of their tan couch and did not look up until Alice finally managed to plop herself down into the puffy white armchair. "It's only for another week, Alice. Six days really. You know that," Maisie explained with disarming grace. "After that, you'll be able to roam as freely and as often as you like. I'll see to it the Nest's new ruling republic will be sure you are supplied with a bunch of security while you're doing that roaming, too. Helena Heathcoat will never get within a hundred yards of ya. That I can guarantee."

"Oh, can you now?" Alice asked rhetorically. "You haven't any more clue than I do about just who in the hell the people will elect to this new republic we're dreaming of. You and I could easily find ourselves on the outs, as far as influence over representatives go, anyway. After all, Mais, you're still just thirteen years old."

"Whatever," Maisie shot back under her breath as she bent back down to lace her last boot. "We shouldn't be talking about this stuff here, anyway."

"Oh, pish posh," Alice scolded her. "If they were listening in and spying on these quarters, we would've been hauled off to the brig by now, don't ya think?"

"We can't know that," Maisie shot back. "Besides, Spurnberg thinks they're playing the long game. And I agree with him. We shouldn't talk about any of the plan here, or what comes after, just to be safe." Maisie's eyes were apologetic and a bit embarrassed as her last comment touched upon the very topic that had Alice all worked up this morning.

She was forbidden to leave her quarters, and thus, forbidden to meet up with the rest of their cohorts in the off-the-charts annex room Spurnberg had discovered in the access tunnels behind the Water Converter Facility down Branch 6. Alice had felt left out of the loop, especially since Maisie had remained such a strict adherent to the no-resistance-talk-allowed discipline in their shared quarters down Alleyway XII in Orange Corridor. Maisie's eyes quickly took on a compassionate veneer, but before she could apologize—which Alice could no longer abide—she cut her off. "I hate being put out of action, but I do understand why. I was just trying to soften you up to the fact that, soon, you might find *yourself* out of the action. That's the gamble with democracies, sweetie."

"Whatever," Maisie told her with all her compassion fled and annoyance taking its place.

Alice giggled at her roommate's truculence. They both knew that after they pulled off the job on Friday that Alice, Stevie, Maisie, and their compatriots had been planning for months, Maisie would surely see to it that whoever ended up in charge would owe their positions largely to her wily guile and cunning charm. She would have her influence, one way or another. Alice knew that for a certainty, despite her warnings. No way would Maisie's forceful personality be brushed to the side again. The young girl had chafed more violently and vocally under the lash of the Witenagemot than any other single resident

since they first took power. She would not stand for her current diminished status to endure after the Witen was in tatters and begging
the residents for mercy. Over their past eight months of cohabitation, Alice had come to understand that Maisie had a fire burning
white-hot deep within her. The passion with which she lived her life
was what fed the ceaseless forge, necessitating she forever remain
at the center of it all, no matter what that might entail.

"Would it really be so awful to have a break from all this responsibility?" Alice asked her young friend. "If the residents all elect some
other eager souls to take the reins of the republic once we deal with
the Witen, then so be it, I say. We'd have done our part, the way I see
it. I'd gladly shift the load to their shoulders and come back here to
raise my baby," she finished, rubbing the mountainous swell of her
tummy with a grin.

"No. That ain't such a bad scenario to hope for, I suppose." Maisie's
hazel eyes locked with Alice, and the older woman never failed to
marvel at the depth of wisdom that radiated from their earth-toned
honesty. She read in them now both understanding and irritation in
equal measures. Then a mischievous smile slowly spread across the
teen's lips. "But if you're so eager to be done with all this responsibility
and what not, then why are you arguing with me now about going out
to the Commissary?"

"I want to be free of the burden of mankind's fate, not free from a
fridge full of sausage and eggs," Alice told her as she scooched and
squirmed deeper into the armchair's cushions. "One of us needs to
get some shopping done. And you and Stevie and Spurnberg and
everyone else already forbade me from the cafeterias, even though
we all know Helena never eats at any of them anymore. And I know
you'll be busy all day, all week really. So, by my math, that only leaves
me for the shopping, kiddo."

"Whatever, *kiddo*," Maisie shot back. "Just be quick if you do go,
'cause Stevie will kill me if you get into some sort of trouble out there."

"I'll be quick," Alice promised. "Don't worry."

"I'm serious, Allie," Maisie said, adopting a more intense manner.
"Stevie and Spurnberg are crazy worried about any exposure just now.
We're so close. Everything is nearly in place. Nearly. We can't afford
for the Witen to be taking any sort of interest in any of us just now."

"I know all that, Mais. I'm just as committed to and nerve-racked about this mission as any of you. Just 'cause I'm bursting at the seams right now and can't do much more than waddle around for a half an hour or so between two-hour naps doesn't mean my heart isn't in this just as much as yours."

"I know that, Alice. Really, I do. I didn't mean to suggest less," Maisie assured her. "I forget how difficult this all must be for you right now. Me and the gang are like ... running around all day and night. With no real time to dwell on our nerves, you know? While you gotta be stuck in these quarters all day with nothing to do but to think about it. Must be hard. I'm sorry, Allie."

"Oh, cut it with all that crap this instant," Alice demanded, waving her arm to chase away the words from the air as if they were smoke. "We all got it hard just now. And it probably ain't gonna get any easier any time soon. I don't deserve any extra sympathy. We can get through all this though, ya know? I do believe that, Mais. I was just venting earlier. You know how it is... Just don't worry about me, kiddo, or the baby, neither. We'll be just fine. You got enough to worry about today, more than any thirteen-year-old should ever have to worry about, in fact."

"I'll be just fine, Alice." Maisie cut in fast before Alice could get going with the argument the pair had seemed to be eternally locked in.

That argument, of course, being about Maisie's youth and how unethical it was for all these adults around her to keep putting her in such dangerous positions. Alice knew how the argument would go before they even picked it back up again. Alice would beg her to forget about everything and go back to being a kid. At which point, Maisie would declare her childhood over on account of all she'd done and witnessed. And when that still prevented Alice from giving up her pleas for Maisie's withdrawal from the resistance, the teen girl would point out the Commander's obvious blind spot when it came to her. There was something in the monster of a man that was once Jasper Montrois, something that wouldn't allow him to treat Perry Sagal's daughter with the same cold dispassion with which he weighed the rest of his serfs. And so, Maisie quickly became the bane of every supervisor and warden in the station. But no matter what they charged the girl with, word would come down from on-high to let her go with a warning. Alice knew Lieutenant Masterson, Orange Corridor's warden, wanted her surveilled and harassed daily, but rumors all said that the Commander wouldn't have any of it. Apparently, he believed letting Maisie off for her various trespasses against his regime was apology enough for killing her father. Alice figured that was about all the sense of empathy the colossal tyrant had left inside his sick soul. But regardless of what caused the Witen's blind spot when it came to Maisie Sagal, their resistance couldn't afford not to take advantage of its opportunities.

So Alice didn't even bother starting the argument. Instead, she wiggled her way up and out of her chair. Maisie stood and met her in the center of the room. Alice snatched her up, engulfing the young teen in a warm hug. Maisie bent herself around her half-brother or sister and squeezed tight. "I love ya, Mais... We'll get through this all somehow. Your sibling is going to grow up in a peaceful world. And they'll have their big sister to thank."

"Her, and their momma too," Maisie added as she withdrew from the embrace. "Be quick at the Commissary today, okay? And go around 1000 ST. I've noticed it's pretty dead in their around then."

"Yes, ma'am," Alice promised with a wink and a sarcastic salute. "Now, go on. Get out of here. I'm sure they're all waiting for you."

"One more week, Allie," Maisie told her with a resolute belief evident in her bearing. "This baby will have their future secured after that. I know it," she added with a hand gently resting on her roommate's belly. "One more week."

THE COMMANDER

The Commander sat behind the massive mahogany desk in the same brown leather rolling chair that his predecessor in power once sat. Hubert Harrington had a narrow, bony ass. The imprint it left behind in the soft cushion was entirely unsatisfactory to meet the Commander's rear-end demands. It was wide with good lumbar support, though, and after months of continual use by its new owner, the chair had warped and reformed in all the right ways. Now the Commander was in danger of passing out whenever he perched himself in the fancy desk chair behind the red-brown lacquered desk. He had to remind himself periodically not to slouch. The authority the chair signified in the expansive executive office demanded a regal stature from its occupier. The office itself, with its soft cream-colored walls, red-brown leather armchairs, and twin end tables and oval-shaped coffee table, all matching the exquisite mahogany desk, carried a similar badge of authority as well. They were the outward symbols of the Commander's supremacy. And while he did respect them and offer them the honor and dignity they deserved, he did revel in them as well. He'd earned them. He'd earned this station … and all that dwelled within it.

The Commander's train of thought had been musing on these simple joys of authority, and so he failed to recognize that the Steward was done with his report and was now just standing before the barren surface of the ten-foot wide mahogany desk with a look of minor impatience written all over his face. "Sorry, Steward, I did not catch your last."

"My own fault, I'm sure, Commander. Perhaps I should've noticed you were busy with the myriad dreadful worries that incessantly press upon your shoulders as the leader of the last band of humanity in the cosmos," the Steward responded in the usual obsequious manner he adopted when speaking with his leader. The Commander was a bit annoyed by the brazen sycophancy at first. Until the Steward explained that when they saw how deferential the Witen's number-two man was to his superior, the Witen's officers, footmen, and citizens would be quicker to adopt the deference they needed them to adopt in order to ensure the Commander's peace reigned unchallenged. He told the Commander they would all instinctively follow suit, and then that same deference would transfer to the Steward, the officers, supervisors and eventually even the footmen. And as the Steward was with most everything, he had been right. "I was just chattering on about an unimportant report, Commander, sir," the Steward went on. "Nothing that I needed to bother your sacred time with anyhow. We do, however, have a citizen waiting with Captain Alvarez and her corridor warden, Lieutenant Dirks, just outside in your lobby now."

"Who?" the Commander asked in a distant, uninterested voice.

"Helena Heathcoat."

"Who?"

"She is the woman who took Elias Sagal in after that rapist's trial and execution all those months ago. She's done a bang-up job with the boy. Made a fine home for him, one replete with plenty of due honor for the Witenagemot," the Steward explained.

"Oh, her," the Commander said, only half remembering what the man was talking about. "How is Sagal's son getting along, then? Any trouble?"

"None," the Steward assured him. "I have him on my personal security detail, well away from his troublemaking sister."

The Commander thought he detected the tiniest hint of disapproval toward his decision-making in that last remark. The Steward had been fairly vocal about the need to seriously punish the Sagal girl for her various civil disturbances over the months. The Commander was having none of it, though. She was just some angry thirteen-year-old, no threat to their ultimate designs, surely. He had been truly fond of Perry Sagal once, despite how angry it made him to remember how little trust the doctor had in the Commander's intentions, so much so that he was willing to try to kill him. He'd thought Dr. Sagal had known him better than that. He'd thought the man respected him enough to trust that the Commander was only taking the drastic actions demanded by the times. But he had, of course, been wrong. Perry Sagal was a disloyal fool who'd forced his hand. But no matter how much that fact angered the Commander, enough respect and admiration for the man remained within him so as he could not bring himself to harm the doctor's children. So he employed a policy of looking the other way when it came to Maisie Sagal's antics, subconsciously at least... Well, partly, anyway.

"The boy isn't showing any signs of insubordination or anything?" he asked the Steward, thankful that the brother half of the Sagal-children equation was being attended to by his subordinate with a much more tenderhearted bend than the one he aimed toward

Maisie. The Commander knew that had to do with the Steward's own lost son. He figured the Witen's number-two man was making efforts to replace the son he'd lost with that of Perry Sagal's, which was fine by the Commander. Everyone had their own ways of coping with the lost world. The Commander filled his own empty soul with his duty, with his rule … with his power. And so long as a person was able to accomplish their duties and live within the Witen's laws, then the Commander didn't care how they coped. And no man or woman of the Witenagemot performed their duties with more steadfast wisdom than the Steward.

"Well…" the Steward began, clearly unsure whether or not to share his current thought with the Commander.

"Well, what?" he prompted.

"Well, we did have a small unpleasantness at his first Third Day as a member of my security detail. I had to rule against a girl the kid clearly has a crush or something on. Remember that bullshit one of Mikkelson's supervisors pulled on me I was telling you about? That whole wergild thing."

"Oh, right, right," the Commander said, remembering. "The boy was there for all that, eh?"

"Yeah. But it's nothing to worry about," the Steward assured his leader. "I had a nice long talk with him right afterward. He was a bit upset, but he came to accept, after a time, that he is just too young now to understand the nuances of justice. He's gung ho about serving on my detail, though, and so was easy to distract. I had him help clear out those maintenance workers who were rioting outside of the priest's liquor stand yesterday. Nothing like the thrill of power to set the boy's head right."

"Good. That's good. *Helena Heathcoat…* Isn't her wife that Alice Stark woman? The one you suspect of leading a resistance movement."

"Yes, sir, that's correct," the Steward reported. "She's the one currently sharing living quarters with Perry Sagal's daughter."

"Right, right. I recall now. Hyun's wife is friends with the both of them, right?"

"Uhh... Yes, sir," the Steward answered after a small reflection. "*Stevie* Hyun is her name. And those three are indeed often spotted in each other's company."

The Commander grunted acknowledgment before swiftly shifting the topic back to the matter at hand. "So, what the hell does this Helena Heathcoat want with us, then?"

"Well, I'm not certain exactly," the Steward answered. "Captain Alvarez wouldn't allow something to be brought to your office without good cause, though. I know that much. Neither would Lieutenant Dirks, for that matter."

"True," the Commander allowed. "Well, bring 'em in, then, I guess."

The Steward turned to face the office's black double-doors and nodded his head at the footman perched alongside them. The footman in question was a female of about thirty years with smooth, dark skin spread tight across a slim, sleek physique. She turned without a word and opened the righthand door. The Commander failed to hear the ensuing exchange, but he saw clearly as his office's inner security guard beckoned for his callers to come forward. Alvarez sauntered in, his permanent look of easy contentment evident as ever. Lieutenant Dirks came striding through the open door an instant later. Helena Heathcoat tagged along behind her, taking two quick steps for every one of Dirks's.

The Commander waited until the trio made it around the armchairs and coffee table in the center of the wide room to stand beside the Steward, directly in front of the imperial mahogany desk, before speaking. "An issue in your corridor, Lieutenant?" he asked in a calm, quiet voice.

"I'm afraid so, Commander, sir," Dirks answered, always being conscious not to lift her eyes to the Commander's without his leave. "I would not bother your sacred time, sir... It's only that I'm fairly certain you will want to hear what Ms. Heathcoat has to say firsthand ... and..."

"Look at me, Lieutenant," the Commander ordered in a fatherly voice. Once the woman raised her thin face so he could make out the reverent honor that lay plain in the whirls of her pale-blue eyes, he continued, "I know I have your trust. And you should know that you have mine. I know you would not trouble me needlessly. Plus, I trust Captain Alvarez's vetting process. It hasn't failed me yet." The

Commander glanced at the handsome, cocksure Regent of the Corridors to see the Witen's number-three man's smirk spread even wider. So," he said, shifting his gaze to the long-limbed woman in the knee-length purple turtleneck sweater beside the lieutenant, "say your say, Ms. Heathcoat."

Helena's short-cropped sandy-blonde hair stayed stiff and unmoving as she flipped her head up toward him. There was a fire plain as day in the woman. The Commander watched as her jaw quivered while she emitted huffing sounds, interspersed with growled attempts to begin a sentence. Clearly, something had her agitated, and her better instincts were trying as hard as they could to tamp down her bursting fury. The Steward had promised him the woman who had taken Elias Sagal in after they stripped him away from Maisie was someone the Witen could trust, "a true-blue pious member of the cause," was the way the Steward had phrased it a few weeks back, in fact. So, obviously the woman knew she ought to behave herself before the Commander, in his own damn office no less, but clearly, whatever brought her in today possessed the power to make her falter before her ruler and forget her decorum.

"Relax yourself, Ms. Heathcoat, and speak clearly ... and calmly, goddammit. There's nothing I hate more than a blabbering fool."

"Yes, Commander, sir," Helena groveled after gathering herself with a swiftness the Commander approved of. "Forgive me, sir." The Commander flicked his hand at the woman, urging her to quit with the apologies and get on with it. "Right, well, sir, you will know from the Steward that I believe my wife Alice Stark to have been Perry Sagal's lover before you ... you uhh... Before you put that traitorous asshole in his place."

The Commander glanced over at the Steward who offered him the tiniest of nods. "Yes, yes. What of it?" he then asked the violet-draped woman.

"Well, I saw her today, Commander. In the Commissary," Helena informed them. "No one has seen her outside her quarters in weeks. And no wonder. She was pregnant, Commander, sir. I confronted her and demanded to know who the father was. She wouldn't say. But it's gotta be Perry. Who else could it be? The timing fits for sure. She was huge," Helena almost screamed this last point and even mimed a large belly around her own relatively slim torso. "She's gotta be eight months along at least. That puts it just about right for being Perry's. Plus, I know it was him just from the look on her face. We've been married for almost ten years. I know her faces. I asked flat out if it was Perry's, and her look confirmed all. She freakin' ran away from me before I could get the truth, but she didn't need to say it. I know. So then, I started to think about all her pregnancy's implications, and I figured she must be going to see one doctor or another in Newton Hospital. But that'd mean she'd be walking right down Branch 1 all the time, plain as day. And if it's Perry's accursed child, then she would not be doing that. No way. So I figured some doctor is coming to her. Unless you all do know about this child and are okay with it?" she posited a bit hesitantly, but the Commander was still impressed by her courage and will to speak it at all.

"No, Ms. Heathcoat. We certainly were not aware of your wife's pregnancy," the Steward answered her while looking at the Commander. "I have a standing order among the hospital staff to report all pregnancies aboard station to me upon confirmation. Such lives need to be cherished and assured the greatest chance of viability. For they are truly the future. But I was never informed of Alice Stark's condition, as you claim it. If what you claim is true, it would constitute a massive failure among my spy web. I am not at all comfortable with its implications."

"One thing at a time, Steward," the Commander told the man. "I'll accept that your wife is indeed pregnant. That fact, especially at over eight months, is pretty undeniable. So I'll trust your eyes there, Ms. Heathcoat. You've been a loyal and valued citizen of the Witenagemot. I have no reason to doubt any of your story really. Yet the fact of this child's parentage still remains but a belief based on some convenient timing and a certain look on your wife's face. Although the thought of more of Perry Sagal's progeny joining our fragile society does give me pause, especially if left alone to grow up in the company of his closest admirers. If what you believe turns out to be true, we really shouldn't allow the child to be raised outside of the Witen's direct control. Moreover, if what you believe turns out to be indeed true, it will have constituted a grave breach of The New Destiny Constitution. Not just on your wife's part, for keeping both her pregnancy and its possible traitorous lineage from us, but on the parts of all those who worked to keep this from us. Steward," the Commander addressed his fellow titled officer of the Witenagemot in a voice rich with sovereign superiority, "send footmen to collect every doctor aboard station. Have them waiting in this office, ready to answer my questions as soon as we return."

"Yes, Commander, sir, as you say," the Steward responded, turning from the desk and reaching for his pocket tablet. He had the tablet halfway to his ear before he did a doubletake and turned back to face his leader. "Did... Did you say *return*, sir?"

"Yes, Steward. I did."

"Oh," the lesser man replied with an arched brow. "Where will we be returning from?"

"We need the truth of Ms. Heathcoat's wife's condition. What better way than to ask her directly?"

The Steward searched for words for a few seconds before a smirk finally ended up on his lips. "Surely there is none, Commander. Shall we go now? I have a handful of footmen just down the Branch doing a bit of training."

"Yes. Good," the Commander said, rising to his feet. "They'll be happy for the break in routine, I'm sure. Inform them they will be joining us. Ms. Heathcoat," he called to the short-haired woman before the mahogany desk, once more barely containing her bubbling fury. She stilled herself at the sound of her name, though. *Gotta give her credit for the effort of manners*, the Commander thought. "You will be coming along as well. If she isn't home, might you know some other places she might end up?"

"Yes, sir, Commander, sir," Helena answered, bobbing her head up and down. "However I can be of service to the Witen, I'm willing."

"Good. Very good," the Commander said, making his way out from behind the spotless grandiosity that was his executive desk. "Lieutenant Dirks." Dirks's head twisted up toward him at the end of her long, slim neck. "Lead the way, if you would, Lieutenant." She dipped her chin an inch in acceptance, then turned on her heels and headed for the door. The Commander came out from behind the desk to follow. Alvarez was second through the door with Heathcoat right behind, but before the Steward could pass through, the Commander clasped a hand on top his shoulder. "Leave the Sagal boy behind to guard the offices," he told his number-two man. The Steward wrestled a confused look from his face with admirable dexterity and managed a confirming nod just as they exited the Commander's executive office.

DOLLY

"These idiots, half the goddamn station knows they're plotting something," Larry Holderman scoffed. "If you don't say something to stop them, every last one of the bastards will be no more than goddamn heads on spikes by the end of the week."

"That's a bit dramatic, don't ya think, Lar?" the priest asked him.

Dolly was sure hoping Father Boyd was right, and Larry Holderman had no reason to come storming into Boyd's living quarters all hot and bothered about the doomed resistance plot rumored to be in the works. Dolly's husband, Gabe Duchesne, was one of those resistance plotters, after all. Dolly did not want to believe their scheme had been sniffed out by the Witen already, as both Larry Holderman and his module crewmate, Jed Redding, seemed to believe. She needed Gabe to return safe to her after he and his resistance pulled off their grand plan. Gabe was her life's North Star; she dare not even imagine going on without him. Of course, Gabe could, and indeed often did, irritate the hell out of her, but she still feared to contemplate living this new, cold, foreign life bereft of his company. It was hard enough making it through each day with the memory and guilty weight of the billions of souls who hadn't been lucky enough to find the sanctuary of Cardinal's Nest. To do so without Gabe to lean on was inconceivable. So she needed Larry and Jed to be wrong. She needed Father Boyd's calm reason to be the day's truth. "Gabe is certain no one in the Witen knows anything of their plans," she told them.

Father Boyd treated her with a wink, then reached out to squeeze her hand. Dolly was resting in one of the room's two chairs, right beside Boyd as he fussed over some bubbling pots perched precariously atop a gray folding table. "Well, let's just all hope that's so, Dolly. No point shouting 'fire' with no sign of smoke. Besides which, I'm not really sure what it is you want me to do exactly, Lar, if you're really right about what the Witen happens to know. I'm a simple brewer, my friend. I want no part of any resistance, or of the Witen's menace, neither. Leave me out of all of it." Boyd looked back to Dolly with that, and an apologetic look spread swiftly and honestly across his face. "Look... Regardless of anything, we shouldn't be speaking of such things here."

Dolly had sought out Father Boyd's company for the exact reason that he tried to keep his shop/living quarters a politics-free environment. He never allowed plotting of any sort to take place in his shop. Dolly knew it was in this way that he remained exempt from any of the Witen and its councilmembers' various harassments. The priest provided his wares to every man or woman, be they resistance sympathizers or Witen zealots. True, it was the resistance sympathizers who hung around the shop for some chitchat, more so than any of the Witen zealots, but both parties knew they were welcome, and a truce of sorts had sprung up. Though, that's not to say the limits of that truce hadn't been tested a time or two. Just yesterday, some maintenance workers seemed to think the priest had been checting them after guzzling down a few of his bottles. There wasn't too much drunken drama, really. The Witen had come storming in with a pack of ten footmen swinging bats and clubs, and the workers had quickly seen the error of their ways. Despite the occurrences of such rare events, Dolly still figured the priest's shop was the obvious choice for an escape from her incessant worry about Gabe and his compatriot's future failure or success.

Dolly had a fondness for Father Boyd. His calm, cool wisdom seemed to come with none of the caveats of lesser clergyman. He was who he was. There was no pretense with the man. Dolly could talk to him for hours. Boyd would stir his pots and fill his bottles, and Dolly would rattle on and on about nothing, really. She had a feeling that the priest enjoyed their conversations as much as she did. They'd become true friends of late, as true a friend as Dolly had aboard station. She needed his company. The two module crewman's intrusion had been entirely unwelcome. And so, she pondered polite ways to ask them to grab what liquor they required and move on.

Jed Redding's low, husky voice invaded her internal deliberations. "They would listen to you, Father," the tall, thin, gray-haired module pilot was saying. "Think of young Maisie, for god's sake. These resistance plotters are so focused on revenge that they've blinded themselves. The very immoral things they profess to oppose are now being employed by them. Sorry, Dolly. I mean no offense," Jed said, stepping close to Dolly. "I just think they've lost their marbles a bit. And who could blame them for it? I mean, I get it. I really do. But still, nothing justifies putting that young girl in harm's way like they're doing."

"They only use Maisie where they have to, Jed," Dolly told him, defending her husband's better judgement. "The Commander has a real blind spot when it comes to her. But I assure you that whatever they are planning, Maisie will be far away from any danger."

"They hope, anyway," Larry sardonically added.

"Enough of this stuff," Boyd's voice rose to its highest volume since Dolly had been in his company that day. "I'm serious. Anyone could just walk in here at any moment. That's the damn point of this place. Now, respect it or go," he finished with a finger aimed at the narrow passage through the cluttered quarters that led to his hatchway.

"I'm sorry, Boyd," Dolly offered in a rush. "And to you, too, Jed. I didn't mean to get all worked up or anything."

"Yeah, me neither, Doll, of course," Jed said. "I'm just nervous for 'em all, ya know? But sorry, Boyd. We won't mention that topic again. Right, Larry?"

"Yeah... I guess," Larry answered after a time. "Sorry, Boyd."

The hatchway swished open the instant after the half-hearted apology faded away. Dolly and the three other men in the living quarters' cleared central workspace turned toward the sound just as Gabe came shuffling through the narrow entry passage. Dolly's eyes locked with her husband's as he rushed toward her side. It wasn't panic she saw there, not exactly, but it was something very close indeed. "What's the matter?" she asked him.

But before her question could be answered, Maisie Sagal jogged in after him, followed by Stevie, and lastly, to Dolly's disbelief, Alice

Stark. "Alice?!" the priest bellowed out, as surprised as Dolly had ever seen him. "What are you doing out? I told you and Maisie and Spurnberg and Stevie, and all the rest how Helena's looking for you. She's got her own little army of spies all over this station. If they spot you here, there's no hiding that belly. Stevie... Maisie, I thought I suggested you guys keep her in her quarters until after you do whatever it is you're planning to do."

"You told 'em, Father," Alice said as she plopped herself down in the room's only other chair with an arm for support from Boyd. "And they did the best they could. But you'll find I'm not to be tamed."

"Oh, come on, Alice. Why risk this now?" the priest asked her in a lightly scolding manner. "Let's just get you back to Orange Corridor right away before any of your wife's friends see you."

"Too late, Boyd," Maisie stated.

"What?" Dolly and Boyd both asked at the same instant.

"We needed food," Alice said. "Maisie's been running around with her hair on fire, busy as all hell, and I didn't want to be treated like some invalid any longer. I deserve to be able to go to the Commissary like any other person."

"You didn't...?" Father Boyd asked in a soft voice.

"We needed food, goddammit! What were the odds that she'd be there at the same exact time, anyway?" Alice defended herself.

"Helena?" Dolly guessed in fear.

"Yeah, she tracked me down in the produce section and ... well ... uhh ... noticed the bump," Alice told them, rubbing her belly.

"What happened?" Jed Redding's deep voice called out the question into the gasped silence that followed Alice's words.

"What happened?" Alice asked back with rank sarcasm. "She blew a damn fuse, that's what happened. Demanding I tell her who the father is and which of the station's doctors have been treating me and all sorts of other craziness. I couldn't do nothing but flee from her in the end. God, I can't believe it has come to this with us. We were so in love once... Once... A lifetime ago."

"You just fled from her?" the priest asked in confusion. "What did she do? Did she say anything?"

"She started to follow me out of the Commissary but then got a better idea," Alice said in a gloomy voice.

"She went and told her corridor warden," Maisie said, looking at Alice with a motherly sort of disappointment.

"And Lieutenant Dirks went right to Captain Alvarez, who went straight to the Commander with it," Gabe added. "Or so the station's gossip line is saying right now, anyway."

"You were with her, then?" the priest asked Maisie, Stevie, and Dolly's husband.

"No," Maisie said, answering for all of them. "We was all walking through the Central Hub when we ran into her on her way here."

"We dragged the details from her there and then," Stevie confirmed.

"And so, Boyd, seeing as how the cat is out of the bag," Alice cut in, still rubbing her belly, "I figured I'd come pay you a visit. I've missed your company, and I'm too stir-crazy to go back to my quarters now. And no point, anyway."

"Well, Alice, I've certainly missed your unique charms, don't get me wrong, but I would've rather our reunion took place in a few days or so," Boyd told her.

"Yeah, now who knows where the hell we'll be next week," Gabe said, sounding genuinely perturbed.

"What do you mean, honey?" Dolly asked her husband, now standing alongside her.

"I mean, the Witen is going to be looking too closely at all of us now. They are going to want to question everyone who might've known about Alice's condition and helped to keep it secret. Why the hell do you think we was forcing her to stay in her damn quarters in the first place?"

Dolly slapped her husband on the thigh for his rude tone.

"We can't know that," Maisie suddenly argued with a little less conviction than she might have otherwise. "Who knows if the Commander and the Steward are even gonna care about some pregnancy? They might have other evil to occupy themselves with. All ain't lost yet."

"Ha. You dream, kid," Gabe responded in a tone that Dolly rewarded with an elbow to his side.

"Especially if Dr. Perry Sagal is the father of that hidden pregnancy," Jed concurred.

"No, Maisie is right," Stevie spoke up. "All is not lost. Even if they come to question us about Alice. We can compartmentalize the two things: the hidden pregnancy and the coup. We'll have to, anyway."

"Or you could abandon your crazy plot that's just gonna get you and probably every last motherson in this station killed," Larry Holderman suggested condescendingly.

"We can't!" Maisie barked back at the round, red, bald man. "We have to take control of the station now while a chance still exists for us."

"She's right," Stevie agreed. "Tomorrow is no guarantee up here anymore. We have a good plan, though, Larry. So rest easy. We can't afford to let it pass us by. But we are certainly taking every precaution as well... And we are trusting friends like you and Jed to keep silent," she finished with a bit of threat in her normally sweet voice. The red-headed beauty stared down Larry for a long time after that, waiting for both him and Jed to nod their heads and mutter promises of silence. Her raspberry hair and light splash of auburn freckles glowed bright in the room's harsh lighting, accentuating the natural regal authority in her crystal-blue eyes. Larry and Jed were no match for them.

"I really can't have you all talking about this stuff in here," the priest announced, sparing the module crewmen. "Really, please. Just take Alice back to Orange Corridor. Try and avoid people as much as you can along the way. I'm sorry. I just can't have this kinda stuff going on here. They watch me."

Right on cue, the hatchway swished open once more and all heads turned toward the narrow passage. A tangible darkness followed the figure who stepped into view inside the small, circular workspace. The Commander's eyes were cold. His gaze malev-olent. The black handle of his long, heavy battleaxe poked up over a round, muscular shoulder. His hulking presence blotted out the room's brightness. His full, dark beard pierced by four linear scars running from deep into the tangled facial-hair of his right cheek all the way up across his milky white right eye replaced the brightness with gloom. And then, all the dread the Witen's leader had brought about in Dolly's heart doubled as the Steward, Captain Alvarez, four footmen, Lieutenant Dirks, and Helena Heathcoat crowded in after him.

Silence sat heavy in the cramped space. The Commander placed himself in the center of the cleared patch of what was once a standard living quarters chamber. The Steward quickly moved to stand alongside him, though Dolly noted he made sure to stay at least one pace back. The four footmen, Lieutenant Dirks, and Helena Heathcoat all stayed along the room's circumference, as did Dolly, her husband, and all their friends. The workspace grew so packed, Stevie's shoulders even pressed up against a footman's, as did the priest's. Dolly looked up to her husband. Gabe gazed back down at her. And when neither could find comfort in the other, they searched the eyes of their friends, hoping against hope. But no, the same fear and panic was plain as rain on theirs as well.

Finally, the Steward cleared his throat. "Good afternoon, Father Boyd," he said through a patronizing smirk.

"Steward, what brings you in today?" the priest asked in a calm, sarcastic voice that proved to Dolly what a deeply courageous soul Father Boyd truly was. "Run dry of all six of those bottles of moonshine I sold you last week already?"

"No, Father, afraid not," the Steward responded with cool threat. "I am not one for overindulgence. My son and I learned how to ration our resources the hard way. No, the Commander and I have come for another reason entirely," he finished, staring at a still seated and hugely pregnant Alice Stark. "Ms. Stark, we've been looking for you. You weren't at your and little Ms. Sagal's shared quarters. And for a moment, we didn't know where to search for you next. Then my network informed me that you and your friends," he added, turning his gaze upon Maisie, Stevie, and Gabe in turn, "were all spotted entering Father Boyd's humble liquor shop. And here, indeed, we find you. On the one hand, it is nice to see the lightning-fast accuracy of my network of patriots in action, but on the other, it's heartbreaking to discover Father Boyd would so blatantly betray the solemn promise he swore to the Commander and myself: to keep no secrets from the Witen. Yet here we find a citizen who's been hiding her pregnancy from us, conspiring with god knows how many other citizens in the process, hanging out plain as day in your little, danky-ass shop. All of which suggests to me that you, Father Boyd, have known about Ms. Stark's condition all along. And that... Well, it hurts my feelings, Father. It really does."

"Well, I'm real sorry about your feelings and all, Steward," the priest shot back, unintimidated, "but I had no prior knowledge of Alice's pregnancy. Your fancy spy network should've had you well informed that this is the first time she's even left her quarters in weeks. How the hell would I know what's going on with her? I barely ever get a damn second to leave this place and grab a bite at the Main Cafeteria, let alone go making any house calls, at least none that ain't work related anyway."

"Right, Father," the Steward agreed sardonically. "And you wouldn't dare lie to me, I'm sure."

"Just tell them who the father is, Alice!" Helena suddenly shouted from her position behind the Steward. "Tell them who you betrayed me with, you sick bitch!"

The Steward whipped his head around. Dolly could see the glare he shot at Helena and noted its fury. Helena had been all worked up one moment, but one glance at the Steward's fiery eyes had immediately stilled her. He let the glare go on for a few uncomfortable beats, long enough for Helena's cheeks to flush red. When he turned back, it was Alice who became captured beneath his unyielding gaze. "Yes, Ms. Stark, please, if you will, tell us all who the father is.'

Dolly's blood ran cold as she watched Alice lever herself up in her chair while staring up at the Steward. "Why do you need to know? Huh? Just why the hell do you care?" she asked him, her voice cracking all throughout.

"Ashamed, are we?" the Steward shot back disdainfully. Dolly noticed a difference in the man's glare. His dark eyes now carried a hint of pleasure and a drip of anticipation. "You know, I dealt with a lot of divorces in the old world, the dead world, the past life, as The New Destiny Constitution refers to it. Infidelity is a bit of a shitty thing to engage in, but it's hardly rare enough as to shame you into not naming your child's father."

"I'm not ashamed," Alice declared, defiance firming up her voice.

"Then tell us who the man is," the Steward prompted with sweet contempt.

No, Alice, don't do it! Dolly's inner voice was shouting as she stared at her chestnut-haired friend, her soft features edged now with bursting turmoil. Dolly could see it plainly in Alice's squinting eyes scrunched up tight behind her tortoiseshell glasses. Alice broke off her deadlock stare with the Steward to glance up and over at the Commander. Dolly expected to find rage and indignation of some degree on the broad, scarred face of the Witen's leader, but instead, she couldn't make out a single feature of the bear-man's face. He was turned completely away from Alice and Dolly, staring intently at Stevie Hyun. Dolly was instantly afraid for that stare's implications, for Stevie Hyun looked radiant, gorgeous even, despite the room's harsh lighting, and Dolly was a woman of the world; she knew the kind of reasons men gazed at gorgeous redheads.

"Dr. Perry Sagal," Alice Stark's firm pronouncement drew the Commander's steady gaze from Stevie. Alice waited until he was looking right at her before she added, "A better man than you."

A tension ensued so great it could've snapped an anchor chain. The Steward ended it with another clearing of his throat. "Footmen, drag them all back to Branch 1's executive offices. I'll have a few more questions for them," he ordered.

"No," the Commander said just as the four footmen were snapping into motion. The word was so small and spoken so low that everyone in the room was certain they misheard it. Dolly was definitely under that misapprehension.

"What?" the Steward asked his leader.

"We'll get what we need from the doctors," the Commander told the Steward, who stared back at him, his mouth agape. "I am willing to forgive everyone in this room ... if she comes with me," he declared, an outstretched finger pointed directly at Stevie Hyun. "Agree to be mine and I'll leave these people alone ... for now," he told her.

"Commander, sir," the Steward began in a voice that sounded far from the confident, sly mannerisms it had been affecting moments earlier, "you cannot be serious. We have to interrogate every last one of these citizens—and most likely a great many more. If they would dare lie about something as brazen as a pregnancy—with Perry Sagal as the father, no less—what else wouldn't they dare to lie about?"

"Nothing that should threaten us, surely," the Commander answered in a calm, grumbling voice. "No. I say no. These people shall remain unpunished for this crime. I am a man of my word, goddammit, Steward. How dare you suggest I impugn that honor? I am a man of my word, and my word is the law. If Stevie agrees to come with me willingly, then I swear the Witen shall not harm her friends here. I'll look the other way–this one time. I'll even allow Ms. Stark to raise her baby as she pleases, provided she keep its father as secret from it until the end of time. But only if you come with me," he finished, stepping close to Stevie and crowding her against a table stacked w th empty bottles.

The Steward wanted to say something. That was clear. But ne held his tongue. He did glance around the room, searching for sup-port for a few seconds, but in the end, he straightened his back and bit his lip. Dolly felt a cold chill ripple down her spine as the Commander stepped even closer to Stevie. He reached out and grabbed ahold of her upper arm as Stevie snapped out of her disbelieving torpor. "Abner! Get Abner!" she screamed as the Commander dragged her toward him.

Maisie snapped into action with no delay. She was quick and small and nearly made it to the workspace's one exit passageway. Lieutenant Dirks managed to clap a hand down on her shoulder and drag her back, held firm against the tall lieutenant's body. "Come qui-etly... Come *willingly*," the Commander told Stevie, "or I'll take them both from her." He used his chin to indicate Maisie and then Alice's bump in turn.

"No, Stevie, forget this jerk!" Maisie cried out.

"Yeah, don't you dare go with them, Stevie!" Alice demanded of her friend, her eyes streaming with tears of rage and fear, much like Dolly's own.

Dirks clapped a hand over Maisie's mouth as two of the footmen moved toward the still seated Alice while reaching for their respective bludgeoning tools strapped tight to their backs. "Stay away from her!" Stevie shouted at the footmen, stopping them dead in their tracks. "I'll come, Commander," she managed, her voice only cracking slightly as she eyed the man with confused horror. "I'll trust you to be a man of your word."

The Commander nodded his commitment to the bargain, his dark, implacable face as difficult to read as ever. Stevie allowed the giant tyrant to lead her by that same hand clasped tight around her upper arm toward the exit path.

No! This isn't happening, Dolly was silently screaming. *Somebody do something.* Then, to her supreme regret, someone did. The priest bolted two steps and placed a hand on the Commander's shoulder from directly behind. "Wait, Jasper. This is mad. You can't–"

The Commander's left elbow plowing into Father Boyd's nose cut off the clergyman's pleas for rationality. Dolly could see, as the rippling brute turned back to face her and her friends, that any chance of reason ever rearing its head aboard station again was as likely as human beings ever breathing in a vacuum. Boyd collapsed to the floor from the blow, as though he was already out on his feet. The Commander moved to stand over where the priest had come to an awkward rest. "I can, Priest," he told the unconscious lump. "Oh, I can. Footmen," he barked to his serfs without shifting his glare from Boyd's sprawled mass, "deliver the good priest his punishment for breaking his oath to me and the Steward. I can forgive all these fools for keeping Alice's little secret, but I won't forgive a man for betraying an oath."

As though they'd been expecting the order, the four footmen snatched out their baseball bats and battleaxes and instantly began a savage and sustained attack on the boxes and equipment stacked up all around them. Glass shards rained down as Gabe wrapped an arm around his wife and rushed her toward the hatchway. Maisie, Larry, and Jed made it to the path just ahead of them, each with an arm or a guiding hand helping Alice along. Dolly glanced back right before she stepped into the narrow passage. Her heart broke, helpless as she was to rescue the priest. Footmen were stomping on the unconscious body of Father Boyd as they dashed around the room in their mad, destructive frenzy, stopping only to stuff full bottles of the priest's various concoctions into the cargo pockets of their crisply-pressed, gold-trimmed gray Witenagemot uniforms.

INTERLUDE

JORDANA

They were back in another series of cramped and stygian access tunnels. Maisie had led Jordana through a confusion of passageways for a good ten minutes upon leaving that paradise of urban tranquility, that homage to peaceful days long past that was the Priest's Clubhouse, all the while, speaking over her shoulder and regaling Jordana with further episodes of her tale aboard station, a tale that grew ever more twisted in the telling. Jordana's head was reeling when Maisie abruptly stopped in a poorly lit alcove.

Though dark and gloomy, the snug little recess was pleasantly warm thanks to the churning and whirring machinery surrounding them on three sides, all of which were far too advanced and uncommon for Jordana to even begin to guess at their possible purpose. The sudden rush of warm air caressing her exposed forearms, neck, and face made Jordana realize she had been walking with her arms crossed and exhibiting an ever so slight shiver.

When did that start? she asked herself. Coming up blank, she realized there was actually very little of their flight away from the priest, Larry Holderman, Jed Redding, and the priest's sweet old wife, Dolly, that Jordana consciously took in. Maisie's story had her enraptured, commanding all her attention.

It wasn't only the young woman's amazing tale that had Jordana reeling. Maisie had her in a state she hadn't been in since the earliest days of the infection, a state she swore would never be allowed to take hold of her again. Confused, disoriented, engrossed, unsure. Pick a word because they all applied, and she felt them all in equal measures, just like in those early days. And just like in those early days, she felt the rush of those emotions threatening to overwhelm her. Jordana just couldn't help herself. The captivating young resistance leader was imbued with an electricity of character unlike anyone Jordana had ever known, save perhaps her leader, Arlo Bailey. Jordana was even realizing that she was now trusting Maisie almost on the same level as she trusted the Bruderschaft's fearless warrior-champion.

She was putting her entire mission into the hands of this hazel-eyed, brown-haired, ivory-skinned beauty before her. The realization troubled her. *Am I letting my heart play tricks with my head? Should I trust this woman? Am I risking the mission? Should I have tried to approach this Witen on my own, despite what my rescuers urged?* Jordana asked herself the questions back-to-back. Such were the queries that piled up in the unconscious corners of her mind during their mad dash through the twisting access tunnel system of Cardinal's Nest Lunar Station. Jordana found herself unable to answer any of them honestly.

Worse yet, she found herself *unwilling* to answer any of them. Something deep and primordial inside of the former Royal Air Force pilot was calling out for Maisie Sagal. Something inside her demanded Jordana trust the lithe and powerfully confident young resistance leader—though it did feel to her, on some level, a betrayal of her Bruderschaft. Jordana knew she was placing the call she heard from deep within her heart, whispering on repeat the name of Maisie Sagal, above her loyalty to the 87 brothers and sisters she'd survived nightmares upon nightmares alongside in the Bruderschaft, but she simply lacked the strength of will to resist the magnetism.

She was following and trusting Maisie now, and that was that. The cards were flipped. The dice were rolled. Pick a metaphor. Jordana still very much accepted she had a mission she must accomplish, and by God, she would accomplish it—only, now she'd be doing it with the help of Maisie Sagal. With that understanding firm in her mind, Jordana let the alcove's warm air settle her shivers, along with any lingering inner turmoil, and turned her attention to the task ahead. Maisie stepped away from the warmth, raising an ill-constructed gray comm device the same shape and dimensions as a set of Bicycle playing cards with a thin blue banding of something she took for electrical tape along its circumference. Turning in half-circles, apparently looking for a signal, the young woman must've found one a few yards away from Jordana, just out of earshot. She was definitely curious who the resistance leader was contacting, but the warm air in the alcove was too comforting to abandon. *She'll tell me when she comes back,* Jordana reasoned.

Maisie ended her communication and quickly hustled toward their warm niche. She cleared her throat between slightly labored breaths, sending echoes crashing down on them in stereo around the cozy little alcove. "Alright, he should be here any minute," Maisie breathed in a low voice.

"Who should be here?" Jordana asked in a matching tone.

"Roddy Sheffield," Maisie answered as she leaned back against a bulky, oblong piece of gray-and-black machinery. "He worked in the Control Room in the days before the Commander won the Tournament I was telling you about. He was only one of a handful of people to survive the raid the former security officers led on the Control Room the week before the Witenagemot *officially* took over the station. The operators who did survive that raid all swore oaths to the Witen... All except Roddy, anyway. They banished him to the cafeterias and a life of scrubbing pots and pans for it. In retrospect, he got off light. These days, the Commander would just chop a man's head off for disloyalty."

"Bloody hell," Jordana said in genuine surprise. "It's really that bad?"

"Oh, believe me, you haven't heard the half of it yet," Maisie told her with a sardonic grin. Jordana took one look at the grin and knew it disguised some true darkness. Then the young resistance leader blinked, and her face wore its determined, businesslike mask once again. "Anyway, Roddy is a man who has no reason to love the Commander or his Witen, that's for sure. And their loss has certainly been our gain, let me tell ya. He set up our encrypted comms network basically single-handedly," she said, indicating the small piece of cobbled together tech in her right hand. "Cainey pretends he helped, but that's Novocaine for ya. Roddy lets him take some credit... And that in turn tells ya the type a guy he is. Arlene Fincannon and him have been good friends to me up here over the past few years, good friends to the Resistance as well. Arlene is newer and lacking in Roddy's specific expertise, but she's been a huge help with some of her connections lately. And she only really joined up because of Roddy—there's a story there, but now ain't the time, I think. Bottom line is: we were very lucky Roddy Sheffield sought us out. We was stuck for a good while before he came into the fold. I trust him completely. So you can rest easy on that account. I would've avoided contacting him, nonetheless, if I could. I don't want to risk anybody unnecessarily or anything, but if we're gonna stand a chance of getting into the Control Room to get that message of yours past the station's apparent cloaking tech, then we're gonna need him."

"He's sure he can hack the terminal on that emergency hatch in the Greenhouse you were telling me about on the way here?" Jordana pressed.

"He says he'll have no problem getting past either emergency hatch... And he hasn't failed me yet," Maisie responded with slightly arched eyebrows.

"Well enough, I suppose," Jordana conceded. "Thank you, Maisie," Jordana said after a time and a bit awkwardly. "I appreciate you arranging this... And all the help, really. I can tell how much the priest cares about you. I'm sure it wasn't easy to go against him."

Maisie smiled as she looked up to lock eyes with Jordana. "He and Dolly both," she said, still wearing the smile. "I hear some orphans resent adults who try to look out for them after their parents pass, but I certainly never felt that way... And I lost mine twice over," she added this strange point in an indecipherable manner. "Boyd and Dolly have been my rocks throughout these years. Even in the beginning, when they were trying to get me to stop resisting the Witen, they still were there for me, emotionally at least. I hate going against them. I really do. But even in spite of how cringy I feel when I think of how egotistical it sounds, I do believe I am doing the right thing once again, just like I was back then... And I think they'll come to stand beside me once again as well."

"What about … uhh … yours and the priest's plans for defeating this Witen?" Jordana asked. "Didn't I hear the priest say something about just needing more time or something?"

"It needs more than time," Maisie answered, shaking her head. "It stretches the limits of the definition of the word *plan* at this point. It's more like an outline and some wishful thinking at best. We got a few key elements in place, true, but it's ultimately hopeless. Ya see, there's this secondary station systems-terminal deep in the access tunnel system, and it's redacted from any floorplans the Witenagemot has access to. The thickheaded goons got no hackers or tech people to speak of, really. They got the codes and can get into AOA's files, but there's plenty of buried shit they don't have a clue is even there, much less that they could ever access themselves. It ain't a full auxiliary control room unfortunately, which is another story all together, but you can access the Grand Rotunda's mega Branch hatchways on that terminal. We figure to use it to open up Branch 2. Ya see, we were hoping to get it open and sneak into the Branch to get the Lunar Garage up and running. We think we know a way to lock the big Branch hatch behind us from the inside, too, so the Control Room can't access it. Of course, this is all after we manage to squirrel away a few months' worth of food and water. But provided we clear that gigantic hurdle, and we were all locked up secure in the Lunar Garage, we would set to work preparing an E-11 Shuttle for departure to take us to some refuge back on Earth, like an island or something, much like your people were thinking. We got a few picked out for possible settlement targets. We even have a former shuttle pilot in the Resistance who volunteered to fly the damn thing. But it's a long shot, to say the least. We have a fair amount of water, but we barely have any food stored. Not to mention the fact that we only have a rudimentary plan for getting the life-support systems back up and running. As it stands right now, we can only find a way to divert enough resources to power the alleyway that cuts down the center of the Branch, along with the Terminal itself … we think. But it doesn't matter 'cause it's too small an area to house as many residents as would want to come with us, as well as all the equipment we would need to bring along. And those oxygen recyclers in there haven't been used in nine years or received any maintenance to speak of. They'll break down in a few weeks, at best, and then we'll all be dead before we could ever get a shuttle halfway launch-ready."

"Yes, I can see that doesn't sound very promising at all. I suppose I'm starting to understand why you were so eager to help me," Jordana said playfully.

Maisie smiled back. "I told you it wasn't much of a plan." Her face grew serious as she added, "The priest has hope even in the most hopeless moments. It's his curse, the way I see it. It stops him from seeing the world before him and the practicalities and necessities you have to accept to survive in it. This community, Jordana, it will not survive another year of the Commander and his Witenagemot. They are fracturing. And when the break comes, it will doom us all. If I'm the only one up here who sees that and is willing to act on it, then so be it. There are so few of us left, Jor. We can't leave our fate to men like Jasper Montrois. I'm not trying to drag your people into a war to save us up here or anything. God knows you've all been through enough. I just... I—"

"The Bruderschaft will do what we must to protect each other and survive. You don't need to apologize to me," Jordana cut in to assure her. "The Commander and the Witenagemot are not your fault. You're the one person up here who seems to understand my predicament and is willing to help. It's my honor to repay the favor and help you deal with these righteous wankers who call themselves your rulers." She treated the resistance leader with a smirk. Maisie blushed in response, dropping her eyes. Jordana felt her own cheeks growing warm as she studied the brunette beauty. "I still can't really believe they took power up here in the way you say they did, not that I don't believe you or trust you or anything," she assured Maisie. "It's just hard to credit that we had more freedom down in the chaos than you've all had up here in techno paradise. Humanity is a strange beast," Jordana surmised.

"It's darkest before the dawn, and good always triumphs over evil in the end." Maisie put in her more hopeful summation with a forced lightness and honest smile.

"Well, I'm certainly hoping that's so," Jordana said with an honest smile of her own spreading across her face. "I am curious, though. You said the Witen was concerned AOA was responsible for the infection. And didn't you say something about this Steward-guy saying it was a supernatural curse from the tech givers brought on by AOA's treachery? Which, incidentally, is pretty close to the mark. But I digress. I'm just wondering why the Witen didn't investigate and expose them. 'Cause they do know a great deal about what happened and are largely responsible for it as well. Yet it seems to me that the AOA hasn't been punished. Hubert Harrington himself was free to come seek me out in the Priest's Clubhouse, for example. Why the hell didn't this madman calling himself your Commander chop *their* lying heads off?"

"I don't know really," Maisie said with a thoughtful scrunch of her forehead. "I remember everyone figured they would in those first few weeks after the Commander won the Final Tournament. I think I can recall people speaking about public executions for the 'Old World Order,' as the Witen referred to AOA and the government heads, just like you suggest, but then things kinda snowballed, and with all the other shit that was going on, I guess we all just kinda forgot about AOA and the infection. The Witen must have, too. Once they were set up all snug and secure down Branch 1, they quit talking about the past altogether. They've been trying for almost ten damn years to get us to forget about a world, or a life, before this place. Plus, they probably didn't want to set a precedent of delivering on any of the bullshit promises they made just before the Final Tournament. People might come to expect it of them," Maisie added with a scoff. "Like the promise of taking Earth back, for instance. They have no interest in anything but holding—and even growing—their power. They are fascists who fear knowledge. They probably just brushed AOA and their culpability away rather than risk some piece of information coming to light that might undermine their propaganda. They're in paradise in their ignorance up here, Jor. They get to pretend they're the heroes and saviors of humanity, while still living the tyrant-life. They ain't looking to rock any boats or go flipping over any stones. Forgive my metaphor mixing, but you get the picture."

"Yes, I think I do," Jordana said with slight hesitation. She was beginning to understand much more had gone down up here in Cardinal's Nest Station this past decade than even her wildest imaginations could conceive.

She felt her curiosity growing and was once more on the verge of asking another question when Maisie suddenly beat her to it. "It sounds like you really trust your leader, then, eh?"

Jordana interpreted the off-topic inquiry as a less than tactful way to broach the subject of just how much power Arlo Bailey had over her and the Bruderschaft and just what kind of leader he really was. "He's no dictator or anything like that, if that's what worries you," she told the younger woman in a sincere voice. "He's quite the opposite really. Every member of the Bruderschaft has an equal say in all our plans. Arlo makes sure of that."

"Sounds kinda utopian compared to us," Maisie said with a wry smirk. "I mean, apart from fighting starvation, freezing-cold, and hordes of zombies that is." The two women warming themselves in the alcove burst out with genuine laughter at the absurdity of it all for a few seconds.

"Well, it has been a relief beyond words to have people you know you can count on during the dark nights and god-awful bloody days," Jordana put in once she regained her breath. Then, in a more serious tone, she added, "People you'll do anything for."

"You'd really do anything for them?" Maisie asked.

"In a heartbeat," Jordana answered with no delay.

"Arlo included?"

"Arlo especially."

Maisie glanced up and down at Jordana before coming to lock eyes with her. "Are you ... uhh..." Maisie began, after a few strange heartbeats. "Are you and him... Are you guys... Were yo— You know what, I'm sorry. It's certainly none of my business. Completely irrelevant. I apologize."

Jordana wrangled a smile before it could stretch its treacherous tentacles across her face. "No, please, it's okay," she assured Maisie. "Arlo is my leader and friend—a good friend, for sure—and a fellow brother in the Bruderschaft ... but we weren't... We never..." Jordana trailed off, her cheeks now bright red.

"Oh..." Maisie clearly wanted to say more, but like Jordana, she must've been struggling for words. Before either could find a single syllable, a dark figure crept out from around a shadowed corner, shuffling toward them. Jordana instinctively thought of the Colt .380

Mustang pistol strapped to her right ankle, but the look on Maisie's face stopped her from reaching for the concealed weapon. The younger woman was calmly stepping toward the hooded figure.

Must be this Sheffield guy, Jordana told herself. *God, you're bloody nervous today, aren't you?* The self-reflection led her back to thoughts of that .380 Mustang at her ankle. *If Maisie's tales are true, it may well be the only firearm aboard this entire station.* Before she could analyze any of the implications of that private knowledge, Maisie was hailing the hooded figure. "Roddy, that you?'

The hole in the darkness ahead stepped into a stray ray of light five paces from Jordana to reveal a man in a charcoal hooded sweat-shirt and slacks. The shadow-laden man spoke as soon as he threw off his dark hood. "Yeah, Mais. It's me," Roddy Sheffield assured her in a soft voice. Sheffield immediately began darting his head back and forth in what Jordana took for a nervous inspection for any eavesdroppers. The man seemed to be made for furtive glances and hushed conversations. He was perhaps five-eight and maybe a hundred and forty-pounds soaking wet. His eyes were impossible to make out, sunken as they were beneath a protruding brow and encircled by a thin, scruffy black beard flowing into a tangle of mid-night-black unwashed locks. "I take it this is the Star Hawk pilot I've heard so much about over our continuously abused comm line."

It took Jordana a second to realize the man was talking about her. She chided herself for being so distracted. Sure, a lot had happened over the past few hours, but Jordana Revere was a professional. She had a duty to keep a clear head. *For the Bruderschaft,* she reminded herself before slapping on an appropriately warm face of greeting as she stretched out her right hand, "Jordana Revere," she offered, step-ping toward the smaller man. "You're Roddy Sheffield, I take it. Maisie was just telling me a bit about you."

"All good, I hope," Sheffield responded, taking Jordana's prof-fered hand.

"She says you're willing to help. That's as good as it gets in my book," Jordana told him as she took a step back to lean against a piece of softly humming machinery.

"Happy to," Sheffield assured her. "I can't take another day of these Witen bastards, much less another couple years—which is the best the priest can offer. No, I hope you excuse my presumption, Ms. Revere, but I believe your coming here is a sign for us to take action right now, before it's too late."

"A sign?" Jordana was puzzled by the sudden flash of zealotry extolled by this resistance fighter, and her voice betrayed that fact.

"Roddy is a dreamer with the soul of a poet," Maisie explained. "He still sees purpose in our struggles up here. The man's been preaching of a sign that will unite us all for years now."

"And here you are, come among us," Sheffield said, staring at Jordana with awe in his face and voice.

"I'm just a pilot with the misfortune to experience mechanical malfunctions with her craft due to poor upkeep. It's no more divine than that, sir, I assure you," Jordana told the man while fighting off a smirk at the thought of anyone ever accusing her of being a prophetical herald.

"Well, whatever brings you here, Jor, we still have a job to do," Maisie cut through the awkward tension in the room to say, wearing an apologetic smirk on her face for Jordana's sake. "Did you bring the VLSE suits?" The question was directed at Roddy Sheffield.

It took the man a moment to realize he'd been queried. When he finally did, he dragged his starry-eyed gaze from Jordana to favor Maisie with a puzzled look. "The suits?" he repeated with apparent misunderstanding in his tone. "No, we can't get the suits for another three hours."

"Another thre—" Maisie cut short her indignant outburst and calmed herself with a deep breath. "Whadya mean three hours? I thought you told me you were getting the VLSE suits."

"I did tell you that," Sheffield responded defensively. "I told you I was getting them from the Greenhouse's control room. I can't very well stroll in there during operation hours, now can I? I mean, I can bypass the security terminal quick as you please, and then the suits are just hanging up in an emergency cabinet in the bulkhead across from the security hatch. I can even access the Greenhouse's control room with no problems once we're in there, but not with every damn worker in the place staring at me the whole time I do. Well, I mean... I could still do it even then, but I don't think it would be advisable."

"Oh," Maisie answered, defeated. "Well, that ain't how you made it sound over the comms."

"Well, sorry, I guess. I mean, I think I was pretty clear, but I was definitely trying to keep my replies short and to the point. You know, the way a conversation over comms traffic is supposed to soun—"

"Whatever, it doesn't matter now. Why three hours?" Maisie cut him off to ask. "Main shift ends in two."

"True," Sheffield allowed. "But I thought it prudent to give the place another hour to die down completely. Not to mention the fact that *Footman Sagal* is curious as shit. The guy's got like some kinda sixth sense about ya. He knows something's up. He's freaking out really, asking everybody for your whereabouts, lurking over the shoulders of those of us known to be your good friends. The dude is insufferable."

"I'm sorry about him, but he's still just a confused kid at heart, lashing out," Maisie answered, giving cover to her little brother.

Wait a minute, Jordana thought, *her little brother! He's still... He...* "Your brother is still one of them, like totally with the Witen?" As soon as the words were out, she wished them back.

Despite how graceless the question had been, Maisie chose to answer without any signs of annoyance. "Unfortunately, yes, he is. The bastards are good at what they do. They took him from me and indoctrinated him. They gave him purpose or their own twisted version of such anyhow. They're using him, and he is just too damaged by a traumatic life no little boy should ever have to live to res st. But he ain't lost," she vehemently insisted, "not yet. None of them are. We just got to turn off the propaganda spigot. The well will dry right up after that. And in no time flat, the spell will be broken. Trust me."

Jordana felt Maisie's discomfort and pain and groped for words of consolation or support. Before she found any, Sheffield said, "Your sister was looking for you, too. The little genius devised some kinda one-way radio that can listen in on our encrypted channel. She heard our whole conversation and tracked me down right after and made me promise to make you contact her. She held me hostage," Sheffield added with a laugh. "Told me she would turn over this listening device of hers to the Witen unless I promised to get you to call her. She told me she was headed to the Priest's Clubhouse and expects to hear from you there within the hour. She was certain someone there would have a comm device. Ha huh, you believe that? And I am a man of honor, Mais, so I will force you to make that call," Sheffield finished with another good laugh.

"So it was a girl, then, Alice's child?" Jordana asked.

"Yeah," Maisie drew out the word as she slumped to the floor to find a pleasant seating position. "My sister, my everything. Hell, Jor, it's like Dolly was saying earlier, I still got a lot more story to tell."

"I guess so," Jordana agreed. "Well, it sounds as if we've a few hours before we can do anything more. Am I right?" she asked Roddy Sheffield directly.

"Looks that way," the small, dark-clad man concurred.

"I suppose you want to hear the rest of the tale, then," Maisie suggested in a knowing voice.

"Might as well pass the time somehow," Jordana said with shrugged shoulders as Roddy Sheffield found his own seat against the warm machinery. Maisie grinned as she blew out a resigned breath. Then, just as she had done only a couple hours earlier, she cleared her throat and lurched into some awkward mumbles before finally finding her rhythm.

CHAPTER 7
MIKKELSON

He spotted her in the Module Garage. Maisie had no business anywhere near the place. Nonetheless, he wasn't particularly surprised to see her come strolling through the Garage's gaping archway. *Did I anticipate it?* he asked himself, so serendipitous was the dark-haired girl's timing. Mikkelson had scheduled the monthly inspection, with which he was currently engaged, at the very beginning of the week. But maybe a part of him had known even then that the girl and her resistance pals were gonna have to turn to Nate Novocaine Barker sooner or later. Perhaps his impeccable subconscious logic had known she'd wait until the last day of Schedule 1, just before shift's end to approach the pathetic little rat. His subconscious logic had probably taken a satisfying pleasure two days back, after the Commander and his goons stormed the bastard priest's liquor shop and snatched up Stevie Hyun. Mikkelson's subconscious had probably rejoiced to see a key player in Maisie Sagal's band of morons hauled off down Branch 1. *Locked far away to muffle her screams, no doubt,* Mikkelson thought, grinning.

A part of him must've known then that whatever the morons were hatching was now lacking one probably important cog in the plan. A part of him probably knew that his 1600 ST inspection around the Module Garage with Supervisor Addison would surely find him in prime position to lay eyes on the bratty little bitch's attempt to recruit Novocaine Barker, a module garage maintenance worker, to her scheme. Mikkelson had always known it would be Maisie to come, as well. It was predictable as a single-sided coin. The whole station knew the Commander let the sexy little troublemaker get away with anything. Of course her *supposed* allies in rebellion would send her as their messenger.

So, no, Mikkelson was not surprised to spot her here and now. He was quite pleased instead. He was ecstatic, in fact, bursting with glorious lust, just as he always was whenever he spotted her firm thighs and tiny, swaying hips bustling her about the station. Which was often indeed, if not in his own person, then by video from citizens who spied on the girl for him as a means of working off one or another of the ingenious debts Mikkelson and his acolytes delighted in inventing.

"Shall I go on, Chairman?" Addison's voice cut through his trance-like state.

"No, Addison," Mikkelson told his subordinate supervisor after quickly gathering himself. "That'll be all with that. You do a fine job here. That's clear," he told the pencil-thin pushover with his pathetic blond beard so thin and scraggly that it massively undercut the grandeur and due respect the shimmering golden suitcoat he wore demanded. Mikkelson did not scold the imbecile for his trashy facial-hair, though. Supervisor Addison was as much of a loyal disciple as Supervisor Chairman Mikkelson could boast. He saw no reason to needlessly alienate the man with a blunt assessment of his appearance. "Go back to your office and gather your two footmen and the one I brought along, and station them at every exit in this garage. I want eyes on Nate Barker. Don't take him right away unless this place is all cleared out. I want it kept private. If he leaves here in a crowd, we will tail him. Tell the footmen to keep their tablets close and stay in contact at all times. He could leave through any exit, don't forget. So, a man at each one, and whichever one Novocaine takes, call it out over the comms. We'll work out a way to corral him somewhere quiet or cut him off somehow once we get a better idea of which route he takes. If he hops on a trolley, then I don't care if you're noticed—one of you bastards best jump aboard with him. Throw some fool off if you have to. I don't care. Just do not let the man out of your sights. Understood?"

"Yes, sir," Addison said with a small bow. "I'm on it, sir," he added, turning toward his office.

Mikkelson watched him go a few paces before turning back to watch Maisie speak to Nate Novocaine. It seemed to him the conversation was wrapping up. Maisie was darting glances all around the garage. *Checking to see if anyone is spying, no doubt, no doubt.* Mikkelson laughed to himself as he crouched out of sight behind a docked collector module. When he dared again to peek around the smoke-gray tank-shaped collector, Maisie was indeed wrapping up the confab. She pounded her finger into the man's chest twice before she turned from him and headed toward the archway. Barker had been cowed by the jabs. *That, and the look in the girl's eyes, no doubt.* Maisie Sagal did have a mature command in her eyes that seemed to tame the natural apprehension of anyone she ever met, that obvious apprehension, of course, in conceding wisdom and leadership to a mere child. And Novocaine had plainly been entranced by those commanding hazel eyes. The short, pig-faced cuck stayed stock-still for a good ten-count after Maisie left before he went back to tinkering with the oblong hunk of space-age machinery hanging from a winch chain alongside him.

Mikkelson watched as Barker went about his work as though no one had ever distracted him. Five minutes on, the shift's end buzzer blared out through giant speakers perched high in the rafters of the Module Garage. Barker still had work to finish, though. The handful of other Schedule 1 Shift 1 module maintenance workers were tossing down their smocks and gloves, grabbing up mugs and lunch pouches and heading for the archway. But Novocaine Barker had been distracted by Maisie for five minutes. It had thrown off his end of the day routine, clearly. The small man was darting around his station, frantic as a fleeing mouse, hanging up tools and wrapping up cords. His delayed departure worked out fine as far as Mikkelson was concerned. *Very fine, indeed,* the supervisor chairman thought as he snatched up his pocket tablet. "Are your men in their places, Supervisor?"

"Yes, sir." Addison's voice came back almost immediately. "Two by the archway and one man each on the access hatches."

"Good. Looks as though he's the last one in here. Is that right? Are we all clear here?"

"All clear, sir," Addison confirmed through the comm. "Last trolley is taking off now. A few pedestrians lagging behind, but everyone is headed away from here, for sure."

"Wonderful," Mikkelson said, his anticipation surging. "Move in now, then. No need to be coy."

"Yes, sir," Addison's voice came back, beaming with pleasure.

Barker hadn't made it ten paces toward the neon-green trimmed archway before all three footmen closed in on him, boxing him in to the front and sides. It took the stupid grease monkey a second to realize the three gray-uniformed citizens surrounding him were not about to let him pass through. He nearly stumbled into Mikkelson's own footman, Terry Lukash, but caught a glimpse of his dead eyes at the last instant and pulled up short, nearly tripping over himself to avoid contact with the bald-headed former bodybuilder with a keg for a gut and tattoos pockmarking his pale arms from shoulder to fingers. Mikkelson had headhunted the man for his personal security detail on day one of the Witen's rule. He wasn't about to be left without sufficient muscle to defend himself. Aponyaschefski had his leashed monster hound in Jasper Montrois, so Mikkelson made sure to secure himself an ignorant brute of his own. Lukash was so thankful to Mikkelson for plucking him out of the shit stews of the swine farm that the man had been eager to be his dog. He'd become as much a loyal man as Addison. That was good because Mikkelson needed to control this situation if he was to have any chance to spin it to his own benefit. He needed it kept private. Lukash and Addison's presence were a great assurance in that regard. *I'm sure Addison's pair of footmen are his most trusted underlings as well. How else would they achieve their status?* he thought, laughing.

Mikkelson and Addison stepped up behind Barker to finish boxing in the weak little halfwit. Novocaine twisted around to face him, and Mikkelson felt a powerful pang to snap a picture, the look on the loser's face was so sweet. He knew the jig was already up before a single word had been spoken. Mikkelson could see that truth plain on his face. Nate Novocaine Cainey Barker was on his list of citizens of note for a reason. He knew that it had been Barker that ratted out those poor Star Hawk pilots and got them and poor, pitiful, suffocated Sargent Marge killed, an anecdote that Maisie Sagal and her resistance friends have surely heard but, for the sake of their pathetic hope, they didn't dare believe. Barker was also a foolhardy gambler. Mikkelson had him by the balls on account of those debts alone. He wouldn't even need to play the rat card.

Though Mikkelson knew he most likely would, just for the pure pleasure in humiliating the fool. He truly did have Novocaine by the balls, and they both knew it. Barker had been ducking his men for weeks now, and Mikkelson hadn't been pressing too strongly for a more vigorous attempt from his collectors. He was letting the fruit ripen so when he did finally apply the squeeze, what came pouring out would overfill his glass. Mikkelson knew now that moment had come. He smiled as he placed a bet with himself that he'd know every word Maisie had whispered to the simple mechanic within five minutes. Then he reflected on just how fun power really was.

His smile spread wider still, thinking about how easy it all was for him. Sure, it had definitely been simpler when he was head of the credit system and AOA was still running things, but Mikkelson knew, as he stood before the quivering loser, that he would still climb to the very top in the end. He was a man who could adapt. He prided himself on that virtue. A weaker man would have thrown up his hands in surrender once the Witen took away his currency and charge, but not Mikkelson. He adapted. He saw right away that in a world with no hard currency, *everything* becomes currency: shifts, food, liquor, clothing, theater vouchers, time in the game rooms, and of course, favors. Oh yes, *favors*—that small word that could mean oh so very much indeed.

"You're a gambling man, Novocaine," Mikkelson began suddenly. "What do you think the odds are on me and my friends listening to any excuse you care to offer in defense of your repeated delinquency? High or low, Barker? What kind of odds you give that proposition? Huh? Care to bet against it?" Novocaine simply stared blank-faced back at him. The look enraged Mikkelson, and he put all his mighty weight behind a slap that drove with a loud, wet smack across the little man's cheek. "You owe me a great deal, Nate Novocaine, and I've decided to collect, in full, today."

"I can't give what I don't have," Barker said in his whiny little way. "I know I owe Supervisor Addison some shifts, and I been logging them. You can't say I haven't been."

"That's hardly all you owe me, Novocaine," Mikkelson cut in before the swinish bastard could get going.

"I didn't say it was," Barker defended himself. "I'm just telling ya I'm paying it down as best I can."

"Don't demean yourself like that, Novocaine," Mikkelson told him with thick sarcasm. "After all, you have the power, right now, as we speak, to eliminate your lofty debt with one small act of betrayal." The module maintenance worker knew what was coming next. Mikkelson could read it in the sudden spasm of his skinny shoulders and the instant bulging of his horrified eyes. "I want to hear every sentence of you and Maisie's convo just now. From beginning to end. Not a word omitted," he informed Barker, confirming the man's worst fears. "Every fucking word ... and I'll lift your debt. Or you can refuse, and I'll let Footman Lukash and his companions loose to wring it all from you in the form of bruises, blood, and broken bones," he added, an arm indicating the mean-mugged footmen. "The choice is yours. But make it fast. My patience with you, Nate Novocaine, has worn very, very thin." When Barker still hesitated, Mikkelson went in for the kill. "You're a fucking fool, *Cainey*, you know that? Why would you even bother to contemplate protecting a bunch of people who only came to you as a last resort?" Barker's eyes bulged even wider as he realized just how much Mikkelson already knew. "Yes, ya fool. I know that Maisie was just here representing her doomed resistance friends. I'm not an idiot. And neither is the Steward, by the way. Everyone knows the Sagal girl represents the secret resistance, and that the fools are all planning something big. We all know, too, that whatever their plot may be, it's apparently so monstrously idiotic that AOA and their pack of pet world leaders wouldn't contribute men or support to its ends. Why the hell would you protect such utterly doomed assholes who only came to you at the last hour and as a last resort? They all know, deep down, that the rumors of you ratting out their precious hero, Sargent Marge Hamill, and those poor, brave pilots is true. For the simple expediency of convenience and an abject fear of losing their last hope, they've all decided to pretend they don't believe the rumor about you. But they do, Novocaine. They all believe it, deep down. And deservedly so. Isn't that right, *Cainey?*" Mikkelson asked, embellishing one of the man's seemingly countless nicknames.

Novocaine had no answer.

"Come on, friend," Mikkelson implored as he plopped a flabby arm across the small man's shoulders. "Last chance. Out with it now." Mikkelson had slurped down a can of sardines just before coming to the Module Garage. It made him smile to see Barker's disgusted face as he took in the obvious odor.

"I never committed to her damn plan in the first place. I told her as much just before she left," Barker finally said in his defense. "You gotta tell the Commander as much, you gotta. It's the truth. I swear."

"What is it you failed to commit to?" Mikkelson asked, leaning in ever closer.

"She... They... They need an extra person now that the Commander made off with Stevie Hyun."

I knew it, Mikkelson thought, vindicated.

"Maisie and Stevie are just supposed to create a distraction during their plan, but they need both to pull it off."

"Is that right?"

"Yeah."

"Who were they supposed to be distracting? By what means? At what time? And distracting from what?" Mikkelson removed his arm from Barker's shoulder and stepped back from the broken little asshole as he asked the questions.

Barker's head fell, nearly to the floor, as he sighed a pathetic little sigh. "They are gonna take over the alternate Control Room in the access tunnels behind the Poultry Processing Plant."

"To what end?" Addison spoke up from obvious curiosity.

"They are gonna do it late at night, so most of the Witen will be sleeping somewhere down Branch 1. Maisie is supposed to act as lookout and distractor for Stevie as she sets off an air-leak alarm in the Module Garage."

"Which would send any footmen on the night watch running in the opposite direction of the Poultry Processing Plant, yet not disturb anyone's slumber down Branch 1, seeing as how micrometeor impacts and general wear and tear sets the air-leak alarms off fairly routinely," Mikkelson said, catching on fast.

"Right," his subordinate supervisor agreed. "Protocol for that warning going off during night shift is every available footman responds to the alarm's location immediately to apply sealant to the leak."

"Yeah," Barker hopelessly confirmed.

"I suppose you aren't a terrible replacement for Stevie Hyun," Mikkelson told him. "You do work here in the Module Garage, after all. That's gotta count for something. Maisie did ask you to replace Stevie Hyun in this clever little scheme, right?"

"Yes."

"What are they gonna do once they gain the alternate Control Room?" Addison asked.

"They're gonna close Branch 1's hatchway," Barker answered simply.

"Then what?" Mikkelson prompted.

"I don't know. Make demands in exchange for food and stuff, I guess," Barker answered, his head still hanging with his chin pressed to his scrawny chest.

"How do they plan to take over the alternate Control Room exactly?" Addison asked with scornful doubt. "They have at least two footmen outside of both of those rooms, day and night."

Barker shrugged. "The resistance guys got like six of them for the attack. The alternate Control Room behind the Poultry Plant is set in a corner where two perpendicular access tunnels meet. They figure they can sneak down one of them completely out of sight before the footmen even know they're there. They've gathered some bats and clubs and stuff of their own, and then it will just be a simple six-on-two since every other footman on duty will be headed the other way. It ought to be easy enough, especially 'cause they ain't using comms either, so the Witen's tech guys can't be tipped off. The attack squad is just gonna be waiting for the alarm to go off as their final go-ahead."

"When do they plan to implement this little coup of theirs?" Mikkelson asked.

"Tomorrow night," the module maintenance worker responded in a barely audible voice.

"Okay, Novocaine," Mikkelson said, after a pause. "You and I are going to take this to the Commander and the Steward, and I'll tell them how you never committed to any of it and were instead planning to rat them out the whole time. I'll swear to that, and you'll be spared any punishment. But ... you will omit Maisie's involvement. You will say that this *resistance* asked you alone to set off the alarm. You will do and say all of this because you owe me as much, but also because, being the pathetic little pussy you are, you are terrified of getting your ass beat by Footman Lukash and his two friends. Is all of this understood, Novocaine?"

Barker lifted his chin from his chest just enough to nod acknowledgment.

"We have a deal, then?"

"Yes." Barker's voice was soft and cracked.

"Good," Mikkelson stated with glee. "Supervisor Addison," he called to his subordinate with a grin in his voice, "you trust these two men?"

Addison turned to his two footmen. Neither hesitated for a moment, each nodding in turn to the scraggly supervisor. Addison turned back to Mikkelson, wearing a grin he was sure matched his own. "We are your men, sir. We keep your secrets, Chairman."

"Very good," Mikkelson said as he began a slow waddle toward the garage's archway. He felt his men fall in line behind him right away, only Barker hesitated. But just before Mikkelson was forced to turn and glare at the stupid loser, he heard the light pitter patter of his footfalls trailing obediently behind them.

"When? Did you say? When are they planning this treason?" the Steward asked in a cold voice from his lazy lean against the side of the Commander's mahogany desk.

"Tomorrow night, sir," Mikkelson answered him, making sure to spice each word with the sycophantic groveling the Witen's top two men both enjoyed so well, only, when it came to the Steward, or Harclay Aponyaschefski, as he was really called, the sarcasm behind Mikkelson's groveling always seemed to make itself much more obvious.

"You were right to bring this to your supervisor, Novocaine." The Commander spoke for the first time since Mikkelson, Addison, and

Barker had been escorted into the Commander's executive office. "And you were right to then bring it straight to us, Chairman," he added, shifting his gaze to Mikkelson.

"Of course, Commander, sir," Mikkelson said, averting his eyes. "I am as committed to our great Witen and the New Destiny Constitution as any one of you." Mikkelson lifted his head with that and let his gaze fall first on the seated Commander and then on the Steward and Captain Alvarez in turn, standing on either side of the massive and desolate desk. "I wish to demonstrate that commitment to you now, in fact."

"Oh do you now?" Captain Alvarez asked with his customary casual sarcasm.

"As soon as Addison came to me with Barker and I learned the truth of this supposed resistance's plans, I knew two things: that I was going to bring it to you straight away, and that I could provide a silver lining to this betrayal these ungrateful assholes have planned."

"A silver lining?" the Commander asked in a slow growl.

"Yes, Commander, sir," Mikkelson assured him. "Well, perhaps nothing will make swallowing their betrayal any easier, but I believe now that we know their plans and have the upper hand, we can at least snatch them all up with little to no struggle. If we take all the conspirators in the act of rebellion, then we can try them before the entire population, and no one could question their guilt, nor our right—I mean *your* right, Commander," he quickly corrected himself. "No one could question *your* right to serve them their just punishment. Such a display will also serve to quell any further rebellions right then and there, surely."

"Perhaps," the Commander growled after a moment.

"And I've devised the perfect plan to thwart them, Commander," Mikkelson affirmed. "You see, all we need do is hide a couple dozen footmen, say in the access tunnel the alternate Control Room is actually set in to, the tunnel hidden from the one the resistance fools plan to sneak their way down. Which they will do as soon as we set off the air-leak alarm. They don't dare use their tablets for fear of us spying on them and giving the plan away. So the idiots will just stroll their way right into a trap once they see the alarms go off. Addison and his men know the Module Garage better than anyone, so I'll go with them to ensure that task is carried out correctly. We'll figure out which specific air-leak alarm is best to set off and how. I leave the ambush details to your infinite wisdom and experience, Commander, sir." Mikkelson paused there to accept the slow, gracious head bow the Commander offered after that unctuous compliment. "I suggest we keep our knowledge of their plans as quiet as possible, though. We don't want to give the game away. I can help you with the logistics, Steward, sir," Mikkelson said, swinging his bulk to face Aponyaschefski, "if you can't figure out how to get that many footmen in that access tunnel late at night without alerting the residents."

"Thank you, Chairman," Schef responded in a shrill voice. "But no, I don't believe your *expertise* will be required. I've got everything well under control."

"Oh, yes, Steward, sir. Of course you do," Mikkelson said, darting an overt glance in Barker's direction.

Aponyaschefski was a pompous buffoon who'd gotten lucky befriending a capable psychopath. Mikkelson had smelled it all over the man the instant he met him. His petulant look and stammering splutters were merely further proof. "W-we... We will contact you all when our plans are finalized, Chairman," the former small-town lawyer finally managed to say.

Alvarez stepped around the desk to face Mikkelson, Addison, and Barker an instant later, corralling them toward the office's black double-doors. "Barker," the Commander suddenly called out just as the thin-waisted, full-breasted, dark-skinned footman standing sentry beside the doors moved to open them, "you're gonna stay with us until this is over. While I am grateful you brought this plot to our attention, I still remember your failings and cowardice. I still remember how you got my friends killed. I don't trust you. So, come on, sit yourself down, and have a drink," the Commander offered the invitation in a sinister growl, belying the welcome offer. The big, bearded brute reached into a drawer beside his right leg and came out with a three-quarters full bottle of the priest's moonshine. "Supervisor Addison," the gorilla hulking menacingly behind the pristine and austere desk then suddenly barked at Mikkelson's ally.

"Yes, Commander, sir?" Addison managed in a squeaky voice.

"Cover for Novocaine as best you can. We wouldn't want his resistance friends to find out he's a rat. They may not trust him the next time around," he added with a strange chuckle. "Oh, and Supervisor, from now on, you will make a weekly report about your sector to the Steward and me directly, in this very office. Is that okay? Or do you have some problem with that?"

"No, sir, of course not," Addison said, steadfastly not looking Mikkelson's way. "I'll have a report for you by week's end, Commander, sir."

"Good, Addison," the Commander said in his rumbling growl as his eyes locked with Mikkelson's. "See that you do. Now, off with you," he added with a flick of the wrist.

"Keep your tablets close, gentleman," Aponyaschefski called to them as Mikkelson and Addison stepped through the now open door. "And stay in your quarters until you hear from us."

Infection Event: Day 354

Novocaine was supposed to meet up with Maisie in a little alcove off of Branch 6's lengthy and expansive alleyway just beyond the Solar Power Generator at midnight Station Time. Mikkelson had gotten that detail from Barker as they waited in the Commander's comfortable lobby outside his executive office last night. The bastards had kept them out there for a good hour. Mikkelson figured it was just to show they could. He hadn't let it bother him. He'd expected no less. And the room really was comfortable with a fat, cushy couch and three pillow-soft armchairs, not to mention the tasty little servant of the Witen bustling her sexy ass around the room with pitchers of coffee and trays of snacks at his pleasure. He was content to lounge around in that massive lobby for another few hours.

He had spent the time there, between snacks and imagined desires, planning his next step, plotting out each word of his appeal and every specific detail of the story to either include or omit. It was in that time that he realized he'd never asked Barker where and when he was to meet up with Maisie Sagal. Barker had named the location as soon as he'd asked, and Mikkelson had instantly known there had been no deception behind Novocaine's answer. It was a perfect meeting spot. A dark alcove just outside the Module Garage's archway from where they could gather themselves and scope the scene. Once there, they'd have plenty of time and opportunity to spot any complications and decide whether or not to go through with their plan.

Mikkelson would've gladly set his trap right in that out-of-the-way little cranny of Cardinal's Nest's immensity. It would've been a lot easier, in fact, to do it right there rather than where he and Lukash currently waited for his prize. But for some reason, the Commander cared whether or not Novocaine's cover was kept intact. So Mikkelson couldn't risk the girl spotting Barker alongside him, not to mention seeing Addison and his two pet footmen in the Module Garage waiting to do her and Barker's task for them. True, once he had her, she'd never be seen again, but he couldn't be sure she would truly come alone, or one of a hundred other unpredictable problems wouldn't arise. So Mikkelson was playing it safe and setting his ambush on the girl for just inside Branch 6's giant archway. Mikkelson would get his people to inform Barker that if anyone involved with the resistance who survived this day's events came asking what happened to Maisie and why he set off the alarm without her, he was to say that he was there waiting for Maisie in the alcove beyond the Solar Power Generator right up until the last minute, and when she didn't show up, he figured she chickened out, and he knew he could complete his task without her. Barker could even claim *he* was the aggrieved one to anybody who came to him demanding answers. He could say he took initiative and should be praised not vilified. Barker would probably be saying something similar without Mikkelson's insistence anyway, being the cowardly little lying bastard he was, but Mikkelson would still have his people make Cainey Barker see the wisdom in never straying from the *official story*. He figured the location of his planned abduction should serve to give Novocaine Barker a plausible enough defense on its own of his innocence in the Witen's infiltration of the sorry little resistance's grand scheme, but the cover story would serve as backstop.

Never a bad idea to cover your ass, no doubt, no doubt, Mikkelson reminded himself. *Especially not when you're a few minutes from enjoying your special treat.* After tonight, Chairman Mikkelson would have managed to feed the clawing hunger within him, that relentless lust that tickled at his reason and sanity day and night. And after tonight, he would have climbed another rung in the Witen's ladder. He would let nothing within his power and control risk the high both of those great aims promised to deliver. The doubts and anxieties that plagued this afternoon and much of the evening seemed to make the promise of those great twin treats all the sweeter still.

His hopes had prevailed in the end, and Alice Stark's sudden labor hadn't been able to destroy all his hard-won plans after all. It was the Steward—*Aponyaschefski*—who was behind the push to piss on Mikkelson's hopes. He had been certain that Alice Stark herself had to be a part of the resistance's plans. Never mind her late-term pregnancy or the fact that Novocaine Barker had named all six of the residents in the resistance's attack squad and Alice Stark had been conspicuously absent, the imbecilic ex-lawyer was still certain she had to be a key cog in their schemes, and they would have to abandon their plans now that she was otherwise occupied in Newton Hospital. But thankfully, the man wasn't fool enough to go against the truth of his own eyes. Once a footman with a hidden camera lurking in the dark shadows of the Grand Rotunda used his device to capture in frame all six attack squad members sneaking their way from Branch 4 across to Branch 3 and the access tunnels behind the Poultry Processing Plant beyond, Aponyaschefski couldn't deny the resistance was indeed going through with their plans.

That sweet confirmation had come over the comms only minutes ago. It had sent Mikkelson's heart fluttering. A blush even crept up his cheeks. He was giddy. He'd never been giddy before, but he knew there was no other adjective to describe his current state. And then the sultry little minx stepped into a bar of light as she passed through Branch 6's purple-striped archway. His heart became in danger of bursting from his chest faster than he would've believed possible. He was in real danger of giving the game away. They needed the girl to take a few more steps into the alleyway before they could be sure to spring out on her and cut off her escape route. If she was alerted by the thunder currently rumbling inside his chest before then, he'd lose the treat he so very desperately needed. Mikkelson reached out to Lukash beside him, gripping the man's forearm. Lukash gazed down at him, but Mikkelson simply looked away and drew in a deep breath as quietly as he could. And somehow, he'd done it. He'd calmed himself. Well, enough to remain unnoticed by the girl anyway.

When she finally did hear and see the two large men jumping from a shadowed corner of the long alleyway, one in a gold suitcoat with black stitching stretched tight across a bulbous frame and the other with basketball's for arms and a thick chest threatening to burst the seams of his finely golden-stitched gray tactical blouse and pants, it was far too late. Lukash was behind her instantly. Mikkelson's bulk quickly cut off any possible path forward. They had her within seconds. Mikkelson clamped a hand over her mouth, stifling her first scream in its infancy. Then he helped to hold her still as Lukash went to work with the duct tape. She was incapacitated and slung over the big man's shoulder a moment later, just as Mikkelson withdrew his tablet and dialed the comm to the private channel he'd established with Addison and his men earlier that day. "Okay, boys, you there?" he asked the tablet in a hush.

Addison's voice came back quickly in the same quiet tenor. "Here, sir. Good to go."

"Okay, okay. I'll switch back to the main channel then to check-in and tell them we're good to go. Standby to hear the go-ahead to set off the alarm," Mikkelson told the supervisor.

"Okay, Chairman. I'll switch over now."

Mikkelson and Lukash locked eyes as he dialed the main channel back on his tablet's comms app. A simultaneous chuckle burst through both men's lips as they glanced around them, not really daring to believe how very easy it all was. "Alarm team ready, Commander. Over," he said into the comms in a serious voice that failed to wipe the smile from his face.

"Roger, alarm team," the Commander's growl came back over the comms. "We are green to green on this end. Set off the alarm now. Out."

"What do you want with me, you sick bastard?!" the girl shouted at him as soon as he peeled back the duct tape across her mouth.

"I think you already have a pretty good idea," Mikkelson answered her, licking his lips. The fear and revulsion that spasmed from every inch of her sexy body was gobbled up by his lust as a sort of delicious appetizer, for he couldn't quite claim his long-anticipated dessert quite yet. Mikkelson still had to report back to the Commander's executive office and supply his mission report. Montrois and Aponyaschefski would probably already be wondering what had him so delayed. They might even wonder why Mikkelson went back to his own quarters before first coming before the Commander's mahogany desk, that is if anyone spotted him leaving his apartments. But Mikkelson knew he could just make up some excuse about needing the bathroom or something, a comment he was sure would quickly still any further inquiry.

It had turned out to be a close call for Mikkelson and Lukash as they made it from Branch 6 with the girl all the way back to his luxury quarters in Branch 1. The Commander and his ambush team had announced over the comms that they were marching back to the Witen's stronghold with six resistance prisoners in tow within a minute of his, Lukash's, and the Sagal girl's safe and unseen arrival at his luxurious apartments off the Grand Alleyway. The night's events had unfolded a deal faster than Mikkelson had foreseen, and so a few moments of anticipatory gawking at Maisie Sagal, helpless and strapped down tight to a kitchen chair in his private living quarters' dining room, was all he could afford to spoil himself with at the moment. But he'd be back soon enough. And then countless hours of fun with the young teen would be in his direct future.

Mikkelson turned from his frightened prey and stepped up close to Lukash staring fixedly at the girl from the corner of the vast and spartan rectangular room. "I better go make my report. Do not open the hatch for anyone other than Addison or myself," he told the man with a finger aimed at his face.

"Yes, sir, Chairman, sir," Lukash managed after struggling to drag his gaze from the forsaken teen.

"You keep a good eye on her, Footman," Mikkelson told him as soon as he had the tall blockhead's full attention. "She's a shifty one, I hear."

"She'll be here waiting for ya when ya get back, boss," Lukash promised.

"You make sure she stays unspoiled while I'm gone, as well. You hear me?" Mikkelson demanded, poking a fat finger into the big man's chest. "Don't you dare touch her. Not before I've had my fun." Mikkelson withdrew his finger from Lukash's chest. He shot a hungry smile Maisie's way as he tapped a few comforting taps against the cheek of his head of security. "Rest assured, though, Footman, you'll get the scraps to do with as you please," he told the man while never breaking eye contact with his new slave.

"Thank you, Chairman," Lukash answered with a wide, thirsty grin.

Mikkelson turned from them without a word, striding toward his hatchway with a gleeful lightness of foot.

CHAPTER 8
ELIAS

The sterile, antiseptic aroma of Newton Hospital lay heavy in his nostrils every step from its red-and-white striped archway to where he now lingered just outside the double-doors of the neonatal ward. Elias Sagal hated the stink. It reminded him of a man he did not wish to think about just then, of times best forgotten. Such memories could only weaken his resolve now, and he would need every ounce of it to face Maisie... *And her traitor roommate.* Elias was furious with them for being so blind. *Why can't they open their eyes to the Witenagemot's responsibility?* He shook his head, releasing the tension threatening to manifest itself in other, more lamentable ways. *They are so dang lucky the baby came last night,* he told himself, and not for the first time. The serendipitous timing of the illegitimate child's arrival was a definite good break. Elias was truly grateful to whichever diviner of destinies was responsible for the lucky turn.

The thankful thought calmed his breath. At length, he reached for the handle of the whitewashed door. Just beyond the double-door's threshold, an unmanned nurse's station loomed on the left. Across the hall, a square room, roughly 20 feet by 20 feet, was sparsely dotted with a few uncomfortable-looking yellow padded chairs, all of them unoccupied. Beyond the desk and waiting room, the wide hallway dissected a pink-trimmed, white-walled corridor about ten yards long. On either side of the hallway, two doors led into one of four birthing suites, or so Elias presumed. There seemed to be light seeping from the small window of only one of the suites though, the nearest suite on the left. With no one to tell him not to, Elias marched toward it and, with a steady resolve, didn't hesitate to shove the door open as soon as he arrived.

Alice Stark rested on the harshly lit suite's lone hospital bed, positioned forward so that she was nearly sitting straight up. Her arms were empty. Elias was glad to see it. He presumed the baby was asleep in the clear plastic bassinet stationed beside Alice's bed, but he darted his eyes away before confirming it. Instead, he inspected every other nook and cranny of the birthing suite. Its white-tiled floor and unornamented walls were clean and basic. The bed was surrounded by the usual equipment one sees in hospital rooms. A small sink and cupboard were tucked away in the corner opposite the door. The only abnormality of any kind Elias's critically trained mind picked out was the lack of a warm bottom seated atop the room's lone visitor's chair. *Where the heck is she?*

Elias was certain he'd find Maisie resting beside the Stark woman. She hadn't been at her quarters or any of the handful of other spots he'd made a cursory search for her. Yet the hygienic chamber revealed no sign of his big sister, not even a coat or a sweater or a purse or a bag or something slung over the chair to show that someone had come and then only stepped away for a moment. *Where the heck is she?* His sister had to be with Alice. It was the only place left that made any sense. The pair seemed to look out for each other. Elias guessed they were friends as well as roommates. *As well as family*, he thought before quickly getting angry and shaking off the unwelcome notion. He had no wish to show his weak, fretting worry to the woman who claimed to be his father's lover. He would show her only the implacable determination the Witenagemot's Integration Program had instilled in him.

In keeping with such training, he waited for the disheveled woman with her greasy mop of chestnut curls to be the first to speak. "Hello, Elias," she managed after a time.

"Alice," he said by way of greeting.

"Have you come to see the baby?" she asked, her arm reaching for the lip of the plastic bassinet.

Elias would not allow his gaze to follow the movement. He kept his eyes locked firm on the bedridden traitor. "No," he told her. The woman treated him with a wounded look, but Elias didn't let it affect him. "I'm guessing you've heard by now about the resistance plot and how the Commander was able to easily stop it, thank god."

"Yes, I've heard," Alice managed in a tired voice.

"It's a good thing your baby came early, then, eh? For you and Maisie both."

The stout woman in the blue hospital gown looked back at him with an odd curiosity in her eyes that Elias couldn't immediately recognize. "What are you talking about?" she asked him in the same tired voice as before.

"Well, you see, I was kinda afraid when I first heard about the attempted raid on the alternate Control Room that I'd find out that you and Maisie were involved in the idiotic treason. I know all these resistance losers are friends with you guys. But then I overheard that you had gone into labor yesterday. And after I hadn't seen your names among the traitors who were captured in the raid—a raid where your jerk buddies were planning to kill two Footmen of the Witenagemot, to murder two of the last five hundred people left in the universe, by the way, when I heard you two weren't one of 'em and had instead gone into labor, I thanked God for the good luck, 'cause as much as you and your friends have been telling Maisie otherwise, I still care about her and don't want to see her hurt."

"I was never part of the plan, Eli," Alice said with a sigh. "I was hoping you'd come to see your new sister, not to make sure Maisie and I weren't trying to overthrow your evil masters."

Elias patently avoided glancing in the baby's direction, even when Alice began to rock the bassinet back and forth on its rollers. With an effort, he found words to shout back at the adulterer. "Just 'cause my dad believed he knew better than the Steward and the Commander don't make it so. My dad blinded himself to our new reality, Alice."

"Oh, Eli," the woman began with another annoying sigh, "please spare me Aponyaschefski's bullshit rhetoric. I'm too exhausted to even work up the strength to properly scoff at the hypocrisy." Elias was snarling, searching for a worthy retort, when Alice's eyes suddenly shot up. She sat bolt upright on the mechanical bed and reached out to snatch his right hand. "Wait," she cried, squeezing the appendage ever harder as she continued, "did you say your sister's name wasn't among those captured?"

"Yeah," he answered as he ripped free from her clutches. "Where the heck is she exactly? I checked your quarters and the cafeteria halls, but no one I asked has seen her. I figured to f nd her here with you."

"You're sure she wasn't captured by the Witen? You're sure her name wasn't on that list?" Alice demanded.

"Yes, I'm sure. Quit messing around now. Where is she?!"

"Something is wrong, Eli. You gotta listen to me," she pleaded, locking eyes with him for the first time. "Your sister *was* a part of the plan."

"What? What are you saying?"

"I've been laying here worried sick that your Commander's mercy when it came to her would finally reach its limits with this new transgression. I doubt he'd ever turn his axe on her, but I thought at the very least she could be locked up away from me. I've been jumping from bliss for my new child, your new sister, one minute, to shuddering worry for Maisie's fate in the next, as well as that of our friends."

"What the heck are you talking about?" Elias demanded, thrown only a bit by Alice's clear distress.

"She went to help set off the air-leak alarm in the Module Garage."

"Oh, you gotta be kidding me. I freakin' knew it! How could you let her do that? You freakin' idiot!"

"She did only what she knew to be right," Alice argued in her and Maisie's defense. "Never mind the why now, Eli. We have a big problem here, kid."

"How so?"

"You were right to come here looking. Your sister would indeed be here if she weren't captured. The only thing that would keep her away is if she were detained in some way. And it seems that your Witen friends knew all about the resistance raid, which implies they knew about Maisie's role in it. And if that's true, then they must've snatched her up with the other plotters. But if they did, why wasn't her name included on this list of the traitors you say you've seen? There could be no good reasons for your sister's omission from that list, Eli. Don't you see that, kiddo? Maisie is in trouble."

"You're just against the Witenagemot for what the Commander had to do to my dad. You can only see them as the bad guy in everything," Elias told the liar in the bed before him. "What reason could the Commander possibly have to keep her name off the list?"

"I don't wish to guess, Eli," Alice said, "but if I had to, I'd say the odds are it's for a reason similar to the one he took Stevie Hyun away for."

"No," Elias breathed reflexively. Alice Stark was surely imagining things. She had to be. *Right? Yes, of course.* Maisie had probably just gotten away clean and was laying low somewhere. The Commander was an honorable man. Stevie Hyun had come to his side willingly. She wanted to be his comfort. Everyone in the Witenagemot was well aware of that.

"Go to them, Eli," Alice implored. "Demand they give up your sister, for your father's sake … and for Carrie Roxanna Sagal," she added, her hand moving once more to the plastic bassinet.

The name stopped the world. His breath grew heavy. A flush washed over every last inch of his body. Before him swam the kind, soft-eyed, freckled-face of Carrie Montrois, along with that of her giggly, sweet, pug-nosed daughter Roxanna. The child had been named after his life's great hero. The woman at the heart of all his motivations. He couldn't stop himself from looking at the baby now. Elias stepped closer to the bed, gaining an angle to look down at… *My sister.* He saw Alice's likeness plain in the tiny face before him, though the facial features Maisie had inherited from Perry Sagal were painfully recognizable in the baby's small and delicate profile as well. Fast asleep as she was, he could not tell if her eyes were as dark as her thin fluff of hair. She had skinny little fingers and toes at the ends of long, slim limbs, currently splayed in a fashion Elias thought looked cramped and awkward.

He was just about to move to the crib and adjust the child into a more comfortable position when Alice's voice stopped him dead. "They tell me she's got cerebral palsy," she stated in an indecipherable tone. "She might need a wheelchair to get around her whole life … or perhaps not. They can't know for sure yet, they say. She's so beautiful, though, isn't she?"

Elias nodded his slow agreement. "Yes, an angel," he confirmed with a tear in his eye.

"Please, find your sister, Eli," Alice begged, once more squeezing his hand. "Go to them. Find Maisie."

Wiping away his weakness with a shirtsleeve, Elias gave his word. "I'll get to the bottom of what happened to her. I promise."

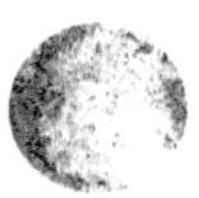

His mind was racing a mile a minute, and he had no clear memory of leaving Alice's birthing suite or even Newton Hospital itself, really. Elias's feet had simply carried him toward the Commander's executive office of their own volition. He had no idea what he was to say or even how to secure entry into the office at all. The Commander kept a footman at his double-doors, day and night. He couldn't think straight to plot or plan. Doubt was swirling about his head, mingling freely for the first time in months with logic and honor. *There is no way he took her,* he'd think one second before a flash of Carrie Roxanna Sagal's tiny, helpless image would spark in his mind, followed inevitably by a flash of her namesake pleading successfully with the security officer at the foot of the mobile staircase leading into the belly of that fateful E-11 Transport Cruiser, and he'd doubt all over again. He had to get to the truth. He had to get into the office and confront the Commander. Elias knew he risked everything with such an act, even his own life, but his legs would not stop pumping. They were carrying him inexorably down the Grand Alleyway straight toward the executive wing. He had to know. He had to rescue Maisie if she was in trouble, for Carrie Montrois, for her sacrifice.

The first thing to catch his attention on his current journey, outside of his confusion and inner tumult and fear, was Supervisor Chairman Mikkelson. Elias turned his head in time to spot the grossly fat man standing outside his quarters, punching his door code into his hatchway keypad. The Chairman's head was turned his way as he lazily tapped his code. There was a look in the man's eyes that broke through Elias's head fog. He had never particularly liked Chairman Mikkelson, despite him being a high-ranking member of the Witenagemot. He knew he owed him respect and deference because of it. But what came natural and felt right to give to the other council members was an effort for Elias to offer up to the swollen Labor Supervisor. He tried to bury the feelings, knowing they were wrong and even treasonous, but it was nevertheless a great effort for him. He, of course, knew the Steward did not at all like the fat man either, which went a long way in alleviating the guilt he felt by his disgust for the Supervisor Chairman. Even so, Elias knew he had no right to stare him down. He quickly darted his gaze back to the white-tiled path before him, though the strange and unsettling look on Mikkelson's face stayed with him for a good few steps.

It hadn't been completely wiped from his mind's eye until he arrived at the shimmering golden archway leading into Branch 1's executive wing. All his prior fears and uncertainties returned with a vengeance, though he only hesitated at the threshold for a single breath. *I gotta do this,* he told himself as he marched toward the Commander's office at the back of the wide complex. Elias was surprised to find the expansive lobby outside the office empty. The footman usually stationed just beside the glossy black double-doors was nowhere to be seen. The lobby door swung shut behind him, stopping a shout of "Hello, anybody here?" from bursting free from his lips while simultaneously pushing him across the lavish space with its wood-paneled walls and black marble floors toward the over-size ebony doors in the corner of the rectangular chamber.

He raised a shaking hand to knock on the intimidating entryway but again stopped just short of announcing his presence. This time, it was the muffled voices on the other side of the double-doors that caused the hesitation. Elias stood frozen in place. A war raged in his mind between his loyalty to the Witen, to his duty to humanity, and the doubts he'd built a wall to hold back but were now loose and unre-strained. He remembered his pride in winning the Challenge Contest and the conviction he'd come to that day to trust his training, to trust the Steward and the other Witenagemot Councilmembers, and lean into his anger and bury his softhearted emotions, but the memory was followed by his first day on the Steward's security detail and how the man he'd come to revere so greatly had sided against Clara

Christie, a girl he'd warmed to during the first weeks of the Integration Program. She'd ended up not having what it took to be a member of the Witen, but Elias respected her attempts. She had at least tried to do her part, but it just hadn't been in the cards for her. Plus, she'd looked awfully cute while trying and had been nothing but sweet and kind to Elias, despite his natural shyness, which was a real rarity among his fellow Program Initiates. Still, he had understood she was out of his league, and anyway, most of his love-crushing energy was spent up on his dear friend Tessa Rodriguez, but regardless, he'd grown quite fond of her in a short time. He had felt deep anguish for her situation, for the claims she laid on that Third Day … or had *attempted* to lay. He had been left dumbfounded when the Steward had allowed her supervisor to pay her off for mistreating her. The war between these two mutually exclusive positions rampaged on in his mind as the voices inside the office grew a little louder, a little clearer.

Elias leaned in closer. "…that goddamn priest," the Commander was saying.

"No one's seen him, sir." That was the Steward now.

"Well, Footman, what say you?" the Commander asked.

The voice that responded was familiar to him. He recognized it within the first few words as belonging to Footman Childress, the exact footman Elias had expected to find standing guard inside the lobby. He knew full well the duty rotations of most every footman and servant of the Witen by now. It had always been his experience whenever he escorted the Steward to the Commander's office around this time of day to find the dark, slim, menacing woman standing straight-backed beside the big black doors. He was wondering just what had the door guard guarding the wrong side of the door when her shrill voice answered the unasked question, "… and no new rumors at all, Commander, sir. I asked around on my down shift, like you asked me to, went to just about everybody, and nearly every last footman and servant seems to agree that the old fraud hasn't left his quarters once since receiving his punishment."

"You're sure?" the Commander's door-muffled voice demanded.

"Yes, sir, Commander, sir," Childress assured him.

"Just as I was saying, Commander." The Steward's voice was fainter than the others and less agitated. Elias leaned in even closer, straining to hear. "The man hasn't left his place once, and no one's been in to see him. He's crushed. Whatever power or influence he might have had is a thing of the past. No one would dare ally themselves with him. Not after the way you dealt with him, sir."

"You think I was too rough, Steward?" The Commander's affronted growl was plain even through the thick door.

"Not at all, Commander," the Steward answered in the same low, bored tones as before. "I only wish I'd hung around to grab up a few bottles of his stuff for myself. As it is now, I'm stuck bartering the shit off those lucky freakin' footman on that punishment team like every other sucker up here," he ended with a barely heard laugh.

Elias registered the Commander's corresponding chuckle as his hand moved, without any clear or remembered choice of his own, toward the glossy black door's shiny black metal handle. And then the next thing he knew, he was pushing the door open and stepping through. All heads turned his way. There were four in total: the Commander, the Steward, Footman Childress, and Stevie Hyun. Childress stood at attention in front of the mahogany mega desk. The Commander sat leaning forward in the leather chair behind the empty workspace. The Steward lurked behind his superior's right shoulder, sipping red wine from a glass tumbler. And Stevie Hyun... Well, Mrs. Hyun was apart from the others. Not just her position in the room, which was slouched forward in one of the office's two red-brown leather armchairs, leaning over the low coffee table in front of her to reach for a half-empty bottle of what Elias recognized as the priest's moonshine, she was also apart in state of mind. She appeared strung out and tired while the Witen members sharing the room with her were alert and invested. Stevie Hyun looked a million miles away. Filling the glass tumbler in her right hand with the moonshine bottle in her left, the motion was her only connection with the physical realm. Elias saw into her eyes as he stepped past her. There was no one behind them. Stevie Hyun, for all intents and purposes, was not here.

However, Footman Childress most definitely was. The wiry guardswoman was on him in two long strides. "The hell do you think you're doing, Initiate?!" she was screaming at him as her callused palm slapped firm against his breastbone.

"Elias? What... Wha-wh—" the Steward managed, licking up the wine he spilt over his fingers during his initial shock to see his hand-picked security detail intern striding boldly into the supreme ruler of the human race's swanky personal office. "What is it, Initiate? Is there a problem? Why wasn't I contacted? My goddamn pocket tablet isn't switched off again, is it?" he asked, reaching for the device in his blouse's right breast pocket.

"Yes, Steward, sir, I have a problem," Elias calmly said, despite the opposition from the strong woman shoving him toward the double-doors with a stiff arm to the chest along with his massive guilt for not trusting this man with whom he owed so much, indeed, these *men* to whom he owed oh so very much.

"You bring your problems to your first-line supervisor, and I'm damn sure that ain't the freakin' Commander!" Footman Childress scolded him. "You know that. What the hell's the matter with you, Initiate? Just what in the hell were you thinking, barging in here like this?"

"What problem, Eli?" the Steward asked, setting his drink down on the red-brown lacquered desktop. "Let him speak, Footman," he called to the dark, thin woman corralling Elias toward the exit. "What's wrong? Was no one else in the lobby? Where the hell is the damn servant? Didn't you tell the girl you were stepping in to give the Commander your report, Footman Childress?"

"No, sir," Childress answered, taking her hand off Elias's chest and turning back toward the massive mahogany desk across the room. "There wasn't any servant in the lobby when the Commander summoned me in, Steward, sir. I mean... I would've told the servant and all ... only, I didn't think it uhh ... uhhmm ... honorable to ... tc ... to keep the Commander waiting and all. You know, his time is precious and ... well ... well, I just came in. Chairman Mikkelson had gone, and I didn't see anybody about or nothin—"

"Relax, Childress," the Commander's voice rumbled through the room like distant thunder on a hot August night. "You made the right call. Now, young Sagal," the gorilla in the brown leather desk chair called, shifting his focus to Elias, "let's see if *you* made the right call as well. Tell us the reason you burst into my private chambers, and I'll judge whether it be sufficient enough cause to merit this unorthodox action."

"Where is my sister?" The question just popped out. Elias couldn't decide if he'd actually said it or if it had merely been a trick of his roiling mind. The looks on their faces quickly confirmed that, yes, he had indeed asked the question. He'd done it. There was no taking it back now. So, Elias leaned in. "Did you take her? What have you done with her? Why was her name not on the list of those captured in the failed raid?"

"Initiate Sagal... Eli, what the hell are you talking about?" The Steward sounded confused and even a little wounded. Elias hadn't been expecting that. A sob of remorse nearly broke through the fiery anger that was currently driving the bus of his cognition, allowing the Steward time to shake his head and try again. "What's this about your sister, now? She's missing? Where have you looked?"

"And why assume that we have her?" the Commander added in a discontented growl.

"I was just with Alice Stark. I thought to find Maisie there. I had looked most everywhere else," Elias kept his gaze aimed at the Steward as he spoke but could feel the menace pouring off the Commander actively fraying his already threadbare courage.

"How's the baby?" The question sucked all the air out of the room in a flash. It came in a soft, slightly slurred tenor, and though Elias was sure Stevie Hyun had been too far gone, in more ways than one, to interject with any coherence, the gentle inquiry could have come from no other person in the room.

Into the fresh silence in the plush office, Elias gave his weary answer. "Not good. Well, good... I mean... Well... The baby's got cerebral palsy, Alice says. But otherwise healthy ... I think. I—"

"You were speaking to the Commander, Initiate!" Childress cut him off, slamming her closed fist into his chest this time. "Never you mind about some traitor's whore and her bastard child. How dare you show this much disrespect in this room and in the presence of our two great titled officers no less. What the hell, Initiate?" she wondered with another fist to the sternum. "I was hearing good things about you from Footman Dollingford and her crew. This display will break their hearts with shame."

"Continue, Initiate," the Steward prompted in a flat, indecipherable tone.

Elias was sweating now, the anger and beliefs that had driven him here becoming harder and harder to cling to. He felt his resolve cracking. *Oh, God, what have I done? What am I doing here?* But he'd come too far to turn back now. He was in way too deep. No way could he slink back out through the ebony doors and pretend all this had never happened. The Commander had demanded his reasons. And the Steward, his usual advocate and ally, was clearly losing patience with him as well. So he forgot about the small drunken woman in the armchair and her split and swollen lip and the purple-and-yellow tinged dark half-circle below her left eye. He breathed out, straightened his spine, lifted his chin, and told them. "Right, well... Well, like I said, I went to see Alice Stark in the neonatal wing in Newton Hospital when I couldn't find Mais nowhere else. But you see, she wasn't there. Alice told me that Maisie had been a part of this planned raid that you guys stopped, and when I told her that her name wasn't on the list of the residents that you guys captured... Well... Well, Alice freaked out and ... and..."

"And what? Assumed we'd snatched her up with the others but were keeping her involvement secret?" the Steward postulated. "Elias... Kid, why in the hell would we do such a thing?"

"Well..." Elias began, very unsure and panicking a bit. "Well, Alice said—"

"*Alice said!*" the Commander cut him off by parroting his own words back at him. "Alice Stark, your father's whore, was quick to believe the worst in us, I'm sure. But you, Initiate Sagal, you should know better than to trust an accusation from her lying lips. But instead, you swallow her bullshit whole and march your ungrateful ass across the Grand Alleyway, only to come barging into *my* private office and hurl unfounded accusations at your lawful ruler! You really ought to know better, Initiate."

"Well, where is she, then?" Elias heard himself ask.

"How the hell should we know, you fucking shit stick?" Childress grabbed him by the scruff of his shirt and began to shake, her eyes disbelieving and horrified. "She's probably off plotting more murders with all her traitor buddies who didn't get snatched up in their pathetic failed raid."

"Alice swears she was a part of the plan. What reason would she have to lie to me about that?" Elias asked, fighting to break loose from the guardswoman's clutches.

"Get your fucking ass in that lobby and wait for me at attention, you disrespectful shit," the Footman told him with a shove toward the double-doors for emphasis. "Sorry about this, Commander, sir. I'll deal with this idiot. I'll set him straight. Don't you worry, sir. Come on," she said, grabbing the back of his shirt collar this time and marching him out of the room.

"Mikkelson." The Steward suddenly spoke the name, but softly, reticent almost. Then more loudly, as color flushed back to his face for the first time since the Commander had shouted, he spoke the Chairman's name again. "Mikkelson. Yeah, of course that disgusting blob didn't tell us everything."

"What? The hell you talking about?" the Commander asked, sounding uncertain for the first time in Elias's reckoning. "What about Mikkelson? What's he got to do with this?"

"Everything, sir," the Steward assured his boss.

The Commander swiveled in the leather chair to face his number-two beside him. "Explain yourself."

"Well, sir, it's obvious that the fat creep knew about her part in the plot and then deliberately kept it from us."

"Why the hell would he do that?"

The Steward didn't answer except to glance across the office at Stevie. Her raspberry curls fell in greasy tangles around her face, so Elias couldn't tell if she knew all eyes in the room had darted her way, but something about the way she sipped her moonshine and stared stock-still at the table before her told him she was oblivious again. The Commander kept his head turned toward the freckled former-beauty longer than anyone else. When the Commander glanced back up at the Steward standing beside him and silently stared him down while slowly rising to his feet, it was clear to Elias that his special benefactor's subtle implication was about to cost him. But instead, the Commander suddenly reached out a meaty paw to slap atop the Steward's shoulder. He stepped around him without a word, only to squat his tall, bulky frame down atop the front of the desk. Elias couldn't make heads nor tails of the Steward's expression. He thought he recognized confusion there, but the man was so seldom confused around Elias that he couldn't say for certain. Whatever it had been, it was gone by the time he squatted his considerably smaller body on the desktop beside the Commander.

"You really buy this Stark woman's story, then? You think Maisie Sagal had a role in tonight's treachery and Mikkelson neglected to tell us for his own ends?" the Witenagemot's chief councilmember asked his subordinate.

"Well, sir... I mean... Well, it wouldn't be unthinkable now, would it?" the Steward began, tactful as an ace defense attorney. "The girl has been rash in the past and has never been very repentant of those transgressions, either. It's easy enough to believe, living with that arch-traitor Alice Stark, that she could find herself mixed up in this scheme. I mean, these resistance idiots wouldn't hesitate to use a child if they thought she could be of use to them. They've no honor or sense of immorality. They are nothing more than incompetent fools grasping at straws. They'd take any advantage they could. Hell, you know what? I bet Maisie was pressed into taking Alice Stark's place in this scheme after she went into early labor. It might've been a last resort kinda thing. I mean, they had already turned to Cainey Barker, for god's sake. Why would they scoff at using a thirteen-year-old kid, especially if it was in a pinch?"

Oh my god, it was Mikkelson. Oh my god, what've I done? Of course it was Mikkelson, that disgusting jerk. Why didn't I see that? Oh my god, what've I done? "Sirs," he bellowed, falling to his knees. "Please, Commander, please, Steward, forgive my doubts, forgive my stupid accusations!" He begged, hands clasped before his face in supplication. "I shoulda known it was him, Chairman Mikkelson. I shoulda known. I saw him in the Grand Alleyway on the way here. It broke my stride, something in his face. I should have known then. I shoulda stormed into his quarters before I ever dreamed of walking into yours, Commander, sir. I-I-I don't... I don't know what came over me, what possessed me. I was just afraid for Maisie. And I'd just saw my ... my ... my new sister... I mean, Alice's daughter... I saw her and I... I... Oh please forgive me, Commander. Forgive me, Steward. I should trust you most of all after all you've done for me. Please forgive me, sirs."

"Emotions always get the best of us, Elias," the Steward began in a calm, instructive voice. "You no doubt had some good cause to lose your composure today, but you still should've remembered your training. You should've remembered that your problems are small matters compared to your responsibilities. You should've sought me out for counsel. And yes, you should never doubt us."

"Forgive him, Jasper," Stevie Hyun said, now alert in her armchair, her drink discarded and her blue eyes shining. "Go get Maisie from that man. Go now. Please." The light left her eyes a blink later. Now it was the fading bruise below the eye that drew attention. Elias watched as she seemed to crumple back into herself. The baggy gray sweatshirt she wore seemed to swallow her up. Her dirty hair fell back over her face, and her hand went once more to her moonshine tumbler.

When he turned back to face the Commander and the Steward from their perches against the mahogany desktop, he found the Steward looking at the Commander and the Commander staring intently at Stevie Hyun. His ruler's brow was furrowed. His mouth set in a thin line. *What is it with these two? What is she to him, really? Why is she still here if those bruises are his fault?* "Very well, kid," the scarred ruler stated, still staring at the drunken mess in his office's armchair. "I suppose I understand. You're worried about your sister. I get that. Plus, you're just a kid. Sure, you shoulda known better, but that's what training is for. Hopefully, you got these poisonous doubts out of your system."

"I'm sure he'll make it up to us in the Integration Program by being Initiate Supreme this cycle," the Steward promised on Elias's behalf.

"I'll expect nothing less for every damn cycle you got left in the program, kid, you understand me?" the Commander demanded as Elias finally found the strength to make eye contact with his sovereign.

"I promise, sirs. I will be Initiate Supreme every year. I promise. I will never fail you again." Elias felt the tears welling behind his eyes but caught himself before they could fall. His actions today were bad enough without blubbering. God knows what they thought of his toughness and character already. He couldn't let them think he was some weak, bawling fool as well. "Please, then, Commander and Steward, please help me get my sister away from Chairman

Mikkelson. Or if not, at least help me get into his quarters so I can find her myself. I hate to press you now, sirs, or anything, but I don't like to think of what wasting another second here could mean for Maisie over there."

"Then let's go pay Chairman Mikkelson a visit, shall we?" the Commander said, shoving up off the desktop. Elias didn't dare move or even breathe. He was hoping he heard the Commander correctly, but this day's emotional turns had him mistrusting his ears. Only when the scarred and bearded behemoth in the gold-lined black uniform moved toward a cupboard cunningly concealed in the wall behind his desk to pluck out his long black battleaxe did Elias begin to believe what he'd heard. "Come on, Sagal... You too, Childress," he said, stepping toward the double-doors. "Steward, you coming?"

"Of course, sir," the man answered in a chipper voice. "Just let me call up a footman to watch the door while we're gone," he added, with-drawing his pocket tablet.

"Your axe sharp, Footman?" the Commander asked the guards-woman with a slight grin.

Childress returned the smirk as she patted the axe handle poking up behind her left shoulder. "Sharp enough to shave with, sir."

"Good. Good. And you, Carr—uhh... Stev—uhh... You," humanity's benevolent ruler called out to the redhead in the armchair, "you just stay right here."

Once again, Elias found himself marching down the Grand Alleyway with no clear memory of setting off or of any step of the journey so far. His mind was back to its earlier buzzing, but whereas before it had been mostly doubt and panic causing the brain-fuzz, this time it was wrath and pride ... and, of course, gratitude, not just to the Commander and Steward for pardoning his totally unwarranted behavior, but to Stevie Hyun for being his unexpected champion. Elias guessed things could've turned out very differently if she hadn't made her timely plea. The woman seemed to have a good deal of sway over their Commander, and today, Elias was the better for it.

He was reflecting on that unanticipated blessing as his party closed on the Supervisor Chairman's hatchway. One look at the big, bald footman standing cross-armed in front of the entryway cleared his fog and reflections pretty quick, though. He saw that the man had rolled up the sleeves of his gray footman's uniform jacket in a clear effort to display a tapestry of ink in every hue and shade covering his forearms. The dim, cruel obstinance in his beady black eyes was oddly chilling. Elias could tell the man was going to be an issue at a glance. What the Commander thought about the boulder of a sentry was unclear. His simple greeting of "Good morning, Footman" gave no hint to his thoughts.

"Good morning, Commander, sir," the tattooed meathead barked back after snapping lazily to attention.

"We're here to see the Chairman, Footman ... uhh ... Lukash, isn't it?" the Steward asked from a pace behind the Commander and two in front of Elias.

"Yes, sir, Steward, sir. You guessed it," the bald man told them with what Elias took for a very insolent grin.

"Well then, Lukash, open the hatchway. We need a word with Chairman Mikkelson," the Steward prompted.

"I'm awfully sorry, Steward, sir, but I can't do that," the bald man stated, still wearing that infuriating grin.

"What's that now?" the Commander asked in his most menacing growl.

"I'm sorry, Commander, but I got my orders from Chairman Mikkelson directly. They was quite specific, sir. I am to let no one enter without express permission from the Chairman."

"Well, you've been given new orders now, haven't you? From a higher authority, from the *highest* authority," the Steward told the man, impatient rage clear in every syllable. "Open the hatchway and stand aside, Footman."

"I can't do that, sir," Lukash informed him calmly through his petulant grin. "I've been given a direct and specific order by a senior member of the Witenagemot Council, and according to Article 3,

Section 7 of The New Destiny Constitution, I must obey that order by any and all means and in spite of any and all challenges."

"Mikkelson told you to say this, didn't he?" the Steward accused, fuming.

Lukash was working up some insolent retort, Elias could see it plain on the footman's face, but long before he could speak it, the Commander's black battleaxe flashed out from where it had been slung low and loose in his right hand only a millisecond earlier. The heavy, brutal blade hacked clean into Lukash's left knee a good three inches. Instantly, the man crumpled, but it took a ten-count before the first hideous shriek erupted from his lips. The Commander ripped his axe loose of the bald man's mangled flesh, but the footman was already well past bearable torment. He did scream as the wicked blade was extracted, but no more so than he already had been. His pathetic, whimpering state had no power over the Commander. Calm as ever, he dragged Lukash toward the hatchway keypad. The man's nearly severed leg left a thick streak of blood for every inch of the five feet he was dragged. Elias couldn't take his eyes from the copper-scented pool. He heard more than saw as the Commander smacked the bleeding footman, demanding he enter the code into the keypad.

The whoosh of air heralding the hatchway's opening brought Elias's eyes up from the streak of gore. "Let me go in first, Commander, sir," Footman Childress called out from her position directly behind Elias. A second later, she was moving, axe at the ready, toward the now open portal.

"Wait one, Footman," the Commander called, stopping her short. Childress looked to her leader, expecting directions of some sort, but a steady stare at the injured man at his feet was all she received. Then, with little to no warning, the black axe flashed, and Footman Lukash screamed no more. The Commander's battleaxe had sunk to the hilt into the top of the bald man's head. With a foot against the corpse and one firm yank, their ruler had his axe free from Lukash's flesh once more. "Okay, Footman," he said, looking up from his recent work, "now you can go in."

Elias was last through the portal. He entered a wide foyer with a tall ceiling and wood floor. Thankfully, the room was empty and spacious, because the three who went before him had all pulled up short just inside the room. Elias had to quickly juke around the Steward to avoid a collision. Once clear, he instantly understood what had caused the sudden halt to their home invasion. Mikkelson stood in the archway set into the room's righthand wall two-thirds of the way back. He wore a red silk robe and nothing more. The garment was cinched high, but not quite high enough for Elias's taste. One of the fat man's hairy tits was flopping out, the left. For the Chairman's part, he seemed to know it and not care. He leaned languidly against the archway, feet crossed and both hands resting atop his massive gut. "To what do I owe the great honor of your visit, Commander?" he asked, picking at his teeth. "I wish you'd warned me. I would've prepared something. I'm afraid I've not much to offer beyond a glass or two of that traitorous priest's harsh moonshine."

"Your footman delayed our entry," the Steward stated simply. "He flat out refused it, in fact."

"Did he now? Oh my… Oh no, no, we can't have that. Lukash?" Mikkelson called through his still open hatchway. "Come in here and explain yourself, Footman."

"The man said he was acting on your orders." The Steward spoke as though Mikkelson hadn't.

"Well, he must've been a bit confused, clearly, Steward, sir. Forgive him. He's a big dumb brute, good for lifting things and scaring fools and not much else. I'll be sure to punish him good, Commander, sir. You'll see. Footman Lukash, get in here now!"

"You know he ain't coming, Ian." The Steward's voice was ice-cold now. The use of the Supervisor Chairman's first name sent a shiver down Elias's spine.

Mikkelson was thrown for a moment by the name. His casual demeanor flickered for a second, just a second, but it did flicker. The sight brought a smile to Elias's lips, followed by an immediate sinking feeling in his stomach. The man had something to hide, and when he remembered just what that might be, he wanted to vomit. "Where is she?" Elias demanded, stepping toward Mikkelson.

"Excuse me?" the fat man in the silk robe asked him with a crooked, indignant eyebrow.

"My sister. Maisie. Where is she?"

"Check your tone, Initiate. Who the hell do you think you're talking to?" Elias saw his eyes go to the Commander and the Steward, clearly hoping for backup.

When they came back to Elias, they were no longer haughty, no longer indignant. They were afraid. Maybe only a little, but Elias definitely saw the fear there. It propelled him to further *technical*-sedition. "What have you done with her? Why didn't you tell the Commander about her role in the raid? Huh? Where is she?!"

"Answer the boy, Ian." The Commander punctuated his order by slapping his axe handle down on his palm.

"But..." Mikkelson began, no longer leaning at all, but instead curling up in his flimsy garb, one hand clasping the ends together just below his throat. "But, sir, I... I have no idea what he's talking about, let alone what's brought you to my private quarters just now. Lukash, get in here!" he added with a shout toward the open hatchway. "This is highly inappropriate. This... This... Sir, this is madness."

A muffled thud echoed out from somewhere in the lavish quarters behind Mikkelson. "What was that?" the Steward asked as though he already knew.

Elias didn't wait to hear the answer. He bolted past the blob in the archway, barely avoiding being trapped there against his flab. He thought he had a pretty good idea where the thud had come from but couldn't be sure. He entered a vaulted dining room and saw two points of egress. One seemed to lead into the kitchen, while the other opened on a narrow hallway. Just as he was telling himself to flip a coin and choose one, another muffled thud could be heard. It was lower than the first, but Elias was nonetheless able to identify the kitchen as its point of origin.

He was just darting through the archway leading into the wide rectangular space when another thud sounded out. His eyes followed his ears' instructions and saw a pantry door set into the wall at the end of a spotless marble countertop. Elias ran to it, flinging it open just as Mikkelson stepped into the kitchen, followed by the Commander, Childress, and the Steward. "What is it, kid?" he heard the Steward ask. "She in there?"

Elias stepped farther into the cramped space but found nothing at all, not even a can of dried peas. "No, sir. Nothing."

"There. You satisfied with whatever the hell this was, then?" Mikkelson exclaimed. "Can we stop rampaging through my home now? The servant only just finished waxing my beautiful floors last evening. Look, I don't know what kickstarted this madness, but I'm willing to let bygones be bygones and not press for any punishment for your boy," he told the Steward directly. "I trust that you'll impress on him the dishonor in leveling false accusations against a councilmember. I would like you all to leave now, please. Oh, and send in Footman Lukash if you would be so kind, Commander, sir. I don't know what the hell the oaf is doing out there. I'll be sure and replace him right away. Don't you worry there, sirs."

The Commander's dark, bearded face flushed a bit red. A bashful look even twinkled in his eyes. But it didn't last. Another thud, this one two quick, unmistakable beats, churned Elias's already rumbling belly, just as it wiped the sheepish looks from the Commander and the Steward, replacing them with victorious smiles. The sound came from right beside the pantry. Elias darted back inside the cramped cupboard to push against the side the noise came from, searching for a trap door or false wall. Finding none, he jumped back out and approached the kitchen wall itself, giving it a similar search. His first shove shifted the wall. A three by six section of it moved back a good six inches. Muffled sobs could be heard immediately. His heart racing so fast it seemed poised to leap from his chest, Elias pushed the section of wall farther. It swung as if it was hinged on the right side, opening up on what he took for a saferoom of some kind. He had time to think it fitting since the girl strapped with duct tape to a wooden chair lying on the small room's cold floor was now officially *safe*. "Maisie!" he shouted, dropping down to tend to her restraints.

Elias was acting on full instinct now. Immediately, he set to work on the duct tape, whipping out his pocketknife in a flash and slicing Maisie's left hand free all in the same motion. As he went to work on the right, his sister stripped the foot-long band from her lips. "Elias!" she screamed in abject relief. The sound nearly broke his heart. Elias knew he had to stop himself from imagining the things Mikkelson had done to his big sister before he showed up. He brushed such worries aside and focused on freeing her dangling feet. "Oh, Elias, thank god!" she panted, wrapping her now free arms tightly around him.

"I can explain, Commander, sir," Mikkelson said, his voice more angry than scared. "The girl owed a debt, a debt she freely took on. This was the way we mutually arranged to pay it off, whatever she might tell you."

"You lying bastard!" Maisie screamed, pushing free from Elias to climb to her feet. "You abducted me, you sick jerk! You fucking touched me! Damn you, you ... you ... you bastard! I'll kill you!" She managed two paces toward the fat man before Elias caught her.

"Of course she'd say something like that now, sir, just to save face with her family, no doubt," Mikkelson said, edging a step back.

"He's lying! Kill him!" Elias's sister screamed in fury, his warm-hearted, dedicated, steadfast sister.

"Commander, sir, might I have a private word with you, just man-to-man?" the rapist in the robe asked his ruler.

"Why?"

"Well, you see, sir, I know you are the sort of man who understands these kinda things."

"What kinda things are those?"

"Well, you know, you and I, both men with a heavy burden, lots of stress... I mean, it has to go somewhere after all, doesn't it?" The fat man laughed, sounding irritatingly amused. "You have found your particular uhmm ... *outlet*, shall we say? You've found your outlet, and I trust a man strong enough to take what he likes wouldn't begrudge a man of *lesser* strength staking his own claim to a *lesser* outlet, as it were. And I wasn't lying before, Commander. I would never and have never lied to you. To either of you, Steward, sir," he said, treating the number-two man with a patronizing smile. "The girl really does owe my supervisors a great deal. I oversee the bartering going on in the Living Quarters Corridor, you see. Somebody has to do it, no doubt, no doubt. Left to their own devices, the nitwits would be at each oth-er's throats in no time. So, I have my supervisors dip their fingers in here and there just to keep everything running smoothly. All on the up-and-up, I assure you. No violations of The New Destiny Constitution at all. No sirs, none. I'm just doing my job as Labor Supervisor, nothing more. Anyway, Maisie Sagal, as it turns out, in addition to her many other infractions over the months, has also wreaked a good deal of havoc on the *barter market*, as I call it. She owed a great deal, as I said. And she fully agreed to work it off by … by … doing a bit of role-playing with me. Nothing harmful, nothing nonconsensual, all on the up-and-up, as I said. I am a New Destiny Constitution abiding man. I only closed the door on the saferoom for her own anonymity's sake. She might well be ashamed to tell some of the people in her life the things she's willing to do for money. I didn't feel it necessary to flaunt her presence. I heard my hatchway open and simply closed the door on her and promised I'd be right back. Obviously, I didn't think it'd be with an audience," he ended with a belly laugh.

Maisie meant to call him a liar or something of that nature, Elias was sure, but all that came out was a snarl, somewhat catlike, only deeper. Elias was really struggling now to hold her back. The Commander, for his part, did and said nothing. He simply stared down at the shorter man with a blank, thoughtless gaze. The Steward, meanwhile, stepped around Mikkelson to edge into the narrow chamber. The saferoom was only roughly seven feet wide and ten or eleven deep. Just enough room for the chair Maisie had been strapped to and a two and a half foot tall circular end table. The Steward stepped right up to the glossy-white metal table and plucked something off its surface. Elias couldn't say what. He was partially blocked by the sister he was still holding back. "And what's this for, then?" the Steward asked, brandishing the item for everyone to see. "What's in the syringe, Ian?"

"He was just about to stick me with it. He said he was gonna knock me out and when I woke up I'd be carrying his baby. He said I'd belong to him for good then. He's a fucking sicko! And he's a lying jerk, too. They just jumped out at me and grabbed me up and dragged me here. The bastards had me tied to this chair in the dining room. I never agreed to any deal. I was in the dining room, strapped down in that damn chair, and that big freaking footman he's got working for him called him over his tablet and told him you were coming. So he whips out this syringe and some small bottle of something and starts dragging me into this room. We get in here, and I see him getting that syringe ready, so I started shouting. And then he slapped me, and then, like, I don't know, just, like, panicked and clapped a strip of duct tape over my mouth real fast and then closed me up in here. I couldn't hear ya through the door, but I figured you had to be in his quarters somewhere, or else I hoped, anyway. I couldn't shout or nothing, so rocking against the walls was the best thing I could think of. Only, I fell over the last time."

"Stevie Hyun came to my bed willingly, Mikkelson," the Commander said, breaking the flow and shooting all eyes his way. "She wants to be mine."

Mikkelson swallowed hard after a long look into his ruler's cold, dark eyes. "Of course she does, sir," he muttered in a fluttering voice. "I didn't mean to suggest otherwise. I... Well, I... I only appeal to my rights under our marvelous constitution. If the girl insists on accusing me, then I have every right to defend myself in a Third Day hearing."

"Wergild isn't getting you out of this," the Steward promised. "The Commander has already approved an amendment to that clause, effective last week. It will be announced at tomorrow's Third Day."

"She came to me willingly!" the Commander suddenly roared. His black axe dropped from his hand as he stepped toward the fat man. Elias would've thought it impossible, with the amount of chins Chairman Mikkelson had, that anyone could ever get their hands around his neck to throttle him, but he'd have been wrong. The Commander's fingers were long and strong enough to accomplish the task. Mikkelson attacked the arms choking him, chopping down and punching up to no avail. He switched to an eye-gouge, face-scratch method but failed there as well, even earning a headbutt straight to the bridge of his nose for his troubles. Elias watched as the blood flowed from his nose and his face turned purple. He felt his sister stiffen in his arms and knew she watched, too. The Steward stepped out of the cramped chamber before Supervisor Chairman Mikkelson even left his feet. He thrashed on, long after Elias's friend and benefactor had left the room.

When it was over and the blob's chest rose and fell no longer, and he sprawled like the bloated carcass of some bulbous sea creature, Maisie shrugged off Elias's hold and strode two paces to the fresh corpse. She stood over the robed butterball for two long breaths. Elias thought to call out to her, wondering what she was thinking, what horrors she was remembering, when she suddenly spat a thick wad of phlegm down on the purple face of her tormentor and began to kick the dead man with heedless abandon. "You bastard! You sick bastard!" she screamed all the while. "He put his freakin' hands on me. He freakin' touched me. He ... he ... touched me," she finished with a final kick to the purple face.

"Now might be a good time for a thank you," the Commander said to Maisie's back.

When she turned from the dead man, Elias had hoped to see relief and satisfaction and gratitude, but his sister's face held none of those qualities. If anything, she appeared even angrier than she had when snarling at Mikkelson. "Thank *you*?" she scornfully asked. "Thank you for what? For believing yourselves to be gods? For killing my father? I am supposed to thank you for giving power to a sicko pedophile like this?" She gave the corpse one last kick. "Yeah, thanks so much, *dear leader*."

"Maisie!" Elias exclaimed, horrified. "My goodness, Mais, he just saved your life, for god's sake."

"Yeah, after you came and begged, I'm sure," she said. With a heavy sigh, she turned to face her brother, giving him all her attention. "Elias, you gotta get away from these people. Come back home with me right now, please."

He didn't know what to say, what to think even. His eyes locked with the Commander for one long, terrible moment. How could he forswear the man right to his face? How did she expect him to abandon a man who had just finished strangling the fattest man Elias had ever known to death with his bare hands? How can she continue to set aside Carrie Montrois's great sacrifice? Now both Montroises had saved her life, and she still couldn't find the grace to be grateful. It was so infuriating, so frustrating. *Why does she always make everything so hard? Can't you just once say thank you and move on?* "I can't come with you, Mais. You know that."

She was on him in two strides, wrapping him in a hug every bit as strong as when he'd first cut her loose. "They are messing with your head, Eli, telling you lies," she whispered in his ear. "They are brainwashing you, little brother. You've got to trust me. I love you, Eli. You gotta come back to me. Please, Eli. Remember Mom. Remember Dad. Remember them and come back with me."

He placed his hands on her shoulders and pushed away his big sister's embrace. "No, *you* remember Carrie Montrois and what she did for us," he shot back. "The Commander is her husband, her love. He is only doing what is best, both then and now."

"Elias, no," she said in a low, broken voice. "He butchered our father. He chopped his freakin' head off, Elias."

"If our father had won, he'd have just helped AOA kill off the security squad, one by one. And then mankind would have no future at all." Maisie didn't respond, only stared at him with a dumb, stunned look on her face. "Plus, he had no business challenging in the first place, Mais," Elias declared, trying with emphasis and inflection to get her to see the light. "Dad was far outmatched by the Commander. The Commander is the First Knight of Fate. No one could've beaten him. No one *can* beat him. Dad was just flat-out wrong, Mais e."

"How dare you!" she screamed just before her slap landed.

It was loud, and it stung, but he mostly felt the pain in his heart. "Come, Initiate Sagal," the Commander's rumbling voice called out. "You've done well today. Let's leave your sister to process her trauma as she will. I suppose she's suffered enough for her foolish choices. You reap what you sow, kid," he told Elias, bending down to snatch up his axe. "It ain't a common phrase for no good reason Now, come on. Let's leave your sister to reflect on that," he said, beckoning him to leave with a short gesture. Elias waited for Footman Childress to fall in line behind the Commander before following in turn. He never broke stride nor looked back when Maisie fell to her knees and began to wail for forgiveness, though he did reach up to touch the spot on his cheek where her blow had landed. The red mark would fade, along with the sting, but the scar on his heart, he knew, would not vanish so easily.

CHAPTER 9
THE COMMANDER

Infection Event: Day 356

His left hand clutched a dewy glass of chilled wine. His right squeezed the arm of his leather wingback chair, gripping and loosening in a steady rhythm. He'd sent that pasty-faced footman after her twenty minutes ago already. The Commander did not like to think about what could have the man delayed. After all, his private quarters were only just across the Grand Alleyway from his office in the executive wing where last he'd left her.

The son of a bitch should be back by now.

Still, it was another three slow sips before the ash-blond stork of a footman finally delivered the woman to his bedchamber. "Here she is, Commander, sir. Sorry for any delay," the footman said, staring at the carpet before him.

"It's alright, Footman Webster. Not your fault, I'm sure." One look at the glazed and distant blue eyes of the woman standing alongside the footman told him that much. "See that we aren't disturbed 'til morning."

"Yes, sir, Commander, sir. Certainly, sir," Footman Webster promised as he bowed at the waist and backpedaled from the Commander's elegantly decorated and plushly furnished bedroom. The wingback chair he currently occupied was part of a matched pair set into a corner of the room adjacent to the California king bed. After the footman was out of the room, he beckoned for the red-headed woman to join him. She came straight away, or near enough to make no matter. "You'll read to me tonight," he told her, snatching a thin hardcover book off the lampstand beside the twin wingbacks. The Commander pushed the worn burgundy book into her hands as she plopped into the open chair. "The page is marked."

"I see," the redhead said. He had never asked her to read to him before, but the woman took it in stride, flipping to the marked page with no hesitation. She did look up from the text before starting, though. "I'll need a drink," she stated without any discernable slur.

The Commander set his own down in order to prepare one for the raspberry beauty. He'd anticipated the request and had a spare glass ready on the lampstand. She'd have to do without ice, but it was the Commander's experience that not many other folks actually drank their wine chilled like him, anyway. He handed her the glass half full and was busy staring into the purple-red depths of his own when the woman finally began the story. "*Chapter 12... James's large, frightened eyes traveled slowly around the room. The creatures, some sitting on chairs, others reclining on a sofa, were all watching him intently.*"

Her recitation whirled throughout his mind, existing somehow in both focus and without. It lifted the burdens from his soul and yet added others. It was working just as he'd hoped, and still somehow not at all. He was swimming through the choppy seas of his dreams and memories, her words registering and fading, snapping off flashes in their wake of half-remembered days gone by. Pain and misery mingled freely with joy and wonder. All at once, he felt back home, back with *them*, and still a million miles away. But it was better than the silence. Anything was liable to creep into his mind in the silence.

"*James had decided that this was most certainly not a time to be disagreeable, so he crossed the room to where the Centipede was sitting and knelt down beside him,*" the woman narrated as a clear memory of a two-year-old Roxanna held out in his arms wearing a heart-melting smile as they waded together in the shallows of Lake Huron one summer's day flicked onto the projection screen of his mind. He hadn't even noticed the tears flowing into the tangles of his black beard until the woman's silence had lingered too long to be merely any dramatic pause in the story. His eyes flicked open to discover the woman staring strangely back at him. He watched as her crystal-blue pools moved back down to the book in her hand. She flipped the burgundy hardcover to the titlepage. Her eyes lingered. The Commander knew exactly what had caught her attention. Below the bold title reading *James and The Giant Peach by Roald Dahl*, a name and date were inscribed in faded royal-blue ink, written in ornate cursive by a neat, flowing hand. *Property of Carrie Hoglund, October 1999*, he knew it read.

"This was your wife's book, wasn't it?" the freckly redhead in the wingback armchair across from him asked. "I imagine she and you would read it to your daughter. Right? You brought it up here with you when you first came up with the prep workers. Maybe the two of them even encouraged you to take it and think of them. This book is all you have left of them now, ain't it? I wonder what Carrie would think if she were to find me sitting here reading it to you. I wonder how your sweet little Roxanna would react if she could see her father today. I truly do wonder just what that kind and noble wife of yours might say."

The Commander didn't answer. He stood up instead. The woman looked up to him, insolence and contempt in every line of her face. A mighty slap from his right hand set that straight. "*You* are my wife," he told her. "Now, get on the bed." She did as commanded, but the look came back. The Commander satisfied himself on that account, several times over, before at long last he fell asleep.

Dark-gray storm clouds were stacking up overhead. The city streets he strode were familiar, but each successive corner he turned around revealed something he was not expecting. He knew, with the certainty of dreamers, that he was searching for something, searching for *someone*, but the cracked and weedy streets and cul-de-sacs he blundered down seemed only to be leading him farther from that which he sought. Cars with flat tires and dust-covered windshields became more frequent as he headed toward the downtown business district of this strangely familiar town. He didn't hear the cries until another two left turns down the abandoned streets. From then on, they grew louder with each step. If the city he wandered through was familiar, the screams and cries were as recognizable as one's own face in a mirror.

"Roxanna!" the Commander bellowed as he bolted toward the fearful shouts. "Carrie, I'm coming!" They came into view as soon as he rounded the T-corner intersection in the heart of the decaying town's metropolitan center. The visual confirmation was not quite the relief his soul had been praying for. It was indeed his wife and child crying out for him to save them, and the sight of their bright faces hit like an adrenaline shot to the heart, but the surge of relief was gone as quick as it came the instant his mind computed the whole picture. His wife and child were at least half a mile down the broken, dusty street—a street packed with hundreds and hundreds of writhing, blood-stained, gray-skinned Damned all the long way to where Carrie and Roxanna occupied a tenuous refuge atop a vine-invaded city bus.

"Daddy!" Roxanna called out on first glimpse of him. Her voice was so close. She was a half mile from him, but it rang in his ears as if she were standing beside him. "Help! Help us, Daddy!"

"Jasper!" His wife's voice exploded in his ears at the same volume as his daughter's. "Monty! Oh god, Jasper! Help us! They're climbing the bus!"

The Commander saw that it was true. The Damned were climbing over one another, scaling the dirty blue walls of the public transportation vehicle. Some were falling through the large, rectangular, smashed-out windows in their fevered quest to reach the flat roof. "I'm coming!" he shouted through cupped hands. "Carrie, hold on! I'm coming!"

Suddenly, there was an axe in his hand, a black axe. He didn't question where it came from, only gripped it all the tighter and began running flat out for his family. The skies let free the instant his initial step hit the cracked concrete. The Commander was soaked before his first axe blow ever landed. His championship blade cleaved clean through that first Damned, and when he whipped the wicked tool back to ready another swing, it smashed into a group of four or five Damned and sent them flying twenty feet through the air. He was strong, oh so very strong, and fast, lightning fast.

With his right arm, he flailed the axe at the demented masses. With his left, he bashed forearm smashes into snarling faces, sending them flying, limbs snapping and bones cracking. In this fashion, as if taking a scythe to a field of wheat, he cleared a wide swath of rutted street all about him on a steady march toward the rotting bus. "Hurry, D! They're almost up here!" He heard Roxanna scream as though standing right next to him, even over the growls and groans of the mindless cannibals pressing close. "They've almost got us, Daddy!"

He was sweating now, sweating buckets. He could feel it even in spite of the driving rain. His heart was set to leap from his chest. He was still a hundred yards away, at least. With a roar so deep and rattling it rivaled the thunder above, the Commander lashed out a straight right kick. It plowed into the chest of the Damned woman before him, sending her flailing violently backward, knocking down other monsters like dominoes. He charged into the gap, axe still swinging, Damned still falling left and right to its wicked blade. "Oh god, Jasper! Oh god, they're on us!" Carrie's voice, so hypnotic and soothing in the past, was now laced in every syllable with panic, horror, and, worst of all, disappointment.

"Nooo!" he screamed, lashing out another straight kick. "I'm here, Carrie. I'm here! I'm coming. Hold on!"

The bus was only a dozen paces away now. He was going to make it. He was going to save them this time. He could see Damned on either side of the mammoth bus. They had indeed reached the roof on both sides, but only just. The Damned were awkward, shambling things, semi-dexterous at the best of times. The Commander saw that he could reach the roof in three quick leaps and likely beat them to the punch. The last two Damned in his path were hacked in two by his axe, their severed corpse halves flying off in opposite directions. "Aghh, Monty! Please help! Jasper, they're on us! Aghhh!" His wife's voice was shouting in his ear as he pushed off his right foot and leaped onto the hood of a crashed conversion van beside the bus. From there, he vaulted onto the blue people-mover itself, landing nimble-footed on the ledge of its now smashed-out back window. Then, with an ease he didn't even momentarily contemplate, he planted his left palm on the metal roof and hauled himself atop the structure in one fluid motion.

He made it up just in time to watch four Damned, two on either side of his precious ones, somehow, impossibly, reach his family ahead of him. They wrapped their arms around them and hauled them over the roof's edge into a pulsating horde of gray-skinned abominations.

"Nooooo!" He was too late. "Noooo!" His wife had been dragged over only a step before his arrival. His finger had even brushed the fabric of her sweater. "Oh god, no! No, please no. Carrie! Roxanna!" The horde had seemed to swallow them whole, gulping them down with one giant, many-segmented maw. No matter where he peered over the edge of the bus's rooftop, he found no sign of his wife or daughter. "Carrie! Roxanna! Carrie!" He was shouting, knowing full well how useless it was. He knew he had to jump in after them, and as soon as he knew it, he hated himself for having delayed this long. But before he could cannonball into the sea of mororic monsters, Carrie crawled back atop the roof.

Roxanna was only a moment behind her mother. They had crawled up on the front of the bus and now stood about even with where the driver's seat most likely was. The Commander had worked his way by this time to the back of the long dusty-blue vehicle. There were maybe ten yards between him and his family now, ten yards of open metal rooftop, ten yards between him and the only thing in all the universe he ever would or could want, but the Commander did not go to them. Far from being the medicine for his panic and tur-moil, the sight of them sent icy-cold shivers shooting down his spine. Roxanna, beautiful, bright-eyed, pudgy-nosed Roxanna, stood atop the roof in ripped rags, stained from foot to neck in what he took for the girl's own blood. Her left arm wasn't there. It ended just after the shoulder in a gory mess. But there was oddly no pain on her face. Instead, his sweet daughter was smiling. And when he looked over to his wife beside her, he found the same strange, mirthless smile on her face as well, along with several long, ragged gashes and two large, meaty chunks bitten out of either of her cheeks, all of which dripped an endless flow of red.

"Now we're monsters like you, Daddy," his daughter informed him in a calm, melodic version of her once playful voice.

Carrie stepped away from her daughter, right toward the Commander. He wanted to step toward her and snatch her up in his arms. He wanted to run away and never look back. What he did instead was nothing. He let his wife of sixteen years stroll across the bus roof in absolute silence, save only the steady rain lashing against the flat metal surface. The Damned were all standing still and quiet. The thunder above was crashing and rolling in a constant pattern. Then Carrie was in front of him. She reached out and took his left hand into her own. The Commander looked down at the woman before him, past the rain-drenched red hair and tattered and ravaged face, straight into the depths of her clear blue eyes. He saw his wife there, and so squeezed her hand.

"She's not me," Carrie told him. "You know that, Monty. She's not me. Come be with me. Come be with us." She pulled him in for a hug before he could answer. He hugged back with everything he had and allowed her to maneuver him to the edge of the roof and then straight over.

He was falling into the gray horde, their thousand hands reaching for him, when he suddenly gasped awake to find himself tangled beneath the silk sheet of his California king bed. Breathing heavily, and resentful of it, he threw the sheet off and sat up. Next, he swung his feet off the mattress and sat perched on the edge of the bed. Then he slapped his pocket tablet resting screen-up atop the bedside nightstand. *0127 ST,* the time flashed yellow in the bottom corner of his tablet's lock screen. He curled his toes, squeezing the soft carpet beneath them, and began pondering how best to rid himself of this most recent onslaught of venomous trepidation. The Commander knew Stevie was naked beneath the comforter on the other side of the mattress. Another go at the woman might just help alleviate any lingering bad vibes, but the sight of her curled up in a ball beneath the covers as far from him as she could manage without falling off the bed, with nothing but the top of her head and tips of her toes exposed, dampened his ardor before it could reignite.

Her sulking and cowering bored him, and the dream was all but faded now, anyway. A thought struck him then, a fine alternative way to hasten the full retreat of his subconscious picture show. A bottle or two of what was left of the priest's wine would do the trick, if, that is, there were any bottles left.

I'm gonna have to tell the Steward to get somebody to pick up where that traitorous, phony, bastard preacher-man left off, he decided, shuffling bare-chested and barefooted across the cushy silver carpet of his opulent bedchamber.

CHAPTER 10

ALICE

Infection Event: Day 438

"At least give me my baby back before you forget yourself and go off screaming and yelling at the man." Maisie seemed to suddenly remember she'd been holding her sister. She handed the precious bundle over to Alice impatiently but somehow still gently. Maisie was the best big sister in the business. How that girl kept her head and maintained her compassionate nature, with her moral compass staying firm to the pure north through countless horrors, never ceased to amaze Alice. Even now, only a few months removed from narrowly escaping rape and kidnapping at the hands of a slobbering psycho, and then being spared the imprisonment her cohorts in the failed raid on the alternate Control Room were currently suffering, she was still focused on the future, on everyone else. It was beyond admirable.

Alice hadn't been involved in the raid herself, not really, just kept a few secrets and passed on a few messages, but she still felt guilty as all hell knowing everyone who had taken part in that ill-fated adventure, save Maisie, had been locked away somewhere out of sight down Branch 1 for weeks now. She knew, too, that her teenage roommate/pseudo stepdaughter had to be feeling that same guilt and helplessness just as strongly as her, if not more so. Maisie had suffered a lot of trauma that night, and a good few others, more than enough for most lifetimes, and yet, she was still attacking each day with the same vigor as the last, no matter how hard the previous night had knocked her down. The girl was indominable, unable to tolerate injustice with a passive grace. Nothing on Earth ... *or the moon* ... could break her will, be it pedophiles, kidnappers, murderers, or despots. The Witenagemot's oppression was her problem to solve, and so solve it she would. So, obviously, Alice's warning that Abner Hyun would not be at all pleased to have them drop in to see him unannounced went completely unheeded.

She had nearly begged Maisie on bended knee to see how potentially dangerous this endeavor could be. Alice had explained that there was no telling how the reclusive, broken man might react to the three of them ringing the hatchway buzzer of the single-tenant living quarters he'd been shut up inside for the past eleven months. The place had once been an empty unit off a lonely alleyway in Maroon Corridor. He'd sought the vacant quarters out and squatted himself inside in an obvious and deliberate attempt at seclusion from the rest of the population after he'd killed Eddie Sarkisian in the Final Tournament and broken his wife's heart in the process. Alice knew many of the cruel and impudent residents were taking bets on which actual day Hyun would finally off himself. There were even a few of the more greedy gamblers that were all for storming into his squatter's sanctuary and checking to make sure the man hadn't already done the deed. Nothing had come of it, so far as she knew, but regardless of just how many visitors Abner Hyun had to his new pad in the past, Alice believed he was bound to be ill-receptive of whoever came calling now.

They were desperate, it was true, and she knew that. Time was running out. But even still, Alice feared this approach. After what felt like a zillion sleepless nights over the past few months tending to the hungry growing baby while plotting with Maisie on how to free the prisoners of the raid, they had come up with nothing. They had failed. Their friends were doomed. But even still, Alice knew full well the man had locked himself away from people for a reason. Maisie hadn't out-and-out dragged her here, but once she snatched her daughter from her grasp and started walking toward Maroon Corridor, Alice hadn't had much choice. Standing before his quarters now, though, the urge to run away suddenly seemed like the best option for all interested parties.

Then Maisie reached for the hatchway buzzer and held it down, ending Alice's last chance at flight. "Easy, Mais. No reason to piss him off before we've even started," Alice said, shifting her two-month-old daughter into the cradle of her arm.

"He might not come otherwise," Maisie responded, finger still holding down the buzzer.

"You'll let me do the talking now, remember?" Alice reminded her.

"I know. I know," Maisie answered, annoyed. "I heard ya the first time."

"He won't be happy to talk to anyone, I'm sure. And I've never met a man who could tolerate being scolded by a kid. So just leave it to me."

"I'm no kid!"

"To him and folks like him, you are."

"Whatever. Just don't let him off the hook. He helped get us here. It's long past time he stopped moping and got off his ass and did something. I'm gonna make sure he knows just what that scar-faced demon has done to his wife ... if the man can even care anymore."

"I'll tell him everything, Mais, all of it, I promise. Just try and understand the man is fragile. Not all of us are blessed with your relentless brand of resilience and courage, ya know."

"Flattery won't buy my silence," Maisie told her roommate with a small smile as she finally lifted her finger from the hatchway buzzer.

"Just let me handle this, Mais."

"Yeah, yeah, yeah..." the young teen was saying as the portal suddenly slid open. A shaft of the alleyway's fluorescent lighting illuminated the bare shins and feet of a pale man. The rest of him was left opaque by the darkness seemingly filling every corner of the room beyond. The man said nothing nor made any gesture of welcome. He stood rock firm square in the entryway, and though she could not clearly see it, Alice had the impression of crossed arms resting atop a smooth bare chest.

A silence stretched on and on. Alice lost her tongue. Maisie was glaring at her impatiently. *You said you'd do the talking, so do the talking already*, that face seemed to say. "Abner Hyun? My name is Alice Stark," she finally managed through a mouth of marbles. "I don't know if you remember me. We met a few times awhile back. Your wife and I are good friends. This is Maisie. She... She—"

"He knows me, Alice," Maisie interjected. "Don't ya, Mr Hyun? God, you and I and Stevie must've shared a dozen meals together back in your guys' place in Silver Corridor during those first few weeks. Mostly breakfasts before I would head over to Father Boyd's place to help him out for the day. You remember that? Stevie was giving me lessons on her keyboard, and the mornings were the only time we were both free. We'd gab and gossip ... and play ... and you'd cook and sing your showtunes before the stove in your dirty blue *Kiss The Cook* apron, whipping up cheesy scrambled eggs and mounds of bacon or sausage ... and pancakes. Oh man, those pancakes. Dang, they was some good pancakes. You remember that, Abner? Do you remember that good man? What have you done with him?"

Alice was tongue-tied yet again and pissed at herself for it. She had known Maisie was liable to be as diplomatic as a hyena at chow time when dealing with Abner. That, after all, had been why she had insisted during the trek through Branch 4's maze of living quarters corridors that if she was going to come along, Maisie would let Alice do all the talking. It was a longshot that the man would even answer the door for them. If they started the conversation with patronizing disgust, it'd be an even longer shot still that they would ever be invited in for a chat. But Alice had hesitated, thrown by the half-seen, and hopefully only half-naked, presence drawn up before them. She had hesitated, and Maisie's impatience, little as it was, had worn thin before she could regroup. Their chance for a reasonable conversation was blown—Alice was sure of it. Right up until the moment Abner Hyun finally spoke. "That man is long dead, Mais," he said in a thick, wheezy voice that clearly hadn't been used in a very long time. "Y'all can come in and look for him if you want, but you ain't gonna find him here."

"We'll look," Maisie said in an uncertain voice as she stepped through the open portal. Hyun stood aside to let her enter, his shins and feet disappearing deeper into the darkness.

"Might we turn on a light, Abner?" Alice asked as soon as she stepped into the quarters' small foyer.

A soft click presaged a burst of pale, diffused light. Abner Hyun stood beside a tall lamp in a corner of what was a living room in most folk's quarters. Considering the four-foot lamp, with its simple black metal rod and stand, was the only piece of what could be called normal living or sitting room décor in the entire hexagonal space, Alice didn't think the small room that opened off the even smaller foyer qualified for the title. It wasn't that the room was barren and lonely–far from it. Nearly every inch of floor space was taken up by discarded MRE wrappings, alongside box after box of still more Meals Ready to Eat. Each box could hold 50 meals. A few were open and picked through, but just as many, if not more, were still sealed. It had been merely chance alone that Alice and Maisie hadn't stumbled into a stack. A foot or two to the left or right and Alice would've tripped over the foodstuffs for sure.

Abner had made his way through the maze with no apparent problems, suggesting an intimate familiarity with the mess. He stood with a hand before a dimly lit face, shielding his eyes from the chintzy lamp's meager light. Although, she figured his appearance would be no less haggard in any light. The dimness was probably even helping him on that account. A scraggly, patchy, greasy black beard covered the lower half of his once handsome face, while a shock of lank, disheveled jet-black hair hung down over nearly all of the top half. Beneath the shag were eyes sunken in dark pits, radiating stress-lines in every direction. Alice wouldn't go so far as to classify him as wasted, but he had definitely lost weight since last she'd seen him. His gray gym-shorts appeared excessively baggy, while the hint of a ribcage could be seen beneath the stretched skin of his torso. "This'll have to do for yas for now," Abner said from where he'd gotten comfortable leaning against a stack of brown MRE boxes.

"It's fine. We can see well enough, I guess," Alice responded as she watched Hyun reach behind the stack and come back with a ratty navy-blue t-shirt.

"What are y'all doing here?" he asked them, tugging the shirt over his dirty head. "Stevie said she'd never send anyone after me. She told me to rot here, last I remember."

"Stevie didn't send us," Maisie told him, "though, as her friends, as the people who *love* her, it is for her sake that we've come."

"A lot has happened, Abner," Alice said in a patient voice she was finally proud of. "I don't know how often you've gotten out of here over the past few months, but–"

"Somewhere close to never," Abner interrupted. "I thought such behavior would send the message clear enough that I didn't want to be bothered, but apparently not."

"*Bothered*?" Maisie shot back, her face flushing red. "Don't want to be *bothered*? You jerk. You big stupid assface. Have you any freakin' clue what has happened? To the station? The other residents? Chr st man, to your own freakin' wife, for god's sake? Have you any clue? God, I knew I should've come here right after they took her. I can't believe I let you and Dolly talk me out of it," she added to Alice as a disgusted afterthought before turning back to Abner. "This is all your damn fault, and you can't be *bothered*?!"

"Maisie, maybe you can wait outside and give Mr. Hyun and me a minute alone," Alice interjected, trying to diffuse the potentially volatile situation. "I'll introduce him to the baby. Give us a couple minutes alone for that, will ya?"

"*A lot has happened*," Abner repeated Alice's earlier words in a strange, ominous tone. "But I take it, seeing on how it's been eleven damn months since anyone has come knocking on my door, that you ain't here because of *a lot*? Something new, something spec fic, something recent has brought y'all here today. And if you're coming to me, and it's just you and Maisie bringing the message, then I can only assume there is some hopeless deed you expect me to pull out of my ass and flash a miracle down into the hearts and minds of our fellow man, like I'm some goddamn wizard. Christ, y'all gotta know that's how I fucked up the first time, taking collective destinies into the palm of my hand, playing god with a war hammer. You have to know that hopeless, evil, sweet self-righteous sort of mission led me to murder my friend and burn my marriage the last time I tried it. Y'all know that full well. And yet, here you are. And yet, you still come to me. Why? Huh? Why would you do this to me? I don't want to hear whatever bullshit has brought you ladies here today. I'm sorry, I just don't. I can't. I checked out. Don't you understand? I checked out. I can't anymore. I can't. I'm not me. I'm *this*... God, why have you come here?"

"Why'd you open the door?" Alice asked, not knowing where the question came from. But once said, it felt right. He had indeed let them in after all. Perhaps that meant something. Perhaps he was open to coming back to the world. Maybe only subconsciously, but he had let them in. "Your wife needs you, Abner."

"I can't fight them. They're too strong, too good, too well equipped, too well secured. This whole place has got their backs now. What could I possibly hope to do? You obviously have no real plan. Stevie sent you here to beg me 'cause all your other plans have fallen through, I'll bet. Christ, I'm surprised you've all made it even this far. There are too few people in this station to expect to keep anything secret from the *Witenagemot,*" he said with a sarcastic sneer for his oppressor's regime. "This is just like Stevie. First, she tells me she'll leave me if I try stopping Jasper and Aponyaschefski, and now, she sends you after me to do that very thing."

"She didn't know what they'd become. None of us did ... and things were different then. *Circumstances* were different," Alice explained.

"Stevie did not send us, Abner," Maisie told him with firmness in her voice. "She can't. He won't let her leave Branch 1. They've even taken her tablet from her." Abner stiffened, staring at Maisie with a furrowed, questioning brow. "No one I know has made any contact with her for a couple weeks now."

"What the hell are you talking about?" Abner asked in a way that made it seem like he knew very well what the hell she was talking about.

"Your wife is *his* now, Abner," Maisie told him, seeming to twist the words like a dagger in the guts. "Your good friend, Jasper Montrois, took her from us and is doing god only knows what with her now."

"No," Abner muttered.

"Yes," Maisie assured him, remorselessly. "While you've been lying here in this filth, feeling sorry for yourself, your wife has become a sexual prisoner of your onetime best friend." Abner stopped and started a dozen times, but no words ever came. "Anyway, Alice and I just thought you'd like to know," she told him, turning back to the hatchway. She made it all the way to the threshold before turning casually back, wearing the face of a lightly disappointed English professor. "If you ever find a way to man up enough to face him, they're hosting a public mass execution tomorrow in The Meadow. He'll be there, with her, most like... Like I said, just thought you'd like to know. See ya around, Mr. Hyun."

Alice moved to join Maisie at the small, sour quarters' still open hatchway. She was only six or seven steps away to begin with, and just two from the exit when Abner called out to her. "What did you name the baby, Alice?"

She turned back to face him and couldn't help the grin from taking hold of her lips. Alice could never stop beaming whenever she spoke of her precious angel. "Carrie Roxanna Sagal," she told the haggard man in the half-light.

"Sagal?" he asked with an upturned eyebrow aimed at Maisie.

"He's Perry's," Alice confirmed. "We call her Riri or Care Bear or Care Care or cutie pie or peanut or angel or a thousand other things," she added with a giggle.

The smile that washed over the man's face was as surprising as it was genuine. "It's a beautiful name. She's a beautiful kid."

"Thank you, Abner," she said, pleasantly surprised on many counts. She knew Carrie's condition was recognizable but always appreciated the people who never thought to mention it, not even in their eyes or their initial reaction. Such folks were few and far between, sadly.

It wasn't that she thought her daughter disfigured or malformed and didn't want to be reminded of this or that she was in need of some sort of special, gentle treatment or anything. On the contrary, Carrie Roxanna was the most beautiful, flawless creature Alice Stark had ever encountered in her life. She had poured her whole heart inside that girl's soul on first sight. It was just that she was planning to raise Carrie with a positive, can-do attitude. She would stay constantly vigilant for anyone who ever dared tell her there was something she could not do. Cerebral palsy would not dictate her life. It would not limit her goals or ambitions. Alice would die to make sure of that. So when people saw only the beautiful, happy, rosy-cheeked baby in her arms and not her unfortunate condition, it made her happy. She felt a certain kinship with such people. Hyun darted his eyes away quickly, though. With them locked on the ill-used room's carpet, he began to wave her out the door. Alice took the hint. She used her left arm to shepherd her beloved stepdaughter into the empty silver alleyway while in her right, she cradled her miraculous baby girl.

CHAPTER 11
ABNER

He had clicked off the lamp just after Maisie Sagal and Alice Stark left. Abner sat there, alone in the dark once again, only there was something different this time. Whereas the dark veil had been a constant comfort in the past, hiding all and gifting him a place that felt apart from the world, the heavy blackness now felt suffocating. He felt its weight heavy across every molecule of his skin. Its former refuge felt like a distant thing of the past. Abner Hyun could no longer even remember the relief of its embrace from only minutes earlier.

He was clicking the lamp back on before he really even knew what he was doing. But once lit, he felt he could breathe steadily once more. It frightened him, the thought of losing the comforts of the darkness, his monastery, but nonetheless, standing square in the lamp's small ring of light, Abner knew he could never go back to his ebony isolationism.

He has your Stevie. He's got your wife.

The thoughts played on a loop. With each repetition, he felt his former torpor and weakness sluffing off his soul while his body was simultaneously invigorated with an equal fervor. Abner felt electricity in his every muscle, in every atom. His mind bounced from absolute disbelief to bursting fury, like a pinball machine falling down a steep cliff. *How could Jasper do this? He can't have. It can't be true. Can it? Oh god, I thought I was safe from these thoughts for good. I was gone.*

*God, what's happened to me? What is happening to me? What has
he done with my fucking wife?*

The conviction of this last exasperated thought had him striding
toward the hatchway without a second thought. Abner had no real
idea where he was headed, no real idea of what he was going to do
once he got there, or what exactly was true and what wasn't. He was
just walking. It felt like moving toward the problem. He was stalking the
alleyways with purpose. What exactly that purpose might be didn't
really matter to him. He had broken free from his hibernation. The
shame of who and what he'd become in that dark place couldn't even
deter him. Once, such feelings had brought him to that low place, but
the thought of Stevie being ill-used by anyone, let alone his former
friend, had somehow elevated his conscious self above his former
emotional weaknesses. He almost felt as though someone else was
behind the wheel, pulling all his levers, and Abner was only along for
the ride. Whatever the case may be, he was walking ... somewhere.
That's all that mattered just then.

He only knew where that *somewhere* was the moment he
arrived right outside its hatchway. Abner punched the familiar code
into the keypad of his former two-tenant quarters in Silver Corridor.
When the hatchway swished open to reveal a dark chamber beyond,
Abner was sad but not truly surprised. He'd believed Maisie the
instant she'd first told him of Stevie's fate, some part of him, anyway.
The dark, empty quarters' confirmation of that fate was still chilling in
its effect, nonetheless. Abner did not call out for her. A small, hopeful
part of him wanted to, but another part of him knew how painful just
uttering her sweet name aloud would be, while the rest of him was
well aware of how useless it would be. Instead, he strode into his
former home with a quiet dignity, the best dignity he could muster in
light of his appearance and condition anyway.

Abner tapped on light switches as he made his way deeper into
the humble quarters, fully accustomed to the light once more, craving
it even. Soon, he found himself in his dining room, standing before
Stevie's painting. Its sunset colors spoke to him in a way it never had
before, yet somehow felt utterly familiar. They seemed to radiate off
the canvas, crashing like successive waves into his retinas. But it
was the lonely ship that locked him firm in place before the splendid

work of art. Something about the small black hull and single mast bearing the somewhat loosely flapping black sail spoke to all his grief and inner turmoil. Something about the way it rocked softly across the placid water reminded Abner of every good memory he'd ever shared with Stevie, more so than any one picture or anecdote could ever dream of doing.

Suddenly, he remembered the New Destiny Constitution and its many bylaws from his hundred hate-readings of that shameful text and understood both why Alice and Maisie had really come to tell him about tomorrow's executions and exactly what he was going to do about it.

Go and get your wife back, you goddamn fool.

"He'll be there," Maisie had said. "He'll be there, with her, most like."

...And so will I, vowed Abner Hyun.

He stood weeping before his wife's finest oil painting for another few minutes before embarking on stage one of his new plan: filling his belly with something warm for once in eleven months, followed by scrubbing himself from head to heal in a long hot shower. *You won't get close enough to talk to the man smelling like rotted cheese left out for a week in the sun,* he told himself after a whiff of his right armpit. *Besides, if it turns out bad and I fail, then I can go out looking my best, dammit. I suppose I can at least give myself that much respect.*

CHAPTER 12

STEVIE

Infection Event: Day 439

Another day she never thought to live had come to pass. This one was unique from the soul-wearying ones before, however. For one thing, she was actually out of her velvet prison, out in the open, unbound and sober. For another, there were people other than Witen officers and footmen around her. Every last one of her fellow residents were now bunched together in a rough crescent fifty yards from the tropical oasis that dotted the geometric center of The Meadow's desert. She longed to be one of them. Instead, she stood apart, stood, in fact, alongside those who stood before them. She ached to lose herself in that mass of humanity but could not move to join them. She *would* not. It would all be for nothing if she tried to run now. She was chained by her own altruism.

She had to stand where she now stood, right beside the Commander and his pet Steward.

They, of course, had taken up residence directly in front of their most recent ungodly creation. It was something Stevie Hyun thought never to see. It was so medieval, so archaic. The juxtaposition of it amid the futuristic superstation was eerie. Worse yet, it did not instill quite the shock in her that she would've thought. She was expecting to see something like it today, she realized. Stevie had overheard the Commander ordering engineers to construct something gruesome for the upcoming executions, but she hadn't known what. She'd been too drunk and too emotionally depleted to care and listen close.

Seeing his end product was indeed a blow to her sense of decency and justice but not at all shocking, sadly. The Commander and his Witen friends had lost their ability to shock her long ago. Still, once she would've bet money never to see a six-stall, fresh-cut wooden gibbet in person, not outside of a Renaissance Festival anyway. Stevie was happy to have her back to the ugly contraption now. Though, trying to ensure she did not have to make eye contact with any of her fellow residents in the crescent-shaped crowd arrayed before her, especially someone she knew, someone she cared for, was proving to be a difficult task. *Still better than looking at the gibbet,* she told herself, studying the white sand at her feet.

The crowd were herded in a manner alluding so closely to mounted cowboys wrangling a head of cattle that Stevie could just about picture the collar and bells tied around all her fellow resident's necks. Captain Alvarez and the Lieutenants of the Witen, with the help of their brainwashed little foot soldiers that went by the patronizing moniker of Footmen, drove the listless mob across the wide, fertile grounds of The Meadow to this dry, destitute spot in the desert just in front of the fresh-built gibbet. They were now penned in by a ring of five footmen spaced evenly between Captain Alvarez and the six Lieutenants of the Witen, all with bats, axes, spears, and clubs held tensely in firm grips, ready to lash out at anyone, for any reason. Stevie assumed it was their clear and unambiguous threat that had the crowd quiet as church mice. All of them knew as well as she did just what the gibbet meant, with its six lengths of black rope tied into bulky nooses hanging from its thick beam of still-green hardwood. The Witen meant to handle their business. They wouldn't have any patience for disobedience this day.

Stevie's attention was drawn, in unison with everyone else, to the maroon-and-silver speaker laying atop the sand in front of the gibbet, only a few feet from where she and the Commander and the Steward stood. Drums echoed from the cedar-chest sized device. Drums so loud, so strong, so booming, and so steady, they rattled her teeth.

Boom, boom, bang, bang, boom, boom, bang. Boom, boom, bang, bang, boom, boom, bang, the simple beat went, relentlessly.

When she finally looked up from the speaker that at one time sat atop the formerly banal tennis court which served as the killing grounds of the Final Tournament all those months ago, she saw even more footmen, come from somewhere, somehow, shoving a path through the center of the crowd's crescent, dividing the arch of people like slicing a rainbow in two with a bolt of lightning. This fresh batch of primly pressed, gray-uniformed footmen were escorting today's condemned, strung out in a line six poor souls deep. Footmen stood, weapons at the ready, on either side of the column, as well as before and after. Even if the failed raiders could somehow break free from their steel magna-bonds, they were not going to get very far, and no one from the crowd was going to get close, either. They were really taking no chances.

The drums are tolling their death-march, she suddenly understood. *No doubt the sociopaths beside me think it's some kinda damn honor*. They were so lost in their own ego, their own fantasyland, that they could convince themselves of anything. She was standing next to a bitter, greedy, sycophantic charlatan and the venal man's object of adoration, a childish, angry fool, lashing out at a world he no longer understood, a world he feared.

All the broken bastard can think to do is attack… Jeez, do I feel pity for him? Stevie was no longer certain. He was her tormentor, her betrayer, her rapist, her abuser … her *lover? God, am I that broken already?* she asked herself. *Have I really given up? Am I really his now?*

No. The definite answer came with his accidental touch. It made her cringe. Only a glance, a brush of hands as he turned to face the marching condemned, but it was enough to let her know she still despised the scarred monster. Though she stood here today unchained, unbound in any physical way at all, she was still nothing more than his slave. Stevie Hyun was sane enough to remember that much. She was not totally broken just yet. The realization gave her some welcome comfort. She even found herself daring to hope only a heartbeat later, daring to dream of rescue, of lasting escape. *Perhaps Maisie and Alice can finally rally the residents out of their meek and pathetic passivity and put a stop to today's madness, and then bury the Witenagemot from all memory once and for all… Or so I will hope*, she told herself. *He can't destroy that in me unless I let him. Just hang on, Stevie*, she silently extolled. *Just a bit longer.*

"Ladies and gentlemen, residents of Cardinal's Nest, citizens of the Witenagemot, I thank you for joining us on this forsaken ground," the Steward bellowed at the silent crowd with gesturing hands and a fatuous grin. "I'm sure many among you are wondering why we've chosen to erect the Commander's justice on this scorched and cursed patch of sand. Well, I'll tell you. It's because the evil planned and attempted by these selfish fools you see trussed up before you today is so heinous, so egregious to the foundations of our species, that we in no way feel they're entitled to their last sights being the beauty of The Meadow's flowering fields or the awe-inspiring wonder of the Grand Rotunda or the majesty of engineering that is the Living Quarters Central Hub. No, sir. No, ma'am. They do not deserve anything but sand. Their souls are as barren as these soft white dunes. This is where they belong. They would've destroyed us all. And not just us, but the memories of the lost loves we carry with us as well. Their souls would never get the rest of knowing their husbands, wives, fathers, mothers, brothers, sisters, friends, neighbors, whatever, outlasted the catastrophe and started over in their names. They would've ensured that the last generation of the human race perished together just when they seemed to finally have a workable system, just when the right people, the right *man* arrived to ensure its security and survival. If these vile traitors had been successful in their pathetic attempt, humanity would be no more. They have sinned against the very core of everything, against the heart of the matter, you might say. They deserve no comfort in their final moments. Now, the Commander and I would spare these traitor's loved ones from having to endure their demises if we could, but as we've come to learn over our weeks of interrogation with the condemned, many of their loved ones harbor views very sympathetic, if not identical to, the very ones that helped land these people in chains today…So endure it you shall. And silently. We shall brook no outbursts here today, no disorder of any kind. The officers and footmen around you have full discretion to deal with dissenters in any manner they see fit. You will all learn today's lesson, one way or another."

The dictator's asslicker paused there to allow the Commander to tap the shaft of the black axe strapped to his back before crossing his arms over his wide, rock-firm chest. The crowd stayed silent. The condemned stayed silent.

The Steward carried on. "These six before you today have been found guilty of various violations of the New Destiny Constitution, not the least of which being treason. This alone is punishable by death. According to The New Destiny Constitution bylaws, that method of execution is to be the gallows. Make no mistake, people—none of this brings us any pleasure. No, my friends, this is a sad day for the Commander and I, for every member of the Witenagemot. We give so much to the cause of mankind and expect so little in return. To be repaid for that service with treachery is almost heartbreaking. Notice I say *almost*, for the Witenagemot will never falter. We may bend with grief and betrayal, but we shall not break, ladies and gentlemen, we shall never break. No one is ever beyond the law of the Commander and his Witenagemot. To those of you in the crowd today who are sympathizers with the condemned, know this: we have wrung from these six every last detail of every plot or scheme you've ever dreamed up. We know your meeting places. We know your leaders and your spies. We know everything. We have shut down and disconnected both of the alternate Control Rooms from the system. They are essentially broom closets now. So, if you need the space, feel free to toss your shit inside. They aren't good for anything else now... And for our AOA and former-government friends, we know about the satellite platforms and your plans to fly a Star Hawk here loaded with munitions and have taken certain steps to avoid that unlikely scenario ever coming true. Well, one step really. That being setting off all of the remaining satellite platform's self-destruct sequences."

A somehow deeper quiet seemed to grip the crowd. Stevie saw eyes darting this way and that. She saw a few former AOA execs and some of what she thought was the British PM's entourage suddenly go pale. Stevie had been at the meeting where Harrington and his people had first suggested their satellite platform plan. She knew the former denizens of Branch 1 were holding it like the proverbial ace up their sleeve. The drums from the speaker had stopped with the Steward's first words, but she swore she heard a bell tolling from it now. It took a good few moments for her to realize it was in her head.

She was hearing the death-song of any dreams at future resistance, and she knew it.

All her prior commitments to not let go of hope no matter what were held together now by only the smallest tensile thread. *They know everything. Ha, of course they do.* The Witen had the prisoners locked away for over two months. She should've realized they'd be using that time to interrogate them. Stevie looked at the condemned, now driven to their knees by their footmen guards in a line five feet in front of the Commander, the Steward, and her. Their backs were to them, but she saw easily what she was looking for, nonetheless. Once a person knew what to look for, one could hardly fail to see it. Each of the shackled doomed before her bore fresh-scabbed cuts, half-healed burns, bruises in various states of fade, and though she could not see their eyes, she knew from how they all hung their heads that a haunted soul could be seen clear in their whirling irises. *God, they've all been tortured,* she knew. Stevie's heart broke for them, but she did not show it. She kept her face as blank and dead. She would not give the Commander the satisfaction.

"All resistance ends today on these hot sands," the Steward said. "You will all witness that end for yourselves, firsthand... Then, maybe, god willing, we can get back to the project at hand: the survival of our glorious species!" the Steward shouted, adding a clenched fist above his head for autocratic emphasis. "Before we list the condemned and then wipe their names from the pages of history forever, we have a smaller matter to make mention of, though not a trivial one by any means, as those who were involved in the matter can well attest. Another long-constructed act of insubordination was also recently dealt with by the Commander. Alice Stark hid her pregnancy from the Witen. In direct defiance of the procedures outlined in the New Destiny Constitution, Ms. Stark conspired with several members of Newton Hospital's staff, including two doctors and a half dozen nurses and orderlies. Each of these hospital staff members have been found guilty after confessing to their crimes. For their deceitful deeds, they have been sentenced to two years of dish-duty in the cafeterias for every single meal: breakfast, lunch and dinner, seven days a week. They will work out any kinks this puts in their health-care schedules on their own. I hope their busy schedules and a bit of hard labor teaches them something of honor, humility, and loyalty, and what kind of noble commitment it takes to be a good Witen citizen. As for Alice Stark herself, the shame of placing so many good people in a position to defy the New Destiny Constitution is something she'll have to learn to live with the rest of her life. If true justice and karma exist, which I am certain they do, she will have to grapple with her selfish choices all day, every day, until she dies No one gets out of their responsibilities in the end. One way or another, karma catches up to you. Well now, I suppose that's as good a segue as any," the Steward said with an actual giggle. "I now invite you to watch karma smack these failed raiders. Thomas Spurnberg," he called to Stevie's condemned friend at the right end of the line of shackled prisoners, "rise and hear your verdict."

Spurnberg didn't rise. He looked up through Stargazer Ceiling instead. This last defiant act cost him a club across the back of his thighs by the gray-uniformed footman nearest him. Another was on its way, but Spurnberg avoided the pain and opted to stand. "Tom Spurnberg," the Commander growled out from beside Stevie, "I f nd you guilty of treason, and hereby sentence you to hang."

"Gayle White, rise and hear your verdict," the Steward called out. The short, olive-skinned woman in line beside Spurnberg rose to her feet right away and stood with her round shoulders hunched and her chin pressed down on her flat chest.

"Gayle White," the Commander repeated her name in the same growl as before, "I find you guilty of treason, and hereby sentence you to hang."

"Alicia Mendoza, rise and hear your verdict." Mendoza was an athletic woman with wide hips and a straight back. Locks of her dark, matted hair fell across her eyes as she stood, hiding her thoughts, though Stevie could only see her side profile from her position anyway.

"Alicia Mendoza, I find you guilty of treason, and hereby sentence you to hang." The Commander's voice was more robotic than an Astro droid's.

Stevie Hyun knew each one of the poor souls ticked off the Steward's evil little list. She'd been plotting and spy ng right along with them before the Commander had taken her. She realized she could have easily been one of these doomed few. The thought was strange and terrifying. Stevie tried to decide which fate she would've preferred: her current tormented and abused road or death in the desert hanging from the end of a rope. No immediate answer struck her. "Thaddeus Mackerelli, rise and hear your verdict." The familiar name of a man she spent many a night brainstorming and flushing out ideas with across a rickety card table in that huge empty ante-chamber Spurnberg had found broke her chain of thought.

"Thaddeus Mackerelli, I find you guilty of treason, and hereby sentence you to hang," the Commander's voice bellowed the formal name of the tall and slender trolley driver. Stevie and all the others only ever called him Relly. Something about hearing his full name called out made his imminent loss all the sadder.

"Robert Boston, rise and hear your verdict," the Steward called the fifth name. Boston, like Spurnberg before him, refused to rise. He was a big man, tall with milk-chocolate skin, a wide face, and broad, sloped shoulders. A man not easily cowed was Bob Boston. Hours of hard labor in and about The Meadow, keeping it lovely and operating smoothly, had strengthened his thick arms into tree trunks. When the footman nearest him whacked his barrel-stout thighs the first time, Boston barely flinched. The willowy kid wielding the club couldn't have been much older than seventeen, and despite the might of the Witen and his armed compatriots all about him, Stevie still saw fear in the young footman's eyes when Bob Boston climbed slowly and deliberately to his feet, staring down the little pipsqueak all the while.

"Bob Boston," the Commander called in his uninterested, robotic growl, "I find you guilty of treason, and hereby sentence you to hang." Boston only turned his head and spat.

"Gabriel Duchesne, rise and hear your verdict." It was this last name that Stevie found the hardest to hear. Her dead-eyed gaze nearly cracked as the husband of her good friend Dolly Duchesne made his way to a stand on shaky, nervous bowlegs.

Stevie thought she heard a muffled sob come from the silent crowd, Dolly's muffled sob, she was somehow certain. The Commander ignored it. "Gabe Duchesne," he said carelessly, "I find you guilty of treason, and hereby sentence you to hang."

"As of this moment, these six names are expunged from all record of our civilization. All trace of them shall be deleted from the work roster entirely. Anyone caught repeating any of these condemned names will be guilty of treason and punished accordingly," the Steward informed the assembled crowd. "Once hanged, these traitors shall be left here to rot as carrion for the flies. This will be the Commander's lesson for all those who still foolishly love and respect them and might wish to honor their sacrifice in some treacherous way. The corpses shall not be touched. Any violation of this decree shall be considered an act of treason and also punished accordingly."

"I challenge the ruling!" a voice shouted from the middle of the crowd, a familiar voice.

No! Stevie silently cried. *Abner, no, keep quiet, you idiot! Please, oh please, someone shut him up.* Her plea may have been heard by some watchful yet indolent deity—she would never know. All she knew was that her husband did not heed her silent wisdom. "I challenge the ruling of these six condemned," he shouted just as he pushed his way through the final row of residents before the gibbet.

"Abner?" the Commander said in a half confused, half pleased voice.

"Hold your tongue, citizen!" the Steward commanded. "Didn't you hear the warning? You were told to remain silent throughout these proceedings."

Abner looked invigorated, determined in a way she'd never seen before. Her husband had lived his life on the very edge, facing danger on what felt to her like a daily basis, so Stevie had seen him keyed up and locked-in before, but the man who stood before the gathered residents of Cardinal's Nest Station was on a whole other level. He was clean-shaven and wearing fresh-pressed black fatigue trousers with black combat boots and a tight black Under Armour t-shirt. A recent buzzcut lined his handsome face. He'd definitely lost some weight, and even a bit of muscle, but in that moment, Stevie would swear he looked better than ever. She fell in love with him all over again. Memories of the park bench he'd scooched up close to her on to whisper some cheesy pickup line she'd long since forgotten on some long ago, unremembered date flashed in her mind. She had fallen in love with him then and there on that rusty park bench, despite all her best efforts. It was the same now, except that she was not at all fighting the emotion. She welcomed it like the kiss of a warm brazier against winter-numbed hands. Stevie's heart only understood in that moment how very much she'd missed him these past dark months. She'd been so concerned with being mad at Abner for so long that she never allowed herself to deal with how much she missed him, with how much she cared for him, with how much she *needed* him.

Abner held her heart in his hands, and she had needed him to know that, to take it seriously for once. Anger and separation were the tools she had decided, subconsciously more than anything, to use in order to drive home that point once and for all. She'd always seen them back together in the end, whenever she allowed herself to picture the future that is. Stevie wasn't really expecting Abner to take her coldness to such extremes. She'd thought he'd come begging a few times until she could be sure he was ready to change and make up to the people for what he'd endorsed and allowed … and done, to his friend… *To poor, stupid, jerkface Eddie Sarkisian…* Then she could forgive him. Instead, the softhearted fool had been so ashamed by his actions and her response that it just about broke him. She wasn't expecting Abner to move into those lonely quarters in Maroon Corridor. Stevie had started to regret her approach, though she certainly couldn't admit to him as much. *No, you were too proud to forgive him. You had to drive him away and leave yourself prey for a madman,* **s**he scolded herself.

But he's here now. Abner is here, my sweet Abbie. He's come for me. He'll take me away from all this. He'll make it alright, a naïve part of her assured. *No, he'll only get himself killed before your eyes and sink the final nail into your sanity coffin,* the more rational part of herself shot back.

"I have a right to speak, Steward," her beautiful, courageous, idiotic, wonderful husband told the scowling Witen Councilmember. "I am a citizen of the Witenagemot, whether I like it or not. Isn't that so, Steward?"

"Yes, it is," the Steward confirmed. "And you are subject to its laws, so hold your tongue, and step back in line."

"Well then, as a citizen of the Witen, I have a right under Article 10, Section D of the New Destiny Constitution that I wish to exercise here and now. Perhaps you've forgotten your own work, Steward, but it is that section of your *Constitution*," he continued, spicing the last with sarcasm, "that clearly outlines the rules and regulations regarding Final Appeal. Shall I recite to you the exact wording? *If any citizen disagrees with a decree or judgement of the Commander, that citizen has the right to challenge the rulings by Final Appeal.*"

"What do you mean, 'challenge the rulings'? The hell is 'Final Appeal'?" the Commander asked his former friend with no trace of his ruler's growl. "Steward?" he prompted, turning to face the much shorter man. "What is he talking about?"

"I challenge you to a death match, Jasper," Abner stated simply.

"No!" Stevie cried aloud an instant later.

"You insisted on the clause, Commander, sir," the Steward told his sovereign in a small voice. "All citizens have the right to challenge your authority over any ruling. But don't worry, sir," he added, brightening to his earlier form, "I was not just a simple country lawyer back in the old world. I know my way around a contract. I made sure a bylaw exists in the very next section which allows you to circumvent the challenge for the sake of whatever insane moron would dare challenge you in the first place. Obviously, any such fool would clearly have to be wrong in the head. What more proof could one possibly need?" he asked, laughing. "There would be no honor in entertaining their madness. As leader of the Witenagemot, it is your duty to care for humanity. And when someone is mentally ill, you do not indulge their fantasies. That would not at all be in their best interest. You could even be considered negligent in your duties as ultimate caretaker of the human race."

"Is that the sort of man you are, Jasper? You're gonna hide behind a technicality? What, are you not man enough? Don't have enough honor to keep your word, to fight for your place? Too afraid of losing? Ha, I never took you for a coward, Monty," Abner said with oozing disdain. "Boy, did you sure fool me..." The butt of Lieutenant Gregson's bat smashed into her husband's side, cutting off his taunt.

Five footmen had moved with the Lieutenant through the crowd and now took up position encircling Abner. Stevie watched, rooted in place with panic, foolish hope, and disbelief. "You call him Commander, you backstabbing bastard!" Gregson demanded, red-faced.

"Thank you, Lieutenant," the Steward called out to Gregson approvingly. "Never mind this trash, sir," he advised his superior. "Abner

Hyun already proved his cowardice in the Final Tournament. He forfeited back then and lost any right he might once have had to challenge you. To accept his offer now would be an insult to all the good men who had to die in that honorable crucible."

"You will fight me, Monty," Abner told the Commander, ignoring the Steward completely and without any sign of lingering pain from Gregson's smash. "You have violated my wife. You have betrayed everything good in the world. You will fight me. If I gotta kill all your bootlicking Gestapo Stormtroopers just to get to you, I will. You will fight me, Monty. You will fight me here and now, you fucking coward, you fucking pathetic, evil bully … you fucking beast!"

The Commander said nothing. Stevie watched a shadow that was never there pass across his eyes. A second later, he was reaching over his head for his battleaxe, still without a word. The crowd seemed stiff now, as well as silent. No one dared move a muscle. The Commander stared Abner down while the tension ratcheted up. No one made a move. No one dared even to breathe. Then the Commander raised his black axe and pointed it at Stevie Hyun's defiant, uncowed husband. "Step aside, Lieutenant Gregson," the scar-faced despot commanded his man. "You five," he said, nodding to the footmen that had accompanied Gregson, "clear this crowd back a bit. Give us some space. Move the condemned right in front of the gibbet. Come on. Make some room."

"Commander, no!" the Steward whispered. "There is no need for this. The man has no right to this challenge. You don't have to do this."

The Commander looked down at the Steward for a long breath. "This ain't about my pride, man," he told his subordinate as though he was speaking with a child. "He has called me out in front of everyone. I can't be seen to be afraid, rightly or wrongly. Fear of this," he said, running the ball of his thumb down his axe's shiny, oiled blade, "is the only thing keeping this all together." When it was clear the Steward had no response for him, the massive man in his gold-trimmed black uniform, with its gilt stars popping off the collar points, turned to shout at the man in the much more modest black garb across from him. "I don't want to fight you, Abner, but I will, for the people, for humanity. I'll get no pleasure in destroying you, my friend, but if you want to go through with this ... then ... then that's exactly what I'm gonna do. I will have no pity, I warn you."

"You will die today, Monty," Abner told him with a grim certainty in his voice.

Lieutenant Dirks had come up to the action by then and did not at all care for Abner's continued lack of title decorum. She slammed her war hammer's butt into his other side. "Easy with that, Dirks," the Commander called to her. "Give the man your war hammer, Lieutenant." Dirks was wary of what she'd heard, but her obedient nature took charge and carried out the request. She backed away from Abner once the weapon was in his hand, as though she feared he'd smash her down as soon as she turned her back on him. "Step back," the Commander told Stevie, a guiding hand on her shoulder making the invocation an order and not a suggestion.

When her gorilla-muscled abuser turned from her to face Abner, Stevie's eyes locked with her husband's across the parched sands. *I'm so sorry ... for everything,* she read on his lips. *It's gonna be okay. I love you,* he silently assured before blowing a soft kiss her way. Then his eyes were on the shaggy monster-man stalking toward him. Stevie Hyun's legs gave out beneath her. She crashed to her knees, wanting desperately to look away, to look anywhere else, to *be* any-where else, but she couldn't. She just had to watch, same as last time. *God, déjà vu's a real bitch.*

Clutching handfuls of scalding sand she barely felt, Stevie screamed her husband's name as the Commander's first slash came looping in toward his head. Abner ducked beneath the blow and used his momentum to roll behind his opponent, all while lashing out with his weapon and driving the steel, 3-inch diameter hammer-head into his foe's left calf. The Commander crumpled to a knee with a growl. The crowd's collective gasp drowned out Stevie's own.

Abner didn't hesitate. As soon as he regained his feet, his war hammer was once more flying in to smash his enemy. This strike failed to land, however. It had to be abandoned entirely, in fact, when a sudden looping slash aimed from one knee came sweeping in to meet him. Abner was forced to step back in a quick retreat. The fine sands proved treacherous footing. Stevie watched with rank fear as her husband tumbled onto his ass. His warrior instincts kicked in immediately, to her small relief. Going with the tumble, he managed a graceful reverse-summersault as the Commander's battleaxe came whizzing just above his head. Abner then found himself kneeling in the sand before an off-balance Jasper Montrois. The mighty slash had flung the massive man's center of gravity way off kilter. He was vulnerable. Stevie could see it, and so could Abner. He sent his war hammer scything in as fast as a whirling helicopter blade. The Commander had only just regained his stance when the flat-faced knob at the end of her husband's war hammer smashed into the side of his lower leg, the same leg the first blow had landed on.

Humanity's ruler crashed once more to his knee, this time bellowing in a strained agony totally alien to the autocrat. Stevie could feel the smile forming on her face. Abner kicked the sand at his feet, sending a spray of minute shards of ageless seashells splashing into the Commander's eyes. Montrois reeled back, holding the axe before his face to shield himself from further showers. Abner followed, not allowing the taller and bulkier man to climb up off his knee. Stevie doubted Monty could, even if her husband were not chasing him backward with a series of looping slashes. She was sure his leg had to be broken. The Commander wasn't putting any pressure on it yet, scrambling backward on one knee as he was, so she could not verify her belief. But that second blow to his leg had landed so flush, as well as so forceful, no leg on Earth could've withstood the collision. She knew it had to be broken. Soon the big, clumsy lug would move a hair too slow, and one of her husband's slashes would connect against something vital. The man couldn't scramble like a dismembered gecko across the white sands forever. His size and injury must catch up to him in the end.

Monty must've realized as much himself. He quite abruptly stopped scrambling and instead snatched the shaft of Abner's war hammer from the air on his next wild swing with what looked like very little effort. Stevie's last hope and one true love tried to rip his weapon free from his enemy's clutches, even grabbing its handle in both hands and giving a twisting yank from the hips, but the Commander wasn't letting go. He climbed slowly to his feet, his grip on the war hammer's shaft never faltering. Abner released his weapon just in time to dive out of the way of Monty's uppercut slash, leaving the larger man all alone in the very center of the ring formed by the elongated crescent of residents butting up on either side of the long wooden gibbet.

The Commander flung the war hammer twenty feet across the sand to land just beside her husband. With a roar, he charged at Abner, limping only slightly on his assaulted limb.

How is it not broken?

Stevie's husband snatched up his returned weapon and met the charge, parrying his onetime friend's mighty axe swing. A clang of steel on steel twanged into the otherwise silent dry air. Stevie spared a glance up at the Steward. She had felt his nervousness beside her only moments before, but a gleam now radiated from his azure eyes. Stevie recognized it for triumph. It was easy to spot, the pompous cretin wore it almost every day. She turned back to her husband's deathmatch just in time to see another one-armed axe slash parried by Abner only moments ahead of disaster. The steel song was louder than ever. Suddenly, Stevie found herself wishing for the drums, anything to drown out that awful clanging battle screech.

Monty gave up on his attempts to hack his opponent down and simply stepped forward into a front kick. The blow landed square in Abner's abdomen and sent him flying back ten feet to crash once more on his ass in the soft sand. Abner had lost his wind, clearly, but somehow managed to cling to his war hammer. It proved a fortuitous break a moment later when the Commander strode two long paces across the desert to smash down an overhead slash into the top of Abner's skull. He was able to interpose his weapon just before the black battleaxe's wicked steel blade could shear into his flesh. He had to squirm and roll to avoid two follow-up cuts before Monty stopped to draw in a breath. He favored his left leg still. Clearly, she'd been wrong, and it wasn't broken after all, but just as clearly, Abner had done some damage.

He needs to exploit that, she knew.

They say married couples start to think alike, and perhaps that's true. No sooner had the strategy dawned in her mind than Abner flung his war hammer at his foe. The long steel tool cartwheeled through the air a few revolutions before the Commander smacked it with a jab from his axe, just inches before it lanced home. The momentary entanglement of the weapons and the sudden confusion from the unusual maneuver had Monty off his guard for a crucial moment. Abner had followed his hurled weapon the instant he'd tossed it, diving feet first at the scar-faced, milk-eyed gorilla-man's injured leg, like a soccer player aiming a red-card worthy tackle at a hated opponent's top scorer.

The Commander snarled as he crashed to the sand, nearly landing atop Abner in the process. But her husband had rolled clear of the felled giant, free enough even to jump atop his chest and drive an elbow solidly through his thick tangle of black beard to slam hard against his square jaw. Abner hammered home two more successive forearm shivers, driving the Commander's massive cranium into the white substrate and using each new blow to secure his position across Monty's torso. A fourth elbow was on its way when Jasper Montrois remembered his axe. He still gripped its coal-black shaft firm in his right hand. Changing to an underhand grip, the Commander smashed the butt end solidly into Abner's chest. Winded once again, it was all Stevie's husband could do to roll off the Commander, snatch up his war hammer, and stumble away to a safe patch of sand.

"Get him, Commander!" a shrill voice called out from the assembled crowd into the hushed atmosphere. "Kill this jerk!"

"Yeah, kill him," a second voice agreed.

"Don't let this bastard destroy us, Commander," a third joined the entreaties.

"Kill him for us, Commander! Only your strength can take us through the darkness," yet another distinct voice added, quoting a ubiquitous piece of Witen propaganda. This final call opened the floodgates, and despite all the Steward's prior warnings to maintain a silent vigil, Stevie felt she was hearing a cacophony of at least half the voices in attendance screaming out some similar desire for her husband's blood. Abner looked at Stevie. Their eyes locked across the sands once more. A thousand unspoken words passed between them in an eyeblink.

"Aaaahhhh!" Jasper Montrois's war cry cut short their silent conversation. "No one challenges me! No one defeats me!" he shouted, spittle flinging from the corners of his grimacing lips. "You should've fucking known that. What's mine is mine!"

"You die today, Monty!" Abner shouted back. And suddenly, the two men were sprinting at each other across the sweltering desert floor. The Commander went high. Abner's slash went low. In near perfect unison, Montrois skipped clear of her husband's hammer as Abner dived to the right to avoid the axe's red bite. A few more summersaults across the rolling sands and Stevie's love was back on his feet and squared off with the Commander once again. They circled each other then, each being careful to stay just out of reach of the others lengthy weapon.

"How could you?" Abner asked, though from the way he said it and the way he refused to look Stevie's way after, she knew he hadn't wanted to. He was trying to be angry, determined, *single-minded* even, not vulnerable and betrayed. When the Commander had said nothing for reply, and it was clear he never would, Stevie saw her man swallow down his distracting emotions and find his rage reservoir once more. "Fuck you, Jasper. What you lost don't make any of this right. You turned yourself into a goddamn monster. Now, fuck off and die." He was running as soon as the last word cleared his lips.

Montrois recovered fast, but his parry still came late. Abner was able to crash his hammer onto the Commander's right hand. The axe tumbled from his grip in what felt like slow motion. Stevie could see real fear behind the milky white darkness of his left eye. He made no sound though, neither did he cradle his injured hand to his chest. He used it as ably as the left to balance himself as he dodged back from three successive slashes. Stevie could see blood dripping from the appendage, however. Her mind could have been playing tricks on her, she knew, but it really did seem to be swelling larger and redder by the second. *Now, that definitely has to have something broken in it,* she assured her hopes.

Abner chased Montrois away from his fallen weapon, and now, the bigger man was running out of room to retreat. In a few steps, he would collide with the first row of compacted spectators. *He's got him,* hope was singing to her in sweet melodies. *It'll all be over soon. Kill him, Abbie. Kill him and end this. You got him. You gotta.* Their nuptial connection was again spot on the mark. Abner charged in to end the madness once and for all. He aimed a wide, looping slash at Monty's side, only to shift its course at the last possible second and direct its path toward his opponents injured lower leg. The move was almost too fast for Stevie to follow. It should have been the beginning of the end, but the Commander, despite his injuries, had somehow known it was coming and hopped deftly over the fearsome slash, landing firmly on the injured leg itself, no less. Then, with his freshly injured hand, he wrapped his thick fingers around the shaft of the war hammer on Abner's follow-through, just above the yellow-taped handgrip, and ripped it from her husband's clutches with little more than a grunt for effort. The man's strength and stamina must've been as shocking to Abner as they were to Stevie because he simply stood in place and stared at his empty hands for two whole seconds after his disarming. It proved more than ample time for the Commander to stride one long pace forward and smash a snapping headbutt down into Abner Hyun's handsome nose.

The blow was loud and hard and sickening, but Abner kept his feet. Though, he did have the good sense to dart back from the man and put some space between them. He was clearly woozy and shaken, and the sloshing sand pulling at his feet was not helping. It wouldn't be long before the Witenagemot's supreme ruler stalked him down and landed another devastating blow. So when he nearly tripped over the Commander's black battleaxe, he didn't hesitate to bend down and scoop it up. Once Montrois saw Abner go for the axe, he went back for the fallen war hammer. The combatants had exchanged wounds and weapons. With their new armaments and shaky legs, they once more charged. The last headbutt told, however; to Stevie's horror, it told. Still plenty woozy, Abner slipped on the treacherous turf with his first two steps, putting him way out of position to fend off the vicious jab the Commander punched into his belly with the end of the war hammer.

Stevie watched her husband's stomach crumple around the hammerhead, saw Abner's face turn beet-red, saw the axe fall from his spasming hand. She watched all this and wanted so badly not to believe her eyes. She wanted to be mad, to be seeing things. Stevie Hyun, proud wife of Abner Hyun, had no wish to witness his left shin shatter under the impact of the Commander's next whipping smash. She needed so badly for it all to be a bad dream, for the image she now took in of her beautiful, loving, adoring husband's neck being throttled beneath the titanic grip of the Commander's swollen and bleeding right hand to be some nightmare, soon forgotten come daybreak. But she did not wake. The nightmare endured. She had to watch his flawless face smashed and battered under a flurry of goliath-sized fists. Then she got an up-close view of her private horror. The Commander flung her husband's half-limp body a third of the way across their makeshift battlegrounds to land just feet in front of where she still knelt atop the blazing sands.

Like a wild beast released from its cage, she crawled across the shifting surface to throw herself atop her chosen partner's broad, heaving chest. "Abner! Abbie!" she bellowed his name, not knowing what else to say. Stevie pressed her head alongside her husband's bleeding cheek and sobbed deep wells into existence in the desert beneath them. "Oh, Abbie..."

"Don't be mad," he cut her off in a croaking, battered voice that still held enough levity to bring a fleeting smile to her lips. "I know I said I had to last time, too, but... Well, when Mais told me what he'd done... Well, I had to try and win you back."

"Oh, Abbie I know. I know, and I'm so sorry," she told him, suddenly inundated with the shame of every time Monty The Monster's skin touched hers.

She had more to tell him, a lifetime's worth of more, but the Commander interrupted their reunion. Acting as if she weren't there at all, he bent down and grabbed Abner's shirt collar in a bleeding fist and dragged him out from under her. Stevie made to crawl after, but the Hyun family's bane stepped in front of her, cutting off her path. She diverted her slog as the Commander crashed down on her husband. Where only moments before it had been Abner on top of Montrois's torso, it was now the Commander, the much bigger man, by three inches and seventy pounds, on top of Abner's. Stevie scrambled to her feet, cursing herself for meekly crawling in the first place, but she was too late to stop the first blow. Montrois's bloody hand added a splatter of her husband's as he drove a punch down atop the bridge of Abner's nose.

"Nooo!" Stevie shouted, kicking at the massive man's side.

The kicks had no effect on stopping the follow-up smash the Commander dropped atop the same spot with his left, uninjured hand. So she started scratching and clawing, thinking at any moment one or more member of the Witen would surely pull her off their dear leader. No one interfered, though. *The moronic cowards still think they ain't allowed to touch me*, a detached part of her mind thought as she went right on kicking and clawing and scratching and punching, just as the Commander went right on demolishing her husband's once-beautiful face.

With a huff of exertion, Jasper Montrois stopped beating the man beneath him. It was sudden and unexpected, and only then did he seem to notice Stevie. She was still kicking and scratching at the man, she realized. Her eyes were on her battered lover and her mind was nowhere and everywhere. Her limbs were acting on pure auto-pilot. It took his blood-soaked right hand wrapping around her throat and her feeling the multiple broken bones within shifting unnaturally against each other as the pressure perpetually tightened before she was fully back in control of her arms. Stevie immediately brought up both of them to try and pry away the vise that was tightening around her neck. When her legs started kicking open air, she understood the Commander was lifting her up off the desert floor. Broken, bleeding hand be damned, his grip only got tighter. She looked at her defiler once, and only once, when she felt the world slipping away. His cold eyes, one inky black and one milky white, locked with her own. They seemed to hold a question. What that question might be did not interest Stevie Hyun one little bit. She used her last burst of strength and final stored breath to spit into his face and croak, "Fuck you." He scowled at that, she saw, dimly. Then her head snapped violently to the left as a loud crack echoed inside her skull. Then all was black- ness and always would be.

CHAPTER 13

MAISIE

She'd been standing on tiptoes, hopping up and down, leaning on neighbors, anything she could to see the action. Maisie wasn't particularly short for her age, but there were still many in the crowd a deal taller, and she'd gotten stuck in the middle of the gaggle. True, she might have been a bit rude and gotten some put-out looks from a few of the adult residents she had used for a leaning post, but Maisie hadn't cared much, not just because most of those adults were Witen sympathizers and collaborators, but because she simply had to see the battle.

Only when Stevie's neck snapped in the Commander's hand like a thumb against a pencil did she regret her behavior. Maisie Sagal would've given a great deal not to see that. Even worse, at the horrible echoing sound of the snap, the crowd around her surged forward as one beast, pinning her in place between two sweaty farm process workers just off shift and still in their silver-and-maroon jumpsuits, stained from neck to toe in god only knew what. Her head was above almost everyone in the crowd, giving her an unobstructed sightline to something she couldn't close her eyes to fast enough. Stevie's head dangled from a floppy neck in some kind of gross parody of a marionette with a cut string. Maisie's eyes had stayed open just long enough to watch the first few inches of Stevie Hyun's lifeless buckling fall after Jasper Montrois, the enemy of all mankind, released his grip.

She might've screamed then if Abner Hyun hadn't beaten her to it, and if his wail hadn't been so heartbreakingly mournful as to sap the breath clean out of her lungs. "Nooo!" he continued crying as he somehow struggled up from where he lay atop the red-stained sand. His face was pulp. Maisie found it difficult to believe the man could even see through his ghastly swollen eyes. But as he pulled his wife into his arms and cradled her lolling head against his chest, he nonetheless showed little sign of the dazed pain that had been suffocating him only moments before.

The Commander lurked above the tattered couple for a few long, breathless seconds before strolling casually away. Maisie forgot about him and kept on watching the tragic scene despite knowing how private it should be. But she was in anguish, too. Stevie Hyun was a close friend. She'd thought of her and Alice and Dolly as surrogate mothers, many times. She loved them all, and Stevie especially.

The wonderful women with whom she had developed friendships were her small consolations throughout her time inside Cardinal's Nest's hotel from hell. They were all thick as thieves in no time flat, and pretty much, for all intents and purposes, the real driving force behind the resistance despite Alice's pregnancy. Well, perhaps not Dolly so much, as far as their resistance stuff went anyway. Maisie still took a good deal of comfort in Dolly's company, regardless, and even though her husband was in fact part of the plot, they talked about everything but the Commander, the Steward, and the downfall of their Witenagemot. Dolly was delicate in that way, but very strong in others. Each woman meant a great deal to her and had helped her, each in her own unique manner, by her own unique means, through some very dark days. They were her family. The rest had died or left her. When Maisie reminded herself that it was she that had gotten Abner all worked up and set this whole horrible event into motion, she nearly vomited all over the bald process worker pressing against her right side.

The ebb and flow of the compact crowd shifted then, plopping her down a good two feet with little warning. She nearly lost her footing and feared for an instant she'd be trampled into the sand by the blood-maddened mob, but thankfully some semblance of calm and reasonable crowd manners were suddenly snaking their way through the residents, allowing her to regain her balance unhindered. Maisie only had to hear Abner's woebegone wails of "Stevie! Oh, Stevie! No! No, please... Oh, god... Oh, Stevie!" all the while interspersed with guttural curses of "You killed her, you fucking bastard! You fucking killed my wife! I'll kill you, you fucking bastard, you fucking monster. You fucking raped her and killed her. How could you?! Who the fuck are you?! I'll... I'll... I'll fucking kill you!" Maisie did have to hear those terrible cries, but she was at least spared having to see Abner's tears mingling with the blood on his face. For that much, and little else, she was thankful.

A purely logical part of her wondered how the man could manage speaking at all. Any other jaw would have shattered under that onslaught of the Commander's mighty fists. She didn't see why Abner Hyun's should be any different. But somehow, he was shouting. And when the crowd started buzzing around her once more, and the jostling began, she knew something was happening out there on those sands that was impossible to believe.

He must've gotten up and is going for Montrois, she thought, the instant before confirmation came in the form of a tall supervisor assistant closer to the action, shouting at the residents behind him pleading for new. "The son of a bitch stood up," he said in a voice at once both amused and amazed.

"He's fucking hopping toward the Commander on one leg," a voice she instantly hated called out with a laugh.

"What does the dumb shit think he's gonna do on that shattered fucking leg a his? I mean, look at the damn thing, flopping around like his fucking wife's head." The laughter that rippled through the residents after that shout made her so angry she nearly swung a punch at the jerk behind her cackle-laughing like he was at one of those stand-up comedy shows her father had taken her to a couple years back, but she restrained herself and got a better idea. The crowd was again pressing in tight together to see the upcoming action, and Maisie didn't hesitate. She leaped up, falling against the bald process worker and clinging tight to his head and shoulders until the other process worker in the thick-rimmed glasses got close enough to pin her up in her elevated perch.

Out on the scorched sands, Abner was indeed hobbling on one leg toward the Commander. Maisie had lost track of the Witen's leader after Stevie was killed and only now saw that he had wandered back to where his black battleaxe laid half buried in a small dune. The giant now held the weapon at his side in his right hand. It stayed right there by his side for Abner's entire curse-laced, pain-spasmed, hopping trudge from where his wife lay to just two feet before the Commander. Abner was out of breath when he arrived and nearly collapsed when his shattered leg took his weight for a second as he lost his balance. The recent widower's once-good friend loomed silently before him the entire time, showing only the slightest hint of favoring his own leg injury. Abner somehow regained himself, and just as he drew in a breath to speak, the ruler of what's left of the world flashed his axe out in a slash so fast, if she blinked, she'd have missed it.

Sadly, Maisie had not blinked. Her eyes were wide open, and her sightline was clear. She saw the heavy blade shear into the side of Abner's bruised and swollen head, just below his left ear. It was through the skull completely and sending the top half tumbling independent of the rest of its body to the hungry white sands faster than the sick sound of the severing bones and tissue could reach her ears. All in attendance had fallen deathly silent and stayed that way as Abner's body fell forward toward the crescent crowd, giving them all a clear show at the former proud security officer's exposed pink tongue and throat.

She did vomit then, and the bald farm process worker did not at all appreciate it. "Agghh, sick! What the fuck, girly?!" he yelled, elbowing the residents hemming him in to open up a small gap in the tight-packed crowd. Maisie plopped to the sand once the pressure holding her up slackened. Somehow, from somewhere, against her every horrified instinct, she found a controlling calm and stood back up very deliberately and very slowly. Her puke-spattered victim stared her down the whole time with a look on his face that shifted between indignation, humiliation, disgust, and rage. Before any argument beyond his initial outburst made itself manifest, Maisie saw in the distance, above the bald head of the sick-covered man in the work-worn jumpsuit, a black battleaxe raised in a bloody fist. And when the crowd saw the same, they erupted, most of them, anyway.

The justifiably irate man before her shuttered, not expecting the unified cheer, and turned to see its cause.

Many around her stayed silent, heads bowed with looks that screamed they'd like to be anywhere else, but just as many were cheering with hoots of glorification and pumping fists of self-righteous euphoria. Above the noise of the willing slaves, Maisie heard *his* voice bark out some command. She couldn't make out the words, but his low growl was unmistakable, and when Tom Spurnberg was led up the gibbet steps trailed by his shackled compatriots only moments later, she could guess what order must have been given. The gibbet's platform was raised about three and a half feet off the desert floor, she judged, so she needn't be leaning on anyone's shoulders to see the condemned led one by one to the spot where their last breaths would be drawn. Each noose was tied at the end of a 4-foot length of black rope. Each rope dangled from the thick wooden crossbeam placed eight feet above the gibbet platform and spanning its entire 30-foot width.

Dolly could be heard sobbing into a hand, unable to contain her emotion as Gabe was chivied to his rope and the noose tucked down around his neck. Maisie knew her friend's cry by now. She'd used it often when lamenting her husband's decision-making and the lives and loves they'd all lost to the Infection Event. Maisie and Dolly had entered The Meadow together with every intention of enduring the day's evil events side by side, but when the footmen and officers started corralling the crowd toward the desert, she and Dolly Duchesne had lost each other. Judging by the fact that she could hear the sobs Dolly was obviously trying to hold in, Maisie figured she was somewhere close by. Though, try as she might, she could not spot her through the dense crowd. She gave up the effort when the Steward strode to the center of his stage. He looked as though he might fall off at any moment, so close to the edge of the platform as he was, but his precarious perch had no effect at diminishing his cocky, satisfied, superior grin.

This freakin' guy loves all this, she understood at last. *None of this would've happened if they hadn't brought this jerk up here. This is all his fault really, him and his pawn Montrois. He's the reason Elias won't talk to me anymore. He's the one who poisoned my baby brother with his power-trip.*

She hated Harclay Aponyaschefski in that moment. And then he spoke, and her hatred grew. "Residents, citizens, I implore you, do not look away." Maisie would've charged at the man and clawed his face off had she been in the front row. Since she wasn't, all she could do was listen to him spew his bile. "This gibbet," he said, tapping the platform beneath him with his foot, "has been constructed with deliberate forethought and purpose. It has been built to these specific dimensions in order to enact true justice. For their crimes, these condemned before you deserve a harsh punishment. The lesson must be learned, people. The message must be received... Below the feet of each of these six is a trapdoor. When this rope is cut," he said, pointing to a taught length of black rope shooting off from the crossbeam upright at the far end of the platform, "the doors will open. Now, you may have noticed that the nooses dangle at the ends of only four feet of rope so that when the trapdoors are opened, most of these treacherous rogues will only plummet a few inches before the rope goes tight. The taller ones may get lucky and fall far enough to snap their necks, but I doubt it... This will not be over quickly, ladies and gentlemen. These six shall strangle here for as long as it takes... Then we will remove the platform but leave the gibbet and the bodies hanging from its crossbeam ... until we feel the message has been truly received."

"We get the message, Steward, sir. Now hang the stupid bastards," the same voice she despised earlier was back at it again. Maisie watched Aponyaschefski try not to grin, but the hint of one was plain to see, nonetheless.

"Very well, good folks," he responded to the anonymous voices that quickly joined in the calls for murder, "keep both eyes open, do not turn your heads, and learn your lesson well." With that, he turned to the gibbet's staircase.

The Commander was already on the second of three steps when the Steward bowed toward him reverentially. Montrois returned the gesture of deference with a quick, and seemingly bored, nod as he climbed the final step. His heavy footsteps boomed out into a crowd hushing with anticipation as he made his way across the platform to the anchor rope. He paused, axe loose in his still bloody and swollen right hand, before turning to face the rapturous crowd. "Witness justice!" he bellowed, thrusting his axe into the air. "*My* justice."

The Witen sympathizers burst out with approving cheers like gleeful wolves or rescued shipwreck victims. Montrois whipped his heavy axe down, shearing the anchor rope and burying itself eight inches into the crossbeam upright. The condemned, Maisie's good friends, fell then, but as the Steward had said, none very far. No necks snapped. Her confederates were all choking to death before her eyes, and there wasn't a damn thing she could do about it.

The Commander turned to watch his work. Maisie stared daggers at his wide, muscular back whilst he stared transfixed at the six stricken faces fading from beet-red to suffocated blue. All six were kicking, swaying, and scrambling for purchase. None were finding any. Not a soul in the crowd did a thing to stop the insanity as the condemned died slowly, second by excruciating second. The crowd barely made a sound. Choked gasps and stretching ropes could be heard clearly above the murmuring din.

Then she heard Dolly crying so loudly there had clearly been no attempt at stifling the outburst. Maisie could not stop her eyes from turning toward Gabe. When she took in the same sight Dolly must surely be seeing, she understood the uncontained reaction. Tears flowed from eyes rolled up in a skull like rushing streams across dirty, purpling cheeks. His hands were tied helplessly behind his back. His short, stout legs feebly struggled to press against the white sands just inches below. He looked pathetic, terrified, tortured. Maisie's heart broke to think that this helpless image would be the last Dolly Duchesne would have of her husband.

If she weren't boxed in, Maisie imagined she might scramble beneath the platform to Gabe and let him use her as a stool to take his weight. But she knew how hopeless a thought it was in nearly the same instant it had dawned. Too many footmen stood by, all too eager to swing their sticks at someone. Too many of the residents themselves would assist the Witen only for the asking. Too much power had been seized by the Commander. There was no stopping the Witenagemot now, no helping friends escape strangulation, no helping anyone, save by their express permission. The resistance had lost. Maisie had lost. It was over.

Even a modern-day hanging can get boring after a while, apparently. Some of her swinging cohorts weren't even done kicking before the crowd started to peel off. The Commander and the Steward had been the first to march from the desert. Though, they had of course been accompanied by an escort of burly, gray-and-gold draped enforcers, with Captain Alvarez, the six lieutenants, and all the remaining footmen in the desert hurrying along at their heels. That signal had told the gathered residents their required time of attendance had come to an end. A few families left immediately after, but the majority of the crowd stayed to watch the spectacle.

But the novelty did truly seem to be wearing off now. Little by little, space opened up around her. Faces she hadn't seen through the tight press revealed themselves. Some bore looks of sycophantic ecstasy, while others mere bemusement. No one spoke much as they left. Maisie imagined their minds and thoughts were just as jumbled as her own. She recognized a few of the residents as they left in a detached sort of way. One that stood out was the tall, dark, smooth-skinned and slender female AOA exec. Maisie remembered her from the impromptu meeting at her and Alice's place all those months back. The woman had spoken with a good deal of authority, she recalled. Hubert Harrington had even looked a bit sheepish beside her, much the same as he looked even now, standing a pace behind the dead-eyed woman. It was those black, unnatural eyes that broke through Maisie's torpor. She saw a fury there, the same half-contained fire that had shown itself at that unproductive meeting. Somehow though, Maisie knew the woman's anger had little to do with the injustice she'd just witnessed.

The platform satellites, their plan... That's what's got her so pissed, Maisie knew.

The pair of AOA executives walked past her just as the crowd thinned enough to spot Dolly cutting across the departing grain, headed for the gibbet. Her dear confidant was once more frantically wailing. Maisie assumed Dolly was about to do the very thing for Gabe that she had wished to do for him minutes earlier. She knew full well how ill it would go for Dolly should she attempt to save her strangling husband, but Maisie found herself unable to either move or shout to the inconsolable woman. She was paralyzed by fear in a way unlike all past experience. Maisie had been afraid these last few years often enough, but somehow, she'd always found the hope and strength to keep swallowing it down and persevering through the chaos. Only now, she felt defeated, truly beaten for the first time in her life. She felt useless. Maisie knew she'd be of no comfort to Dolly, of no help at all. The Witenagemot had won. So she just stood there, still as a spineless toad, watching her friend in deep anguish struggle toward her near-lifeless husband.

Thankfully, Larry Holderman, Jed Redding, Aziz Patel, and a short, bowlegged Asian woman Maisie knew worked with Dolly in the Rec District's Mini Caf kitchen weren't so immobilized by weakness as she. The four of them caught Dolly from behind within a dozen paces of the gibbet. With an effort heretofore unnecessary in the relatively short life of Maisie Sagal, she dragged her gaze from a thrashing and forlorn widow in the desperate clutches of four strong friends and the gory injustice that hung amidst the dry air behind them. Never again, Maisie Sagal vowed, would she look at that awful scene. The desert had become a dead zone in her mind. Her eyes would not twitch its way, not so long as the corpses rotted below that thick green hanging beam.

A trolley. I need a trolley, she thought, jogging across The Meadow's footbridge toward the line of waiting transports. *Home. I need to get home.*

The Number 9 magnetic-rail trolley floated to a stop along a silver-and-orange streaked bulkhead inside Annex VI in Orange Corridor at the junction of Alleyways XI and XII after a long six-minute journey, and then, after ninety or so steps down Alleyway XII, Maisie finally found herself standing before the cramped, new-age apartments she had called home for the last fourteen months. *Carrie Roxanna,* she chanted her sister's name as she punched in the door code. *I need you.*

A passed-out Alice could be seen sprawled across their living room couch in a pair of faded red sweatpants and a stained gray Dartmouth College t-shirt as soon as Maisie crossed their quarters' threshold. Maisie saw no baby in the bassinet beside the low wooden coffee table, nor inside the composite-material swing at the end of the couch that an engineer friend of Alice's had crafted for her in private. Without a word of greeting, for the sake of both the tired woman's rest and Maisie's own desire for silent solitude, she marched toward the spare room at the end of the long hall.

Maisie didn't want to discuss the day's events just then, or perhaps maybe ever. She wanted quiet but also the best comfort she could think of, the only company she cared to share: the warm, soft skin of her sister's cheek pressed against her own, the emotional blanket that enveloped her whenever she cradled her adorable infant sister in her arms. She needed to see Carrie's bright hazel eyes looking up innocently into her own, knowing pure security and trust. Maisie longed for such a feeling herself, and if she could not find it in her own life, she would try to taste its savors through the medium of her small, double-chinned, munchkin of a sister.

Maisie knew Alice would be understanding in all things, even in Maisie not wanting to talk about anything just then, but she was still as grateful as she was currently capable of being that Alice was now indeed catching some winks in between Ri Ri's naps. Her roommate would no doubt be eager to hear all the day's news. Alice had vowed loudly and often these past few weeks, including directly to the face of her corridor warden Lieutenant Masterson, that she would not be attending the mandatory punishment ceremony. Maisie was sure the frog-faced lieutenant had reported the intended breach of orders to Captain Alvarez at least, but she wasn't really very surprised when

Alice received no real pushback for her defiance. The Witen had been treating her like an outcast of sorts, like a non-person almost, like she didn't really exist as far as they were concerned, perhaps due to some small vestige of decency inside Jasper Montrois's heart, some lingering empathy for Perry Sagal and his loved ones that stopped him from allowing more harsh forms of punishment meeting Alice Stark's defiance. Maisie couldn't say. Or maybe the idiots really thought exiling her from their worries, cares, and responsibilities really was a worse punishment—who knew? Whatever their reasons or infirmities, Alice alone among the residents had stayed home for the hangings. And even though Alice did truly despise Montrois, Aponyaschefski, and all their evil machinations, she did still live on a lunar station, and its realities led one to crave gossip, the fresher the better.

But thankfully, Alice was fast asleep, and Maisie was able to make it all the way to the spare-room-turned-nursery without waking her. Carrie rested in a bowled pad inside her crib, fast asleep herself. Her sister was swaddled in a crochet blanket their Alleyway neighbor, Miss Kinsner, knitted right after Alice had come back home with her. Maisie set to gentle work, unwinding the soft pink-and-purple wrapping before scooping her baby sister off the pad. Carrie gave only the softest, purest, most loveable whimper as Maisie rested her small head atop her shoulder. Backing into the room's rocking chair with her Ri Ri resting lightly on her chest, Maisie began patting her back and softly humming. There was no real tune she followed, just sweet hums of peace and safety.

Ri Ri managed another soft whimper. Maisie couldn't help herself from wrapping her arms across her tiny back and basking in the clean, guiltless scent of her cherished relative. In Carrie Roxanna's blood flowed her father's, the same blood that pulsed through her own veins. Maisie could almost imagine their hemoglobinic similarities calling out to one another and inducing bursts of rejuvenating endorphins whenever they were within a certain proximity, as if they knew. In this cold, dark new world, where the very air itself was no absolute guarantee, it was easy to feel lonely and abandoned. Ri Ri thawed that frosty emptiness better than anyone or anything Maisie Sagal had left in this life.

The relief of her embrace brought on the tears, rivers and rivers of tears, so many tears, cried so hard and so viscerally they woke the sleeping child atop her chest. "Everything is lost, Ri Ri," she sobbed. "Everyone is dead... Elias is one of them. They've taken him for good. Nothing I say gets through to him. They've won. They beat me, Ri. They beat us all. I'm so sorry, but I gotta give up. I gotta... Oh, Carrie," she wailed, clutching her confused sister tight, "we just gotta take care of each other now, as best we can. That's all we can do. I'm sorry. I can't fight them anymore. I give up."

"Maisie, that you?" She heard Alice calling from down the hall over her own hysterics. "Maisie? What's wrong?! What happened?" This last was heard clear as a bell despite her state, as Alice had made it into the nursery.

Alice went for her child at once, snatching a fussing Carrie off Maisie's shoulder. "I'm sorry," Maisie muttered as Alice cooed and rocked the shaken infant. "I just needed to hold her, Alice. I needed her."

"It's fine, Mais. Carrie's fine. Everything's fine," Alice said, dismissing Maisie's apology with a flick of her wrist. "Just tell me what happened? Tell me you're alright, at least."

"We got them killed, Allie," Maisie said after a few moments spent settling herself.

"What?" Alice asked, obviously hoping she'd misheard.

"Abner and Stevie, the both of them, we got 'em killed," Maisie told her in a numbed daze. "He killed them both. Then all the rest, too. They're all dead, Allie, and it's all my fault. Snapped her neck right in front of everyone, and no one did a damn thing. They won, Alice. I can't do this no more. We can't fight them. They beat us. I gotta give up... I do. I... I... I give up."

"Oh, no you don't," Alice boomed back at her with a certain vehemence for which Maisie was ill-prepared. "You will keep right on fighting, Maisie. We will keep fighting. For the sake of this beautiful child," she added with a soft kiss planted on the baby's pale brow. "For Stevie's sake," she said, nearly breaking, "for Abner and all the rest, you will keep fighting, Maisie. You will not give up. We can't. Their fates are not our doing, but I gotta believe we can still make their sacrifices mean something. We have to," she implored, still cracking with her own grief. "*You* have to, Maisie... You are gonna create the world

Carrie deserves, the world we all deserve. I just know it." Alice bent down in front of Maisie still seated in the maroon La-Z-Boy rocking chair. Carrie had been sent back to dreamland with her mother's kiss and did not wake, even when Alice leaned forward to pull Maisie in close with her free arm.

"You are far stronger than you know, Mais. You're gonna save us all someday," her cherished roommate and surrogate mother attested in a husky, tear-brushed whisper.

CHAPTER 14

BOYD

Pink Floyd's "Lost for Words," from the Division Bell album, rolled its mellow way around his echoing new home. Boyd was waiting patiently, or at least attempting to, for Dolly and a few other sorely missed faces. His massive hidden hall had only a low end table, laden with six glasses and two full wine bottles, beside a single recliner across from a three-seater fold-out couch, and arranging their delivery hadn't been easy, so the blue plush couch would have to serve for all his expected guests. The two larger pieces of furniture were positioned at either end of a 14 by 16-foot black carpet dotted with white stars and galaxies done up in oranges, blues, violets, and grays. He was seated in the navy-blue recliner facing the matching couch, with a clear view of the rectangular hall's lone entrance hatch.

Music helped him clear his head and ready his thoughts, good music anyway, and Pink Floyd definitely qualified. He wanted to be sharp and lighthearted. His guest's reactions to seeing him in this strange place were quite unpredictable. They needed the best of him. Music always helped bring that out. Good music, a good song, his favorite song—one of hundreds—was the closest thing to real magic.

Once I would've prayed, Boyd thought, thumbing his stereo remote to the next track the shuffle feature cared to serve up as the final chords of "Lost for Words" were strummed. It wasn't that long since he'd stopped, only three years and a couple months since he'd survived that first day of total liberation, though it had often felt like a lifetime ago, and in many ways had been. Bending to his knees, clasping his hands and pressing them reverently to his bowed brow while he spoke with his savior and creator had been such a central part of his life ever since he was old enough to form long-term memories.

Boyd had been so nervous that first day, almost shaking after skipping that first check-in with *the boss*. But when the day had progressed the same as the thousands before, without any catastrophic floods or fires, with no sudden impulses to rob, cheat, steal, and kill his neighbors taking hold of his impressionable mind, he'd gotten lost in the monotony of daily living in a world where everyone was just doing their best to be their best and live their best life, and he realized that he had actually forgotten to be nervous about divine retribution.

Boyd hadn't felt completely cured of his holy shackles just then. It had taken a bit more exposure to ideas and information he had been steadfastly avoiding in the past, but he did get there in the end, burying Father Raymond Boyd for good and all, metaphorically at least.

After all, he still wore the damn collar. He'd sworn his life to it, an oath of honor. Boyd couldn't stomach the shame of forswearing an oath. Their sanctity hadn't waned with his new enlightenment; if anything, they'd grown. All a man truly had was his word—break it just once and you never got it back. Unless, of course, you were dealing with a known dishonest quantity, like the Witen for instance. Forcing an oath defeated the purpose. One had no duty to uphold a bargain wrung through intimidation. *There is nuance in all things. Never forget,* he reminded himself. Or perhaps that rationale was simply a cowardly lie he told himself in order to avoid the whole ugly confrontation. Boyd knew his track record would certainly point toward the latter explanation.

The Church, or more precisely, Cardinal Joiner had sent him up to the moon for some "heavy contemplation and penitent reflection" once his diocese's bishop ratted him out to his superiors. Boyd had been skipping out on his duties, feeling like a fraud, like a wolf among lambs every time he put on the robes. The bishop hadn't been pleased. The weaselly bastard sat Boyd down in a stiff green folding chair inside his sweat-stinking office and demanded he provide him with some reasons for his recent behavior. Boyd had then responded with calm honesty, saying, "I am pissed, Bishop, at myself, at you, at the whole damn system going back two thousand years. I despise the fact that I am stuck in an order of pedophilic, sexist mythmakers and grifters."

Those words—whether they were wise or not is a question for the philosopher to puzzle over—had set off a chain-reaction that made it all the way to the Cardinal level. Hell, maybe even the Pope himself had been told; Boyd couldn't be sure. But as fate would have it, he had a reluctant friend in Cardinal Joiner. Once the eminent vicar with the Pope's ear had been a humble Massachusetts priest, and a young Raymond Boyd had been his eager protégé. Not wanting to face the fact that his tutelage could've truly failed so utterly, Joiner, being one of the few church officials who knew of Cardinal's Nest's construction and The Vatican's part in it, had pushed for the convenient Lunar Base solution rather than a simple defrocking.

Lucky me, he laughed to himself, flipping the song yet again. Boyd knew the piece within the first few notes, he was sure of it, but cut the song short before he could puzzle out the title and artist. The white wheel on his entrance hatch was spinning. They were here.

"I don't know what you could have behind that hatch, Doll, that would excuse this creepy hike ya dragged me and my baby girl on, but it better be damn good," Boyd heard Alice Stark saying as the large steel hatch swung slowly open on its reenforced spring.

"Would a glass of chilled red wine qualify, Alice?" he called, standing up, bottle in hand.

"Boyd!?" It was Maisie Sagal who was first to shout his name in shock. Alice was busy picking up her jaw from the floor.

They both tried squeezing through the hatchway at the same time, Alice with an arm across her baby girl strapped to her chest in what Boyd knew was called a baby carrier. Giggling, the girls shimmied their way through, never taking their eyes from him. He had missed them a good deal more than he'd known. The sight of their happy faces, not to mention that of the pink faced little angel dangling in her baby carrier, brought about a groundswell of happiness Boyd had not at all been prepared for. Then Dolly stepped in behind them, and the feelings almost came flooding out in tears. He caught himself, though, remembering his determination to stay lighthearted, so that by the time Larry Holderman stooped through the hatch behind Dolly, Boyd was once more master of his emotions.

"No Jed?" he asked the collector module navigator with an unaccusatory smile.

"He'll come around ... eventually," Larry Holderman told him as he turned to shove closed the spring-loaded hatch.

"He's scared. I totally understand. Tell him I said as much, will ya?"

"Father Boyd," Alice Stark called in a booming voice demanding obedience, "you tell me right this instant just what in the heck is going on here and why you let us all go on imagining awful things about your fate."

Father, she calls me. He nearly corrected the record once and for all. The words were on his tongue, but before they passed his lips, he remembered just who was in charge of The Church now. *He*, Father Raymond Boyd, the priest, was its authority and could make the title mean anything, stand for anything. He could kill all the dogma and make love, grace, and reason the only stipulations. He could embrace the title even... *Or am I just being a coward again?*

Maisie's shout saved him from having to answer that question. "Why didn't you tell us you was here, Boyd! Why just Dolly? ...Wait, did you know, too, Mr. Holderman? Why didn't you tell us on that long-ass hike through that maze out there?" she demanded, pointing through the hatchway.

"I thought y'all knew... Or else I didn't really think about it all that much. I got a lot on ma mind lately, thank you very much. So excuse me if I drift a bit on walks. Hell, Dolly only told us this morning anyway, for Christ's sake." Turning to face Boyd, he shot his eyes to the floor and began to half speak, half mumble. "We tried to get Jed to come, and he demanded Dolly tell him exactly where she was taking us and ... and..."

"And I did," Dolly confirmed. "I thought it might persuade him to follow me. I'm sorry, Boyd. He promised not to tell anyone what I told him, though."

Before Boyd could brush off Dolly's concern, Alice spoke as she was lifting her daughter out of the carrier strapped to her chest. "Well, damn, Mais, what does that say about us? Dolly barely had to ask us fools twice."

"You complained every step of the way here, Alice," Dolly reminded the voluptuous brunette now cradling the baby in the crook of her pale arm.

"Whatever," Alice dismissed Dolly with a playful wave of her hand. "Well, Boyd," she said, adopting a more serious tone, "I suppose I got no place being angry at you really, do I? I mean, it was my fault the Witen showed up at your shop that day. If that's why you've been avoiding me, then let me say I understand, and I was only shocked earlier and everything. I'm afraid I don't always react well to things in the moment. I just... Well... Hell, Boyd, it's just good to see you, and I hope you can forgive me. I'm sorry I didn't come looking for ya or try and demand the Witen tell us what happened to ya." He wanted to stop her there and assure her there were no hard feelings, but Alice was worked up and so barreled on. "I guess I just figured the stories of you hiding away in your quarters were true. I figured you hated me and wanted to be left alone."

"I didn't." Maisie Sagal spoke, moving toward the couch before Boyd had a chance to open his mouth. "I was sure the Witen killed ya and paid off that maid to keep up the pretenses. I tried to ask the chick like three times, but she never even speaks to me, just acts like I'm not even there... I knew you wouldn't blame any of us or hate any of us," she said, plopping down on the soft couch. "You're a priest after all."

Boyd laughed then. It felt good, so good, like medicine, so he went with it, chuckling all the way back to his chair. "Yeah, Mais, I am that... Oh did I ever miss you all, oh so very much."

"I guess Dolly a little more so though, eh?" Larry Holderman said in a cheeky voice as he sat his plump behind on the arm of Boyd's new couch.

"I reached out to Dolly through certain means right after those bastards killed her Gabe," Boyd told them, locking eyes with the handsome woman in the sandy-blonde bob. She treated him to a smile that could've melted his heart if he'd let it. Boyd needed to distract himself with pouring drinks for his four guests in order to stop the flush of love from revealing itself on his cheeks. "We've been in close contact ever since," he concluded the topic. "I would've brought you all here sooner, or at least made you aware of my fate, if I could have, but I've only just now deemed my position secure enough to risk this meeting. I've been doing a lot of scrambling behind the scenes. That silent maid you've been so rudely rebuffed by, Maisie, my dear, is working for me."

"She's what?" the young teen asked, horribly confused. "She works for *you*? Why?"

"Keeping up appearances: dropping off groceries and dusting and vacuuming and shit like that, to make it look as though one hermit is living in there if the Witen ever decides to raid my old shop again."

"And just what good would that do when they charge in and you're nowhere to be found?" Alice asked him as he handed her a glass of his finest vintage.

"Oh, I'll know what raids are planned far ahead of time," he assured Alice, Maisie, and Larry, all of whom were shooting him very skeptical side-eyes. "I have my return in such an unlikely scenario already planned out. Don't worry there. If the Commander gets impulsive one day and barges in suddenly... Well... Hell, that's just the gamble I'm taking, the one I'm hoping you'll all soon take with me, in a way. But I don't see it happening any time soon. I am in every Witen Council meeting. I may as well have myself a chair right there amongst 'em. I'll know what they plan. I've not been idle in my seclusion. I've set up a network of spies, using my stored supplies of alcohol and other fun things as a fund for the enterprise. Through some fine finagling, I have coerced, bribed, and cajoled a web of individuals unknown to the Witen since they all had no part ever in the resistance. I diversified my portfolio, so to speak, or at least contracted out my labor, storage, and direct operational management. You will have noticed, no doubt, that the Billiard Lounge has suddenly discovered a more than adequate supply of liquor from seemingly nowhere in the past few weeks, as though its managers had been stashing it all away somewhere."

"Well, yeah, actually," Larry said, bemused.

"Tastes a bit familiar, too, don't it, Lar?"

"Yeah, now that you mention it."

"That's 'cause it all funnels through me. My recipes. My process. My brand. I'm directing the manufacture and distribution from back here, behind the scenes as it were," Boyd told them, not able to control the cocky slant of his voice. "The left hand don't work without the right, but the right don't know where to find the left without me... That's a grand over simplification, but you get the picture, I think. I've had to make a few dirty deals and gotten a bit of filth on my boots. I'm in no way proud of it, but my friends, we are reduced to lurking in the shadows of dark and dingy annex tunnels and antechambers now. Our endeavors, our hopes have to live in the shadows. So, we gotta become creatures of those shadows, and such people must necessarily associate with other shady, shadowy folks. But never fear—the perks of insider business with me and the threat of me ratting on them to the Witen for what I've already convinced them to do for me will keep all my shady friends in line. The network can be trusted. It will hold, or else crumble when I say, believe me, guys."

"What the hell are you babbling about, Boyd?" Larry asked after a hearty swig of wine.

"I'm saying I was wrong. We can't be indifferent to the Witen. They won't let us. I'm asking you all, here and now, to join in a new resistance with me, even though I know I have no right to ask anything of you, especially since I've been so unhelpful in the past. Six good folks are hanged dead. I might've been able to do something about that, had I tried, had I not looked away from it all and focused on my little liquor shop. I did try to affect change from behind the scenes later, I swear I did, but my situation wasn't as secure then, and I... Well, I figured it to be too high a risk to expose myself so soon. I did nothing, then and now, and they're all dead. Maybe that's on me, and maybe that's how it should be. So I know you have every right to tell me to fuck off and throw them deaths at my feet, but I'm asking you instead to join up with me. Join me in a *new* kinda resistance, a *long-haul* resistance. Hell, there ain't no reason to let humanity fail just 'cause we all got a bit too impatient. I'm asking you all to help me devise and enact a scheme to secure us a way either off this barren rock and back to Earth or a peaceful cohabitation here, in these halls and chambers, if the former ain't feasible... So, Larry, Alice, Mais, I'm asking you to help me, and if not, to at least keep my secret."

"Of course we'll help ya, you big jerk," Maisie told him with a look of flabbergasted indignation.

"Yeah, Father. None of us are blaming you for anything," Alice concurred. "Shit, I was certain you were mad at me," she added with a laugh.

"I'd like a few more answers first," Larry cut into the good mood with harsher tones.

"Absolutely, Lar. What do you want to know?"

"Well, for starters, how the hell did you find this huge place, all empty and off the books?"

"Ah, yes, my new digs," Boyd said cheerily. "You like?" Once they all nodded their heads, Boyd smiled and carried on. "Well, a few months back, when Spurnberg first told me about the secret meeting place he'd discovered for you guys, it got me thinking. I started wondering just what other secret rooms or tunnels or whatnot this place might be hiding. So, through my various connections, I was able to get my hands on an original set of unredacted blueprints for Cardinal's Nest. On those blueprints, I found where Spurnberg's place was and then scanned the rest of the prints for a similar setup. That access tunnel system just beyond that hatch," he said, indicating his hatchway with an outstretched hand clutching tight to a half-full glass of wine, "well, it fit the bill perfectly. And when I checked it out, lo and behold, this place was just sitting here, empty and begging to be found. It's become home now, slowly but surely anyway. You wouldn't believe how difficult just getting this chair back here without the Witen noticing was."

"I can imagine," Larry allowed. "Have these shadowy connections of yours told ya anything about who ratted out the resistance's raid on the alternate Control Room?"

"They all figure the Witen had some resistance folks bugged. They even think it's possible the meeting spot itself Spurnberg found was bugged. I mean, the Witen's goons did track it down and block it off the day after the failed raid. It all made me worried about this place's anonymity really, but I had someone sweep it for listening devices and hidden cameras before I moved in. I ... uhh ... spent some nights sleeping in the tunnels themselves back in the beginning," he told them, tossing the hardship off with a chuckle. "I took some steps to make sure this little sanctuary stays off the books, too... Well, the books the Witen can access, anyway. Never mind, long story. Suffice it to say, most everyone I know to ask who would know anything about it all say the Witen was eavesdropping on the resistance. I tend to agree. There were a lot of you," he said, looking at Alice and Maisie. "They probably figured out who one of your people were and slipped a device on them, easy as that. I can't imagine anyone would have betrayed you. Hell, everyone involved in the raid got rounded up anyway, save you, Maisie, thankfully," he quickly added to his onetime business partner.

"That ain't exactly true," Larry said. "What about Cainey? Didn't I hear y'all recruited him at the end when Alice went into labor?"

"You're pretty well informed for someone who declined to help us," Maisie told him with the gathering's first traces of hostility. "I did get Cainey to help, but that fat, stinky, creepo slob Mikkelson grabbed me before I ever got to meet up with him that night. Mikkelson and his goons never saw him. Cainey is just incredibly lucky is all. If Mikkelson would've grabbed me farther up the alley, they might've seen Cainey and reported his involvement to the Commander and the Steward."

"He didn't talk about any rat when he had you at his place then, Maisie?" Boyd asked, before realizing how insensitive it was, making the poor girl relive even a moment of that awful day. "Forget I asked, Mais."

"No, it's okay. The slimy jerk only touched my leg a little bit, and only at the end, right before my brother showed up … and the Commander."

"Really, Maisie, it's okay. Let's just drop the subject," Boyd said, scrambling.

"No, it's fine, Boyd, really," she insisted, and to her credit, she did look sedately composed. He stayed quiet and let her continue. "I heard quite a bit of talking while I was his prisoner. Him and his idiot henchman never shut up, really. But nobody ever said anything about a rat, much less that Novocaine Barker was one."

"Sensible to believe the weaselly little fella isn't working with the Witen, I'd say," Boyd affirmed Maisie's conclusions. "The bastards all hate his guts far worse than any of us."

"So no rat, then?" Larry asked, more to himself than anything. "Good to know, I suppose." Boyd thought he would leave it at that, but after an obnoxious sip of fine wine, he decided he had another question. "You say we gotta work with shady people now. Does that include AOA and the government bastards? 'Cause it seems to me just 'cause your shadow friends don't know about any rat don't mean there really wasn't. There most likely had to be at least one, any way you shake it. And if it wasn't Novocaine, then Harrington and his gang are the next obvious choice. They were none too happy with the resistance, the way I heard things. And forgive me, but let's not forget they had Stevie Hyun locked away down Branch 1 for weeks, and I'm betting she knew a good deal."

"Keep Stevie's name out of your mouth, Larry," Alice told him in a voice that somehow remained light and steady for the sake of the baby cradled in her arm. "She spent the last months of her life in Hell, literal Hell on Cardinal's Nest. She was no rat."

"No, Alice, she most definitely was not," Boyd proudly confirmed. "My people all tell me Stevie never spoke but a handful of times her whole imprisonment. She was defiant to the end. She never gave up anyone."

"Okay, so that leaves AOA, then," Larry said, unabashed.

"My informants tell me the Witen is listening to almost everything they care to, and believe me, Larry, my informants are in position to know such things. You wouldn't believe the lengths some of them make me go to for privacy's sake. So, yes, sadly, we may have to team up with AOA and the government heads from time to time. They are an obvious asset any way you cut it. We ain't in any kinda place to be turning away help. Don't get me wrong: we'll be pragmatic about partnering with 'em, as we will with all our decisions, but we can't ignore how useful they are in terms of their knowledge of this station."

"Okay, Priest, okay," Larry barked between belches. "I may have some other questions for ya later, but for now, let's just say I'm with ya."

"Wonderful, Larry," Boyd gushed. "I appreciate your trust."

"God, it's good to see you, Boyd," Maisie broke in, suddenly sobbing.

"It's great to see you, too, Mais," he said, rushing to her side.

"It ain't been easy lately. I nearly lost my faith, Alice'll tell ya," she cried into his arm. "They nearly broke me, Boyd."

"Hush, girl," he consoled. "You go on and cry. No one deserves a cry more than you. It don't matter how many tears fall, neither—you're still the bravest and brightest kid I've ever known."

"It is good to have you back, Father. We've had sore need of your wisdom," Alice agreed with a smile as she lovingly squeezed her adorable baby girl tight.

Boyd glanced over at Dolly after Alice's compliment. The blonde woman in the pink joggers and black sweater glowed as close to anything one could describe as a heavenly being, standing as she was in a well of light just beyond the couch. Boyd couldn't stop his own tears any longer. Keeping his eyes on the beautiful woman behind the sofa, he wrapped Maisie Sagal in a big, warm, long-overdue hug. "Alice," he called to the new mother as soon as his tears dried, "I appreciate the sentiment, but a truly wise man tries to know everything while also knowing he'll never get close… I should've risked coming to you sooner. I've heard stories about how bad the Witen is making things for you. I'm sure you've been struggling with it all, and I could—and will—definitely help, through my network of connections. I was just afraid for my own skin. I thought I was being extra-responsible, staying away from y'all. I thought I knew best. But my *knowing best* left you in the lurch for far too long. I'm so sorry."

"Oh, pish posh, Boyd," she said, flicking his apology away with one hand while the other, the one that cradled her daughter, flicked the last of her tears. "I had Maisie and Dolly and a few other good people helping me through. I'm fine. Don't you dare risk whatever possible plans for escape we may hatch on my discomfort. You hear me?"

"Yes, ma'am," Boyd responded to her wagging finger and sly grin.

"It ain't really been all that bad. I'm just excluded from public services, laundry pickup being the hardest blow on that account. I've had to wash my damn things in my sink like it's the 1930s or something. Most people look away from me as I pass them in alleyways. They try and comply with the Witen's directive to treat me as though I don't exist. It can be a bit annoying, but I've been finding a way to enjoy the silence. I ain't gonna let the bastards break me. And no one has been stopping me from getting food from the Commissary or any of the cafeteria halls yet, so Carrie and me and Mais are eating just as well as ever. Once that stops, we may have some problems, but for now, I'm good… Maisie's still got her services, thankfully. She wants me to throw my laundry in with hers, but I told her I am not letting them use that as an excuse to exclude her from public services, too." She paused there, and the two women in question exchanged looks of well-tread ground. "Not being able to take Carrie to the hospital has been the worst of it. Some good folks I know by our quarters quietly gave me their old baby stuff, which was a godsend really. I don't know what I would've done otherwise," she continued after a gulp of wine.

"I know of a couple nurses who owe me favors," Boyd said, moving back to his chair. "I'll send them your way tomorrow, secret like, probably at night, when most of the station is asleep. I'm afraid nurses is the best I can do for now. I'll go to work on the doctors immediately though, I promise."

"Thank ya, Boyd. I'd appreciate that. Carrie seems fine and all, but she ain't had a check-up since we left the delivery wing. Babies need their check-ups. Babies with cerebral palsy even more so, I'm sure."

"And Carrie Roxanna will have hers, I promise," he told her. Clearly, his knowledge of her child's full name was a bit surprising. The slight shock didn't last, though. Alice shot a wink his way just a few heartbeats later as she kissed her daughter's pudgy cheek.

"So, what now, then?" Larry Holderman asked, holding out his empty glass toward Boyd.

Standing back up, Boyd moved to fill the man's cup. "Now, we set to work. Brainstorming is usually the first step," he added, plopping back down in his chair and hoping he wouldn't have to scramble out again soon. *Slow down on my good shit, ya lush*, he thought of Larry's liquid capacities. "So, does anyone have any bright ideas?"

CHAPTER 15

HELENA

The voice woke her from a deep sleep. She hadn't heard it bouncing off the walls of these quarters for over three years. It was faint and muffled, the words indecipherable, but she could definitely hear it. This was no dream. Helena had no need to pinch herself to understand that much. Tossing off her covers, she bolted out of bed, ripping her robe off the pinewood rocking chair beside her room's hatchway.

Some instinct made her creep toward the sound of the oh so hated and oh so missed voice. Her robe was cinched tight after three creeping steps down the long haul outside her bedroom. Two steps from the dining room, the voice cleared, words suddenly becoming discernable. There was no doubt.

Alice Stark was speaking to someone at her dining room table.

And when that conversation partner finally revealed himself, Helena's whole world flipped upside down. *No, he wouldn't. I'm dreaming. Please, god, tell me I'm dreaming,* she silently pleaded. Fate would not do this to her. How could it allow the same woman to poison the new life Helena had built in her wake? It was all monstrously unfair. *I'm dreaming. I have to be dreaming. This is a nightmare, Elle. He would never speak to that whore. He has nothing to say to her.* Though, apparently, he did.

"Thanks for letting me spend some time and see her, Alice," Elias Sagal's voice both charmingly and treasonously said.

Helena froze in place, just out of sight. Elias must've been seated at table's end, near the archway. Peering her head around the austere frame, Helena confirmed that suspicion. She also discovered that although Alice's voice was in her quarters, physically, she was not. Elias held his tablet on the tabletop in an outstretched arm. Alice, along with the ugly daughter bearing the deformity for her mother's whorish ways, took up the entire screen.

"Of course, Eli. You're welcome to visit in person any time you like as well," Alice told Helena's charge and plutonic companion.

"I doubt my sister would like that very much."

"Your sister would like that a great deal, I'm sure," Alice said, snuggling tight to her foul offspring.

"I meant Maisie," he told her with a chuckle.

"So did I... Oh, don't give me that look," Alice added when Elias began to demur. "I'm telling you that you have it all wrong Maisie loves you and only wants you to come home. There are no strings attached, Elias. I wish you'd trust me when I tell you that."

"I've heard different."

"From people who wouldn't have any way of knowing, I'm sure," Alice said, nagging the boy. "Forget it, Eli. I'm sorry I pushed. Whenever you want to see Carrie, you just let me know, and we will work something out so Maisie don't find out, even though I think you're making a huge mistake," she finished with one of her treacherous smiles.

"Thanks, Alice. I really appreciate getting to talk with her," the boy said. "She's getting so big and nearly talking sentences. I just... I want her to know me, ya know? She's... She's like ... all I got."

It felt like being shot. Though Helena had never actually been before, she was sure it had to feel like being smacked to the heart by those cold words from the lips of her one last bit of family. Alice had taken him from her. Alice had destroyed her life once again. Alice Maybelle Stark, who'd first shown her how to love before teaching her what it meant to hate, had struck again. She was the buzzsaw at the end of all Helena's lines of fate. She was her bane. She had to die.

She has to die, and that ungodly demon spawn of hers, too. They have to die. It was the only way to conquer her destiny.

"Gotta run now, though, kiddo," Alice's voice came ringing out once more from the tablet.

"Yeah, me, too. Helena will be back from the Commissary soon, I'm sure."

"Well, we can't have her seeing this, now can we?"

"Oh, hell no," the evil boy laughed. "See ya later, Ri Ri. I love you."

"Buh bye, Ewias," the ill-made child gurgled as the screen went black.

Helena Heathcoat never expected to be thankful for a migraine; the torturous spells plagued her most cruelly. Yet if not for the whopper that swam up on her shortly after breakfast, she would, in fact, be at the Commissary and never know how badly these two she loved most in all the world had played her for a fool. *Thank god for small mercies.* Before Elias could discover her lurking just beyond the archway, she darted back to her chambers, where she brooded and dressed, and brooded and strapped her sneakers tight, and brooded for what felt like hours, but was really only a handful of minutes.

When she reemerged from her room, her quarters were quiet, seemingly empty. *The bastard boy must've went back on shift,* she reasoned. Helena's mind was set. Without a flutter of hesitation, she went about her mission, marching first to the kitchen for the oh so important knife. Then, a beeline for her quarters' hatchway. So steadfast and heedless as she was, she even knocked over a yellow porcelain lamp from an end table in the living room. Not even its shattering crash slowed her. Helena was a master of her fate. She could not afford to take her eye off the ball for one single second. She bashed at the hatchway's keypad, mashing several keys at once. The hatchway got the picture, however, and slid open a moment later.

The bitch'll be near her quarters. She ain't safe anywhere else, ostracized and excluded like she is, Helena deduced, setting her feet for Orange Corridor.

The Central Hub housed only the smallest of delays, though it still angered her having to push through the zealous freaks crowding around the Glorifier. The hairy prophet set up every day in the same place. Unfortunately for Helena on this day, that spot was just beside the capacious archway leading into Orange Corridor. The Glorifier—as his people named him—usually had sparse enough crowds with roughly the same dozen or so lazy loafers showing up to hear the cockeyed wild man lecture every day, but they were always herking and jerking and dancing about, making it a trial to sneak past into Alleyway X. Today, the fools seemed especially worked up. Helena figured her timing to be terrible. They had to be coming to the pinnacle of their daily devotions.

"Praise the maker for providing us the Commander and all the loyal and mighty officers of the Witenagemot," the ratty-haired self-appointed preacher was saying.

"Praise for the Commander," his fawning ghouls chorused back.

"Glory to humanity's rebirth, glory to us, glory to the Witen's people!" the nut-brown zealot in the skin-tight golden joggers and little else, save a pair of plain black flip-flops, called, spittle pooling up in his gray beard and patchy-haired bare chest.

"Glory to the Witen!" The worshiper's return calls echoed down the alleyway. Helena heard it all clearly, even fifteen strides past the mad mob.

"Hail the Commander, our salvation. Praise to his ebon axe of justice, the deliverer, for it has spilled the blood of the old world so the new might live. We exist here, in this place, on the very edge of that razor sharp axeblade, my brothers and sisters. Yet we fear not, for the axe is held in the unconquerable hand of the Commander! Praise and Glory to him. And praise for our Nest. Praise the maker. Hail and praise them!" the Glorifier was wailing when his infamous televangelistic voice finally began to fade.

Helena shook off the distraction as she approached Annex V. Dodging around its Information kiosk, she readjusted her grip on the butcher knife. By the time she strolled into Alleyway XI, the Glorifier and his raving pack were forgotten. Alice Stark, her personal plague, was once again her sole object of focus. Not even the handful of odd looks she received from passersby at the glimmering, 10-inch kitchen knife gripped firmly in her spasming right hand affected her concentration.

Expecting a long, protracted surveillance of Alice's quarters before her final emergence, Helena was then taken off guard when she stepped around the bend halfway down Alleyway XII to see Alice pushing her daughter's wheelchair as their hatchway slid shut behind them. Thankfully, Alice was headed the opposite direction and never saw Helena, making her feel a bit foolish for darting toward the shadows beside the alleyway bulkhead.

The pair would be an easy tail, easy to keep up with. *Or catch up with,* she told herself, realizing the ideal situation ahead of her. A young couple, seemingly returning from a Commissary trip, were about twenty yards down the alleyway from Alice, moving toward her. Other than that, it was just Helena and her quarry. She smiled to think about the wheelchair, which she had so often complained to her Corridor Warden about, and even the Steward himself in several Third Days, it being obviously deliberately fabricated for her by someone, which was a clear violation of the Witen's orders to treat Alice and her daughter as non-people. It was pleasing to think that wretched piece of machinery would now be Alice's undoing.

She won't be making any quick getaways pushing that thing. Helena Heathcoat was relishing the moment.

Mapping out the distance in her head and rehearsing her attack, she set off toward the slowly rolling pair. Helena wanted to arrive before Alice passed the young couple, thus avoiding any possible interference on that end, though she knew such a thing was incredibly unlikely. *Still,* she thought, *better to get this right. Leave nothing to chance. This is your one opportunity for a new start, Elle.*

Taking tiptoed long steps, Helena crept up behind a slightly stooping Alice carefully pushing her daughter in the illegal custom chair. Alice might've heard her coming just before the end, she would never know for sure, but suddenly, she stopped cold and stood up straight. Helena knew every inch of her wife's polyester-covered back. Her lips had touched its every surface, several times over. Never in all those moments did she ever imagine herself plunging a butcher knife into that achingly satisfying skin between her shoulder blades, but that is exactly what she did. Alice had only a gasp for answer, as if her wind had been punched free. The long knife stayed there until Helena's hand clutching unimaginably tight to its wooden grip became washed in red.

Looking down at her hand to see it covered in her wife's blood, the woman she promised to love, the woman who promised to love her and then betrayed her, Helena shrieked. There were no words, not really, just a torrent of anguished wails. As soon as she withdrew the knife from the back of her destiny's scourge, the betrayer collapsed as though her legs had turned to water. Alice was not dead, though, not yet. She had enough strength to clutch Helena's ankle as she walked around her, moving in for the final kill. Her grip was feeble. Helena kicked loose with little effort. "No, please, Elle," she might've heard her wife beg. Helena didn't care to confirm if the plea had merely been in her head or not. She had a mission to complete. She was almost free.

The child was young and deformed but was not too stupid to realize what had happened. Fear was everywhere about her. She made no sound, just gasped, clearly trying to scream "Mommy!"

End it, Elle. The miserable child will thank you for it on the other side. The crippled toddler leaned as far back as her wheelchair and affliction allowed but remained well within range of Helena's slash. The butcher knife should've cut straight across the tiny throat a good inch or two deep. She'd measured it perfectly, figuring it to be the most humane way. Only, the knife stopped a foot from her target. Her whole arm had stopped, in fact, trapped by a firm hand around her bicep. When she looked over her shoulder to see who had interfered, who she had missed, she wasn't sure which she felt more: anger or inevitability. The boy must've tailed her. He must have been quiet in his room as she left their quarters. Helena had a sudden flash memory of the yellow lamp shattering.

The boy couldn't have failed to hear that.

Elias Sagal, one hand still clutching her upper arm tight in an uncommonly strong grip, stared deep into her soul with something in his eyes Helena had never seen before.

She took it for disgust. A rage swelled in her so as to make the tide that drove her to stab her wife seem like a ripple from a tossed pebble. Elias was judging her, even after all she'd done for him, after all the times he swore he loved her and appreciated her, after all the times she'd cried over dinner about her treacherous wife with him right there, consoling and co-grieving, even shedding tears of his own. How could he have chosen Alice over her? *Because of the devil child,* she told herself. The understanding brought with it a new spark of determination to destroy the bastard creature.

Helena ripped her arm free of the boy's slightly loosened grasp and immediately tried once more to slash the throat of the now screaming beast. "Helena! Elle! What the heck are you doing!?" her charge shouted, preventing her lethal cut yet again.

"Let me go, Elias!" Helena raged. "You'll understand once she's gone. Let go of me, dammit!" This time, she aimed her follow-up slash at Elias's face after she wrenched free. Originally, she had thought only to back him off and give herself space, but his scornfully superior look changed her mind. She saw a taint of Alice there. She would never be free of her destiny unless she removed every last vestige of her wife from this world. Elias had backed off a step to deal with her slash. Helena closed that gap, leading with the butcher knife at the end of her outstretched right arm, aimed directly for the ungrateful boy's stomach.

It happened fast, too fast for even her to follow. One second, she was nearly stabbing Elias through the gut, and in the next, he had bent her arm back in toward her own stomach. The knife pierced her high on her belly, just below the ribs. Her feet went out in an ironic invocation of Alice's own death throes. The pain was on its way, but it became background music the instant she looked up into her murderer's eyes. The boy looked pathetic. *How could the Steward think him so worthy?*

Lights dimmed all around her. The baby's cries and the young couple's shouts for help grew softer and softer. Alice Stark had indeed destroyed her. The thought was funny as much as enraging. In the end, it had not mattered that Helena had cared for the boy when no one else would. Alice still got him to kill her.

At least I take the bitch with me.

The happy knowledge allowed her to die with a smile on her face.

CHAPTER 16
THE STEWARD

It was no longer necessary to conduct Third Day proceedings every three days, as the name would imply. Peace now ruled every corner of the massive station. His laws and edicts had proven their merit, several times over, shrinking the amount of necessary public courts to every thirty or even sixty days. The Steward kept the original title, nonetheless, believing it to have a deal more gravitas than say a "Sixty Day" ever could. The slimming down of the court schedule made it so the odds of a tumultuous event worthy of its hallowed proceedings having taken place a mere hour before an actual Third Day was set to begin was truly a grand coincidence. The Steward held off deciding just what to make of that bit of serendipitous timing until after the imminent trial.

Surveying the fast-filling benches of the viewing gallery, he was struck by just how worked up the people seemed. The incident he'd been partially briefed on by Footman Dollingford just before the bulk of the crowd started piling into Justice Hall was obviously a bigger deal to the people than he'd first imagined ... to some of the people anyway, namely the friends and cronies of Captain Alvarez. The man in question stood before the first bench, right beside the aisle. If the Steward hadn't been warned by his head of security that the Captain would be bringing a petition on this day, his demeanor and position in the cherry-paneled courtroom would've alerted him regardless. But Dollingford had passed on what she heard rolling its way down the station's gossip grapevine, so the Steward knew his protégé was not standing beside the Corridor Regent by choice. The two young, dead-eyed lackeys in their pristine gray footmen uniforms sandwiching the peach-fuzzed teen and never failing to maintain at least one eye on him at all times drove home the point that Elias was not there of his own free will.

For his part, the boy looked remarkably composed, despite the agitation pouring off Captain Alvarez and his men. He seemed to be paying his guards little mind, in fact. Elias had eyes only for a dark-haired girl near his own age seated across the aisle four benches back. A shift in the residents occupying the row just in front of her opened a momentary sightline of the budding beauty.

Tessa Rodriguez, I should've known. The Steward had long understood the boy had the hots for the shapely young woman.

He'd even fast-tracked her graduation from the Integration Program to please Elias. Of course, neither he nor the Rodriguez girl knew of his fudging of a few of her test scores. The girl seemed like a real believer, a true worker, much like the lovesick boy currently staring deep into her eyes. Plus, her parents were steadfast in their observation of the New Destiny Constitution and their deference to the Witen, not to mention both of them occupied key positions in the air recycler facility. They'd been up here since the very first of the prep crew. The Steward didn't have any desire to unnecessarily risk their expertise in such a key station system. The Witenagemot knew which of its citizens were important. So approving Tessa Rodriguez for this year's Integration Program graduates seemed to be doubly beneficial, and thus, an easy decision. The Station was well guarded by the footmen, and one slightly ill-prepared girl wouldn't disrupt that.

No, it was the right call indeed, like all your calls, he chuckled to himself, remembering the smiles on Mr. and Mrs. Rodriguez and Elias alike after he'd informed them of Tessa's status.

Elias only broke contact with the pretty girl's chestnut eyes after she treated him to a sweet yet uncertain smile. The Steward tracked his gaze, watching it land on a shabby young woman in the second row. Most heads would've turned from her in a blink and then for-gotten her completely a blink later. Once she might have been beau-tiful, no longer. Clara Christie had gone from trim and lithe to bone-thin and haggard. The greasy sweatshirt she hunched inside was torn in several spots and fraying at the cuffs. How Elias recognized her, *if* he recognized her, was a mystery. But undoubtedly, his gaze did linger on the tattered shell of a woman. *Jeez, I hope he ain't wondering how a chick who inherited a supervisor's wergild could look so destitute.* The boy had more than enough in his life already to confuse him. *Damn that bastard Naughton and his fat, rotting friend.* The Steward lamented the work he'd have to do in order to right the ship of loyalty in the boy's mind this time. *His shit-eating sister always pestering him is bad enough. Now there's this whole mess, too, dammit. His stepmother dead. Will he care about that? I know he never hated her like that Heathcoat woman did, the woman he lived with and just ... just ... and just ... that he kil—that he had to kill. Damn that bastard Naughton, the fucking deadass Chairman, and Alvarez, too. Fuck, it's hard at the top,* he lamented. The last thing he needed on top of it all was Elias to go poking around Clara Christie's situation.

How will I explain her state now? Hell, man, you know, a focused campaign attacking her character. What else? he told himself with a sigh. *The girl seems a pathetic thing now anyhow. There ain't no saving her. Best for everybody to make her a casualty of the cause and get the kid to write her off.*

Okay now, Alvarez, you sly bastard, what are you playing at here? the Steward silently pondered, shifting gears back to the current crisis. He snatched up his gavel, thinking to enjoy the simple, powerful act, but before he had a chance to bang the stimulated crowd into silence, a chanting ululation came wafting down the alleyway, straight through the Third Day Courtroom's still opened double-doors. "Praise the Commander. Praise the Steward. Praise their justice. All glory to The Commander," the call and response went, growing ever louder. The Glorifier himself was first of his pack of jackals to enter Justice Hall's sacred grounds. The rest of the minimally clad fools weren't far behind. The lot of them burst through the doorway shouting "Praise and glory to the Commander!"

Oh great, these lunatics, now. Yeah, this is just what I fucking need. The Steward didn't think much of the wild-eyed prophet. He resented him, truth be told, and his *followers.* In his estimation, they were just a bunch of loafing degenerates shirking their labor duties. The

Commander, however, saw things differently. He got off on the vanity stroke of the bearded fraud's sycophancy. They all freaked whenever they spotted him walking the station, falling over themselves to show their esteem. And the Glorifier himself was the worst of all on that account. The Steward had seen the shirtless cult leader kissing the Commander's boot, even licking the floor where their scarred ruler tread. And his shrieking voice always displaying that holier-than-thou tone, it all drove him crazy. But the Commander approved, so indulge the useless mouths the Steward must.

Time to bring an end to their babble though, he thought, smashing his gavel atop his lofted adjudication desk. "Silence! Silence! I will have silence in this courtroom. Take a seat if you can find one, *Glorifier,*" he told the underdressed madman, putting an insolent stress on his name. "If not, stand against the wall and hold your tongue. We shall have order here in this hallowed and sacred place, ladies and gen-tlemen. Don't make Footman Dollingford take out her war hammer. You'll never get her to put it away again. Few things in this world she loves more than using it to crack some skulls," he chuckled, catching Dollingford's eye with a wink. The gallery, even the Glorifier and his followers, got the picture. A solemnity spread throughout the court-room with a rapidity that made him smile. "Good. I declare this Third Day open, then," he said with another bang of his gavel. "Is there a petitioner who wishes to be heard?"

"I invoke my right as third-ranking Witen councilmember of first petition," Captain Alvarez bellowed before anyone else could so much as think.

Third-ranking councilmember he calls himself. Oh, Petey, you ought not be so obvious.

"Captain Alvarez, we're not often graced by your presence at these proceedings. To what do we owe the privilege?"

"I have a charge of murder to lay on a Witen citizen, Steward, sir," Alvarez told him with a sneer, shoving Elias's shoulder toward the defense desk. Stepping up behind the plaintiff desk, the Captain then took a few breaths to straighten his uniform and glance about the hall with an arrogant smile. "This boy, your baby-faced secu-rity guard, murdered Helena Heathcoat," he said with a smugness the Steward knew he would never have dared only a few months earlier. *The bastard's influence with the Commander has grown, and worse yet, he knows it.* "Two witnesses saw him stab her to death in Alleyway XII inside Orange Corridor," Alvarez continued. " , and a few of my footmen, were first on the scene. Lieutenant Masterson, Orange Corridor's warden, arrived shortly after, but as I already had the situation in hand, he rightly stepped aside, knowing it'd be best for me to deliver the killer for justice."

"Well, as I'm sure you guessed, Captain, knowing this place almost every bit as well as I do, that word of Elias Sagal and Helena Heathcoat's interaction reached my ears before the start of today's court," the Steward said in his most condescending, patronizing, and I-know-you-know-what-I-know voice. "And from the way I understand it, young Footman Sagal was simply acting in self-defense. Graduating top of his class in near every discipline last year, as we l as being the youngest ever to graduate the Integration Program, the footman in question is thus extremely well trained by every measure of interest to the Witenagemot. You see, Captain, what I fear you may be overlooking is the simple fact that the Integration Program trains our footmen to react on instinct in situations such as the one Footman Sagal found himself in this morning. The read I get from said altercation is mere proof of the Witenagemot's Integration Program in action. The program and training work, clearly," he finished with a smile.

"According to the two witnesses, Steward, sir," Alvarez said, adopting a patronizing tone of his own, "the unfortunate and well-honored Helena Heathcoat only 'attacked' him after the *footman* grabbed her roughly by the arm."

"Yes, I'm aware of what your witnesses will attest," the Steward said, mad he let his annoyance show, even a bit. "But you must know as well as I that they will also testify that the footman only grabbed her arm when she tried to kill the young child, after recently stabbing its mother to death."

"I know of no child, sir," the Captain responded with a pressed grin showing he was clearly ready for the argument. "Neither this child you speak of nor its mother exist. How can one kill nothing, Steward, sir?" Alvarez posed the question knowing full well the Steward would never take the bait. "The boy should have minded his own damn business," the handsome and irritatingly charming Captain continued. "It was far past time a brave citizen, a loyal citizen of the New Destiny Constitution and the officers and supervisors of the Witen, had the balls to do something about the apostate lurking in our midst, poisoning our glorious society from the inside out," he added with a shout and gesture toward the Glorifier.

The man stood out among the sea of faces like a rose on a dirt pile. From his position against the back wall, the gray-bearded prophet in the gold sweatpants happily took advantage of the proffered opportunity. "All glory to the Commander. Glory to Captain Alvarez. Glory to the Regent of the Corridors. His eyes are blessed to see the rot before it can corrupt us all. Praise the maker for the Regent's wisdom. Praise and glory to each Witenagemot citizen who commits themselves to the law. Weeding out the rotten fruit is our duty, my brothers and sisters! Praise to those who destroy the corrupt. Praise and Glory to the Commander!"

"Glory to the Commander indeed," Alvarez said loudly, not so subtly telling the man his oratory services were helpful but complete. The bare-chested zealot got the hint, leaning back against the bulkhead with a contented smile spreading across his craggy brown face beneath his storm cloud mane. "I submit that Helena Heathcoat did nothing wrong, merely defended herself when that boy, who she'd loved and cared for despite his traitor father and sister, when that cold boy violently grabbed her," Alvarez said, pointing toward Elias behind the defense desk to his right all the while. "Who here could blame Ms. Heathcoat for being angry to see the boy who owed her so much betraying her so utterly? I would've slashed at him, too, had it been me. And anyway, it's most likely that Helena, being the loving woman we all knew her to be, was simply trying to scare the boy off and give him time to rethink his traitor ways."

Ha, what a lie that is. The woman was an introvert who barely left her quarters after her wife's adultery. Alvarez didn't know her from Adam. *He'll say anything. The man is utterly lost. He just wants the power.* The Steward began to realize just how serious a threat Captain Alvarez posed. *Humanity can't be left to his devices.* The Steward would have to knock him down a peg or two. *But how best to do it?*

"Helena Heathcoat deserves justice," Alvarez's smarmy voice cut into his musings. "As Regent of the Corridors, I believe it is my duty, in order to maintain the peace in the Living Quarters Corridors, to ensure Ms. Heathcoat receives her justice, even if, sadly, it must be posthumously."

"Here, here," a voice from directly behind the Captain at the plaintiff's desk called.

"Justice for Helena," another voice, this one in the back of the room shouted. *Most likely one of the Glorifier's bunch,* the Steward guessed.

Soon similar calls were ringing out from all over the gallery. He found them impossible to track, and so gave it up, banging his gavel instead. "Silence! Silence in my courtroom! Captain Alvarez, I thank you for bringing this matter before the court today. You have never flagged in your in commitment to tranquility within the Living Quarters Corridors. Everyone knows that full well. The Commander and I thank you for it," he added in an offhand manner sure to piss off the Captain. "I can see how the events of this morning could lead to some real tumult in the alleyways if not dealt with at once. It was only right of you to usurp Lieutenant Masterson in this, as you say. Yet I have to disagree with your interpretation of events." Before Alvarez could unleash his hot retort, the Steward held up a hand and continued. "I am not submitting that I suggest the situation did not unfold just as you say. I would never question your integrity in that way. You are the *third-ranking* member of the Witenagemot, after all," he said, making mock of the man's earlier brag. "Your word should be stone to everyone in this room, myself included. I simply interpret your testimony, and the earlier briefing I received, in a different way. Vastly different, sad to say." Breaking off his combative yet playful grin, he turned then to address the gallery. "Alice Stark and her daughter were not citizens of the Witen, this is true, but the New Destiny Constitution clearly instructs its citizens to do all that is within their power to prevent disruptions. The tranquility of this station was not threatened by Footman Sagal's intervention, but by the reckless acts of Helena Heathcoat. Murdering a woman in cold blood, citizen or not, surely upset many of the more moral and emotionally tuned-in citizens among us. Violence of any kind, on any person, be they citizen or no, is a threat to the tranquility of the station, the oh so fragile tranquility that Captain Alvarez imagines himself protecting by charging my outstanding young security guardsmen with murder. We cannot have bloody mayhem in the halls. Footman Sagal was merely performing his duties as a Footman of the Witenagemot. He would've gladly stopped it at that had Helena not forced his hand. I'm sure of that. Trust me, folks, I didn't pick the boy to protect me for no damn reason. I picked him because he was the most qualified, the most honorable, the most loyal and steadfast. Sure, he is young, only just 14, but that only adds, in my opinion, to his impressiveness. He may be baby-faced, as you say, Captain, but he is as strong and tall as any twenty-year-old would wish to be. I am in good hands with him and Footman Dollingford watching my back. I know, too, that Footman Sagal loved Helena Heathcoat. He took care of her as much as she did him. It was she who engaged in betrayal when she tried to stab him. Now, I can understand these words will not fall kindly on the ears of some of you gathered here today, and that is fine. Debate and differing points of view will help us to keep driving forward. But I do expect you to respect my words and ruling. What happened today was a tragedy all the way around, an unfortunate occurrence that we must put behind us. Helena Heathcoat will be remembered as the loyal citizen she was, while Alice Stark's name shall fade to oblivion. Let that be enough justice." Turning back to Alvarez, he added, "Don't take out your frustrations on my footmen, Captain. I hate to scold you in front of a crowd, but as this petition's plaintiff, it is you I must address. This could've all been handled a deal better, I think. What do you say?"

Alvarez held his gaze for a long time. The Steward was sure he was about to say or do something very foolish, but he turned away abruptly, that charming grin once more animating his face. "Perhaps you're right, Steward," the man agreed, turning to address the crowd. "I only thought to do what was best for my Corridor residents. Maybe I overreacted accusing young Sagal of intentionality. I have a soft spot in my heart for Ms. Heathcoat, a sweet lady, and perhaps I let my anger over her demise rush me into an unnecessary course of action. I apologize sincerely, to you, Steward," he said turning back to the raised throne, "and most of all to you, my fellow citizens," he added, turning once again to face the gallery. "I hope I have not lost your confidence."

"Never!" the Glorifier wailed.

A chorus of such nonsense followed. The Steward let it play out, neglecting to gavel the room's quick silence. "Helena Heathcoat shall be honored, and today's unfortunate events shall be forgotten. So say this court," he pronounced, banging his gavel a few extra times just cause he could. "Return to your duties, Footman," the Steward told his teen guardsman. Sagal turned to go without a word, headed for his current posting beside the Steward's living quarters hatchway. Tessa Rodriguez scrambled from her bench to follow him out. The Steward smiled to see it, especially since Clara Christie had been shooting him puppy-dog eyes all the way out of Justice Hall.

The Rodriguez girl can go a long way in alleviating whatever affection Elias may still harbor for Christie. I'll have to keep that in mind when next I speak with him.

Snapping back to the present moment, he once again pounced his gavel before calling out, "Any other petitioners for today?"

CHAPTER 17

ELIAS

Raspberry scented air filled his lungs. Their lovemaking had left him breathless, but he was glad of it. Tessa Rodriguez laying atop him, bare chest to bare chest, panting in tandem with Elias, while that sweet, rich aroma that revived him was an ecstasy all its own. They had laid together in the center of the sprawling patch many times, it being their favorite spot in all of Cardinal's Nest, but they'd never made love there. True, there'd been some necking before and a bit of explorative touching, but they'd never stripped nude to roll about the springy meadow floor in one another's arms, stifling well-earned moans between long, hungry kisses. After all, they had only ever done the full deed twice now in total. Perhaps that was the reason he felt better in that moment than he ever remembered feeling before. Maybe the novelty of the act was blowing his contentment out of proportion. Although, squeezing tight to the flawless beauty just now sliding up and off him, he could not bring himself to believe it.

Tessa rested her soft hand against his cheek as she snuggled into the crook of his arm. "I love you," she told him.

"We're too young to know what that word really means." It was an oft uttered response. Tessa had grown numb to its surface insensitivity long ago.

"We're both sixteen now, Eli, full citizens of the Witenagemot," she innocently reminded him. "And I'll be seventeen only next week. Most folks 'round here think that qualifies as old enough."

"I think even the oldest man can realize he was wrong. 'It ain't just age that makes you wise,' the Steward says. All we can do is make the best decisions in each moment of our lives based on our experience and emotions."

Tessa only smiled back at him. "Okay then, right now, in this moment, I love you," she qualified her endearment.

"Right now, I love you, too." Elias tried to convince her of that statement's sincerity with a piercing, fullhearted gaze. "And I'm gonna try real hard to love ya in every moment to come," he further promised. "At least until you realize how little I deserve you."

Tessa pulled away from an incoming kiss, softly smacking his chest. "You're the best footman in the Witen, Eli. Everybody knows it. How much more deserving of love could a man be? And anyway, it don't really matter, 'cause what I love about you ain't how good of a fighter you are or how smart or tough or any such junk. It's the soul I see behind these hazel eyes here and now that I love," Tessa said, scooching up to bring her sightline even with his. "I saw you in there, deep behind the melding pools of your irises, the first time we met. I felt like I'd always known the boy in there. I knew fate had put us in this station together for a reason."

Elias's smile could not be tamed, not until his finger, roaming every immaculate curve of her gorgeous, dimple-chinned face, ran over the 2-inch scar on her left cheek. Shame and unworthiness marched their way into every corner of his consciousness. He could not help himself then from seeing the slight misshapen structure of Tessa's stubby nose. She must've noticed him stiffen beside her. And when she looked up to see the inadequacy living in every line of his *technically* young face, Tessa had to know what he was remembering.

"I earned this scar," she told him gently, touching the fading gash with the end of her index finger. "As well as the broken nose," she added, moving to the aforementioned appendage. "They were not your fault, for the hundredth time. I am a Footman of the Witenagemot every bit as much as you. 'What does not kill me, makes me stronger and wiser. My pain is a gift, a reminder of the covenant I have sworn to ensure the endless generations to come. Their futures are guaranteed through our discipline and commitment. I am one of the blessed chosen few. My place in this station is a miracle, to which a great debt is owed. Pain and scars are nothing next to that,'" Tessa made her point by quoting part of the Footman's Oath. "It was my choice to fight. We look out for each other, you and I. We always have. It's what I love about our relationship more than all the rest. More than this even," she added, tugging his spent tool with a flirtatious giggle. "But there are things we have to let each other face on our own, and I would really like you to make an effort to understand the difference." She was still smiling, but Elias knew just how serious she really was. "It was never your place to save me from my duty. Just as it was never your place to save Clara. She brought on her situation with her terrible choices. Heck, Eli, it was the Steward himself who told ya she'd been whoring her body out only six months after inheriting the wergild. Never helped her parents out at all, either. Went through all that property and trade-goods in less than two damn years. Lieutenant Dirks was telling us all about her this morning. She says bad things happen to bad people, and there ain't no more to it. Best to forget her entirely."

"I knew something was wrong when I saw her all those months back in that Third Day when Captain Alvarez tried to get me in trouble for murder... for murdering..."

"You defended yourself, Eli. The rest was trained instinct. Everybody knows that," Tessa cut in to rescue him from starting down that dark road. "Even Captain Alvarez himself said as much at the end."

"I did what I did. Let's just drop that for now."

"Let's drop it all," Tessa said, picking a raspberry from a nearby branch. "We got just enough time for round two before we gotta be back from break," she said, munching down the raspberry with a dangerously sexy grin. "If we stop talking and get to it, that is."

Elias found himself pulling back from her lips. Clara Christie's bloated body found floating around The Meadow's circular river last night popped back into his thoughts, unbidden and definitely unwanted, mastering even his fiery lust. The news had been all over the station this morning, the day's hot gossip. Elias had thought of little else for hours after. That was until Tessa had pulled him along to their favorite spot in the meadow at the start of their early morning shift break with whispered promises of how best they might use its offered privacy. Obviously, he'd since been thinking of little else than every curve and bump of her naked body. Only now, once more, Clara's demise had him second-guessing himself. "I knew that day something was wrong, Tess, and I never even spoke with her, never even looked really. I might've been able to help."

"She was on a runaway train toward Hell, Elias. She was a temptress sent among us to test our mettle. You know that."

"I know that's what they say."

"That's what the *Witen* says. Shit, Eli, it's what the Steward himself has told you time and again," Tessa said, clearly annoyed at his obstinacy both toward her sexual desires as well as what every member of the Witen knew to be true.

"I know. You're right, I'm sure," Elias finally said. "I just wish I could've helped her."

"No one can help a drunk druggy who gets so wasted they stumble into the only open water on the whole freakin' Moon."

"Maybe," Elias allowed. "She was always nice to me, though. And that Naughton guy is a real jerk. He might've been angry at her for the wergild stuff. He could've manipulated things to see her destroyed. It would take more than an alcohol addiction and some pot to blow through the amount of goods she won."

"Supervisor Naughton is a member of the Witen council in the highest standing. Why would he risk that just to punish some girl who is hellbent on destroying herself anyway? Naughton ain't to blame, Eli. Clara is. She probably gambled it all away, most like."

"Maybe. I don't know anymore. Naughton gives me a bad feeling, though. I tried to put it in the back of my mind, but the man just isn't right somehow. If he was violating the New Destiny Constitution and victimizing poor Clara, then it was my duty to confront him. I should've at least talked to her myself about everything. And now I never can."

"Trust the Steward and our Witenagemot, Eli. It's all we got."

"Yeah... I guess you're right," Elias agreed.

"You know, another girl might get jealous that a guy she's currently lying naked beside, playing with his junk, would spend all this time talking about some other girl, an older, more *experienced* girl, no less," Tessa declared with mock outrage.

"I'm sorry, gorgeous. I'll never forgive myself for the distraction," he quipped before kissing her neck. Tessa let out a half moan, half giggle as they rolled around, their hands racing over every inch of their partner's skin. Then, breaktime be damned, they stayed hidden inside their raspberry patch until both were good and satisfied.

His dark-haired lover was still working on the last button of her gray footman's uniform top as they approached The Meadow's footbridge. They'd dressed in a rush, although, exasperatingly, a rush peppered with agonizingly long searches through thick, towering raspberry bushes for missing articles of clothing. Now they were both late. Dollingford would have his hide before the Steward ever got a chastisement in edgewise. Tessa was the lucky one. Lieutenant Dirks ran an admirable operation, to be sure, albeit with a bit less emphasis on rigorous attention to time than most former military personnel. Dirks went her own way, as far as the other corridor wardens were concerned. Her unique way of operating, while unconventional, had been often praised by his mentor in Elias's hearing as "working admirably"—a high compliment in the Steward's vaunted opinion.

Despite his easy acceptance of Lieutenant Dirks's unorthodox approach to her governance of Blue Corridor, the Steward himself, nor his bulldog head of security, Footman Dollingford, were fans of tardiness themselves. His shift partner, Simmons, might cover for him a bit if she was in a good mood, but Elias knew counting on that was a risky proposition. The fresh graduate of the Integration Program took her placement on the Steward's detail for the privilege it was, and so wasn't the type to let an infraction slide. No doubt the stout, teak-skinned, short-woman had earned her placement with her fearlessness and skill with that longspear of hers, but newbies always take a while to loosen up a bit. Elias figured it depended on her hairstyle for the day. It always seemed a good indicator in the past, anyway. When her glorious 4-inch afro was free, the footman could be relied upon to be in a good mood. Catch her with her tight cornrows though, and god help ya.

Let's pray for an afro day, baby, he chuckled to himself before growing serious. *God, I hope there's a trolley waiting.* Elias stretched his five-eleven frame as far as physics allowed and still needed to go on tiptoes to peer over a gaggle of four women in bright, clashing colored sweatsuits out on a powerwalk. "Yes!" he cried at first sight of the half full transport. "Thank goodness. Hurry up, Tess. We gotta catch that trolley."

He only made it one step toward the giant archway. Tessa went jogging past but stopped after five or six paces after she realized he wasn't alongside her. "Eli, what is it? I thought you just said you wanted to catch the trolley? ...Eli?" she asked, puzzled.

Elias didn't see the confusion on Tessa's face, though he heard it all the same. His eyes were locked on the brown-ha red pair with matching hazel eyes peering at the thundering rapids below over the clear rail of the footbridge ten yards away. One stood with her chest against the top of the rail, head extended out over the precipice. The other sat in her custom-made wheelchair, peering through the clear pane of glass.

She's so ... so ... so ... big. Dammit, I've missed so much. Carrie Roxanna Sagal had grown out of her old wheelchair since last he'd seen her across the width of the Central Hub. Someone had made her a new one. Elias wondered just who her mysterious engineer friend was, and not for the first time.

Maisie pushing off the rail and turning his way stopped his pondering. She pulled up short upon registering his presence. Carrie felt her elder sister's discomfort and swung her chair around to discover its source. Elias smiled to see her face. She looked so much like their father, so much like Maisie. Luckily, Tessa had come back beside him by then. Her hand gripping tight to his own helped him stop the tears that begged to flow.

"Eli!" Carrie burst with excitement. "Mais, look it's Elias."

"I see him, Ri Ri," Maisie said, her eyes never leaving him.

"Hello, Carrie." His greeting came with a cautious step in her direction. "You ... you ... you've gotten so ... so big."

"You've missed a lot, little brother," Maisie snarkily informed him.

"I know," he answered dumbly. "How've you been, Ri Ri?"

"I just g-g-got-got a walker I can start using soon!' his baby sister updated him in a rush. "After that, I'll just need f-f-f-forearm-cwutches, that's all! Then I can walk awound this place all by myself."

"Oh, wow, kiddo! That's amazing," he was saying as he closed the gap between them to less than a single pace. Tessa walked with him, step for step, her hand never leaving his. "They tried to say you'd be in a chair your whole life."

"I kn-kn-know. Nurse Gilmore says I'm a miwacle child."

"She's obviously right," Tessa said as Elias beamed.

"No, it's no miwacle. Wight, Mais?" the five-year-old little girl asked her big sister.

"That's right, Ri. No miracles. Just hard work and never taking no for an answer," Maisie confirmed.

"And always doing *wa-wa-one more*," Carrie eagerly pointed out her guardian's important omission. "Maisie and I do our exer-ex-ex-ercises every d-day in our quarters. Weally, I'm l-l-lucky compared to most people with cewebral p-p-palsy. I just g-g-got the stutters a bit and a bad g-g-gait, the nurse calls it. I'm lucky my mind works the way it does. Ma-M-Maisie would l-like it if I could stop gwinding my teef, but I am twying."

"You got a heck of an outlook on everything, Ri," Elias told her with genuine awe.

"It could be worse, Mais says, and I think she's wight."

"That's always true, I guess," Eli had to agree.

"Y-yo-y-you know I kept on begging Mais to bwing me to The M-M-Me-Meadow for a walk. Isn't it cwazy that on the day she does, I see you here?"

"Yeah, that is ... uhh ... quite a ... coincidence..."

Carrie plunged right on before he could think what else to say. "I'm glad it happened though. I missed you, Eli."

"I can't believe you remember, Ri Ri. You were so little."

"I make Maisie t-t-tell me about you all the time," she said in that innocent demeanor all children have.

"That trolley is about to take off. If you two were trying to catch it, I'd go now," Maisie announced in a stern voice.

"I'd like to spend some real time with her, Mais," Elias appealed.

"You can spend all the family time you want with both of us just as soon as you come home." Her stubborn ways could serve up no other response, Elias knew. "We're a package deal. Ain't we, Carrie?"

Their baby sister didn't answer. No one said anything for an uncomfortably long time. Then Elias broke the awkward spell. "You know I can't go home with you. Carrie is still considered an apostate.

And Dad's death still has you out of your right mind and irrational. The Witen knows you're trying to hatch some scheme. They know you've never stopped your useless plots. I can't be seen with you. It would be as bad for you as me. They might get truly fed up with you once and for all."

"Yeah, they'd have to kill me if they saw me getting too close to their golden boy, wouldn't they?" she asked with a monstrously cruel scoff. "You know, little brother, Dad's death really oughta weigh a lot heavier on *your* soul and mind than mine. You serve his murderer. You've willingly made yourself an abject slave of a psychotic and evil man, a slave to a man who could not more clearly be your own father's worst enemy. Perry Sagal is as much ashamed of you as I am. I'm certain of that. Did you really think I was gonna let you vid chat with Carrie behind mine and the Witen's backs like Alice did? Don't you remember what that cost her in the end, you stupid jerk?"

Tessa pulled him away from Maisie's scorn. Elias went with her after a few tugs, keeping his eyes on Carrie Roxanna every retreating step. "Good bye, Eli," Alice Stark's daughter called to him, cold, dead Alice Stark, another one of his failures.

"Good bye, Ri Ri... I love you."

"You can always come back home, Elias. I'll forgive everything." Maisie's voice was tinged with heartbreak now. It was hard to keep walking away from. "We can be a family. Come home, and stop listening to those despots and murderers. They are lying to you, Elias! Come home."

He did stop walking toward the trolley then. Tessa also stopped pulling.

Only, when he went to step back toward Carrie, he found himself frozen in place. Nothing worked. Every limb was frozen, even his gaze, locked on the girl in the wheelchair. Somehow though, in that strange way of dreams, he knew no others were aware of the freeze. Then he blinked, and he was no longer looking at Carrie. His gaze was now locked on The Meadow behind her. All was frozen still, all but a few tall blades of dewy grass parting as a ship's keel cleaves a churning sea a hundred yards into the pasture just over Carrie's shoulder. He never saw the giant wolf until it bounded free of the bright green stalks.

Nooo! He wanted to scream. Instead, the cry merely rattled around his mind as the wolf loped across the gaming fields in a dozen long strides. Elias knew who the wolf hunted. He knew its prey. Oh to scream, to shout, to have the use of his legs, anything, oh what he wouldn't have given. But he stayed frozen. He remained silent. The wolf's jaws locked around his baby sister with a snarl he knew reached his ears alone. Her blood was black. And all at once, the thing in the wolf's jaw was not his sister. Circuits popped and sparks flew as metal crunched between the massive jaws. An adult human skull fashioned from steel and festooned with scraps of living flesh warped before his very eyes into unrecognizability beneath the powerful bite. His voice had returned, he knew in that unquestioned, impossible way, but before he could use it, the scrap of sparking steel between the fangs of that mythical beast abruptly erupted into a white ball of blinding light.

Color and contrast slowly returned to the world, a changed world. It was the same Meadow, yet certain patches of flowers were now in bloom dotted throughout its massive expanse that had not been so moments before, the fruit of certain vines and bushes appeared larger and riper as well. The same precious hand was locked within his own, but there were no scars on her face, no broken nose, and her hair was cut in a fashion he hadn't seen in months. Tessa was saying something to him. Elias could not hear her. She was but a foot away, yet no sound came from her moving lips. The gaming fields were prepared for a Footman's Monthly Tourney. The square had been marked and a few dozen footman were gathered where there had been only a few relaxing citizens before. When Ricky Allanson stepped up beside him just as his hearing returned, Elias knew where and when he was.

His instinct was to toss Tessa over his shoulder and run like hell, far away from the battlegrounds, but it seemed as though he was merely along for the ride. Someone else was controlling his body, an autopilot or some sadistic replay. The Elias in control said, "You got something to say to me, Allanson?"

"Well, little Eli, since you ask, I was just telling the fellas how convenient it is that you find yourself ineligible for the one Monthly where Lieutenant Woodson is Game's Master," the tall, blond, hawk-faced footman with the wormy lips and chalk-blue slits for eyes responded. "I'll bet you had the Steward jigger the schedule to spare you having to deal with an actually fair official. Woodson ain't like the other lieutenants who all just want to suck up to the number-two man. No, he remembers you from the Program, Sagal. He knows what a cheat you are. He might've exposed you here today had you not had the oh so very convenient foresight to fight the last two months and make yourself ineligible for today's tourney."

"He fought the last two months because he was challenged," Tessa defended him.

"He entered himself into the pool twice in a row, did he not?"

"Elias enters every pool he is eligible for. He's got nothing to fear from any of ya!"

"Oohh, watch out there, Rick. Eli's got himself a wild one defending him," MacAlister, one of Allanson's punkish cohorts, said with a burst of laughter. Footman Erkov beside him immediately set to cackling his twerpy cackle at the sexist insult. Kyle Erkov's nose still bent sharply left halfway down its length even now, five years removed from meeting Elias's boot. How the gawky footman could walk around with the evidence of his pitiful defeat plain as sunshine right in the center of his face was as puzzling as it was shameful. Elias had lost respect for the Silver Corridor footman long ago, if indeed he ever had any.

"Rodriguez ain't nothing to fear, Mac," Allanson told his friend while still staring Elias down. "The bitch only got past the program because of the Steward, too. Everybody knows that, just as much as they know Sagal is a pathetic cheat, unworthy of his uniform."

"I passed on my merit, Ricky. Check my scores, why don't ya?" Tessa released Elias's hand and stepped forward to poke a finger into Allanson's shoulder.

"The Steward fudged 'em," the wormy-lipped bastard sneered.

"Watch what you accuse the Steward of, Ricky," Eli told the wannabe tough-guy with cold reason. "The man is our lawgiver and program director. Everything we are as Footmen of The Witenagemot is thanks to him. Speak another ill word of him and—"

"And what? You'll rat me out like the tattling little bitch you are?"

"I will report you, yes… But only after I've beaten your ass within an inch of your life," Elias answered in that same cold voice.

Tessa laughed. Taking up his hand again, she came to stand proudly beside him. The two of them faced Allanson, MacAlister, Erkov, and one other of Lieutenant Woodson's Silver Corridor footmen whose name Elias never cared to learn much less remember. Ricky's petulant gaze never left Tessa, unnerving Elias. Before he could think he might've gone too far, Allanson spoke, confirming it. "Just what the hell are you laughing at, *Tess*? You chicks over in Blue Corridor are just as pathetic as Eli here, you being the worst of the bunch. You ain't a real footman. You've never even entered a Monthly."

"She's entered a bunch of Monthlies," Eli protested.

"Yeah, the fucking obstacle course months. No one's ever seen the chick inside a battle square. Hell, the scrawny bitch couldn't even lift the pugil stick, I'd bet." Allanson laughed.

Elias reacted without forethought or reason. He simply saw red. His left arm shot out to shove Allanson's shoulder, knocking him off-balance. An instant later, Eli's hand was around his throat. "Call her a bitch one more time, motherfucker!" he heard himself shout.

"Elias, no!" Tessa screamed as the assembling footmen all turned toward the commotion. "Let him go. I can speak for myself." Elias calmed instantly at her touch, releasing the slightly taller boy and stepping back. "If this dickhead thinks he can talk about me like I ain't even here and badmouth my people in Blue Corridor, he can think again. I did plan on entering today's tournament pool anyhow. Now I can hope to get the chance to call this jerk out and bash his ass."

"Bash his ass, she says," MacAlister's bloated girth burst out with another chuckle. "She's gonna bash your ass, Rick."

"Ha, yeah right," Allanson croaked, still panting slightly, only now through a devious grin. "The bitch won't enter. I'll believe it when I see it."

No! Fuck him, Tessa. He's nothing. Let's just run, the part of his brain aware of the dream screamed. She didn't heed the silent advice. Tessa was tugging him toward the battle square on the old soccer field. He could not resist her, then or now. That Footman's Monthly Tourney flashed by like pictures in a carousel projector: footmen slashing and swinging their padded staffs at one another's loosely protected bodies, the dense, inch-thick padding at the final foot of the

6-foot ash staffs smacking square on jaws, guts, thighs, and ribs alike, then Allanson defeating the puppet who challenged him with ease, then him calling out Tessa, as Elias knew he would, and then, to his absolute despair, Tessa strapping on the converted catcher's chest protector and home-crafted padded cap donned by each Tourney contender, Tessa stepping up to the center of the battle square to face a man who had thirty pounds and six inches on her, Lieutenant Woodson catching Elias's eye before shouting the match's start. All of it going as quick as it came, yet lingering in some residual, shadowy sort of way as well.

Tessa never stood a chance. She was a scrapper and could pack a punch, great with a longspear to keep her enemy at bay, but Allanson had the same long, padded staff she held. She never stood a damn chance. Woodson should've blown the match dead, ten times over. Tessa stayed on her feet, despite Elias's constant noisy pleas to the contrary. Every blow she took, he felt, and he could not fight back. Always, Woodson kept his eye locked firm on Elias, hoping he might dare interfere. Then all his enemies would win. Elias would be expelled from the order, his citizenship stripped away. The footman tournaments were sacred things. He had to watch his love, his one absolute left in life, beaten and battered. What kept her up, god only knew, but he cursed it all the same.

The crowd around him drifted away like smoke on a breeze. Allanson remained inside the black-painted square walloping his staff into Tessa's sides as she weakly flailed in an act of ineffective self-defense. When the final smashes to her face began to land, the ones that cost her the broken nose and scar across her otherwise blemish-free cheek, even Woodson, the Game's Master as well as his former Integration Program Leader and current adversary, also turned to smoke. The very ground beneath Tessa melted away as she crumbled down, out like a light, disappearing into darkness. Then her accoster faded. Then even Elias himself.

He was adrift in nothingness, attached to nothing, empty, boundless, gone forever, when suddenly, there came the ever-swelling howl of a mighty baying wolf. The sound filled the world. And just before it became too much to bear, the crash of a shattering lamp marked the start of a new silence. The physical world rushed back into view. As soon as he was whole, Elias knew it was the old faded-yellow vase-lamp that once rested atop their living room end table that had fallen before he even stepped out of his room in he and Helena's shared living quarters. *Not this day,* he begged his dreaming mind. It either could not hear or did not care to listen. Elias was helpless to do anything other than exactly what he'd done this day. One glance at the antique shattered lamp Helena was so fond of told him something was very wrong. *She must've been home this whole time. She must've heard,* he told himself back then.

The thought brought him to the hatchway. He made it out of the portal just in time to see Helena round a bend in their alleyway about thirty yards to his left. Elias took off in pursuit. After a few steps though, he was no longer Elias. He was a wolf on the prowl. Not the giant carnivore of dreams past, but his own beast, a smaller cousin to the other. The coat that covered his forelegs and the part of his muzzle he could spy in his periphery was a deep coal black. A far cry from the smoke-gray pelt of the legendary canine he once rode atop.

He was a new thing in an old time. Silently, on padded paws, he stalked Helena Heathcoat through every twist and turn of her weaving path. She never saw him back there, never so much as felt him. The Elias-wolf was certain of that. When her destination loomed ahead, Helena stopped her march, ducking toward the shadows for refuge. A deal more gracefully and agilely, the lone wolf did the same twenty yards behind her.

Tackle her now, confront her now. It don't gotta end the same. Save her. Save them both. Save them all. Stop her! the dreaming boy silently implored. But a wolf was a hunter, not a hero. He only watched, fangs bared, as Helena stuck the knife she'd used to prepare a thousand meals for Elias deep into her wife's back. It was only then that he pounced as the murderer moved in on her next kill. His gruesome jaws locked around Helena Heathcoat's neck in the same instant his forepaws raked loose ropes of glistening entrails from her thin belly.

Elias awoke with the coppery taste of her blood still in his mouth. Groggily, his right hand scrambled atop the mattress beside him. When it reached the edge without contacting anything, Elias changed from unsettled to a touch melancholy. The sheets were warm. Tessa had truly been beside him at one point. That much wasn't a dream at least. There were many mornings when she left in the wee hours or didn't stay at all. So not finding her beside him just then shouldn't be particularly alarming. True, they were, for all intents and purposes, already married. But his lover's parents were still a touch old-school and thought them too young for that kind of commitment just now. Tessa loved her parents and had wanted to humor them at least. So they were set to wed just as soon as he turned eighteen in a few months. Then the whole song and dance of sneaking in and out and pretending they weren't already having sex could finally end.

Still, Elias and Tessa spent near every night, as well as every free minute of the day, in each other's company. Elias felt the imposition of delaying their marriage was easy enough to handle under those conditions, and so rarely complained. Tessa had sworn herself to him as well, time and again, and Footman Elias Sagal believed her. The torments of nights apart were lessened a few degrees by that understanding. The worst part, though, was the dark dreams of haunted days gone by which visited whenever he was alone in bed.

Tessa knew that by now. She'd gotten that truth out of him a few weeks back. Elias figured that this night of all nights would be one in which she'd skirt her parents' half-hearted curfew. She knew how important today was for him, after all.

Yes, she does, dumby. She knows. She wouldn't be gone now for no good reason. The Steward's probably recruited her into taking part in the ceremony, and she wanted it to be a surprise. The belief was some balm for his current distraught mood at least, enough to get him out of bed and moving anyway.

When he stepped into the bathroom, any remaining resentment at Tessa for not being here this morning vanished. A fresh-pressed gray footman's uniform hung from the hook on the back of the door with a napkin converted into notepaper tucked into a breast pocket of the tactical blouse. "Good luck today, *Ethling* Elias. This footman loves you very much," it read with a barrage of X's and O's and mini-hearts filling up near every other square inch of paper. The smile never left his face throughout the rest of his morning routine. It was an actual struggle to pry it from his lips before stepping out of his quarters a half hour later to face his destiny.

LIEUTENANT GREGSON

"Ethling? Ethling!?" Captain Alvarez asked in disgust. "The fuck is that exactly? Sounds made up." The Captain turned from the gayly ribboned and pompously adorned dais erected in the geometric center of the Grand Rotunda atop the golden Old-English W, which itself was painted directly atop the maroon-and-silver AOA logo. "But who the hell among us know enough about goddamn medieval history to refute the son of a bitch? I've always hated the damn subject. Goddammit!" he whisper-shouted. "Ain't nothing was ever said about no damn Ethling when we was forming the Witen. Any of you guys remember anything about any Ethling ever being mentioned before?"

"The clause is in the New Destiny Constitution," Lieutenant Dobechek pointed out. "The Commander had to approve it all. He had to know about it."

"Did he?" Alvarez rhetorically asked.

Burger Gregson stood in a loose circle in front of the dais alongside Lieutenants Dobechek and Schwambach. Captain Alvarez leaned against a chair set for the coming occasion directly across from Burger. Servants of the Witen flitted all about them, preparing the scene. The four officers had even pressed their footman escorts into joining the labor. The faster they got the place set up, the sooner they could leave, they all agreed. And if the lowly bastards really hustled, they might be able to get back to their quarters for a decent breakfast before they had to drag their asses right back here to witness the "momentous occasion."

"The clause didn't exist until last month, Dobechek. Wake the fuck up," the Regent of the Corridors disdainfully told his subordinate.

"What are you talking about, Captain?" Schwambach asked, leaning back on a viewing gallery chair of his own.

"The bastard wrote it in last month and then updated the copy on everyone's tablets," Alvarez informed him. "The damn thing doesn't exist anywhere else. There ain't no hard copy. He can fudge it at will."

"I'm sure the clause was always there," Dobechek insisted, clearly uneasy. "Who the hell can remember every damn rule and bylaw in that constitution?"

"It showed up in there the day before the Steward announced the little traitor-seed's ascension," Burger spoke for the first time in minutes. Three heads turned his way. "Before that, all it had to say about succession was the challenge process."

"Come on, man," Schwambach uttered with disbelief plain on his tired face. "How can you possibly know that for sure? Did you take a screenshot of an older version or something?"

"Can you even do that?" Dobechek asked in a childish manner.

"You might be able to," Lieutenant Gregson allowed. "I wouldn't know. I certainly didn't take no screenshots myself."

"Then how the hell can you be so sure?" Dobechek demanded, plopping fully into an orange padded chair.

"Because I read the fucking thing. Often," Burger said in his mellow yet threatening, easy sort of way. "I like knowing where I stand."

"Well, if you're really suggesting what I think you're suggesting, then why haven't you brought your suspicions to the Commander? If his second-in-command is playing him, and you're aware of it, then you got an obligation to inform him."

"It ain't no use. I brought my beliefs to the damn Commander, Lieutenant, months ago," Alvarez said, sounding near full exasperation. "Whatever I tell the man, the Steward is there to say the opposite."

"So you think he won't believe you either, then, Burg?" Schwambach asked, forgetting himself. It took him a minute to pick up on the awkward silence and catch the evil eye Captain Alvarez shot his way. "Sorry. Lieutenant Gregson, I mean. The Commander really won't believe you?"

"It ain't so simple as all that, Lieutenant Schwambach," the Regent answered for Burger. "It ain't so easy to believe in the first place, especially without any actual proof. Hell, you and Dobechek both expressed doubt. How much harder do you think it is to convince the Commander that the man who gave him the keys to the world don't have his best interests in mind?"

"Someone's gotta do something ... before it's too late," Gregson crossed his arms and said in a low voice.

"Something like what, Lieutenant?" Dobechek warily asked.

"Like eliminating the threat before it can infect the Commander," was his simple answer.

"It's our duty to do as much, the way I see it," Captain Alvarez agreed.

"Eliminate the Steward?" Dobechek clearly couldn't believe what she was hearing. "We shouldn't even dare to talk about that, much less actually contemplate it."

"Stiffen up, Lieutenant," Alvarez ordered. "We're just venting here. Just talking among friends. Don't go running your mouth about some harmless talk now."

"I ain't no rat, Captain," the square-shouldered officer insisted. "I just don't think it wise to even take the risk of talking like this. The Steward hears everything. You guys know that."

"I know that's what the little nerd likes everyone to think," Alvarez shot back.

"No one will know about our private conversations, Lieutenant. Not unless you tell them," Burger Gregson said, uncrossing his tan-complected, muscle-heavy arms and taking a step toward the seated woman. "And if anyone ever does find out, we will know just who to blame." The dark stare he gave her after that ominous warning could've frozen a hotplate. Burger had witnessed it happen often enough. And though Lieutenant Dobechek was one tough cookie, a onetime Final Tournament victor even, she was no match for his intensity.

Ultimately, she threw up her hands, insisting, "I ain't no damn rat, Lieutenant. Relax."

Alvarez broke the spell with a two-fingered whistle. "Alright, people," he called to the now milling servants and footmen, "be back here in one hour. The guests arrive a half hour after that. We will be ready for them, folks. I want a nice, clean, and orderly ceremony today, or it's your asses. You hear me?"

A few listless voices shouted back in the affirmative.

"Good," the Captain barked. "Get the hell out of here, then," he ended with a dismissing wave.

"I'll see y'all back here in an hour, I guess," he said, turning back to face the small group. "Gregson, why don't you come with me? Lieutenant Woodson is meeting at my place for a drink or two in about five minutes. I think the three of us might just find we got a lot to talk about."

CHAPTER 18

JED

Jed Redding startled awake. He could not say why. No hint of any bad dream lingered in his memory. And it wasn't that his eyes flashed open to discover he was not in his own bed in his humble quarters at the end of the long, meandering alleyway in Blue Corridor. Far from being shocked by the revelation, Larry Holderman's bedroom had become as familiar as his own. And even waking up to discover the room empty apart from himself was not all that rare an occurrence either. Larry was an early riser, his mid-ride or midday naps being a byproduct of the habit.

Lying alone in the sleep-tossed silk sheets, Jed found himself wishing this morning could've been one of those rare occasions where Larry snoozed past his normal wake-up. It would have gone a long way just then in calming his unwanted feelings of unjustified unease to be able to curl up into his partner's comforting girth and run a hand through his thick white chest-hair to lull himself back to sleep for a few more winks. But sadly, Jed was alone. And besides, the Ethling Ceremony was only an hour away now. He'd already slept long past anything resembling a sensible hour.

There ain't no avoiding today, Jeddy old boy. It can only be endured, not shunned. "The Witen expects every resident to attend," he reminded himself by quoting Supervisor Addison's end-of-shift briefing to the crew working in the Collector Module Garage yesterday.

Jed needed every last one of the winks he had managed to snatch, he realized, swinging his feet to the floor. The room spun and his head pounded. Last night's fun was going to cost him today. *God, I need an aspirin,* he thought, stumbling toward Larry's bathroom. It was no surprise Father Boyd and Dolly Duchesne's nuptial ceremony last night in the priest's secret clubhouse had not taken the same toll on his partner. Larry Holderman was a serious drinker. All day, every day, he tugged back pull after pull from his little leather flask. A night of boozing was nothing to him. *Lucky bastard,* Jed told himself with only partial sincerity. After all, the man's drinking got in the way of a good many nights they could've shared together. It was the thing the two argued about the most, the few times their discourses ever got as far as could be classified as an argument anyway.

Last night's marriage was long overdue in Jed's opinion, and he knew that was hardly the minority among their small group of trusted and close friends. Even though Jed did not involve himself in their resistance plots, the gang still considered him a close and trusted enough compadre to make the short guest list. Jed was glad of it. They had a blast. Too much fun, really, he realized, clutching his pounding head in his hands as he stood before the bathroom sink, looking forlornly into the mirror at his miserable state.

Larry was most likely running one errand or another or on some important mission for Boyd this morning. He'd most likely get to the ceremony with just moments to spare. Jed knew Larry would be counting on him to save a spot. So, setting his mind to the inevitable, Jed choked down a few aspirin and set the shower running as hazy flashes from last night's party played inside his head: Maisie drunk as a skunk for the first time in Jed's company and dancing like she'd never danced before, Dolly and Boyd never once taking their hands off each other, Roddy Sheffield reciting poetry like a lovesick puppy in the priest's borrowed library to Arlene Fincannon—the newest member of Boyd and Maisie's inner circle was a twenty-something, toe-headed, big-chested, and fit daughter of a former friend of the hippie-haired Sheffield, who also once worked as a computer engineer for AOA—or the newlyweds taking small sips of the priest's strong wine from one another's goblets, as well as many snaps of Larry and Patel off in the kitchen just chilling and controlling the music.

Larry and Patel. Larry and Patel. The memory of those two together all night stuck with him all through his shower and subsequent dressing efforts. They were friends, good friends It should not be odd that they spent time at a party together. Yet the more images of that wedding came back to him, the more troubled he became. *You're just hungover and not thinking right, man. Get over it,* he tried telling himself. But the words fell flat the instant after he thought them. Jed was just about to depress Larry's bedroom hatch-release when something beside the door caught his eye. Larry was a slob, so the mere fact of a pile of dirty clothes stacked up by the door wasn't what pulled him up short. It was the article of clothing barely poking out from the middle of the pile which gave him pause.

He didn't want to bend down and investigate, for his hangover's sake as well as that of his peace of mind, but he found himself stooping regardless. When he tugged the shirt free of the dank pile, all his worst fears were confirmed. Larry Holderman could never fit into the small neon-orange polo he held out in his hand. Hit with a wave of what he rationally knew to be unjust sorrow, Jed dropped the item, watching it fall in seemingly slow motion to the bedroom carpet. The shirt belonged to Aziz Patel. It could be no other's. Not only was it the small man's size and imbued with his signature musky cologne, but Jed had actually seen the saturnine mechanical engineer wearing it many times. Although, now that he thought back on it, the shirt hadn't made its appearance in the slow-tempered man's limited clothing rotation in several months. The implications of that deduction rolled over Jed like a runaway stallion.

They've been fucking for months. Hell, who knows, probably for years even.

Jed Redding knew he had no right to be upset. Larry did not belong to him. But Jed had always been faithful and supposed there was a part of him that expected his lover and module partner to reciprocate that loyalty, a part he never allowed himself to acknowledge before, a jealous part. *God, who am I? Relax, man, Larry still loves you. Just 'cause he's fucking Patel don't change that,* he tried to tell himself. Jed knew he could never confront Larry with what he'd discovered, knew it would change everything between them, but as he marched out of Larry Holderman's quarters, he knew full well it already had, at least in his own heart.

The Trolley Depot loomed up before him. Jed had no memory of his trudge from Larry's place in Green Corridor to where he now stood in the Central Hub. His feet had known his destination. While his mind bounced from despair over his lover's betrayal to shame over feeling betrayed at all, his legs had simply taken one long stride after the next. Jed came back to the moment, darting around a stationary trolley, headed for Branch 4's massive archway and the Grand Rotunda beyond.

"Hey, Jed, wait up," a feminine voice called to him from somewhere in the mildly populated Hub.

Turning toward the call, Jed saw Maisie Sagal and her little sister headed his way. The pair moved slowly, so Jed stopped where he was and waited for them to join him. Carrie had been on forearm crutches alone for months now, a real inspiration with her tenacity and never tiring determination, but she still could not quite move as fast as an unincumbered or unafflicted person. Still, it wasn't more than a handful of seconds before the two Sagal sisters were standing just in front of him.

"Are you going to Elias's ceremony, Mr. R-R-Red-Redding?" the adorable child asked him.

"Everybody's got to," he answered.

"That's what I told Mais, but she wasn't gonna let me c-c-come anyway. I had to make a bet with her to let me."

"A bet?"

"Uh huh. Ya see, Mais has been h-h-home-home-schooling me, and we were doing algebra, and we came to a problem that M-M-Maisie said had her stumped when she was in s-ss-school. So I bet her that I could solve it, and if I did, she'd have to take me to Elias's c-c-cere-c-ceremony."

"What would've happened if you failed to solve the problem?"

"I would've had to eat gwoss broccoli for a month with every d-d-dinner," she told him with a look of pure loathing, obviously recalling the vegetable's foul taste.

"Well then, in that case, that's a heck of a gamble, don't ya think, Ri Ri? I mean, algebra is hard enough for most adults, much less a seven-year-old kid," Jed pointed out.

"Oh, I knew I'd solve it," Carrie said, shooting her sister a sly smile. "Haven't ya h-her-h-heard, Mr. Redding? I'm a prodig-g-gy."

Maisie and Jed both burst out laughing, spreading the child's grin ever wider. "Yeah, now that you mention it, Maisie did tell us something like that before," Jed said, still chuckling a bit and immensely grateful for it. "I'm surprised you made it out of bed at all, Mais," Jed addressed the brunette woman, her handsome features untarnished by last night's festivities. "I barely made it out myself."

Maisie barked a few low chuckles as she agreed. "Yeah, it was up in the air for a few hours there. I'm probably still drunk, as a matter of fact. Might be why I let Carrie convince me to take her to this clown show."

"I won the bet, Mais," Carrie reminded her big sister. "And you gave your word. You h-h-had to let me come. It woulda been dishonorable otherwise."

Maisie could only laugh at that. Jed joined in. The natural remedy was working its magic indeed. His headache was pushed to the background, as well as his pain over Larry's infidelity. "Come on, then, girls. We better get to stepping before the place fills up. I gotta save Larry a seat."

"Dolly wants us to save her a spot, too," Maisie informed him as the trio took off toward the towering archway.

"Her, too, eh? Jeez, I figured Doll and Boyd wouldn't be able to pry themselves apart long enough to allow her to dress and make it down there, the way they was all over each other last night," Jed quipped.

"Gosh, they were adorable last night, weren't they?" Maisie happily sighed. "I'm glad somebody up here can find a bit of joy in the middle of all this madness."

"You and me both, kiddo," Jed agreed. "Let's pray it lasts."

THE COMMANDER

Garlands of pine boughs woven with gold silk wrapped themselves around the railings and edges of the 50-foot by 30-foot dais. Thick gold-and-black ribbons were laced around every post and beam. In the center of the stage, five feet from the edge of the wide platform, sat a podium draped in three banners, the front of which was black and bearing a gold Old-English W, while the side two were gold with a black W. The Commander himself stood at the back of the stage, a good twenty feet directly behind the podium. Behind him hung three more massive tapestries, black-and-gold to match their twins adorning the podium. The central peak of the black tapestry's gold W came to a point directly over his head. The Commander did not need to look up to know this. The Steward had insisted on a damn rehearsal the night before. The pedantic old fart fussed over every little detail, shifting the Commander an inch left, only to correct two inches right. He had no wish to endure the Steward's whiny pleas for him to correctly position himself, so he'd memorized his spot and made sure he hit his mark after marching up the steps of the dais's lone staircase as drums pounded out from the maroon-and-silver speakers resting atop either side of the stage.

Some, he knew, thought the Commander yielded far too much to the Steward. Such people would no doubt squirm to see him play out his part in the ceremony exactly as directed. But the Commander could not worry about such people and their ignorant thoughts. He had a species to rule. The weight of their safety and eternal prosperity were ever on his shoulders. The Commander was grateful for the Steward's organizational skills. He knew things would look a lot different without him. He had no wish to see such a future come to pass. So he humored the man. The Steward was a showman, where the Commander was anything but. In such situations, it only made sense for him to yield to the more eager man. The Steward had gotten him this far, after all. If memorizing a few stupid steps and phrases in some "necessary ceremony" was the worst of it, than that was little enough to endure. It was a cost-benefit ratio kind of thing the way the Commander saw it.

Unfortunately, it had been the limited deference he showed his number-two which emboldened the man to force this day upon him in the first place. *Shit*, the Commander had to laugh, *fate is as circular as it is inescapable*. Many of the officers and footmen were growing resentful of the Steward of late, he was well aware of that. Though it was just as clear that, deep down, all their complaints were merely power lust. They just wanted to be second in line. It had been that very conviction, along with the Commander's desire to keep the ship running as smoothly as ever, which the Steward manipulated to get him to agree to this Ethling Announcement Ceremony. "Naming Eli Ethling eliminates any future competition among the officers and footmen. It settles the matter before it can even become a vocal argument. Trust me, sir, it's best to get out in front of this thing," the former lawyer had told him.

The Commander had been entertaining a pair of young Witen servants that night, both of whom were all too willing to share his wine, but when bedtime came, they decided to deny their ruler his rightful due. The fucking he laid down on both of their tight little bodies had him all worked up. The bitches had cried. He hated that. It was their duty to receive his seed. A baby born of the Commander's line was a blessing. The Steward had placarded that edict in every Cafeteria Hall and gathering place Cardinal's Nest had. They had to know by then why they were there. They had to have seen the signs. They had no right to cry and ruin his mood.

But they did bawl, and he did grow irritated, so much that the whole time the Steward made his pitch later that night in the quiet of the Commander's office, his mind could not focus. He did agree that many of the officers would be after his throne, but he was in no way sure naming a future successor was by any means the right fix. But the Steward was smooth. The man could talk. It had always been a benefit to the Commander in the past, that slick-talking manner, but when he finally found himself on the losing end, he did not like the taste.

Whatever, he was here now. No way would he show his people a disorganized or ill-disciplined Witenagemot. He'd made his choices. Best to just bite the bullet and get it all over with, he knew. So he stayed rock still, arms crossed, staring into the crowd through one milky eye and one clear, wearing a sharp-pressed black uniform, his array of seven stars on either collar popping with a golden-stitched twinkle to highlight the four long gashes running across the right side of his face, drawing one's eye to the shaft of the black battle-worn bearded axe poking up behind his right shoulder. These people were his. He would show them his control. He would let them see his barely caged power and no cracks in the armor. And no matter who went home with what title after this bullshit ceremony, the people would know who was still in charge.

The drums, rolling in a blistering rhythm, suddenly cut out. Five seconds later, after the music's echoes bounced back off the gargantuan bulkheads, a silence permeated every molecule of air in that circular chamber. *So it begins*, he thought with an inner moan he in no way physically displayed. Confirming his suspicions, the Steward stood up from his chair in the wings of the freshly built stage to sedately march toward the podium.

Last chance, man, he told himself. *Nah, on second thought, the boy is young and naïve. I can deal with a threat from him easier than a few of them others. If it's got to happen, let it happen... Just don't drag this shit out, Harclay.*

"Good afternoon, my fellow citizens," the Steward bellowed in a manner evoking some crooked politician. "Today is a glorious day for our Witenagemot, for the new age of man. It is our privilege and honor to share it with you all." Stopping there for the perfunctory applause, the Steward took the time to wipe his lips and clear his throat. "After today's short ceremony, the Main Cafeteria Hall will be serving a special meal for us all. I know we never fail to eat well up here in the Nest, but the cooks have been planning and preparing this spread they got for ya today for weeks now. Our friends that manage the Billiard Lounge have also kindly stocked the hall with enough beer, mead, vino, and moonshine to kill you all stone dead. And speaking of stones, the Hookah Lounge will also be providing some sweet ... uhh ... *herb*, cost free. Limit ten in the lounge at any time, though. Our recyclers can only handle so much. So take your puffs and run on back to the cafeteria hall for seconds and thirds," he laughed. The crowd got the hint after a moment and loosed a few giggles. "It's said that no one knows the precise sources of either of these independently managed lounge's blessed supply. Whether that's true or not, I'll leave for you to puzzle over. But for now, so long as both lounges stay well stocked with their precious herbs and nectars, the council won't press them too hard to spill the beans on their little underground supply chain. For now, we see it as a harmless subversion of a few New Destiny Constitution provisos. The moment that ends, however, the Witenagemot shall intervene. But our strong belief that the hard-working, emotionally exhausted, good, kind-hearted people aboard this miracle station deserve their pleasures. You folks, the first generation of the new world, are the most deserving people in history of an easy way to take the edge off after a long day. This belief keeps our heads turned the other way … for now." He laughed once more but after a noticeable pause. The gallery was left bemused by the display and mostly remained silent.

"So, don't nobody go running on home after. I hope to see each and every one of you at the afterparty. Okay, now, we shift to a more solemn gear. The Commander and I have not come to the decision to name an heir, an Ethling, as we call it, lightly. Obviously, we've both always known that no one lives forever, that this society will have to endure long after we are gone. The Integration Program was step one in the commitment we swore to ensure this station's everlasting vitality. Step two is settling our society's greatest question mark before it can become an issue. Every empire and kingdom throughout all of history was brought low by such an issue in the end. So, we embarked on a years' long quest to seek out the most worthy among you. We needed this successor to be strong, brave, cunning, wise, well-disciplined, young enough to still be virile when his time came, and of course, absolutely committed to the future of humanity. One candidate in the end checked all these boxes, time and again. You've all heard his exploits from the Footman's Monthlies. I'm sure word has spread about his record completion of the Integration Program and his ascension as the youngest member of the Footmen to date. You've all no doubt heard about the many disputes and arguments and sticky situations he has defused over the years in his role on my security detail. I don't have to sit here and list for you one accomplishment after the next. You've no doubt heard, and even shared them yourself. So instead, I will simply invite the man, your future ruler, up on the stage with me, and we can get on to the fun stuff."

Elias Sagal stood up from his reserved spot in the front row of the viewing gallery. The Commander could see the beads of sweat from all the way back where he stood beneath the black banner. *The boy is nervous,* he deduced. *Good. Very good.* Elias's footfalls echoed off the oculus back down on them, the only sound to be heard. When he came to stand at attention beside the podium, the Steward cleared his throat, ending the thick, anticipatory silence. "Footman Elias Sagal, do you know why you have been called here today to stand before the Commander?"

Pedantic bastard, the Commander silently scoffed.

"Yes, Steward, sir. I come willingly and with great humility," the tall and athletic seventeen-year-old boy answered.

"You know that by accepting the title of Ethling, you swear your-self to one day take the same oath as our Commander and sacrifice your name to give your every effort wholly to the safety and enduring prosperity of our species?"

"I know, and I do so swear," Sagal stated the scripted remark firmly, never flinching in his flawless stance.

"By swearing the Ethling Oath, you will have written your fate in blood, a forever indissolvable ink. But you have not forsworn your present. You may be next in line for head of the Witenagemot Council, but for now, you are still a footman. Your duties and responsibilities—and authorities," he added, emphasizing the point with a long stare out into the crowd, "have not changed. Is that understood?"

"Yes, sir, Steward, sir," the boy barked back. "I shall always do my part for the Witen, whatever that part shall be."

"Very well, then. Commander," the Steward called, turning to face him, "I leave the rest to you, sir."

The Commander only nodded for answer. Drawing out his axe from its custom sheath, he took eight long paces toward the podium. Arriving behind it, he leaned the black axe against its cherrywood back. After only a second's worth of pause, the Commander found himself clearing his throat and tapping the microphone jutting out from the podium's top on a bendable rod. He hated when people did that. It made them look lost or ill-prepared. This really pissed him off because he knew damn well what to say. He wasn't lost at all. The tap and throat-clear had been involuntary ticks, nothing more. Needing to reclaim a bit of what he pegged as his lost dignity, the Commander decided to lean into the pause, breathing heavily into the mic and gazing over the masses with a dead-eyed stare that had grown especially menacing since his maiming. Finally, he said his part. "Elias Sagal, as Commander of the Witenagemot and head of its council, I hereby offer you the title of Ethling. Will you claim it?"

Elias made a perfect, crisp military turn, all heels and snappy pivots, to face the Commander. "I will claim the title, Commander, sir," he responded, falling to one knee.

"Then speak the oath."

"I, Footman Elias Sagal, do swear, from this day until the end of my days, to serve the Witenagemot and its citizens in all things, to give my life, honor, and identity to the survival of our eminent species. I commit myself fully to your will, Commander, sir. I shall be your avatar in all matters you deem fit until the sad day I must replace you."

"Very well," the Commander conceded as he snatched up his battleaxe. Raising the wicked blade high above his head, he spoke his last bit. "I hereby name you Footman Elias Sagal, Ethling of the Witenagemot." The axe stayed poised above his head. Memories of himself in similar positions in years past came back in a roaring tide. Some of them felt so real, like he was living them all over again, that after he'd gently brought the axe down to tap the blade on each of the boy's shoulders, the Commander was shocked he hadn't lost himself in the daydreams and hacked Sagal's damn head off the way he'd done his father's.

The crowd burst out cheering, jumping to their feet. The deed was done. He'd done his part. Now he could move on to other more satisfying preoccupations, namely the pretty dark-skinned girl with the copper eyes seated in row two. *How have I missed her before?* he wondered. The Commander snapped his fingers at the stage wing where Footman Childress was standing ready for his orders amid a gaggle of servants acting as stagehands for the immensely and unnecessarily garish little ceremony. Catching her eye, he then pointed toward the young girl in question and nodded once. Childress knew what he wanted. She'd handle the rest.

The day really had not been all that bad in the end. His fears had made him dread it for months. In retrospect, he needn't have worried. True, the Ethling idea hadn't been his own, but the Commander was starting to think perhaps the Steward wasn't too far off the mark after all. *Well, we shall see, anyway*, he thought with a resigned grin. *Maybe I'll even join the festivities in the Main Cafeteria Hall.* His people would get a kick out of rubbing shoulders with their supreme ruler. *Maybe I just will... Maybe ... after*, he thought, gazing at his afternoon's rights with an epically justified pleasure.

CHAPTER 19
LIEUTENANT GREGSON

Infection Event: Day 3,048

The Bowling Alley had been chosen as the ambush site almost from the very beginning. After nearly a decade of serving in the Witenagemot Council alongside the Steward, they all knew a fair bit about his habits. The chubby little bookworm had been shuffling down to the Rec District's Bowling Alley twice a week just before midnight for years now. He liked to keep as secluded from the people as the Commander himself. Plus, he was a night owl and an early riser. The dude never slept really, as best as Gregson could figure. Every Tuesday and Thursday, late at night, long after the lanes had closed, the Steward would show up. Whoever his body-man for that particular shift was would turn on the power and get the lanes up and running for the pretentious twerp. Every last one of his personal security footmen knew how to operate the Bowling Alley better than most of its rotational attendants by now. Lieutenant Gregson heard he couldn't bowl for shit despite all the practice, though. But the man could be relied upon to make his bi-weekly visits to the dark and deserted Rec District's afterhours scene. That was what the three conspirators had keyed in on. They knew he went with only one security footman, a single body-man, as well. There was really no other choice for the attack.

And now, here he was, standing just outside its 8-foot archway with a localized EMP cannister in one hand and his hand-forged steel longsword in the other. The pivotal moment might have had others shook, but not Burger Gregson. That's why Captain Alvarez and Lieutenant Woodson had nominated him and his handpicked team to lead the killsquad. Burger always got the damn job done. There wasn't a situation this world could concoct heavy enough to rattle him. Almost as soon as they'd known the Bowling Alley was the ambush site, Lieutenant Gregson expected it'd be him leading the attack. He had been ready for this moment for weeks now. All the planning was done. Soon Harclay Aponyaschefski, the man insultingly still referred to as the Steward, would be dead and forgotten.

"Take a lesson, Eli," the voice did not come from his comm but from the Bowling Alley beyond. The Steward had set up shop in his usual lane right in front of the archway, so his voice floated clearly to Lieutenant Gregson and his three handpicked footmen.

The soldiers in question were Footman Torrez, Footman Algernon, and Footman Simmons. The first two both worked under him in Maroon Corridor, steady men who knew how to swing their axes. The last was different. Both of the men now inside the alley would recognize her. Luckily for her, they wouldn't be leaving the place alive. Footman Simmons was a stocky black woman with tight cornrows and a wicked spear. It had been Lieutenant Woodson who'd first approached her for the job. The Witen's footmen had themselves a bit of an underground grapevine of sorts, and the word Silver Corridor Warden's people had snatched from that prescient vine all pointed to the iron-jawed woman as the source of some grumblings over Elias Sagal and Harclay Aponyaschefski's lawless mentor-protégé relationship. It hadn't really taken much convincing to recruit her. She was no fan of Sagal. If Burger had a nickel for every time she called him "soft" or a "lazyass," or her favorite insult of "arrogant, entitled little shit," he'd be a millionaire.

He had to loose a soft chuckle even now as he thought about how sweet it was going to be to see the wounded looks on both of their miserable faces when they recognized their once trusted colleague. Sagal himself had not been a specific target. The Ethling was merely icing on the cake. It just so happened that on the Thursday they planned to set their ambush into motion, the "arrogant, entitled little shit" was pulling close guard duty on his master. Two birds with one stone, Woodson, Alvarez, and he all realized when they reviewed today's duty roster.

Though Woodson, and a footman of his named Allanson, were a bit irritated that they wouldn't be the ones to deal with Sagal. They had made a few half-hearted attempts to take Burger or two of his men's places, but really, they all knew who was best for the job. It was going to be an easy piece of work anyway. No need to get two Witen officer's hands dirty for some routine bullshit. True, Sagal might've been the best natural fighter in the entire station next to the Commander, but Simmons's skill with her longspear alone would sorely try him. Once he and Footmen Algernon and Torrez added their blades to the mix, the boy would be toast in no time. Then they could take a bit of time with the Steward.

"Practice makes perfect," their target told Sagal inside the alley. The signature sound of ten pins clattering to the hardwood lone quickly followed the statement.

"I will try and remember that, sir," Sagal answered sarcastically. "What was the score the last time I played you here, again? Remind me."

"Watch yourself, Ethling. You ain't Commander yet," the Steward said with a smile in his voice.

Lieutenant Gregson turned his back on the cheesy jabber to face his footmen. "Okay, listen up, just like we planned now. I toss in the cannister, and we come storming in right on the heels of the pulse. Knock the Steward down right away but try not to kill him if you can. We just want him subdued so he don't go running off while we turn to deal with Sagal. We cut the pretender boy down as a unit and then we should get a good three or four minutes with the Steward before the power comes back online. We need to be out of sight of this place long before that happens. The last patrol passed here two minutes ago, so we don't got anything to worry about on that end for at least thirty minutes, but once main power is back on, the cameras come back online and a signal is sent to the Control Room informing them of the momentary outage. Someone will be sent to check it out soon after that. But we will be long gone before even the Bowling Alley's or this alleyway's cameras can catch a single frame of any one of us. I've had the scrambler running since we left Branch 1, so any cameras along our route here will show nothing but snow. But we better get the show on the road before someone notices this alleyway's cameras have been malfunctioning for far too long to be any system blip. The scramblers ain't the failsafe the EMP is. Might be, with all the cameras 'round here, one or more might snatch a couple clear frames of us between the fuzz. We've already stayed here too long. Now's the time. Okay, y'all ready? Five minutes, in and out, and by the time Captain Alvarez presents his four patsies to the Commander tomorrow morning, we'll be asleep in our beds, resting a deal easier than we have in quite some time. Ain't that right?"

"Yes, sir," all three answered, grinning.

"Okay, flat against the wall," he ordered. "EMP out in three, two, one." Gregson stepped to the edge of the archway, reaching around to toss what looked like a blue-labeled SpaghettiOs can toward the large hall's only two occupants. The electromagnetic pulse cannister was as key to the plan as the assault location. The blue-gray can-shaped devices all flashed a controlled EMP burst, knocking out all electronics in a 60-yard radius. Their quarry wouldn't be able to radio for help if their radio comms weren't working. The Bowling Alley itself would lose power, but that was a benefit more than a detriment. In the three seconds it took for the backup power system to kick on, pitch dark would fall on the trapped pair. Plus, the camera network wouldn't come back online until main power was restored. Those bonuses, along with the sheer surprise of the ambush itself, would be huge advantages.

It's a damn good thing the Captain had the foresight to hack the access chip out of Sargent Marge's arm before they sent her corpse to the mulcher, he thought as the cannister wheeled through empty air. *The mulcher was too good for that traitor,* he decided. Burger didn't like the idea of having any part of Sergeant Marge Hamill still existing among them, whether that part be rotting fertilizer or not.

Alvarez had long suspected the Steward had been holding things back. Aponyaschefski and the Commander had told every Witen officer that all of the video-scramblers, shockdiscs, tranqdarts, minidrones, and EMP cannisters had been aboard Gillian Gerwitz's Star Hawk when it exploded. Captain Alvarez, at least, hadn't bought it. He made sure he could access the weapons locker. The Captain had checked inside it years back, and so had known about the Steward's lies for nearly a decade. *Sleep well, Captain. Tonight, we set your weary mind at ease*, Lieutenant Gregson silently promised his superior as the dull metallic clink of the cannister striking hard-wood reached his ears.

It would have been sweet to watch the little can crack apart and burst loose its payload as the two idiots stared slack-jawed at their doom, but Burger knew he had to save his sight for the coming slaughter. He'd seen localized EMPs go off before, from a safe distance through field-glasses, but enough to know just what Harclay and Sagal were now seeing. Burger and his killsquad covered their ears. The explosion wasn't deafening, but a high piercing ring did ripple out ahead of the subsonic pulse-wave. If Sagal and the Steward were doing a similar thing in response to the painful whine, then they definitely weren't able to shield their eyes from the ball of bright light that expanded into the device's 60-yard radius until reaching its limit and instantly collapsing back on itself.

The power cut out the second the flash had faded. "Now!" Lieutenant Burger Gregson shouted, charging through the wide blue-and-orange striped archway. He felt his footmen on his heels. He was six paces into the Bowling Alley, his three compatriots right behind him, when the backup power kicked in. Dim, hazy blue emergency lighting snapped on all around them. Everywhere there were shadows, darker than he'd been expecting, but it hardly mattered. The target and his pet footman stood a yard to either side of the EMP cannister, squinting shut their eyes and pressing firm hands against their ears. Gregson was first to them. Neither were aware of him until his front kick folded the Steward in half, sending him flying backward toward the oil-slick lanes.

Footman Algernon wasn't a particularly tall man, but he did have long arms. He could really generate some torque with his long axe. He'd also had time to aim a running swing. Yet somehow, Elias Sagal dropped his hands from his ears, took one step back, and caught the axe-shaft in two vise grips. Torrez was on him next, aiming his double-bladed axe for the Ethling's knees. It found Algernon's back instead. Sagal and Algernon both had firm hands on the axe, but rather than try and rip it free, Elias had simply tripped the useless bald bastard, manipulating their grips on the weapon to maneuver Lieutenant Gregson's most senior footman directly into the path of his second-longest tenured footman's double-bladed axe.

It stuck there, deep in the small of Algernon's back. Torrez tried to wriggle it free, eliciting shrieks from his friend and shift partner. The five-ten, long-legged, pot-bellied Torrez panicked upon hearing the screams and realizing what he'd done. Releasing his grip on his weapon entirely, the footman fell to the floor beside his downed partner. Gregson had stepped back toward the fray the instant after kicking the Steward, but as he and Footman Simmons arrived to help their squadmates, Elias Sagal was already taking several steps back for space, holding Algernon's steel-shafted battleaxe defensively across his body.

"Get up, man. The hell's the matter with you?" Gregson barked at Footman Torrez. "The job ain't done."

"Who's the job exactly, Burger?" The Steward coughed the question from his seat atop the hardwood. "Me or the Ethling?"

"You were the top priority, if it makes ya feel better to know you was worth killing, but we'll take the Ethling as our little cherry on top."

"Our?" the Steward asked still coughing painfully. "Who did you hatch this murder plot with, Burger? Huh? I know you ain't got the brains to plan a picnic. Who planned this madness? I know it ain't the soon to be dead morons you brought with y—" The Steward pulled up short after catching his first clear view of Footman Simmons. "Simmons? Wha... Why?"

"Et tu, Brute?" Elias Sagal spoke for the first time since the EMP's blast. "I dared to believe we was friends, Simm."

"I was just your bitch, nothing more. You were the golden boy who could do no wrong. I was your forgotten shift partner," she growled. "How many damn shifts did I cover for your ass? Huh? And how many did you pull for me? Huh? Does none sound about right to you? You and the Steward have put y'all selves above humanity's future. I seen it for a while now. I'm just thankful the good Lieutenant's got the balls to do something about it. And I'll be happy to see your overrated ass bleeding to death at the end of my spear," she finished with an impressive twirl of her six-foot-long oak-shafted and leaf-bladed spear.

"Jealousy is an ugly color on you, Simm," Sagal told her, tossing the axe halfway down the lane behind him so he might draw out his war hammer from where it was cunningly sheathed behind his back. "You wanna see how you look in red?"

"Fuck yourself, Eli. Torrez, stand the fuck up and pull your axe out of his back." She kicked the still befuddled footman. The smack got the man to his feet. He did have an anguished look on his face as he ripped his axe from his dead friend's back, but he nonetheless ripped it loose. Once armed, Torrez regained some of his earlier poise. Gregson went wide to Sagal's left and saw Footman Simmons mirror him to the right. Torrez rubbed his nose with the back of a hand as he took his place in the center of the triangulation.

"Just set the weapon down, boy," Gregson suggested. "I promise we'll end it quickly."

"You want my war hammer, Lieutenant, you come and take it."

"Don't be stupid, Elias," Simmons implored. "You're barely a match for me. Let alone three of us."

"I didn't have much trouble with him," Sagal responded with a lift of the chin to indicate the bloody lump heaped beside a ball-return.

"You'll fucking pay for Algernon, you son of a bitch!" Torrez roared.

"Why me? You're the one who killed him?" Sagal mockingly asked.

"Come on, you fools. He's just buying time," Burger told his two surviving accomplices. "Let's get him."

Torrez and Simmons charged with him, all three rearing back deathblows. Sagal did the right thing. He chose one opponent and went charging in himself. Torrez was met halfway into his bullrush by Elias Sagal's left shoulder. The breath left the footman's lungs in one big huff. Simmons and Gregson both had to change direction and re-aim their swings. Burger's cut empty air. Simmons had pulled her thrust up short. Elias had gone down with Torrez, landing on top of the slimmer man. As he rolled off his victim, Sagal added a kick straight into the side of Torrez's head, snapping his neck.

And just like that, it was two on one, and the damn Ethling hadn't taken a scratch. "Aghhh!" Gregson screamed as he charged the boy yet again. Elias interposed his war hammer, deflecting Gregson's wild swing, but Simmons, thank the heavens, was there an instant later with a vicious and speedy thrust. Sagal was only able to con-tort his body out of the thrusts path a limited amount. The razor edge of the spearhead sliced a clean foot-long gash across the Ethling's belly. Whipping his war hammer back and forth and retreating, Elias pressed a hand to the fresh wound. Lieutenant Gregson knew it had done some real damage. The Ethling's gray uniform quickly soaked black as the red blood drank up the cotton.

"You're done, Eli. Drop the damn hammer." Simmons tried negotiation one more time.

Sagal lifted his blood-drenched hand from the gash and spoke in a calm voice that irritated Burger something fierce. "You're a traitor, Simmons. You had glory with us," he told her, indicating the Steward still on the hardwood bent over in pain. "And now, *traitor* is all anyone will ever think when the name Footman Simmons is spoken in future days, if, that is, it's ever spoken again. And I'm never done, Simm. Two years oughta taught ya that much by now."

Gregson had enough. He needed to get this job done. Time was ticking. Before Simmons could think of a reply, the lieutenant flung his single-runnel, three and a half foot longsword as though it were a spear at Elias standing ten feet in front of him. It was wholly unexpected—that much was obvious. Sagal made some weak effort to deflect the huge projectile, leaving him off-balance. He tried to right himself, but a ball-return came up just behind him. Elias toppled over the automatic-retrieval contraption, landing on his back. Burger and Simmons didn't waste any time. They darted after their downed foe. Burger made a quick detour to snatch up his longsword, so Simmons was first on him. Sagal was only just able to roll clear of the thrust she aimed down at him.

Scrambling on his back, rolling and jerking away from Simmons's spear, Sagal bumped up against the ball-return from the next alley over. They had him. Gregson caught up to the fray just as the Ethling's coming fate was dawning in his eyes. Burger sent in a slash that would've hacked through plate steel straight for the boy's thick neck. Elias did manage to deflect that blow just in time with a flail of his war hammer, but the thrust Simmons jammed deep into his chest just below his left shoulder after he exposed himself was just as satisfying to Burger Gregson as if it were his own blow that landed.

"Ahhh!" the weak man-child hollered in pain.

"Elias!" the Steward croaked in helpless panic.

Burger was certain the stab was an unrecoverable blow, or else he might've whipped another slash of his sword back at the boy's head sooner. Instead, he watched while, just as Simmons plucked her spear from Sagal's chest, the boy reached up over his head and grabbed a bowling ball from the return rack. Simmons had her follow-up and clearly mortal stroke ready to go fast enough; it was only that she was in no way expecting Elias's move. The surprise cost her a knee. Sagal chucked the heavy ball straight into it from two feet away. Simmons fell like someone had abruptly cut the airflow on an inflatable dancing man. Gregson tried to recover fast, but his swing thudded into the thin metal of the ball-return. Elias had rolled and scrambled right over his old shift partner and now stood, his left arm cradled to his chest and his right clinging tight to his steel war hammer with its 3-inch hammerhead and 4-inch long pointed-claw on the inverse end.

"Drop the sword, Lieutenant," the Steward said, obvious pleasure in his pained voice. "Maybe we can still forgive this ... after a bit of penance. Your coup is over, but your life don't have to be. Drop that pretty longsword."

"You think I'm afraid of your little pet here?" He used the tip of his blade to indicate Elias. "Think again."

"I know you are, Burger," the Steward said, climbing awkwardly back to his feet. "Everyone is. It's why we named him Ethling."

Lieutenant Gregson only spat for answer. Then, fast as he could, Burger ducked down to snatch up Simmons's fallen spear. From a knee, he then used this much more fitting armament as a projectile weapon. Only this time, when he followed the toss, he would still have his blade in his hand when he arrived. But Sagal hadn't done what Gregson was expecting. He hadn't stood in place and smacked the spear out of the air with his hammer. No, he ducked and rolled, fast as a greased banana despite his stab wound. Gregson only just managed to jump over the looping slash Elias aimed at his legs as he arrived where Sagal had been only seconds before. Burger whipped his sword at the boy's head when he landed, giving himself some space to regain his balance.

As soon as he had it, Sagal was on him. One looping thrust followed the next, interspersed with thrusts aimed at Gregson's gut. He managed to deflect or avoid the flurry of attacks and was just about to launch into his own counteroffensive when the back of his legs collided with another low ball-return. Burger's arms went out for balance, exposing his substantial belly. Elias launched an impossibly powerful thrust with the end of his war hammer directly into Gregson's solar-plexus. His preciously rare longsword instantly fell from his hand. His whole body spasmed in pain. There was no holding onto anything in the face of that involuntary reaction. Sagal had his war hammer whipping back down a moment later to shatter his skull, but Harclay Aponyaschefski's voice halted his demise.

"Wait, Eli. I want to talk to him. Just the knees and shoulders oughta do for now."

A smile stretched across the boy's cruel, pressed lips. He reared back the war hammer to smash any hopes Gregson ever had of walking again, but Simmons was not out of the fight yet. She had snatched a 5-inch knife from her belt while Harclay spoke and dragged herself over to the ball-return Burger was sprawled atop. Leaning up on her side, she jammed the knife into the meaty part of Sagal's thigh. "Ahhhh!" the boy squealed for the second time. The war hammer was heedlessly dropped, clattering to the hardwood as he bent down to knock Simmons's hand from the blade jutting out his thigh. Elias ripped the knife out just as Burger pushed himself off the return to throw his body into Sagal's.

They fell to the hardwood together, but when he landed, Gregson felt a deal more pain than any short fall should be able to illicit. It was only when Sagal twisted the blade in his rotund, rock-firm gut while scrambling out from under him that the lieutenant understood what had happened. The pain darkened the world around him. Something vital had been compromised. He could not catch his breath. Burger was only semi-aware of Simmons wrapping her arm around Sagal's neck as the Ethling tried to climb to his feet. They were struggling, he knew, distantly, and she could definitely use his help, but Burger could do no more than curl up around the horrific pain in his belly. He did manage to turn his eyes toward the wrestling match in time to watch Elias climb atop Simmons's chest with a bowling ball held above his head in both hands. The world didn't go dark until the woman's head was no more than a mass of red pulp beneath the mint-green orb. Lieutenant Gregson's last labored breath in this life came only a beat later.

CHAPTER 20

MAISIE

"**D**id you get it?" The swine-faced weirdo didn't answer right away. Nate Novocaine Barker felt demeaned by her presence; that much was plain in his ugly scowl. Maisie knew the spineless creep felt he warranted a face-to-face with *the man* himself. She and Father Boyd, aka *the man*, disagreed. To say they didn't trust ol' Novocaine was an understatement, but they were desperate, they were always desperate, and Cainey Barker, weaselly little perv though he may be, was useful to them just now. They wouldn't have wasted Maisie's time with this simple meeting if it were otherwise. Still, they could not credit letting the notorious gambler and cheat anywhere near Father Boyd just yet. Maisie was who the pencil-thin man in the silver coveralls across the table would have to deal with. *Take it or leave it,* she thought, knowing his answer.

Cainey Barker had made friends and enemies in every Corridor. More enemies than friends, sure, but point was, he knew everyone, and more importantly, knew where their pressure points were. Father Boyd's network wasn't always quite the all-seeing eye in the sky that either of them might like. Never leaving his quarters put the priest at a disadvantage in certain scenarios. A man on the ground was always useful. Cainey had been lobbying for such a role within Maisie and Boyd's resistance for years now. Finally last week, he'd caught his big break. Word had gotten to him about the resistance being hard-up for some inside info from a particular Maintenance Depot employee. Barker, as fate would have it, had himself a few run-ins with that employee over the years aboard the Nest. Clarence Overway was the name of the man in question. Now a vice-driven, dark-complected sot with sunken cheeks and a whiskey nose, Overway once had himself a much cushier job than his current gig of scraping vents and traps and crushing and mulching trash in the Maintenance Depot. Clarence Overway was once a control tower monitor in the Terminal of Branch 2's Lunar Dock.

Sheffield wasn't certain he could start up the refuel docks properly, which was a major snag in their already flimsy plan to lock themselves down Branch 2 until they could get an E-11 ready. It was a convoluted and stage specific process. One misstep in the recharging and they could bring the whole station down. The stored fuel on that Dock could be their doom as easily as their salvation. They needed someone to lay out the process for them, step by step. When Cainey heard about their need, he must've jumped for joy, realizing his ticket into the resistance. This ex-tower monitor happened to owe Cainey—for what exactly, Maisie didn't think she really wanted to know—but whatever it was had been enough to get Overway to cop to information he swore to the Witen by his very life never to divulge.

Maisie and Boyd and the rest of their cohorts needed that info. So, they needed Cainey. But not enough to merit entry to the Clubhouse. Maisie had instead tracked him down on his second shift break in the Main Cafeteria Hall. Barker had been taken off guard for a good ten-count after she slid into an orange padded chair across from the small man seated alone at one of the halls many wide black tabletops. His seclusion probably wasn't wholly ostracization in action. After all, the mammoth hall only had a handful of residents scattered throughout the pink-tiled expanse.

Cainey had pulled the late shift this month, which only ever had a skeleton staff. As sparsely populated as the cafeteria currently was, Maisie still would bet that at least half the residents pulling the late shift were most likely grabbing a mid-shift meal in this very hall just like Novocaine. It made sense, being the only cafeteria in the Nest open twenty-four hours. Maisie was well aware of just what conditions to expect in the hall during the shift break and judged it an ideal time to approach the weasel. Few people would see them together, and those that did would simply see two people eating lunch. What could be more natural in a cafeteria? She'd even rushed through the buffet line and mindlessly plopped dishes on a tray to keep up the illusion.

"Well, Barker, let's have it if ya got it," she prompted again in a clear voice, pitched to a normal volume. There wasn't anyone close enough to hear, and no way Maisie was about to get in tight and whisper with the guy.

"Why should I tell you anything? I'll deal with the man in charge or nobody," Barker said into his mashed potatoes.

"If you truly can deliver what you say you can deliver, then maybe Boyd will invite you for a visit—if, that is, what you believe about him operating my shadow resistance from somewhere in the station is in fact true and he ain't just locked up in his quarters with 12-inch nails and a beard down to the floor like the rest of the residents believe," Maisie said, picking at a burger she discovered on her tray. "But first things first."

"Fine, have it your way," the creep said after Maisie let a silence stretch, "but you tell Boyd I know. Everybody knows. The Witen is probably just pretending they don't know, but they gotta know, too. So tell him I ain't too happy about being treated like I'm an idiot. You guys need me… Obviously. You better start respecting me a whole hell of a lot more. I don't like being surprised during my dinner like this by some snarky brat either. You tell him I said as much."

"If I promise to, will you just spill it, Cainey?" she asked, snarky as ever. "Did the dude tell you the process and protocols or not?"

"Oh, he told me," the ugly weirdo said with casual pomposity. "He even showed me a rundown of the operating program. I know everything about the Lunar Dock now. I already did know more than any of you. I probably coulda figured out the system on my own, anyway. But whatever, I got it covered now, for sure."

"So start talking. Break ends in ten," Maisie urged.

"It's too damn much to go over here. I told ya: I need to see Boyd. This ain't something I can give ya here and now," Novocaine Barker was complaining as a dull roar reached Maisie's ears.

"What's that?" she asked, turning toward the cafeteria's neon-pink and orange-banded archway. The sound was growing louder by the second, coalescing into jabbering voices, many of them. Even as she watched, Maisie could see residents at the end of the short annex tunnel connecting the Main Cafeteria to the Central Hub, all of whom were scurrying toward the long Main Branch Alleyway. That would have been a strange sight on its own, let alone in the dead of night. Many of the residents were still in some form of pajamas even. "What's going on?"

"How the hell should I know?" Cainey rudely retorted. "What the hell are they all doing up?"

"And where the hell are they all going?" Maisie added.

It wasn't until Maisie and Barker stepped out into the Central Hub's maroon diamond-patterned silver dome that the first hint of an answer to their questions was answered. The Glorifier stood beside the archway leading into the Main Branch Alleyway, windmilling an arm to direct traffic down the long hall, all the while shouting, "Praise the Commander! Praise the Steward! Their authority is proven again! Hellfire to the traitors! Rejoice, my brothers and sisters, the sinners are burning even now. Praise the Steward. Praise the Commander. Praise the Ethling!"

Praise the Ethling? That's new, Maisie thought. She wasn't normally the type to simply follow a crowd, but she found herself intrigued despite her principles. *What happened? What's Eli got to do with it?* she was asking herself as her feet carried her along with the flow. Though she was desperate to discover answers to those questions and more, it was Cainey who was first to ask one, picking a bald man of average height walking near them wearing flannel pajama bottoms and a hooded sweatshirt. "What the fuck's going on here, Jerry?"

"Dunno, really," the man apparently named Jerry told Cainey. "Some of the Glorifiers people came shouting and banging on hatches down my alleyway, saying to head to the Grand Rotunda. Where was you, Novocaine?" he asked, noticing Barker's coveralls.

"I was grabbing a meal during shift break," Cainey told the bleary-eyed man walking beside him.

"Ah, pulled the late shift, did ya? Ha, poor bastard," Jerry laughed, waking up a bit.

"Why does the Glorifier think he can demand the people show up somewhere? And why the hell are we all going along with it?" Maisie asked, almost to herself.

"It's the Steward who's calling us all to the Rotunda," a dark-haired woman in a pink muumuu said from a few yards behind them. "The Glorifier's people were first to find them. The Steward ordered them to wake up the station right away."

"Find them?" Cainey asked

"Yeah," a fifty-something woman in a gray tracksuit answered for the muumuu-draped resident beside her, "I guess the Steward got attacked by some traitors in the Witen. He only survived 'cause of the Ethling, they say."

"Attacked?!" Cainey responded in shock. "Who would attack him?"

"I don't know," she admitted. "The Glorifier's disciples didn't say much. They had a lot of people to rouse, they said. But I know one pretty well. Maddie Aranzono is her name. She's a servant of the Witen as well as a disciple."

"Sounds like one committed broad," the man named Jerry quipped.

"Oh, she is that, for sure," Pink Muumuu spoke back up to agree. "I know her, too. She's connected as hell. She knows what's what around this place."

"Oh, you better believe it," Tracksuit Lady affirmed. "And she told me as much as she could while the disciples were in my alleyway."

"Where was he attacked?" Maisie found herself asking. "How?"

"Maddie says it was a lieutenant and some footmen. They tried to assassinate him while he was bowling. But thankfully, the Ethling was there."

"Which lieutenant?" Cainey sounded like he needed to know.

"I don't know," Tracksuit Lady admitted. "Maddie might have, but she didn't tell me who, or who the footmen were neither, and believe me, I asked."

"All glory to the Commander! Burn the traitors. Glory to the Steward. Hail the Ethling, warrior and protector of our guiding light!" the Glorifier was saying as Maisie, Cainey, Jerry, Pink Muumuu, Tracksuit Lady, and the dozen odd people near them turned the corner where the Main Branch Alleyway came to a T intersection, heading for the Grand Rotunda a couple hundred meters farther on.

"I heard the Steward told the Glorifier what to say as they woke us all up, too. I guess those is his words that shirtless prophet is shouting," Pink Muumuu said in a hushed voice. "Apparently the disciples ain't too pleased. No one tells the Glorifier what to preach, at least no one has before, except that the Steward can order anyone to do basically anything, so can most of the Witen Council. So really, there are a lot of people who can tell the Glorifier what to say," she added with a naughty giggle, darting glances about her like a spy during a top-secret handoff.

"The Steward can tell him what to say and do, alright, but the Glorifier is the Commander's messenger in the end. You don't want to shoot the messenger," Jerry said in cautionary tones.

"The Steward's got the Commander under his little thumb," Cainey added his two cents. "I'll bet we'll be hearing more preaching about the Steward and the Ethling in the Glorifier's sermons in the future, you watch. The man knows the Glorifier wants to cozy up next to the Commander. No way that sly bastard lets that happen."

"Watch that shit!" Pink Muumuu whispered at Cainey. "Don't be calling any of the councilmembers names around me."

"Relax, Deandre, the man's just talking," Jerry told Deandre, formerly Pink Muumuu.

"The man's gonna get me killed. So he can take his talk like that somewheres else," Deandre stated, crossing her arms and diverting her gaze.

"Relax? Relax, he says?" Tracksuit Lady asked in Deandre's defense. "Do you have any idea what kind of man the Steward is? Believe me, the Glorifier ain't going along with the Steward reluctantly. He is every bit as afraid of him as he is the Commander. That wild-haired prophet idolizes those he fears. He saw what the Steward did before ordering him and his disciples to send everyone to the Grand Rotunda. He knows full well the Steward ain't a man to tempt. It ain't just that the Steward hears everything around here. Him and the Ethling were outmatched and surprised, and both of 'em come out the other side. The Glorifier don't see that as coincidence, I'm telling ya... He wants to say every last word he's saying, trust me."

"What exactly did he see the Steward do?" Cainey asked, sarcasm heavy in his weak voice.

Tracksuit Lady only nodded her head. All those around her turned their gaze the indicated direction. Maisie had expected to see the crowd milling around the massive golden Old-English W beneath the oculus, but the sixty or seventy residents who'd arrived before her were instead gathering just in front of Branch 1's impressive archway. The Steward stood before them, his back to the opulent arcade of the Grand Alleyway. Elias stood beside him.

The sight of her brother caught her breath. His gray uniform blouse was now rolled up and acting as a sling cradling his left arm. Above it, on his upper chest just below the shoulder, a square bandage covered a wound. How bad, she could not say, but even as she watched, blood darkened its fabric. Red trickles were leaking from the patch in several places at once, rolling down her little brother's stout chest to blend with a nasty gash cut across the center of six well-defined abs. This wound was oddly left unattended, but a closer look did reveal subtle signs of hasty attempts to staunch the bleeding. Another bandage was present on her baby brother however, in the form of a crude wrapping around his right thigh. Somehow, unbelievably, it seemed even more soiled than the other. Yet, for all of it, Elias looked none the worse for wear. He stood there, still as stone, staring dead into the growing sea of residents, showing not even a twirge of discomfort. It was that cold, absent stare that caught her breath more than any of his injuries.

What have they turned him into? Oh, Eli, my sweet little brother, what has he done to you?

Maisie looked back then to Harclay Aponyaschefski, the corrupter-in-chief. She forgot her anger in a flash, however, when she noticed the gore-dripping head clutched by the hair in the grasp of the Witen's lawgiver. Realizing just what he held sent a bolt of the most absolutely genuine shock through her system. From the Commander, Captain Alvarez, or any of his lieutenants, Maisie would expect such a thing, but the Steward was the steward. He kept the books. He didn't dirty his hands. She supposed that had been why it took her so long to notice his gruesome prize. The sight of her battered brother was bizarre enough.

The mind sees what it wants to see until it's too damn late, she told herself, thinking the line came from a novel she read once, or perhaps a poem.

Once she mentally pinched herself by looking around to make sure everyone else seemed to be seeing the same thing she was, Maisie looked back to her baby brother. Elias was tall now, six-two at least, and probably not even done growing. His arms were commensurately long. The tops of the heads of a few residents closest to him had obstructed her view at first, but now she saw what was gripped in the right hand at the end of Elias's brawny arm. She knew then who the lieutenant that attacked them had been. A few more steps and she might have made out the face on the decapitated head dangling from the Steward's hand, but one look at the longsword answered the question first. Only one man in the whole station had himself a sword. It had cost Lieutenant Gregson nearly two-thirds of all his goods and property, but the metal worker he commissioned for the job did deliver an intimidating looking weapon in the end. It was probably the single most expensive item aboard station, as far as the barter network went anyway. *Eli's now, I guess,* she surmised as she stepped up to the swelling crowd.

No sooner had she reached the sleepy mob then the Steward abruptly lifted Lieutenant Gregson's head up high. His accompanying howl was alien to the clerk. It was fierce and baneful. His eyes were not his own. Maisie had never seen such a fire behind them. It burned so bright she swore she felt the heat. "Betrayer!" he shouted his first discernable word. "Traitor! A dead man! All of them, dead! Burning! They dared to risk everything, to risk our very fate! This traitor," he yelled, holding the head out to stare down the crowd with the whites of its lifeless eyes, "this man was so vain, so lustful, so power hungry, he risked everything, human destiny itself!"

"Booooo," the Glorifier moaned from just behind her. Immediately, his disciples joined in, adding "Traitor," and "They're burning," and "Death to traitors!"

"But the Witenagemot has proved its worth again!" the Steward shouted, silencing their fawning. "Even against a foe so devious they'd hide in plain sight among us, even against such a foe, the Witen has prevailed again. The Integration Program has molded a warrior with the strength, wisdom, courage, and skill to defeat any threat. My friends, my brothers and sisters in the Witenagemot, I give you my savior, my hero, and your security, Footman Elias Sagal, Ethling of the Witenagemot."

"Praise the Ethling!" The Glorifier didn't hesitate. "Hail our warrior, our knight, our light to burn away the darkness."

The disciples joined in echoing each call and mixing in a few of their own. Soon enough, most of the gathered residents were hooting some similar unholy adoration. The noise rolled up to bounce off the Rotunda's dome and crash back down in waves. Anyone who had missed the Glorifier's wake-up call had to be hearing this at least. When Elias raised the longsword above his head with only the merest grimace of pain, the enraptured throng's corresponding bellow rattled her teeth. The Commander, Captain Alvarez, and the rest of the lieutenants, along with a handful of footmen currently guarding the Branch, certainly heard the commotion. As a group, they were marching down the Grand Alleyway just over the Steward's shoulder.

One by one, the crowd began to notice their coming, shutting up accordingly. By the time the Commander finally arrived alongside Maisie's brother and his dastardly hypnotist, the rumbling of her neighbor's belly could be clearly heard. "The fuck's going on here, Steward?" the Commander asked, rubbing his milky eye with the end of his palm. Montrois wore no shirt nor shoes, only his black tactical trousers, yet he still remembered his battleaxe, clutching it loosely near the blade with the hand not on wake-up duty. Alvarez was a bit more dressed but conspicuously lacking his signature morningstar. The lieutenants were attired in a range of varying degrees to that of Montrois and Alvarez.

"Commander, sir," the Steward said, lowering the still-dripping head of his former councilmember, "today is a glorious day. The Ethling has proved his worth yet again, and we have weeded out some treacherous rats among our ranks."

The Commander must've seen the head and the longsword already, but he made a show of gazing at both items now. "Is that Lieutenant Gregson?" the bear-man growled dangerously.

"It was, Commander, sir," the Steward allowed. "What he is now is nothing save a trophy of the Ethling's victory. I present it to you now as irrefutable proof of this deed. I called you all here to witness this presentation," he said, addressing the crowd once again, "to see the blood, to see the grisly consequences of daring to challenge, daring to doubt the Commander and I's commitment to humanity's future and nothing else. Your rest, while understandably precious, is not more important than your absolute comprehension of that simple fact. Forget it at your peril. Challenge it at your peril," he told them, holding out the exsanguinated head again.

Maisie watched the Steward's eyes when he wasn't looking at the crowd. Time and time again, they returned to Captain Alvarez standing beside the Commander. When she scrutinized the Regent of the Corridors a little closer, Maisie thought she understood why the Steward was so interested in him. The Captain was not his usual, casually cool self. It wasn't just sleepiness, either. There was something in his face that looked ... *afraid.* That was the only word she could think to describe it. *He had a part in this attack*, she knew, with a conviction she couldn't rationalize or explain but she felt just the same. *Not just that, the Steward knows he did, and Alvarez knows he knows.*

It made her happier than a nerd on new-phone day to see the blossoming division within the Witen, though she did her best not to let it show. Elias's poorly treated injuries were dampening her ability to show much joy right now, regardless. *End this impromptu worshipfest and get him to Newton Hospital,* she silently extolled. The Commander must've heard her. In the very next heartbeat, he snatched Gregson's head from Harclay's clutches and stared down her brother while he spoke. "The man always seemed so loyal." He was presumably talking about Burger Gregson, but his eyes were there to disabuse one of that belief.

"Oh, he was loyal," Aponyaschefski said. "To whom? As yet, I can't say. But rest assured, Commander, sir, I will find out." Alvarez diverted his eyes as the Steward's sought them out. *Oh, this is really good,* Maisie thought of the clearly developing rift.

"Where's the rest of him?" Montrois asked, tossing the already-rotting head to the pristinely waxed floor.

"In the Bowling Alley, Commander. Footman Sagal dispatched Footmen Algernon, Torrez, and Simmons, as well as Lieutenant

Gregson. Their corpses lay where they fell," Aponyaschefski informed him, pride in every syllable.

"Very well. Send 'em to the mulcher and expunge their names from the Witenagemot's roster," the scarred and bearded brute ordered. "Everyone back to their quarters," he growled at the residents with a flick of his wrist.

Instantly, residents set about complying. The press cleared so fast that Maisie could clearly see the flicker of uncertainty in the Commander's eyes as he turned from Elias and Harclay. It was gone just as soon as a slim brunette girl of about sixteen years with ivory skin and no waist to speak of stepped up from where she'd been waiting patiently behind him to grab his hand and grope his rock-hard chest and stomach. When he picked her up as easy as King Kong would a Barbie doll and began marching back toward his luxury quarters, the obliviously victimized girl began giggling and kissing his neck. Maisie almost would have preferred the poor child to scream and squirm. It would've been just as hard to watch, but at least she could believe the man had been receiving some pushback for his abominable behavior.

God, I hate that man, she silently declared. *I'm sorry, Carrie, but he ain't your husband no more, and I hate his fucking guts.*

Maisie was the last to leave the impromptu conference, apart from her brother and his master. Their eyes locked across the twenty yards of gleaming Rotunda floor, all three of them. The Steward's beady blue gaze bounced back and forth between Maisie and her brother. She had nothing to say, nothing she hadn't said a thousand times before, anyway. For the moment though, words did not seem to matter. Staring unambiguously and without any judgement or condescension through the windows of Eli's soul felt as though she were making more progress than all the years of pleading combined. The Steward must've seen the siblings' mental connection. Maisie had been paying him as little mind as she dared, her focus on her injured brother, but she did notice Harclay snapping his fingers at a group of white lab coat clad station residents speed-walking toward him down the Grand Alleyway.

Nurses and orderlies, the lot of them. Two of which stepped up on either side of Eli only seconds later. The one on the sling side wrapped an arm around her blood-stained sibling for stability. The other came up on Elias's right side. The stocky man in a tight-fitting lab coat whispered something as he pulled Gregson's longsword from his grasp. Once in hand, the orderly then placed Eli's right arm over his shoulder. Slowly, her brother allowed the two medical staff members to take his weight. Maisie thought she saw his lips form some silent message to her then, but the four other healthcare workers had all rushed up to assist in helping him shuffle to Newton Hospital before she could make out what it had been. His show of unaffected calm had been just that: a show. Now the toll this night had taken was plainly evident. Elias's diminished state broke her heart all over again, a heart already broken in a million pieces.

Oh, Eli, Eli, I'm sorry. Just come back to us.

"Back to your quarters now, Ms. Sagal," Aponyaschefski dared say to her.

She wished as strongly as she'd ever wished before that her angry glare were a physical weapon. Maisie had wanted to curse him, to charge him and throttle him, to laugh at his pathetic attempts to intimidate her, his pathetic attempts to cover his own inadequacies. Kicking him in the balls right there and then would have been a pleasure beyond description, but she did none of that. She had not worked so hard for so long to throw everything away for a bit of fun. So, he got an icy glare, best she could do in the moment. Harclay wasn't breaking first. He knew he had her. Finally, she cut her losses, though a juicy spit was hocked in his direction as she turned back toward Branch 4. Maisie Sagal just couldn't help herself. She hated the bastard. She would destroy his Witenagemot if it was the last thing she ever did.

CHAPTER 21
JORDANA

The collegial and excitedly nervous atmosphere evaporated the moment they both noticed the Colt .380 pistol in her hand. "What is that?" Maisie asked in a slow, uncertain way that led Jordana to believe she knew full well what the weapon was. She just didn't know what else to say.

"I had it in my ankle holster. None of you ever searched me," Jordana explained. "I thought it might be useful just now."

"There's no one left in there. That's why we waited, remember?" Sheffield's voice was stern but clearly shaken. The short, shaggy tech-wiz even displayed a slight tremor as he pulled his hand back from the white wheel of a 2-foot by 4-foot hatch.

Maisie had finished her story about fifteen minutes before their three-hour timetable was up. No one said a word after. Maisie had simply stopped speaking, then slowly stood up. She managed a nod at Jordana and Roddy Sheffield, both of whom took it as a cue to follow her. She'd led them here, to this cramped hatchway in this crepuscular annex tunnel. Right away, Sheffield had gone for the hatch's wheel. The first word spoken since Maisie ended her tale had been her question: "What is that?" The solemnity had died with the gun's appearance.

Sheffield had definitely found his voice. "You can't use the damn thing anyhow. The Witen bastards shot off six rounds in the main Control Room back before the Final Tournament. They got two operators killed and it was only blind luck that the other four bullets didn't clip something critical. You can't use it up here, Ms. Revere," he said, softening his voice. "I'm sorry. Maisie and I should've figured you'd be armed, it's pretty obvious in hindsight, but the one good thing the Witen did was blow up all the guns. This station may look incredible, eternal even, but in reality, it is extremely fragile. The tech up here seems just short of magic, for the most part, but I've seen all the blueprints. I know how delicate the systems really are. The fuel they use to power this place could crack the damn moon. There are redundancies and backups upon backups, but main power is the one thing you can't get around in the end. There is a core at the heart of this station, Jordana, constantly charging and distributing. This process cannot be interrupted for even a microsecond. There is no telling what one stray bullet could do. If it knocks out a conduit to one system, it could trigger a collapse in the next, and before the backup systems can divert power or contain the spread by severing a Branch before the cascade reaches the power core ... well then ... we might see the flash before we're turned to particles in the blast. I don't know. No one's ever survived such an explosion to give us their report."

"I get it, Mr. Sheffield," Jordana calmly explained. "I wasn't gonna fire the bloody thing. I'm not an idiot. I've scrutinized this station's specs every bit as meticulously as you, I'd wager. The threat could prove useful, though, if it happens that you're wrong about the Greenhouse's control room being empty, say. Not to mention there will definitely be people in the main Control Room, will there not?"

"Two." Maisie spoke for Sheffield.

"So that's two operators at the very least we'll have to deal with. And two is just your hope in the end, really," Jordana corrected. "It was well known, even before the cannibal hordes began walking the Earth, that all plans fall to shit as soon as the first shot is fired. And relax, Mr. Sheffield, that was only a metaphor," she added before the shaggy tech-nerd could object.

"She's right, Roddy. It could come in handy in a pinch," Maisie said from her newly achieved perch atop the guardrail of the shadow-laden annex tunnel. Sheffield didn't answer. Jordana thought she might've seen a nod, but she couldn't be sure in the gloom. "You really won't shoot it, right?" the slim-waisted, full-breasted cherub asked Jordana from her lofted perch.

"Cross my heart," Jordana promised with a cheeky wink.

"You gal's ready, then?" Roddy Sheffield was asking as Maisie's rickety comm device started chirping. "Turn that thing down, dammit! There could be a footman passing by on their inspection just outside this hatch right now, and we'd never know it."

"Sorry," Maisie squealed, snatching the device off her hip.

No sooner had she muted her comm then Sheffield's began to chirp. Before he could quiet the super walkie-talkie, a child's voice burst through. "Maisie, don't you dare ignore me," it said. "I'm serious, Mais. Answer me, or I'll make good on my th-thr-threat. Mr. Sheffield better have told you about it. Y-yo-y-you're already two hours late as it is."

"I told her, Carrie," Sheffield said into the comm with a smile in his voice Jordana could not perceive in the dimness. "Don't you try and pin this on me now."

"Thank ya, Roddy. Can you put my sister on, please?" the innocent voice asked ever so sweetly.

Maisie hopped off the railing, deft as a dancer, then stepped three paces to snatch Roddy's comm device from his hand, all in the span of a single second. "Ri Ri, what in the hell are you doing on the comms? Whose device is this?"

"I traded Mr. Barker a few minutes on his comm for some wine I had stored up from a few deals I made last month," the little girl said unabashedly.

"You did what? *Wine*? Why do you have wi— What deals? Who are you trading with in our Corridor? Whoever it is better damn well *be* in our Corridor. If I hear you're even leaving our alleyway without me, I'll... Ughh, wait, you ain't even there now, are ya? You must be at Boyd's if you're with Cainey."

"I already told ya all that much, Mais," Sheffield said, affronted. "Told you to call her over the encrypted network, too. Don't believe her shock, Carrie," he added, a bit louder.

Maisie paid the man as much mind as the shark does the remora. "Ugghh, Carrie Roxanna," she called, so exasperated she used her sister's middle name, "what in the hell are you doing at Boyd's? And Boyd, what in the hell are you doing letting her in?" The last question was spoken a bit louder in the clear hope that the man himself was listening somewhere close by.

"I was snoo-snoo-snooping on you guys this morning and overheard all the craziness that's going on." Wisdom rang clear in the girl's young voice. "You were gonna raid the dang Control Room and not tell me? You could get yourself killed, Mais. Now, I'm not telling ya whether you should do this or not, big sister, but you could've at least said goodbye. Don't I deserve that mu-mu-much?"

Jordana saw the pain in Maisie's eyes as she sighed and pressed the small, blue-taped device to her forehead. "Of course you do, Ri," she answered in a pure and honest manner. "I didn't think it was good parenting to worry you with something like this, though. And by the way, how long have you had this eavesdropping device of yours? Where was I when you were making that?"

"Where are you ever, Maisie?" The answer wiped the smirk forming on the resistance fighter's pouty pink lips. The young child, who Jordana figured could be no more than eight or nine, must've picked up on how hard her big sister had taken her last point. Her voice was comforting when she broke the lingering radio silence. "I'm sorry, M-Ma-Mais. I didn't mean that, really. I know you're working hard for us, doing what you think is best. This is just a big step here, sis. It really could get ya killed."

"That won't happen, Carrie," Maisie promised her sister in a voice struggling to push back tears.

"It better not," the little girl demanded.

"I'll see ya real soon, Ri. I promise," Maisie told her sister, her voice now recovered and determined. "You just get your butt back to our quarters this minute, and don't let anybody see you leaving Boyd's."

"You take care of yourself, Mais, you hear me?" the priest answered for the child.

"I hear ya." The smile in the resistance fighter's voice was bright and unmistakable. The darkness literally rolled back from its majesty.

"Be careful, Maisie. You, too, Roddy. And you, Ms. Revere," Dolly Duchesne-Boyd told them over the radio waves.

"We will," Maisie swore for all of them.

"I sure hope you know what you're doing, kiddo," Boyd's voice came back to add in a fatherly, offhanded manner.

"Me, too," Maisie said after a moment's breath. Jordana watched her hand as it muted the gray device and tossed it back to Sheffield. There was a slight tremble there, much like Roddy's own. Jordana chocked it all up to nerves. She was certainly feeling the stirrings herself. Neither of the hand-tremors lasted, though. Each of her compatriots had firm control over every muscle now. And when Jordana stepped close enough to the younger woman to see her eyes and the dogged resolve that lay within, she knew they were indeed ready. *Time to get this show on the road.*

"Here we go," Sheffield whispered as he began turning the hatch's white wheel.

It swung open four revolutions later. The tech-wiz immediately stooped through. Maisie was next, then Jordana pulled up the rear. The .380 was snug in the palm of her hand, arm out and braced at the forearm by its counterpart, her eye straight down the barrel. Nothing appeared behind the iron-sight as she scanned the vast space around them. To their left lay their next destination. To the right and in front lay rows upon rows of potted produce. Barely discernible in the near-distance from this vantage point, through the towering flora, were dozens of acre plots of cultivated land in the process of growing corn, beans, wheat, beats, peppers, potatoes, and every vegetable in between. Jordana could even make out a half dozen fruit orchards at the far end of the colossal Greenhouse. She had no time to marvel, no time to drool, no time to remember the nights beyond count, struggling for a few hours' sleep through the cramps of an empty belly, no time to resent the splendor before her and the pampered residents who'd enjoyed its literal fruits. Jordana had her mission to complete. So she turned left, along with Maisie and Sheffield, straight toward the security hatch leading into the Greenhouse's control room.

Sheffield pulled out a piece of slapped together tech from his pocket as he approached the hatch's keypad. Jordana had thought the comm devices looked rickety. This thing looked like a shoddy chunk of jury-rigged trash. Three wires with strange metal pads a centimeter in diameter attached to the ends hung off the back of a 6-inch by 6-inch vid-screen. A numeral keypad was currently displayed on the lower half of the screen while a 3-inch blank box took up the top. The shaggy, poetry-loving resistance fighter then whipped out a flat-head screwdriver from another pocket. The keypad's cover was off in a flash, and Sheffield was placing his strange hacking device's clearly magnetic metal pads to specific conduits within. Instantly, six green digits popped up in the blank box on the vid-screen's top half. With each digit spooling rapidly in both directions, it was impossible to ever make out a single number. Right up until the spooling abruptly stopped. Six green numbers were left still as stone on the screen, and the instant Roddy Sheffield punched them into the keypad on his vid-screen's lower half, the security hatch softly slid open with a gentle whoosh.

Jordana was last through the hatch. She assigned herself the rearguard duties, but the place was empty. If there were footmen on patrol, they weren't around here. *Not yet anyway*, she was thinking before the pristine austerity of the humming monitor equipment all around her caught her breath. There were six terminals in the room, five surrounding a larger central terminal. All were simply touch-screen monitors embedded into gleaming white desks, but their eerie futuristic arrangement gave her pause as to whether she could ever navigate the system.

Sheffield moved with no delay for the central terminal. "The VLSE suits are in the emergency cabinet against that wall," he told Maisie, a finger pointing out exactly where.

Maisie caught Jordana's eye before going for the suits. She couldn't be sure, but she thought the younger woman had a certain look in her eyes. The mystery alone gave her a thrill. Jordana was feeling that look in a fluttering heart. She prayed now that it hadn't been in her head, even as she forced herself to turn away from the brilliant beauty and cover the now-closed hatchway. "What are you doing, Roddy?" Jordana heard Maisie ask on her way to the wall-embedded cabinet.

"I just want to see what kind of access this thing really has," he explained.

"We don't have time for that," Maisie insisted.

"Oh, it'll just take a second," Roddy retorted.

"Fine," Maisie said after a hiss of released air rippled through the rectangular control room. "But put your damn suit on while you look." Jordana turned from the hatch then to see Maisie tossing a fat maroon-and-silver cone-shaped bag at the short tech-geek. She got within ten paces of Jordana before tossing an identical bag at her chest. Jordana caught it against her side with her unarmed hand. She had to set the gun down atop a nearby terminal in order to unzip the cone-shaped bag and extract a set of Vacuum Life-Support Equipment.

Okay, so far so good. They were suited up, helmets locked and air flowing, standing in front of the Greenhouse control room's external hatch. True, Maisie and Jordana had been ready for a deal longer than Sheffield, who finally gave up whatever fruitless endeavor he was attempting at the room's central terminal after a few curses and three fist-pounds atop the smooth, composite-materia desktop, but the delay had been negligible really. A few more seconds to prepare her head for the next much harder part wasn't such a bad thing just then. But they were ready now, and once all three locked eyes through the thin layers of their polarized face shields, Sheffield wasted no time. He punched in some protocol into the external-hatch's keypad that cut the room's white light.

Flashing red took up a pattern immediately, interspersed with near pitch darkness. A blaring klaxon could be heard for only the briefest of moments before she felt air being sucked up around her, nearly lifting her off the floor. Artificial gravity cut out a beat later. She did lift off the floor then. Jordana had practice in light lunar gravity, however, and so was able to land gracefully. Maisie wasn't so lucky. Jordana arrested her tumble and had her on two firm legs only a second later. The dark-haired resistance warrior offered up a grateful, self-deprecating smile in thanks. They both looked to Roddy after that, who, if he lost his footing at all, was certainly not showing any signs now. Another shared look and unanimous nod let Roddy know it was time to open the hatch. The thin maroon VLSE suits allowed for ample dexterity of every last digit, and so the man had no problem working the hatch's keypad.

Jordana was again the last through the portal. She might've been first through if she hadn't nearly forgotten the pistol still resting atop the terminal by the entry hatch. She bounded back across the dead room in two long strides. The weapon was pretty useless until they returned to somewhere with Earth gravity and an atmosphere, so she would've preferred to tuck it away for the moment. Unfortunately, though the suits were comfortable and not at all limiting in range of motion, they had no external pockets or pouches of any kind. Jordana had to just hold the pistol, time being. For now, that wouldn't be a problem, but when they finished their 300-yard jaunt across the surface of the Moon and then had to enter the main Control Room without first cutting out the gravity and creating a proper air lock, as they had done just now, the pistol would surely be a hinderance as she tried to scramble through a hatch whilst a whole massive room's worth of air was trying to rush out. *One problem at a time, Jor*, she scolded herself as she placed her feet atop lunar dust for the second time in her life.

Her hand was sweating inside the gloves of her suit, but the tacky palms of her maroon life-support gear kept its firm grip of the Colt .380. Jordana stood to Roddy's left as he hooked up his hacking device to the main Control Room's external-hatch keypad. While Jordana had bounded from the Greenhouse over to the operations center at the end of Branch 1 with the pistol gripped in her right hand, Roddy had held both the screwdriver and his slapdash device in his left. Maisie alone went unencumbered. She stood just to Jordana's left now, the hatchway directly before both of them. Jordana looked down at Sheffield's hacker just as six green numbers went still on the vid-screen.

She could barely see his eyes behind the darkened face shield, but his nod was unmistakable. Jordana looked to Maisie before returning it. The two shared their own private nod before turning to Roddy as one to confirm their readiness. Sheffield's helmeted head turned back to his device's screen. Jordana's eyes went to the heavy-duty sliding hatchway before her. A moment of calm followed the door's retraction. Then all hell broke loose. The well-lit chamber beyond went black as a rush of air socked into Jordana hard as any screaming passenger train. She and Maisie were knocked backward through the light gravity a good twenty yards. Every last molecule of air fled her lungs as she crashed on her back in a shallow dune. Gray dust kicked up all around her, falling back down ever so slowly to bury her.

A breathless agony had her in its grips for what felt like a very long time. She could do nothing but let the dust take her until a tormented breath finally filled her aching lungs. Jordana was up in a flash after that. She knew they'd grossly underestimated how powerful the vacuum would be. Scanning the powdery ground all about her for a sign of where Maisie had been blown, Jordana's gaze fell first on Sheffield. The blast had rocked him, too, clearly, but he'd been beside the hatch, not in front of it, and so had only tumbled back a half dozen paces. Maisie shot past Jordana a blink later, ending her search. The hazel-eyed tigress was heading for the open hatchway. She understood Maisie's haste immediately. With the red flashing lights blaring throughout the Control Room, she only got snap images of the scene, though it was enough to understand an operator was being sucked across the floor straight toward the open hatch. The next red flash told Jordana that the man was unconscious. His limp body crashed against white computer terminals on its inevitable path. They were still in daylight just now. If the man was sucked onto the surface, his skin would roast in the 250 degree solar kiss, if he didn't suffocate first, that is.

Jordana forced her legs into action, catching up with Maisie just as they reached the hatchway. Air was still rushing out, strong as a waterfall, but they managed to hold their ground at the threshold. An instant later, the operator crashed into them. Jordana and Maisie had just enough time to brace for the impact, and so were knocked back only a few feet. With the thankfully small operator clutched tight between them, they struggled toward the room. Sheffield rushed up behind them then, adding his weight to the slog. Jordana saw deeper into the expansive rectangular Control Room as they pushed past the threshold. Another operator had an ever-slackening grip on a leg of a terminal desk in the room's far right corner. His slipping hold held up in the end, though. Jordana never actually turned to see it, but she assumed Roddy had closed the hatch behind them. The rush of air died away fast as a snap, accompanied by the instantaneous return of her body's Earth gravity weight in tandem with the lights.

Not a one of them took their helmet off until the still-conscious operator started drawing in large, obvious breaths between whooping coughs. "Well, guess we shoulda seen that coming," Sheffield tried to make a joke of their foreseeable blunder as soon as he tugged off his silver helmet.

Maisie didn't laugh. Jordana was kicking herself for the miscalculation and barely registered the quip. Falling to her knees, Maisie tended to the injured man. He was still unconscious, but he was breathing again. Jordana and Sheffield set to stripping out of their VLSE suits, only remembering the other operator when he shouted at them in a cracked voice. "You idiots! What the hell did you think you were doing! You coulda got me killed!"

Jordana had somehow clung to her pistol throughout the blowing madness. She tossed it from hand to hand now as she pulled her arms free of the maroon suit. It fell around her waist as she stopped to point the pistol at the operator now marching toward them with both his hands trying to massage his throat. "Hold it right there," she told him in an accentuated version of her rich English accent. "Not another step."

The Control Room's sole conscious operator was a man of middling height, weight, and years with yellow tinged teeth and a product-laden hairdo. His eyes bulged as he realized just what Jordana Revere was aiming at him. "Is that a gun?" the dope asked.

"It's a gun, alright," she told him. "The kind that shoots bullets. So you're going to listen closely and do just as we say, or I will use this gun to fire one of those bullets straight through your skull. Is that understood?"

The operator wanted to protest. He was incredulous. Clearly, not even in the man's wildest dreams had he ever envisioned a scene like the one that greeted him now. He'd only just recovered from near suffocation while clinging for dear life. A stranger with a pistol pointed at his face was obviously more than his mind could keep up with. So he said nothing, just propped up a chair that had been blown around in the rushing wind and collapsed into it.

"He'll be alright... I think," Maisie reported on the unconscious operator at Jordana's feet. "Let's just get to work. Someone out in the Grand Alleyway could've heard the alarm klaxon. I want to get Jordana's message out and the Lunar Dock up and running before the Witen descends on us."

"Why? They can't storm the room, not after I reset the daily pass-code and insert my own, anyway," Sheffield said.

"So, reset the damn passcode, then," she implored. 'Come on, the Bruderschaft coulda left already. Jordana said they were coming no matter what, after all. They could've been sniffed out by a horde of Damned and moved up their departure. Nothing is certain down there, I'm sure. We've delayed long enough." Jordana's smile almost hurt it was so wide. Maisie caught it and grinned back.

Sheffield might've seen the exchange, but he gave no indication as he headed for this far grander Control Room's central terminal. "I'm on it," he affirmed.

Jordana moved toward the seated operator. Reaching into her flight-suit's right cargo-pocket, she pulled out two zip-ties, one of the many items nearly always on her person, including her 5-inch hunting knife sheathed in her right boot, two bandage packs in her left cargo-pocket, a small bottle of water-purification tablets—also in her left cargo-pocket—a book of waterproof matches were in her right, along with two Bic lighters. The Colt .380 was one of those always-items as well, with its extra ammo clip strapped to her ankle holster just above her left boot. The operator was not at all happy to see the two convenient ties, though he hardly made a sound as she pressed his wrists and ankles together and drew the ties tight. 'Are you going to be trouble? If not, you can sit in that comfy chair with your mouth free to breathe easy. But if you do insist on being a bother, then the floor will be your new home after I rip a strip of your shirt and use it to wrap around your mouth. So, which will it be: chair or the floor?"

"The chair," the weak-chinned Witen operator said to his feet.

"Good," was all Jordana managed for reply. She could tell he wasn't going to be an issue before her warning, really, and so had shifted her focus to the room's three-sided windscreen. The massive window was stanchioned with a white support every ten feet, but even so, the view of the gray lunar hills beyond felt nearly unbroken. The Control Room was a perfect rectangle, thirty meters deep and a hundred meters wide, placed like a capital T at the end of Branch 1. Its stanchioned windscreen took up the top half of the three outer walls. The walls themselves were at least twenty feet tall. A platform was embedded all along the three walls, just below the windscreen. A short stairwell along the far right bulkhead led up to the 5-foot wide platform.

Taking two stairs at a time, Jordana was up on the platform in three strides. The view from just beyond the hatchway had been sur-real, but this new, closer angle left her mesmerized. "Some kinda view, eh?" the yellow-teethed man asked, ruining it for her.

"I believe Ms. Revere told you to keep quiet," Maisie said, joining Jordana on the long viewing platform. "Good thing neither of 'em were standing up here when we was hoofin' it across the surface," she said after a moment.

Jordana turned to follow her gaze and had no argument when she saw what Maisie was seeing. The Greenhouse loomed off in the distance, half of it anyway. Its control room and the hatchway they'd exited was plainly in sight at least. Jordana could even make out their footprints up to about a hundred yards out. She followed their path right up to the hatchway. "Damn good thing," she concurred with Maisie. They would've stuck out like a mouse on a dinner plate to anyone watching from the narrow platform. The view was beau-tiful and electric, no doubt about that, but after a time, she was sure even its wonder would grow dull. Three people bouncing across the surface couldn't help but draw the eye then.

Jordana's gaze went left now, away from the far-off Greenhouse and their marked trail. In front, taking up the entire hundred-meter-long windscreen, lay the pristine, yet oft-bombarded Moon. In the far left, taking up most of that bulkhead's thirty-meter-long windscreen, was the Lunar Dock. It lay half in shadow, but Jordana knew just what she was seeing. A massive tarmac, five hundred yards wide and four hundred long, housed three E-11 Transport Cruisers, one Star Hawk, four launch/refueling pads, and a large oblong hunk of half-lit machinery in the tarmac's very center that Jordana knew had to be the Dock's power core. The three vent stacks protruding up into the airless sky from its length left no doubt. The Terminal could be seen before the windscreen ended, but the rest of Branch 2 was blocked from her current vantage point.

"Okay, passcode's reset. No one's getting in without our say so," Roddy Sheffield called from the central terminal. It sat atop a stepped-platform a good three feet above the other terminals, but the women taking in the view still had to look down on him.

"Great job, Roddy. That's awesome," Maisie gushed. Only then did Jordana realize just how nervous the woman was inside. "Get to work on Jordana's message."

"You idiots won't ever get no damn message out," the strapped-up operator condescendingly told them. "If there even was anybody to get a message to, that is." He stopped there to laugh. All three collaborators let him. *What am I, invisible?* Jordana asked herself. Even with evidence of other survivors staring him in the face, the fool was still obstinate. *Some folks just don't want to see the truth*, she reasoned. "Nothing comes in, and nothing goes out. There is an invisible barrier around this entire station. No signal of any kind can get through."

"You're talking about the cloaking tech," Maisie said, jumping off the viewing platform and marching toward the operator.

"That's right," he stated simply.

"We know all about it," she said, wiping the smile from his face. "Now, shut it down."

"I can't," he responded, his smile returning. "He can't, neither," the rotten-mouthed man used his tied-up hands to indicate the unconscious operator, "even if you all hadn't knocked him into some kinda coma. No one can. Not even your treacherous little coward of an ex-operator you got there," he added with a chin to indicate Sheffield.

"Fuck you, too, Stiveson," Roddy muttered in a semi-perturbed, semi-disinterested sort of way, eluding to an existent acquaintance between himself and the off-putting operator apparently named Stiveson.

"Why not?" Maisie asked once the man had stopped chuckling.

"Because AOA are the ones who put it up. It's their tech. It only comes down with a specific code, plus a retinal scan from Hubert Harrington himself. That piece of junk you used to hack the hatches ain't worth a shit against its security measures. Believe me, we've tried, like … a lot. The cloaking shit simply kicked in the moment the Witen took control of the daily passcodes, some kinda impenetrable failsafe against external transmissions or detection, I guess. Or hell, it mighta even been up the whole time. Even simple Roddy over there oughta be able to remember that back when AOA was running things, all transmissions were vetted before any of it ever came across our terminals. They coulda been feeding us bullshit data from the jump for all anybody knows. Alls we know is it's up, and it ain't coming down."

"So the Witen really knows AOA has been hiding us away up here, like for sure?" Maisie asked. The sweaty prisoner only nodded for reply. "Why didn't they tell the people? Why keep AOA's lie for them? It would've fit Harclay's narrative."

"You know why, Mais," Sheffield answered for Stiveson.

Maybe she did. She made no verbal confirmation, just a sigh and a shake of her head, but Jordana could guess at her thoughts. "What happens if the Commander decides he needs it down for some reason?"

"Then the Commander would make Harrington take it down, I guess. Either that or carve out one of the bastard's eyeballs," the obnoxious man laughed.

"We'd better contact Boyd and the rest in the Clubhouse, tell 'em Harrington and AOA and the government bastards ain't to be trusted." Roddy Sheffield decided in a flash what Jordana had been advocating since she'd first arrived. "Hell, they should probably clear out of there completely. If Harrington and Rafferty decide they need some cred with the Witen, they could easily serve up the priest. They sure won't want word of their cloaking scheme spreading. Whoever ain't a Witen zealot already might be pushed to the Darkside by that news."

Maisie turned from the sycophantic twerp to look her friend square in the eye. "Toss me your comm. I'll let 'em know." Sheffield flipped the ramshackle contraption through the air with casual non-chalance. "Can you get past it or not, Roddy?" she asked the shaggy man at the lofted central terminal as soon as the comm was safely captured in her hand.

"I'll try," he managed after a time, his eyes fixed on the monitor, fingers flashing around the keyboard in a blur.

"You'll fail," Stiveson joked.

Maisie cuffed him for it. Jordana had left the viewing platform and approached Maisie and the operator just as he finished speaking, and were she closer, she would've done the same. Still, it was a surprise to see the savage behavior from the younger woman. "One more word and you're lying on the floor with a gag in your mouth!" she shouted at Stiveson on the heels of her slap.

Jordana rounded up two other fallen chairs and set them beside the bound operator. Maisie took the padded seat with an overt pleasure, even offering Jordana a wink in the bargain. No words were exchanged, but Jordana felt them grow closer with each silent second, of which they had an abundance. After Maisie's radio conversation back to the Clubhouse, there had to be at least ten minutes of quiet time beside one another in the middle of the massive white-walled and white-furnished Control Room. The quick update and warning had turned into more of an argument than she cared to have, judging by her body language throughout. Her impatience seemed flattering in some illogical way, though. The stubborn priest finally did acquiesce to Maisie's pleas to hide themselves away, but it was a bit like pulling teeth to get even that much. But afterward, they did get to share those satisfying, though tragically limited, moments of companionable silence.

Until Sheffield spoke, ending the spell. "The bastard's right, Mais," he said. "We need Harrington. I might be able to crack the passcode with a bit more time, but I'll never get past the retinal scan."

The shamed look of failure on Maisie's face was touching. Jordana would've wished it played out differently, but she blamed the hazel-eyed goddess for none of it. "It's alright. Not your faults," Jordana said in an emotional voice. She really needed Maisie Sagal to know that. "We can still get the Lunar Dock ready, can't we? That should be enough message for my people when they arrive. It'll have to be."

"Yeah, I can get it running from here," Sheffield confirmed, a relieved lightness entering his voice. "Only thing is, once I start the process, the power core's venting will be noticeable. Someone somewhere will be looking out a viewing port and see the exhaust."

"It doesn't matter," Maisie said, rising to her feet. "The Witen was always going to find out we'd been here. A siege was inevitable, really. They probably already know, truth be told. How many check-ins have you missed so far?" she asked the operator in a tone that showed she already knew.

"Only the one," the greasy tech-guy answered with an unctuous grin. "But that is more than enough. The Steward don't stand for missed check-ins. Whichever lieutenant is pulling staff duty today will be all over the radio checks, believe me. You can bet someone has reported the lapse by now. You retards are cooked. I'm gonna be watching y'all's heads roll in no time," he added with a laugh.

Jordana gladly took her turn at the slapping duties, shutting the foul-breathed turd right up.

"Just start the power-up process, Roddy," Maisie told their IT man. "Jordana and I will handle everything else."

No sooner were those words past her lips and Roddy Sheffield's fingers blurring over the touchscreen keypad in front of him once again when a muffled chirp began to sing out from somewhere in the operator's jacket. "That'll be them," he said, still smiling a victorious smile. "You people are so dead."

Maisie snatched Stiveson's tablet from a side pocket of his red-and-black flannel jacket as Jordana pulled her knife from her boot. The operator's eyes went wide just as his smile took off faster than an adulterer when the husband comes home early. She had no intention of carving the man up with it, though, just his shirt. Jordana ripped his jacket apart with one good tug, sending buttons tumbling off in every direction, then sliced off the lower third of his white cotton t-shirt. Maisie's eyes were smiling at her as she wrapped the unwashed scrap around the operator's mouth. They didn't need a word exchanged between them. Both knew to grab hold of the man's shoulders and tip him off his chair onto the threatened floor. He groaned contemptuously as he smashed down on the cold, white composite-material floor. Neither Jordana nor Maisie cared much for the cocky jerk's discomfort.

The tablet was still chirping. Maisie stared at it for a few thoughtful seconds before tapping something. Jordana saw its screen light up and saw a face fill the picture. "Who the hell is this?" the woman on the screen asked.

"I believe you know me, Lieutenant Dobechek," Maisie told the stern-faced woman.

"Maisie Sagal? What the hell are you... What... How did you... Where are the operators?" she finally managed a full question.

"One is out. Hit his head pretty good, but he'll live. The other is right here." Maisie pointed the tablet at the sprawled out and moaning ignominy of Witenagemot Operator Stiveson on the floor beside them.

Aiming the tablet back at her own face, she then treated the brutish ginger woman on the other end apparently named Lieutenant Dobechek with an innocent grin. "You have gone way too far this time, girl," Dobechek finally said after a monumental pause "You and whoever the hell you got with you need to come out of there immediately with your hands in the air. You get this one chance, Ms. Sagal. Don't make this get ugly."

"You turned it ugly long ago, Polly." The smile spreading to uncharted lengths on her face told Jordana that Maisie took a good deal of joy in calling the lieutenant by her given name.

"You are dead, you little shit," Dobechek snarled. "You're all fucking dead."

"Not at the moment, Polly. And that's all that matters," Maisie Sagal declared, ending the video transmission.

"Okay, that's it. We should see it firing soon," Sheffield called out a breath later. Jordana's eyes went to the Lunar Dock She felt Maisie beside her do the same. A thick stream of some steaming gaseous substance vented from each of the three exhaust ports atop the power core. Massive stadium lights clicked on all around the tarmac a beat later. The full majesty of the E-11s and the sleek sophistication of the Star Hawk were spotlighted in glory. "So far, so good," Roddy updated, still clicking away. "Once the power core boots up fully, I can start diverting fuel to the launchpads and powering up life-support systems in the Terminal. No promises, though. This shit has been lying dormant for nearly a decade now. It might all boot up only to crash or leak... Or something worse... Or it might not work beyond this much."

"This mission is a gamble, Roddy. We all knew that. Just do your best," Maisie managed in a low, burdened voice.

Jordana watched the venting flow up and up and knew someone seeing the display was indeed an inevitability. Hell, she knew beyond any shadow of a doubt that every last soul in Cardinal's Nest Lunar Station were even now witnessing the flow. In her mind, she pictured residents all over Branch 4 racing to portholes or stopping in the Grand Rotunda or The Meadow to watch the steam float over the oculus and then Stargazer Ceiling in turn. One look at the gorgeous and brave brunette next to her told her their minds were in tune. They were in the endgame now. Jordana only prayed the powered-up Lunar Dock would be enough signal to her brothers and sisters in the Bruderschaft that she had indeed arrived before them. As for what to do when their E-11 made its fated appearance, either unheralded or forewarned, well, Jordana Revere and Maisie Sagal were going to have to figure that out together.

To be concluded...

BOOK CLUB QUESTIONS

1. Can there be any moral authority in an autocracy?

2. Are the adults around Maisie in the first half of the book being reasonable when they include her in their plotting?

3. Is morality determined through the filter of circumstance?

4. What are the implications of AOA's culpability in the cloaking tech?

5. Why have AOA and the government been so content to play a background role for most of the decade of time laid out in this novel?

6. Is any of the tech described in the novel grounded in a possible future?

7. What events do the Bruderschaft's arrival necessitate in the concluding volume of The Despot Chronicles?

AUTHOR BIO

Andy T. Hanson is just your average Mid-Michigan native and Army veteran who, in his own words, "discovered a way to travel the universe without ever leaving the comforts of home. It's a bit like magic in that way, a fantastic sleight of hand. I only regret waiting until my thirties to get started." Residing in Bay City, Michigan, Andy is an avid Detroit and Michigan sports fan. In between Lions games, golfing, grilling and chilling with his big family, in particular his lovely wife Lauren and son Teddy, and devouring science fiction, historical fiction, and fantasy novels, he writes sci-fi novels of his own. He's inspired in large part by George R. R. Martin, Stephen King, Bernard Cornwell, Lee Child, and Sara Rosett, with a bit of Stephen Fry, Richard Dawkins, Kurt Vonnegut, Neil Gaiman, and Craig Allanson for spice. Andy is attracted literarily to well-fleshed out characters, especially gray characters, while his favorite part of writing is simply being present as the story grows of its own organic volition. The Despot Chronicles novels, a three-part, dystopian, apocalyptic epic is what grew from those twin joys.

Discover more at
4HorsemenPublications.com

10% off using HORSEMEN10

www.ingramcontent.com/pod-product-compliance
Lightning Source LLC
Chambersburg PA
CBHW022003310726
48972CB00006B/1498